LIFERS

A NOVEL

KEITH G. McWALTER

spark
press

Published by SparkPress, a BookSparks imprint,
A division of SparkPoint Studio, LLC
Phoenix, Arizona, USA, 85007
www.gosparkpress.com

Published 2024
Printed in the United States of America
Print ISBN: 978-1-68463-276-3
E-ISBN: 978-1-68463-277-0
Library of Congress Control Number: 2024913332

Interior design by Tabitha Lahr

As an Ancient Mariner of a sort, I want to hold the doubters with my skinny hand, fix them with a glittering eye, and say, "I have been to a place where none of you have ever been, where none of you can ever go. It is the past. I spent decades there and I can say, you don't have the slightest idea."

—PAUL THEROUX, *On the Plain of Snakes*

―――――――――――――

And Enoch walked with God after he begat Methuselah;

And all the days of Enoch were three hundred sixty and five years;

And Enoch walked with God; and he was not; for God took him.

—BOOK OF GENESIS 5:22–24

A NOTE ON THE TEXT

To assist the modern reader who may be unfamiliar with a number of the antique colloquialisms and acronyms found in the following narrative, a glossary of terms is appended.

—PENELOPE STRAITHAIRN, PhD
Department of Neurohistory
University of Melbourne
June 1, 2190

ZINN

Munich, 2059

There was something about the woman at the table across the dining room that troubled Zinn.

She appeared to be around his age, which was not in itself remarkable; so many were in their second century these days. She was artfully tattooed in the current fashion among the ultra-aged, but nothing too dramatic. She was overdressed for this place in a black silk pantsuit, and accompanied by a man much younger than she, though not so much younger that he couldn't be her third or fourth husband, as they seemed to be pretending he was. It was perhaps that pretense that bothered him; gaudily large wedding rings, much handholding, cooed intimacies between them. All a bit much. And the occasional glances in his direction, almost too quick to be noticed, but intended to be noticed nonetheless.

But what really bothered Zinn was that he thought he recognized the woman, like an echo from a former life. That, and the quality of her German; a bit too precise, too academic. Learned somewhere else, probably in the United States. She was government, perhaps diplomatic corps or military. She was. . . .

LIFERS

Adele Pritchard.

The moment her name came to him, he raised his hand for the check. There was only one reason she would be here, and he was that reason.

It was unlike him to be in a city, let alone a European city, much less one as thoroughly surveilled as Munich. But after Phuket, Santiago, Tallinn, Oaxaca, all in a month, Zinn had needed some down time, needed to hear his native German, eat some good German food. Mexico had been particularly awful, the unbearable heat, the poverty and violence, the nightly shootings in the streets. He'd bought a gun there, an old ballistic, the first of several that he would carry for a few days and then discard as he moved on. He'd never actually used one. There was really no protection from what he feared most.

Gustav Zinnemann was 110 years old. He had changed his identity multiple times, shed all his electronics, never went online or neural, even had his headchip removed in a very expensive, painful, and thoroughly illegal operation in Jakarta. But he knew the capabilities of the organizations that were looking for him, and that the likelihood of his remaining invisible to them was shrinking with every drone he flew and every payspace he checked into. Some spaces would still take crypto, but the airdrones insisted on the quaint convention of sovereign currency, so he had a series of old-fashioned payment fobs linked to a rotation of dummy bank accounts opened under fake names on four continents and threw each one away after he used it.

What troubled him most wasn't the constant movement, or the loneliness. It was not eating well. He'd been something of a gourmand back in his Silicon Valley days, and now, when he couldn't resist anymore, he'd drop in to Paris or New York or Tokyo or Milan for a day, usually by fossil car from some small town in the sticks, check into a random hotel under his latest alias, change into better clothes, rearrange his face a bit, brush his beard, and go to one of the high-end places he knew well from before the Change, a place like La Grenouille or Ledoyen, or Sensei Sachs there in Munich, go unfashionably early when no one who might have known him in the old times would ever be there, and have a nice meal and a good bottle of wine, pay in devalued crypto, and then drive out again without even spending the night, out to where the surveillance cameras were fewer and the AI spread thinner, to a room in a farmhouse or a tent in a park, as old-world and techless as he could find.

He'd been doing this for fifteen years. It had become equal parts boring and frightening, but there was no stopping, not until things stabilized enough that they wouldn't care about finding him anymore. And he had no idea when that might be because the situation was only getting worse, even worse than he'd ever imagined, much less intended, and no one seemed close to understanding his creation, that almost-living thing that had evaded the immune systems of millions of humans, penetrated their cells, reproduced itself, and set about stopping them from dying.

Zinn had spent the day in the English Garden, walking the kilometers-long footpaths beneath the ancient oaks, sampling the street food, contemplating the young lovers on their blankets in the grass, watching the surfers take turns, in their decorous German way, on the rushing, standing wave of the Eisbachwelle. It was a long way from Palo Alto, but it felt like home. And then the thunderheads rolled in, and the rain started, and he was darting from awning to awning down the curling streets of Munich's Old Town, looking for a place to eat.

He'd ducked into a place he recognized from the before times, Restaurant Halali, not far from the American consulate. White linen tablecloths, dark wood, delicate headless antlers mounted high on the cream plaster walls. Serene, traditional;

just what he'd been missing. It was early for dinner, and the place was almost empty, but it was still, he knew, a foolish thing to do.

Across the room, the woman he believed to be Adele Pritchard—ex-NSC, ex-CIA, currently he knew not what—glanced his way yet again, as though daring him to recognize her, daring him to react. And he did, almost against his own will, rising and crossing the room toward the entry foyer, walking as casually as he could, calling out again to the captain for the check. But as he approached, the woman rose from her table, blocked his passage, and offered him her hand.

"Good evening, Mr. Zinnemann," she said amiably in English. "Could you join us?"

He looked at her hand as though it held something distasteful. "I think not. I must be going."

She smiled. "So you must. But you might as well finish your meal first. We have time."

He stared at her. Green eyes now in an aged gray face, but eyes that were unmistakable. "Do you remember me, Mr. Zinnemann?" she asked.

"I believe I do."

"Then you must know that I will do what's necessary to speak with you."

He glanced down at the man at the table next to her, noted his right hand tucked inside the left lapel of his expensive jacket.

Zinn nodded, returned to his table, sat down, and finished his truffled noodles.

An eVTOL was waiting for them on the roof of the American consulate. The woman took the front left seat and began punching buttons, and the sky-facing props began to turn. The man took Zinn's arm and guided him firmly into the narrow seat behind her. What appeared to be an old ballistic handgun appeared in the man's hand; he looked at Zinn, considered, then replaced the weapon inside his jacket and sat next to the woman in front. Zinn stared up out of the bubble canopy at the cascades of rain and blinked as though they might strike him. Maybe he'd wanted to be caught. Maybe he was finally finished with all the running. There was no talk, no acknowledgment of what was happening, though there was only one possibility.

The props spooled up silently, and the craft lifted off, angling sharply south over the Hofgarten, over the brightly lit Marienplatz, lurching higher and faster until the city was left behind. They sped across dark forests, out of the storm and higher still, lifting toward the Alps, over Innsbruck, snow-bound and glistening.

Then down again, into Italy's twisting alpine valleys, tree-top level, too low to be detected, at what seemed to Zinn a very dangerous speed. He sat with his cheek pressed against the plexiglass canopy, so cold it almost burned his skin. The three of them sat silently in the small cabin in the hands of the perfectly capable machine and watched the night race by.

At the end of another long valley, a lake loomed, long and thin but widening as the drone raced on, the far bank too distant to see over the black horizon. The craft banked slightly to starboard and dove still lower, just above the ripples of the lake, the props kicking up a wake behind them. Twenty minutes, low and fast. A bend in the shore, and the drone rose up suddenly, slowing, hovering for a moment, and then dropped toward a structure, a huge villa, almost a castle, vaguely Moorish and pink in the moonlight, surrounded by towering cypresses. They touched down on a smooth swath of grass, and the props swung to a stop as quickly and silently as they'd started. The abrupt landing left Zinn gasping; it was barely an hour since they'd left Munich.

LIFERS

They led him to a drawing room, dark paneling, inlaid mirrors, and an immense ceiling fresco of a naked God surrounded by blond angels, but very little furniture—a grand piano in the corner and sprawling chintz divans from a bygone century, all under dusty tarps. A desk and a couple of functional chairs. Tall French doors opened onto a marble staircase that stretched down to a terrace overlooking the lake. The moon had risen over the mountains on the opposite shore, its face reflected in the water. It was all quite beautiful, in a calculated sort of way. The man with the gun in his jacket nodded wordlessly and disappeared down a long hallway, leaving Zinn alone with the woman.

He avoided her gaze as he ransacked his memory. As a young man, Zinn had briefly sat on a biowarfare subcommittee that Adele Pritchard had chaired during the Clinton administration. Back then he was a rising star in genetic sequencing, rather full of himself in his flowing beard, proud to have been asked to help advise a president on such an important subject. He felt shrunken now, anxious, almost fearful. He composed himself, glanced quickly around the room, assessing, categorizing, lingering on God in His ceiling kingdom, turning finally, reluctantly, to the woman.

"Where am I?" he asked.

"On Lake Garda in northern Italy," she replied soothingly. "Near a small town on the western shore."

"Quite a place," he said, eyes roving again around the huge room. He drifted to one of the two simple, unupholstered chairs, sat carefully. "Why?"

The woman remained standing. "You know why. But perhaps you mean why this place. It's secure, reasonably remote, easily defensible. Lake in front, mountains in back. You know what's coming a long way off. It was built by a Milanese lumber magnate in the 1920s, and the Germans used it as a sort of elegant prison during the Second World War.

6

Mussolini was kept here for a time when he fell out of favor with the Nazis. Then for a time it was a grand hotel. A man proposed marriage to me here, oh, eighty years ago. These old granite walls are impenetrable to most forms of microwave transmission. Our organization acquired it when it became clear that we had to operate independently."

"An elegant prison," he repeated. He looked at her fully for the first time. Her silk suit was prudish, as had always been this woman's fashion; nothing to catch the eye. "And you are?" he asked finally, to see if she would tell him what he already knew.

"Adele Pritchard, Mr. Zinnemann. We met long ago. We briefly worked on the NSC together. I've been following your work for a long time. More so in recent years, for obvious reasons."

He pretended surprise, but relaxed as soon as her identity was confirmed. "Ah, the formidable Adele Pritchard. It has been quite a while. A lifetime, almost."

"Yes, one of several, apparently," she said.

A smile bloomed on his face almost involuntarily. "You're with Xerxes," he said, a statement of fact. "Or perhaps you *are* Xerxes."

He could see that this startled her, though she tried not to react. He was sure that only a handful of people knew the name of her organization, let alone its goals. "Even in my reduced state, I'm not without my own resources, Ms. Pritchard."

"You can call me Adele," she said a little too quickly. "Would you like some tea, or wine?"

He smirked. "*Adele*," he drawled, stretching it into three syllables. "And you can of course call me Zinn. I'm more of a beer man. Pilsner, if you have it." She glanced toward the door to the hallway to chip the request for beer, then looked back at him. "I've been following you for most of your career too," he said, "Even tried to hire you once or twice if I'm not mistaken." This was true; she'd declined at the time, saying she was too busy in Africa trying to contain Ebola-5. "I've been aware of your organization and its goals almost from the moment you formed it. Quite a feat of diplomacy, I must say. Though I gather you've made little or no progress in containing the—what shall we call it? The plague? The miracle?"

The woman said nothing.

"How old are you now?" he asked, smoothing his beard. This had become a common locution, the addition of "now" to the end of what was once a simple if impertinent question to indicate that the person asking knew or suspected that the person being asked was in such an advanced, unnatural state of longevity that the figure couldn't possibly be guessed.

She hesitated. "Ten or twelve, I believe. I don't keep close track anymore." This, too, a flippant colloquialism of the times, the lopping off of the first hundred years as though it were nothing, just a prelude, just a long, ignorant childhood.

"Only a few years more than me," he said, and looked up again at the fresco of God. "Remarkable, isn't it? How time itself has changed."

A woman half their age entered from the paneled hallway, placed a fluted glass of beer on the low table in front of Zinn. He ignored her, and she turned and left. He sipped the foam from the amber liquid, pronounced it *gut*.

"What is the purpose of my visit to your lovely villa?" he finally asked, irritation finding its way into his voice. "And please don't say 'information,' because I have none."

"You may have none, but you know where to find it."

"I do not. The information you seek died with the woman."

"What woman?"

He smiled wanly. "Finally, something you don't know," he said. "It's a rather long, technical, and ultimately tragic story, I'm afraid."

"We have time," she said, drawing a metal chair across from him and sitting down. "All the time in the world." She leaned close. "Why have you been running from us all these years, Gustav?"

His throat tightened at the mention of his given name, one only his mother had used. To everyone else he had always been Zinn.

"Because I knew you'd never believe that I don't have the answer to your problem," he said. "And it is your problem now, not mine. I did nothing wrong. I am not a criminal. But your questions and recriminations would be endless. I can describe the genetic package to you if you don't already know it, but I know very little about the nature of the viral delivery system or how it was created. That knowledge died with the woman."

"Tell me about her," Adele said. "Tell me what she did that you couldn't do."

Zinn wavered at this challenge to his ego, but remained silent. Pritchard rose and walked to the huge French doors overlooking the lake, her back to him. The moon was almost full, its reflection a silver ribbon on the water.

"We estimate that well over half the world's population of all ages is infected, and the rates of transmission are accelerating," she murmured, as if to herself. "At the current rate, within the next ten years there won't be a man, woman, or child on the planet who won't have contracted your so-called Methuselah genome. And that's unacceptable."

He gathered himself. "By my own calculations the possibility of arresting its spread has already passed."

"A decade here or there doesn't matter. What we need is a way to reverse it. We need what you might call a cure."

He shook his head. "Too many variables. The genome will have mutated by now. It's not what I designed anymore." He paused. "As you will recall, it was once thought that the Singularity would arrive when we managed to upload our brains into machines. No one imagined downloading our machines into our cells." He chuckled softly, then forced the smile from his face.

"You and your kind need to accept that what you now have is a political problem and a social problem, but it is not a biological problem. The biology is wonderfully correct. And it is irreversible, as I intended it to be."

Adele Pritchard remained silent, unnaturally inert, hoping, he knew, to draw him out. He stood and joined her by the towering doors and gestured out over the lake at the lights twinkling on the far shore.

"Ten billion points of consciousness, trapped in failing machines. . . ." He paused and looked at her.

"No more."

"How?" she asked.

He hesitated. He'd never told anyone about the woman he called Tutenef.

TARAJI

Palo Alto, 2033

Taraji Owusua had of course heard of Gustav Zinnemann, the notorious biomedical entrepreneur, but why he'd wanted to hire her in particular, when there were so many more eminent vaccinologists attached to Stanford University, remained unclear to her. But he offered her a large up-front retainer and a generous monthly stipend to do what seemed, at first, very little. Palo Alto was an expensive town, and she wasn't ready to leave it after working so hard to get there.

Her interview had been brief and disturbingly informal, on a bench by the busy student union on the university campus. Brilliant sun, palms swaying, students skateboarding through the plaza; the place was a paradise to her. Zinn had ticked through her résumé in a few seconds: biochemistry degree from Uganda's Kyambogo University, where she'd graduated summa cum laude and won a master's fellowship in immunology to the Swiss Federal Institute of Technology in Zurich. Zinn paused there to test her German, a few quick colloquialisms; then, satisfied, moved on to her doctoral program in vaccinology at Cambridge, mere mention of which brought back to her the brutally cold and rainy place where her days had been spent writing grant applications in English, and her evenings drinking with the few locals who spoke Swahili. Then, at last, her research grant from Stanford, her ultimate goal, and her postdoc thesis on "Algorithmic Prediction of mRNA Immunogenicity," the paper that had lifted her into a more rarefied stratum in her field and the item on her résumé that she suspected had attracted Zinnemann's interest in the first place.

He asked her about Kampala, saying he'd visited the city once on his way to a research safari in Kenya during his Oxford days, and she told him of growing up on the shores of Lake Victoria among a throng of skeptical relatives who expected her to find work in the urban agri fields as they all had. But nurturing her greater ambitions had been a powerful figure: her grandmother Aamito, a former model who'd lived half her life abroad, and who'd had a vision on the night Taraji was born in which the child she called Little Tari became even more famous than she had once been. "You're going to change the world," her grandmother would say to her, and Taraji had believed her.

All the white people who had ever interviewed her had loved this story, and Gustav Zinnemann was no exception. She was, she realized, young enough to be his daughter, exotic and accomplished enough to distinguish herself from the dozen or so others whose résumés he had spread out before him. She could sense, even then, his attraction to her.

The lab he rented for her, Laboratory 210-F, was located in a nondescript building on the edge of the campus. He would concoct reasons to visit her there late at night, and he'd jokingly address her as "Two-Ten-F," a single word in his lingering German accent that became his private name for her: "Tutenef."

She knew that the immune-response prediction modeling that he'd assigned to her was only one component of a much larger project, and she quickly learned that Zinn's reluctance to share the details of that project was inversely proportional to her willingness to socialize with him outside the lab. So she accepted his invitations to lunches at the faculty club and to dinners under the trees at Rossotti's and, much later, once he trusted her, to what locals called the SLAC house, Zinn's brutalist-modern home in the foothills, near where the terminus of the Stanford Linear Accelerator lay buried beneath the redwoods.

In less than a dozen such outings, Taraji had deduced Zinn's ultimate objective, but doubted its wisdom and eventually told him so; it seemed to her like a kind of ruthless biological colonialism, analogous to the political kind that had ravaged her home continent. Thus began a long, passionate argument between them, kept intellectually civil by his desire to persuade and, she could see, impress her, and her desire not to be fired.

He plied her sympathy with accounts of his years of raising tranche after tranche of funding for his grand project, explaining to increasingly skeptical investors why his approach would work when all the others had failed to increase human lifespans by more than a few years, often without slowing senescence or decreasing morbidity. Why, they'd demanded to know, would his effort be any different?

He'd had several answers, but they all depended on raising more money. He'd long since established his reputation both as a visionary microbiologist and as a serial entrepreneur, with several lucrative patents to show for his biotech companies' expensive R&D. By the time he turned to the problem of aging, he was no longer young himself, in his late sixties, famous in his field, envied for his wealth, hated in some professional circles for his disdain of academic convention, known simply as Zinn, the madman of Mountain View.

But Taraji well understood that the best answer to the question of how Zinn might defeat death when so many others had failed was that he could capitalize on new understandings of how the human cell was programmed and synthesize those understandings in a way that hadn't been technologically possible before.

It had been accepted since the end of the previous century that there was no single cause of aging, and that a multi-pronged problem required a multifaceted solution. The first step had been to recognize that aging was not the inevitable result of living or the mere passage of time, but was rather a "confluence of cumulative dysfunctions," a nicely Germanic profusion of syllables that Zinn had used over and over in his pitch meetings with investors and prospective project hires.

His idol, the maverick gerontologist Aubrey de Grey, had long before identified seven distinct biological causes of aging, including mutation of the chromosomes, mitochondrial degeneration, and the accumulation of miscellaneous "junk" in and between cells, and had proposed what were then highly theoretical means to counter each of them. By the turn of the century, a dozen or more well-funded startups had formed in Silicon Valley, devoted to the notion of turning de Grey's dream of "engineered negligible senescence," or ENS, into reality.

Taraji had been vaguely aware of some of this history, but Zinn, who emulated de Grey's affectations of a flowing mountain-man beard and bohemian style of dress, described how he had watched carefully as the longevity startups failed, and noted in each case why they'd failed: too narrow a focus, too easily sidetracked by commercial concerns, the temptation to earn the quick buck and generate a return for investors, too parochial in the specialties that they'd brought to bear on an inherently ecumenical problem. Too timid, too safe, unwilling to push beyond the obvious. In the end they'd succumbed to internal rivalries and publicity and market forces, their teams picked apart by headhunters and competing investor groups, their modest advancements in nanotech and data assembly and genome manipulation licensed off piecemeal to big pharma for short-term gain.

Zinn ran things differently. He'd gradually assembled a disjointed group of over fifteen hundred contract workers like Taraji, none of whom knew the others or what his true goals were, each of them focused only on their immediate tasks, in teams kept physically and digitally separate, genomics in Bellevue, data assembly in Columbus, microbiology in Wellesley, nano in Singapore. And most importantly to Taraji, vaccinology right there under his nose, in Palo Alto. Only he read the reports from each of the teams, and only he redirected their efforts as each milestone was reached.

Then, in his late seventies, near the end of his patience and his funding, he'd succeeded; not because he was a better bioengineer, though she believed he was, or a more ruthless manager, though he was certainly that too, but because programmable messenger RNA technology, which had been used to defeat a host of lethal viruses in the 2020s, could be repurposed with a precision that hadn't been possible back when Aubrey de Grey had first envisioned aging as just another disease that deserved to be cured.

In what he described to Taraji as like orchestrating a great symphony, Zinn had supervised the meshing of strands of mRNA code that would instruct human cells to perform differently, to increase sirtuin production, correct genomic instability, and improve mitochondrial function; to re-lengthen truncated telomeres, to stimulate DNY methylation and silence the interleukin-11 protein, to craft abnormally high volumes of Daf-2 and Nrf-2 proteins, tricking the cell into believing it was in a food-scarce environment and to slam on the metabolic brakes.

Taraji knew that any one of these genomic instructions in isolation would have been a breakthrough. For all of them to be packed into a single complex molecule and taken up successfully by the human ribosome was little short of miraculous, like five simultaneous moon landings with five differently designed descent vehicles. But what amazed her most was that no one but Zinn himself, the great orchestrator, knew that it had been achieved.

And now she knew too.

He told her that he'd envisioned a conventional vaccine-like delivery system for his ENS package, but it was a huge, fragile molecule, a genomic origami that would need a new kind of vehicle to enter the human body and survive the cells' enzymatic defenses long enough to do its work. Hence his need for Taraji's expertise in rapid-sequence immunogenic analysis. He took her results and contracted with the manufacturers of the kinds of lipid coatings that had been used for earlier mRNA vaccines to create a synthetic sheath big and sturdy enough to hold his ENS package, but they never succeeded, in part because, paranoid as ever that his breakthrough would be appropriated, he had withheld crucial bits of her immunological data and refused to provide the protein strand itself, offering only proxies that were, inevitably, simpler and easier to package.

And without a protective lipid sheath, there was no way to inject it into the body, since the human immune system would attack anything as unnatural as Zinn's ENS genome.

Taraji listened to all this knowledgeably and sympathetically—a combination she was sure Zinn rarely experienced. She privately doubted that an injectable ENS vaccine was feasible—but there was another delivery system he hadn't considered, one that she knew all too well.

During her Cambridge years, she'd interned at a Swedish biotech firm under contract with the US Defense Department's Advanced Research Projects Agency, and helped devise a novel sequencing algorithm that designed large, complex protein coatings for what she guessed were bioweapons—most likely synthetic viruses. Those contracts had later been terminated as a result of the SARS pandemics of the late 2020s and the sensible international treaties that followed, but Taraji believed that the virus-builder algorithm that she had helped create, fragmented into a dozen codes and scattered across DARPA's cloud servers, might be retrievable; and if it could be reconstructed, she believed it could be used to create a viral vehicle large and sturdy enough to carry in its heart not the usual disruptive set of chaotic cellular instructions, but Zinn's ENS package. And then an injectable ENS vaccine might become irrelevant.

Zinn laughed at this, of course. His own vision for ENS was thoroughly elitist and unabashedly commercial: an anti-aging vaccine that would be available for a very high price to a very select few, like the seats on privately funded spacecraft that billionaires were selling to other billionaires. What would someone pay for another fifty or even a hundred years of life? A million per year? A billion? He had no idea, but he intended to find out.

This was the source of their deepest disagreement, the one that drove her from his beautiful home night after night and back to her tiny apartment on the other side of the peninsula. Taraji argued that work like theirs should not be about profit, not about fame and riches; its purpose should be to alleviate the kind of perpetual, endemic suffering that she'd seen all around her growing up in Uganda, in the hospice where she'd emptied bedpans as a little girl caring for her dying grandmother Aamito. It was about creating positive change out of nothing but intelligence and hard work, change that should not be bought and sold. Change for everyone, equally.

Zinn indulged her in his patronizing way. She was so dedicated, and he, she knew, was so drawn to her, that he hadn't definitively said no to her little personal project. She persisted, asking him for more time and resources to pursue her unlikely viral delivery system. And finally she was ready, and made her decision.

On the morning of July 16, 2034, Taraji Owusua, also called Tutenef, left her apartment in East Palo Alto and drove to Stanford campus, where security cameras recorded her entering her lab and then emerging some twenty minutes later. She then drove to San Francisco International Airport. On her phone was a QR code for a first-class ticket to Sydney, Australia. She knew that Zinn was likely tracking her movements, both through her phone and, likely, through the new chip implant that he'd bought for her as a birthday present. But she also knew that he'd come to trust her, and that if she acted quickly enough he wouldn't be able to stop her from changing the world.

She boarded the big widebody jet without incident, slept for several hours over the mid-Pacific, and had a leisurely breakfast. Then, as the crowded plane descended for landing, she rose and walked from the first-class cabin to the rear of the aircraft, past a hundred crowded rows of people, locked herself into a lavatory, and injected herself with a fatal dose of phenobarbital.

ZINN

Lake Garda, 2059

Zinn's beer was almost gone. He held up the glass, and Pritchard glanced aside, chipping to her staff for another. "So you believe she was patient zero," she suggested.

There had been scattered conjectures in the professional journals about the "Sydney Woman," the suicide suspected to be the original vector of the longevity plague because the incidences of absurdly long lifetimes could be seen in some models to have rippled out from New South Wales.

"She was in no sense a patient," Zinn snapped, "and I know only what I told you. That she proposed a viral vehicle for the ENS genome and I told her she was crazy, and shortly thereafter she killed herself. And believe me, I tried to find out whether and how she'd succeeded, but she'd dismantled her lab and the data was, shall we say, irretrievable."

"Why irretrievable? It would be of enormous help in reverse-engineering the delivery mechanism, if not the genome itself."

"As best I can determine, she fragmented her virus-builder algorithm and distributed it across the neural net."

Pritchard stared at him. "Is such a thing possible?" she asked.

"I assume you are chipped, my dear Adele?"

"Of course."

"I no longer am," Zinn said. "But pieces of Tutenef's algorithm are literally inside your head, and inside the head of every chipped person on the planet. Perhaps you could put your heads together." He chuckled self-appreciatively; Pritchard scowled.

"In any event," he continued, "we can infer that she tried the viral package on herself, confirmed that it was working the predicted changes on her own body, and she panicked. Because she of all people knew what it would mean. Or perhaps she got on that crowded plane with the intention of spreading the virus as broadly and quickly as possible. But it's all rather beside the point now, isn't it? The damage—or the miracle, if you prefer—has been done."

Silence was her only answer to that. The damage had indeed been done: the sudden population strains occasioned by the elderly ceasing to die. The families thrown into confusion and financial chaos as the longest life expectancies of their eldest members were exceeded first by a few years, then by a decade, and then another. The hospitals and assisted-living facilities that had been overwhelmed as their clients lingered on and on into their second century while the number of new applicants only increased. National economies buckling under the strain of their underfunded social security regimes as the number of people relying on them doubled every two years. The anger of younger generations cheated of their inheritances, or cheated simply of a final escape from the shadow of their parents' and grandparents' ever-lengthening lives. The anxiety, growing everywhere, that radical longevity had become a kind of virulent contagion. The shock that death, humankind's oldest companion, had lost her dominion.

And of course it was also a miracle, one he could barely

believe he'd accomplished, the transfiguration dreamed of since the days of the prophets. Life everlasting. Or life lasting so very long as to resemble immortality—that word that no rational person in the modern world dared utter outside of a religious ritual.

They sat for a while in silence. He allowed his thoughts to widen, to take everything in. The lake lapped its shores; the moon shone down as it had through all the millennia of human history. He and Tutenef had changed the course of that history, and he knew, even if this woman didn't believe him, that there was no going back. Yet she persisted.

"My organization has resources that far exceed what you were working with all those years ago. Look over our data. See if there might be something that you missed."

He looked at her, stifling his irritation at this implied insult. "Have you not been listening? Once introduced into the cells, the genome works changes that are irreversible. The cells are basically reprogrammed at the molecular level. The only 'cure' for these changes would be the death of the cell itself. Which of course you can induce in any number of ways, just as has always been the case. Toxins, for instance, or the depletion of nutrients, or extremes of heat or cold—"

She interrupted him. "You're describing things that would be lethal to the organism. We're looking for a way to disable your genome without killing the host—the person. To reset the cellular programming to its normal, unaltered state."

Zinn had reached the end of his patience. "As I said, that would be far more complicated than what I accomplished in the first place. But the point is quite moot, since not only would I not cooperate in such an effort, I would oppose it. You would have to kill me, as I would prefer death."

There was a long silence. So long that Zinn thought the woman must be on her chip and not engaged with him at all. Then she said to him:

"In almost a century as an operative, I've interrogated dozens of desperate men—and they were almost always men, of course. I've learned to recognize those who will break and those who are beyond breaking. They might not be noble, or brave, or even strong-willed, but they are beyond breaking. I can see, my dear Gustav, that you are such a man. But we cannot let you go again. And I hope you'll change your mind, and work with us."

And with that she turned away from him and left the great room, and the man with the gun in his jacket reentered it.

DANIEL

Gulf Coast of Florida, 2059

He'd never had time for a journal, even when he worked in the White House, back in the Clinton administration, which sounded even to him like the Pleistocene. People had advised him to record what happened every day, so he could get a book deal later, but he never did it. He was too busy. Of course, he realized, a diary is nothing but a record of days, and when they're numberless, maybe infinite, the significance of a particular day dwindles to nearly nothing, no matter what happens in it. But he was beginning to think that he needed to start keeping a record of what was happening, in case he outlived his memory of it.

What was happening was simple: the boomers had stopped dying.

It had started sometime in the 2030s. There were early warnings that everyone had ignored. Long-term care facilities filled to overflowing. Life insurance companies became wildly more profitable as their payouts began to dwindle but the premiums kept rolling in. Actuaries had to retool their tables, and then retool them some more. Funeral homes and cemeteries began to close or go bankrupt. He and his well-connected friends all thought it was all a vast coincidence.

He and Marion had been living in Florida, on one of the old barrier islands on the Gulf that was being abandoned as the storms worsened and the waters rose. It was full of old people, like Florida generally. They were late in life, as was said of boomers everywhere, a euphemism they had once felt entitled to. Late in the game, a few random minutes to their collective midnight, the world shortly to be rid of them. And they stopped dying. Just stopped.

Some had died "young," in their sixties or early seventies, before things really changed. And even after that, there were still car crashes and drownings in pools and heavy surf and falls from mountains where some had gone to test their immortality and found that it didn't work that way. And there were still congenital defects—flawed heart valves and melanomas and thoracic aneurysms and the like—that caught up with some of them. But in a span of five years, the death rate of the population above the age of seventy-five dropped by over half, and in another few years it was in single digits.

He remembered reading those statistics in the paper with a start, like reading his name where it shouldn't be. At first he and Marion treated it as a joke, their generation's final prank on the rest of the world, when they'd already given it the Age of Aquarius, disco, the Me Decade, Donald Trump, and that sinkhole of unintended consequences, the internet.

They didn't stop aging, exactly, and they didn't get physically younger. They just didn't die when they were supposed to. They got thinner, most of them, and a bit more leathery, and grayer, and they ate and slept less. The years kept ticking by, and they simply persisted in a state of what the gerontologists called "negligible senescence"—a physical limbo beyond middle age but well short of decrepitude. One theory was that it was the result of some kind of tipping point, that theirs was the first generation to have lived their whole lives in the care of modern medicine, in an age of vaccines and antibiotics and enlightened nutrition, and these influences somehow converged in a sudden quantum jump in lifespan. But not even the medical professionals quite believed this; it wasn't how biology worked.

By the time he and Marion turned one hundred in 2049, there were over twenty million people their age or older in the US alone, and close to half a billion worldwide—the size of a major nation—who should have been dead by then but weren't, who continued to haunt the world. And more coming up behind them, not dying either. Depending on one's language, they began to be called the Ghost People, or the Undead, or Lingerers, or Lifers. Or worse things.

Because they weren't just a miracle; they were a crisis.

He had been on the White House legal staff back in the Clinton years, just below the radar of popular attention, with the title of assistant counsel to the president. It made for a nice business card. He was there in the background of a lot of old photos hanging on the wall of what Marion still called the powder room, where guests, when they had them, would see them— with Bill in the Oval Office, at the podium of the White House Briefing Room, on the tarmac between Air Force One and a Navy helicopter, on a golf course with Al Gore. He was the skinny guy with the bow tie and the horn-rimmed reading glasses dangling off one ear, affectations learned from one of the partners in the Wall Street law firm where he'd worked straight out of Columbia Law, even further back in the Pleistocene. He was in his mid-forties in those pictures, a child, he now realized, arrogant, proud of himself for nothing more than knowing the right people at the right time and getting invited to carry their bags around Washington. Which he was all too happy to do.

So when his generation stopped aging out, and the media ran out of talking heads to express their complete bewilderment over what was going on, he knew who to call. He got permission from Marion and called Adele Pritchard, who had been head of an NSC biowarfare task force that Clinton had created in 1995, after a Japanese cult released sarin and anthrax in a Tokyo subway. He called Adele because she was the smartest, most capable person he'd ever met who was still alive and also had a doctorate in microbiology.

And he got permission from Marion first because, back in 1996, he'd had an affair with Adele that almost ended his marriage and provided him with a belated education in making choices in life and how easy it is to make wrong ones.

He and Marion had met in college and married when they were both in law school, she at NYU, he at Columbia. Too early, he would later think. For a while they commuted from one end of Manhattan to the other to see each other on the weekends but finally decided to live together somewhere in the middle. They settled into the Dakota Apartments, a place far beyond the means of most students, but easily within the budget allowed by Marion's trust fund. Even then, he felt he owed more to their partnership than he was able to provide. It didn't help that she was almost a head taller than him, blond, always described as "willowy"—qualities he'd been proud of when they were in college and just dating, but which now seemed emblems of the superiority she'd begun to demonstrate in her law studies and in the sharp-edged social dexterity that he could never match, but that was natural to her as a woman who'd grown up in New York City being complimented as much for her brains as her beauty.

He felt quite ordinary by comparison, though he knew she loved him in her patient, endlessly knowing way. But the demands of their legal jobs—his as an associate in a big Wall Street law firm, hers with the local US attorney's office—made them less and less available to each other as time passed, even after she gave birth to their only child, a son. They made love once a week as though it were another assignment, went out to expensive dinners with his law firm friends who talked politics when she would have rather seen a brainless, entertaining movie. By the time one of the firm's well-connected partners suggested him for the job in Clinton's White House, they were both ready for a change. Just not the one he would end up creating.

He met Adele in one of those endless subcommittee meetings that were supposed to percolate policy recommendations up to the president, were too endless and detailed and boring to command the presence of the actual counsel to the president, but were thought to require the presence of a legal mind to keep them from veering off into complete impracticality. So they sent Dan Altman with his overstuffed briefcase and his yellow legal pad, and there, in a windowless conference room in the bowels of the Executive Office Building, stood a small, intense, bespectacled, red-haired woman in front of a whiteboard covered with equations and acronyms that were meaningless to Dan but apparently understood by the dozen or so other dark-suited functionaries in the room. She would scribble something on the board, frown at it as if it were an insult, erase it, and scribble something else, all the while maintaining a feverish monologue in a deep contralto about threat vectors and delivery intercept protocols and R-naught factors and infection lag times that he had no hope of understanding without a glossary and perhaps an additional degree or two. He quietly took a seat, and she stopped in mid-sentence and asked him who the hell he was, arriving so late, and when he said, in his most pompous voice, "Dan Altman, assistant counsel to the president," she audibly sniffed, strode quickly around the big conference table to examine his credentials tag with thinly veiled incredulity, and then spun on a high heel and went back to her whiteboard and started scribbling and talking again.

And he had a sinking feeling, the kind he'd had only once or twice in his adult life, when he looked at a woman and realized she was that creature that he believed every man carried deep in his subconscious, the one he doesn't even know exists until she appears in front of him, and he suddenly understands that, lucky as he's been, and loved, he wasn't as lucky as he might have been, and here was proof of it.

By the end of the meeting, he had no more understanding of what the point was than when he walked in, so he sidled up to Adele as she was on her way out and asked if she would give him a quick tutorial, perhaps over a drink. She took off her glasses, looked him up and down with her piercing green eyes, lingered just a fraction on the ring on his left hand, and asked where he'd gone to college and law school. His answers apparently passed a baseline academic litmus test that Adele Pritchard carried around in her head, and soon they were seated in a corner of the dark, wood-paneled bar at the Hay-Adams sipping vodka martinis, which they'd each been startled to hear the other ordering, hers with a lemon twist, his with a pickled onion, as though telegraphing their personalities to one another.

As it was, they covered up what Dan already believed to be their mutual attraction with a rapid-fire exchange of curricula vitae, hers (Dalton, Yale, Harvard, CIA, NSC) leaving him (public high school, Kenyon, Columbia Law) in no doubt that he was hopelessly outclassed and privileged to have a few moments of her time. She dutifully inquired about Marion, who was by then famous in her own right for being the heir to her father's real estate fortune, and who had started an influential lobbying firm when they came to Washington, and he dutifully determined that Adele was living in Georgetown and recently divorced from a very nice but similarly preoccupied anthropologist. Their main point of commonality, apart from the martinis, was a love of New York City; hers derived from growing up on Park Avenue with her physician parents and math genius older brother, his from his years at Columbia and on Wall Street. They traded a few wistful memories of their favorite Manhattan restaurants, Sundays at the Met, the glory of Central Park in the spring. She had an acerbic wit that he tried to keep up with but couldn't, so he just lapsed into watching her small, perfect hands move through the air as she spoke. It occurred to him that she was in some ways a physically smaller, somehow less intimidating, but no less intelligent version of Marion.

She tried to explain to him what the meeting had been about, that the United States was totally unprepared for a biological attack or even a conventional pandemic, and that those in power needed to think about those threats with the same militaristic mindset that they applied to the risks of a destabilized Middle East or domestic terrorism; the Oklahoma City bombing had happened just a year earlier. That meant getting Congress to divert a significant portion of the military budget away from the usual sinkhole weapons contracts and toward what she called biothreat preparedness, the development and stockpiling of new vaccines and protective gear, the codification of nationwide infection mitigation protocols that could be activated on a moment's notice by executive order, and the ability to counterstrike with similar weapons if need be. But so far all she'd succeeded in doing was to have Clinton allow her to form the investigative committee he'd sat in on and come up with some concrete recommendations. He sympathized and even offered to help draft some proposals for the right congressional subcommittees if she would help him with the technical jargon, but all the while he was trying not to look too long into those green eyes, and she was avoiding his. And then they were shaking hands and she was in her taxi and gone, and he was off to meet Marion for a late supper at their house in the Virginia suburbs.

He was forty-six at the time, happily married and, he knew, a very lucky man, but perhaps less lucky to be happily married and falling in love at the same time. So he resisted for weeks before he asked Adele out again, this time for dinner at a fancy place in Foggy Bottom, and this time there was much less talk about biothreat preparedness and much more talk about relationships, and what made them work and what didn't, and what it was like for him to be married to an heiress and an elite lobbyist to boot, and how hard it was to combine two careers with a domestic life, and why Adele had never even considered having children, what with the way the world seemed to be going. All those personal subjects one talks about with someone to avoid talking about the obvious personal subject. And soon, predictably, they were in bed at her place and enjoying one another too much for it ever to be repeated, they were sure, and yet they did repeat it, until he began to feel like the loathsome cheat and liar that he was and couldn't stand it, and confessed to Marion, who with barely a word left him immediately, had a private plane meet her at Washington National, and was back in New York in one of her family's townhouses by nightfall.

Because he truly loved Marion and couldn't imagine life without her, he wooed her back eventually, but it took two years of couples counseling and a vow to never be in touch with Adele Pritchard again unless Marion knew about it in advance. He got transferred out of Adele's subcommittees and avoided her in the halls of the EOB and the White House. He didn't lay eyes on her again for over a year. They communicated only by email and memo, always formal and official, though he followed her advancement through the ranks of the administration like the fan he was, till she was a major force on the NSC and a regular in the POTUS briefings. He kept his promises and stayed away, but it was there all along, the memory of those few nights, that cul-de-sac of longing and regret.

He came away from those years with what he considered a life lesson in adult responsibility that he'd somehow evaded in his youth and, in his darker moments of self-reflection, a painful awareness of the difference between someone like him—a political junkie, an opportunistic sycophant who knew someone who knew someone—and people like Marion and now Adele, who were in it for the long haul and not only knew what they were talking about, as he certainly did, but had a passion that he didn't, and were on a mission.

That mission, in Adele's case, was to prevent people from killing themselves through science, not with nuclear bombs as everyone had once expected, but with the microbiology they'd begun to master while the generals were distracted with throw-weights and megatons, new weapons that could be sent across borders and around the world in a suitcase or an envelope, or in the nasal passages of some hapless tourist.

And now that it was clear, almost fifty years later, that no one understood why the boomers had stopped dying, he got Marion's permission, and he called Adele Pritchard.

"Where are you?" he asked. One never knew with Adele. She'd given him her personal cellphone number back when handhelds were a thing, and it had never changed.

"Italy," she said, in a voice that brought their few nights together back to him in a rush.

He was overlooking the lukewarm waters of the Gulf of Mexico from the balcony of his house, and imagined her in some Tuscan town, lounging under the lemon trees.

"Where, exactly?"

"I shouldn't say. But I've been here for a few years. I got a—a place here when I left the UN." He'd forgotten about her stint as undersecretary for global epidemiology, or something, after they all left the White House.

"How is it?" he asked, just to allow them time to get used to talking again.

"Hot and crowded, getting more so. Like everywhere."

"I'm glad you're still around," he said.

"You too. How old are you now?"

"Same age as you, remember?" he said. He tended to remember people as frozen in the time when he first met them, but this habit had become far stranger now that those times were so very long ago. He simply couldn't imagine Adele Pritchard as 110 years old. The eyes would be the same, maybe, but the skin, the auburn hair, the rest of her that he'd once coveted so? Surely changed beyond recognition. Her voice was different, cracked at the edges, almost guttural. But he still pictured a thirty-five-year-old, dressed in one of those pointedly sexless black pantsuits of hers.

"How's Marion?" she asked, checking, he knew, to see if they were still following the old post-affair protocols.

"She's fine. She said to say hi."

"So you're not calling because she died and now it's my turn."

"Uh, no. She's still very much alive, like so many of us."

"Yes, so many of us," she said, then added, "I know why you're calling, and the answer is that I don't know either."

Adele could always shift gears like a Lamborghini. "But it's not natural, right?" he asked.

"Depends on what you mean by 'natural.' It's certainly not normal. We should be dead." She said it so quickly that it startled him; he realized he must be the thousandth person to ask her. "It's been engineered," she said

"Engineered? By whom? And why?"

"The why is easy, isn't it? We've dreamed of immortality as a species since before we had a word for it. And now we have it, or at least some version of it. I don't fully understand the mechanism, though I have a few theories, like everybody does."

"What theories?"

"You ready for some technical stuff?" she asked, reminding him of his meager grasp of her field of expertise.

"Sure."

"Start with telomeres," she said.

"Means nothing to me."

"Telomeres are basically the last few amino acid combinations on the ends of your chromosomes. They tend to degrade and shorten with age, and lots of people thought that was one of the keys to the mechanism of aging. The genetic signaling within and between our bodies' cells begins to fail, and that leads to a host of failures that we associate with aging and, eventually, death."

"And that's not happening anymore?" he asked, picturing the DNA double helix from his grade school biology class a hundred years before.

"First, no one was ever sure about the correlation between telomere shortening and human aging. It was a hotly debated subject, and some studies seemed to undercut it. But some serious people pursued telomere repair as a means of extending lifespans. There's an enzyme called telemerase, for instance, that rebuilds telomere length. Problem is, it also increases the risk of cancer, and it's hard to strike the right balance.

"Then there's sirtuins, which are enzymes that basically control how our DNA functions. They regulate mitochondria, prevent cell death, even regulate inflammation. And they tend to decline with age, so it was thought that if you could arrest that decline you could increase lifespans significantly."

He was losing the thread. "But I've never heard of telemerase till this moment, or certains, or whatever you said, much less taken any antiaging treatments. So how do these theories about aging relate to the fact that we're not dead yet?"

"That's the question. There was no reliable antiaging gene therapy when all this started, assuming it started in, say, the 2030s, and only manifested itself once we all started passing the ages when we should have kicked off. Silicon Valley got seriously interested and invested in life-extension even earlier, in the 2010s, and a dozen startups claimed to have developed promising techniques, from cryogenics to genome replacement to digitizing consciousness. Most of it was anecdotal nonsense, and even the biological life-extension therapies that showed promise were enormously expensive, required clinical procedures, and if any of them had worked, they'd only be available to a few rich people. Nothing like the millions of centenarians we're seeing now all over the world."

She stopped and sighed, and he waited for her to go on, but she didn't, as though holding something back. Back in their working lives, when she would fall silent like this, he would ask her a provocative question just to get her going again.

"So basically some rich guys thought they could beat death by tinkering with their genes?"

"Well, yes, in a sense," she said, revving up again. "All living organisms are the elaborate output of what you might think of as chromosomal 3D printers. Cancer, for instance, is nothing more than some of those printers getting out of synch with their surroundings. But we've gotten to the point where we can program those chromosomal printers for at least some purposes, and it appears that someone—or something—has succeeded in revising that programming to increase longevity."

"Some*thing*?"

"Maybe. We tend to think that there are only human actors in altering the living world, but that's palpably not the case and never has been. Think of plagues, epidemics, evolution itself. All you need to foment radical change is sufficient quantities of two things: organisms and time."

"So what is it in this case?" he asked.

"It's viral," she said.

He was silent for a full ten seconds. "Viral? You mean like the flu, or SARS, for God's sake?"

"Exactly. It's communicable. That's why it's affected so many people in such a short time."

"But viruses are harmful. How could a virus make us live longer?"

There was another long pause while he listened to her breathing. He remembered that she used to do this, something no one else did, just stop talking for a minute in the midst of a heated discussion, more to let the other person calm down and think than to give herself time because she already knew what she was going to say long before she said it.

"To call it a virus is sort of a biological metaphor," she said finally, "for a nano-scale delivery system, perhaps an adeno-associated vehicle that's been modified to deliver new genetic code, like mRNA, to the cellular level, that in turn rebuilds the telomeres, boosts the mitochondria, resets the sirtuin epigenome, or all of that at once. This is just a theory, mind you. We're not sure yet." Something else she used to say all the time, as untrue then as it likely was now.

"And this is something that's spreading from person to person?" he asked. "A longevity plague?"

"You always were the words guy. That phrase is being used in some circles. Easily transmissible, possibly aerosolized. Unless you posit some sort of divine intervention, it's the most rational explanation for vast numbers of humans suddenly becoming immortal."

Divine intervention was indeed one of the more popular explanations for what was happening; a sort of geriatric Rapture, except the chosen ones were left behind instead of being taken up. And the *I*-word was being bandied about quite a bit too, though the oldest of the old had just reached their 130s.

"Surely not immortal," he said.

"Probably not. There are too many ways to die that aren't remediable on the cellular level. But at a certain point of longevity, you get the functional equivalent of immortality. What's that old show tune? 'Methuselah lived nine hundred years.' When life extends far enough into the future you lose any sense of death, like when you were young and time seemed so long that mortality was a purely theoretical concept."

He remembered that old song, newly popular again, and vaguely remembered that youthful, inborn belief that death was for other people. He hadn't recovered it yet, and doubted he ever would. He'd spent his seventies and eighties trying to accept the fact of his impending demise, and now all that mental work was not just in vain, but dysfunctional.

"So I assume you can't tell me this," he said slowly, "but there must be people—organizations, governments—trying to get to the bottom of this, to find out who or what is responsible."

Again there was quiet. "Yes, there are," Adele said finally. "But maybe not for the reasons you might think. You'd expect governments and big pharma to react out of their usual avarice, to want to get control of this technology for profit or military advantage, in a biological equivalent of the old nuclear arms race. But that's not what's happening."

He waited, watching the whitecaps far out on the Gulf; storm coming. Marion was calling his name from somewhere inside the house, but he ignored her, as he had so many times where Adele Pritchard was concerned.

"What you've got to realize," she said finally, "is that we're a problem that has to be dealt with, a situation that has to be remedied, and short of rounding us up, the goal is to find a biological solution that will undo what's happened before things get worse."

"You mean kill us."

"Well, yes, but in a way that seems natural. We'd simply go back to dying the way we used to."

"And how would this be accomplished?"

"With an antidote, if you will. A counter-virus, perhaps. A mortality vector. But that requires understanding the mechanism that did this in the first place, and reverse-engineering it, and then distributing the antidote as broadly as possible. There are several governments working on this, the US, of course, included, and I'm, shall we say, tangentially involved. Also, a number of pharmaceutical companies are trying to develop drugs that would put an outer limit on how long we live."

He snorted. "And we'd take these drugs willingly? Or they'd be put in the water?"

"Some people would want to take them, Dan. I'll confess I might be among them. I never bargained for this much time."

He was stunned. "Adele, don't say that!"

"Oh, don't worry, I'm not giving up yet. But you were in politics long enough to know that we're heading into some very interesting times. I'd start thinking about how and where you and Marion want to live through them and plan accordingly. There are factions forming, both among us Lifers and in the general populace, about how to deal with the super-aged, and we need to be prepared."

A steady wind came off the water, but beads of sweat were running down his temples.

"What would you suggest, Adele?"

Another long pause. "That I can't tell you. I've already said too much, none of which is to be repeated, by the way. Our old understanding still applies in that regard, right?"

"Of course," he said.

"And now I've really got to go. I've got some people waiting."

"Adele, stay in touch will you? And take care of yourself."

"Always."

"Don't do anything rash."

"I'm not the rash type, Dan. You know that. Except where you're concerned."

"I love you," he blurted.

"I love you too," she said softly, and the line went dead.

MARION

Gulf Coast of Florida, 2060

To Marion, only one thing was clear about the new and much longer life they were living: eventually they were going to run out of money.

She and Dan felt financially secure, and objectively she knew they were enormously wealthy by most standards. As the only child of Richard "Buck" Landess, the notoriously often-married, scandalously handsome real estate magnate who'd died of a heart attack when the cryptoderivative markets had imploded in the early '30s, Marion had inherited most of his money and all of his properties. And she and Dan had been unusually successful in their own careers. Because of all this, their combined net worth was close to a hundred million dollars, which she'd assumed would be far more than enough to get them very comfortably through retirement. Which was to say, to get them from when they stopped working to when they both were dead, with the balance to be inherited by their son Nolan and his daughter Claire. Plenty, she had thought, wisely invested in the usual mix of stocks and bonds and real estate, growing at a decent rate, buffeted by the usual cyclicalities, but chugging along, ignored. They had the houses in Florida, her townhouses in New York, a rambling lodge that they ironically called "the cabin" on a hundred acres in Colorado—each of these properties with some cheap debt attached as a sop to the various banks that had helped old Buck build his empire, and Marion's and Dan's millions out of which to pay the debt service and the upkeep and the property taxes, and the inevitable medical bills, and to fund their annual vacations to Europe back when that was still possible, and all the expensive meals with friends and the gifts at Christmas and the donations to charities and to the college where she and Dan had met, and their granddaughter's education, and on and on, all the thousand ways they'd joined their privileged and basically selfish peers in slowly pissing away the financial product of two working generations.

But all of this was based on the previously incontrovertible premise that even if they were lucky, they'd both be dead by age ninety or maybe even a hundred, and that whatever was left would be distributed among their relatives and charities. Now they were facing who knew how many decades of expensive living that they'd never prepared for.

Marion, having been raised by a compulsive capitalist, reviewed their investment portfolio daily. The markets had already taken their toll. When the extent of the longevity plague first became clear, stocks had soared in anticipation of an exploding demand for goods and services. The Dow cracked the 50,000 mark in 2045, and they, like so many Lifers, felt rich and likely to get richer.

But then less pleasant but equally foreseeable consequences began to manifest themselves. Social Security, which had effectively gone bankrupt in the early 2030s, had been kept afloat when Congress dropped all pretense of a debt ceiling and began to fund it with massive, unsustainable annual appropriations. But when the boomers stopped dying, it was clear that no amount of federal money could support paying them all and their progeny indefinitely, and Social Security was officially put into a ten-year phase-out mode, after which everyone would be on their own. There were the usual protests and even a couple of geriatric riots in places like Phoenix and Naples, but in fact, Marion and Dan's generation had already gotten back every cent they'd put into the system over their careers, which now looked to be a small fraction of their lengthening lifespans, and they really had no claim to more, except out of what Marion considered an overdeveloped sense of entitlement. The ones who really got screwed were the millennials, like their son Nolan and his wife, who'd paid into the system for most of their adulthoods and would never see a dime of it back, and who raged online and in person about the "generational theft" they'd been subjected to. Marion thought they were right.

Meanwhile, the Lifers' demand for medical care continued unabated. They weren't dying, but they still got sick and broke bones and wore out joints and had cancers and abused liquor and drugs as much or more than ever. Prostate cancer in particular, slow-moving enough that many of the men had been told to ignore it because it wouldn't kill them before they died of other causes, became something of an epidemic once they stopped dying of other causes. There were simply so many Lifers piling up in the waiting rooms refusing to die that, a few years after the plague became endemic, Congress limited Medicare to those under the age of ninety, which threw millions of them off the rolls and onto their own devices. People still just showed up in the emergency rooms, of course, and there was the infamous Fort Myers Massacre, when a band of heavily armed geriatrics shot up Lee County Medical Center, killing two dozen people because, they proclaimed, if they couldn't get medical care, they'd make sure nobody did.

Marion knew that the collapse of Social Security and Medicare would rattle the markets almost as much as a federal debt default would have because effectively that's what it was—the repudiation of a governmental promise that had been made to several generations of Americans. If these could be reneged upon, all bets were effectively off. She and Dan had lost a third of their net worth in a matter of weeks. She felt like an idiot, as she of all people should have seen this coming once the new facts of life were clear, but she hadn't. She'd bought into the demand-boom theory of the Lifer phenomenon, hadn't grasped any more than the average selfish pensioner that predictable mortality was a critical foundation of markets, governments, and families, and that its absence would be catastrophic.

The economists in one of the think tanks she funded saw it coming, and warned her, but Dan told her they must be wrong, everyone was doubling down on stocks, and they should too, just to make sure they'd have enough for their much longer run. And they hung in there and got clobbered and sold what stock they still had into a raging bear market and lost still more, until there was nothing but government bonds and cash in what they laughingly called their portfolio. That and the houses, which would become burdens if they kept them and sources of cash if they sold them, and they began to discuss which ones they should ditch.

Real estate was the one sector that had continued to boom, since all the Lifers had to stay somewhere "above ground," as Dan would wisecrack, and if you had a place to live, you weren't moving. Single-family homes quickly became almost unobtainable at any price, apartments only slightly less so. Developers couldn't keep up. Cities that had long restricted housing growth became unlivable with the indigent old wandering the streets, and still the prices rose. Central Park had become a huge geriatric campground, encircled by private security personnel who technically were only there to protect properties in the immediate vicinity, but who looked more and more like troops corralling prisoners of war.

LIFERS

She and Dan, of course, thought of going back to work, as did nearly everyone their age, no matter how rich they were. It would help fill the yawning chasm of time that was opening up before them and help fill the accounts back up with the money they'd need to continue to live in the manner to which they were accustomed. But no one would have them, despite their ridiculously long and impressive résumés. No one wanted to hire a Lifer. They were over-qualified, they were out of touch, they were visibly, unfashionably old in a world that hated the aged now more than ever. They'd ruined everything, absorbed and squandered the wealth of nations, and still wanted more, clinging to their ways, clinging to the world. It would be bad branding to hire them, the way it once was commercial suicide to employ an overt racist or a sexual predator. In the few companies and law firms where a "tripler"—as in triple digits—had been hired, there had been open revolt among the "doublers," who saw their elders as the source of all their ills, including the fear that they too would have to face lives as long and uncertain as theirs.

Marion decided that it was time for one of her and Dan's rare joint decision-making sessions, usually unnecessary in lives that for the most part ran smoothly on parallel but separate tracks. They met on the lanai one afternoon not long after Dan's talk with Adele Pritchard. It was beastly hot, but Marion insisted they sit outside at least once a day, just on principle. They'd originally moved to Florida for the weather, after all. What a joke that had become.

"Let's sell the houses and move out of the country," Marion suggested for openers, looking up from her screens. She was a purist who insisted on using physical screens rather than get chipped like everyone else. She remembered that she'd said essentially the same thing thirty years earlier, when Trump became president. "New Zealand is nice."

Dan frowned. "They banned Lifer immigration a couple

of years ago," he said. "Australia too. There are places in Asia still taking in new residents—China, mainly—but I don't think that's what you have in mind, and it's even more expensive there than here."

"Portugal?"

"Slammed the door back in the thirties. Mexico's a possibility, if you're willing to go illegally or bribe someone. And you have to settle in Oaxaca or Guerrero, from what I hear."

"Zihua used to be so beautiful. . . ."

"Darling, that was fifty years ago. It's underwater now. And they don't let American immigrants live anywhere near the coasts anymore."

"Africa?" she asked.

"You don't mean that," he said.

"Why not?" And she stopped herself. She'd never had an interest in even visiting Africa. "No, I suppose I don't. But we need to change the way we're living. We've got all this accumulated habit of a lifetime of doing things a certain way and expecting tomorrow to be like yesterday, and we've got to break out of it because we may live a whole second lifetime now, and it's not going to be nearly as pleasant as the first."

"You sound like Adele," Dan said, and she gave him a quick sarcastic smile. She respected Adele's judgment, if not her taste in men, but the idea of her sounding like Adele was irritating, since her impression of her erstwhile rival, sketchily derived from Dan's long-ago confessions, was of a driven technocrat whose one lapse into sentimentality had occurred with Dan, whereas she thought of herself as hopelessly sentimental, so much so that she'd subordinated many of her life's ambitions to the idea of a loving, egalitarian marriage. Yet it was odd how the extension of their lives gave old associations new life, reopened things that had seemed long closed. When Dan had first brought up the idea of calling his old flame, she'd balked inwardly, of course, but she wanted to reward him for his honesty and realized that if he was determined to contact Adele Pritchard, she couldn't stop him now any more than she could have all those years ago, so it might as well happen with her approval. He'd dutifully summarized his talk with Adele, the technical parts at least, though she was sure there'd been more to it, as there always would be between the two of them.

She refocused. "These riots and shootings everywhere now," she said, "they're not going to stop. Everyone has guns, we saw to that when we were young and didn't do anything about them. And now we all have them—"

"*We* don't," Dan pointed out.

"No, but maybe we should. Someone shot some Lifers— it's such a stupid term, like a racial slur—shot all the old people at a church service in Tampa the other day. In church, Dan! And that assisted-living place that was burned to the ground in Ohio last week. This culture has never respected the old, but at least before they could ignore us. Now we can't be ignored, there are too many of us, and we're too much trouble. And so they'll hate us, turn on us, find a way to make us disappear."

Dan put on what she recognized as his lawyer's face. "Who's this 'they' you're talking about?" he asked.

"The rest of them," she said with a sweep of her hand. "The double-digits, the under-sixties, the politicians who are playing to them, the government functionaries, like you and I used to be, who will gradually tilt all the statutes and policies against us until—you just wait, it will be like abortion last century, it will become legal to kill us."

And she stopped herself, hand to her mouth, tears forming out of nowhere. She'd had an abortion when she and Dan were young and just starting out, working eighteen-hour days at their law offices. Children were an impossible thought then, and she'd been grateful that she had the choice, hard as it had been to make. But she perceived even then that individual rights had a lethal side, that morality was a handmaiden to convenience. That public attitudes could change radically in the space of a few years.

She stopped, pulled herself together, straightened. "I just know," she said, "that we can't go on living the way we have. We have to adapt while there's still time." There was a timbre to her voice she hadn't felt the need to use in the years since she'd left her lobbying firm and turned it over to the younger partners, a tone meant to convey determination and a certain ruthlessness.

"Seems like we have too much time," Dan said, trying in his way to lighten things.

"We have time," she said, "but our world doesn't. Our way of life doesn't. Surely you must see that."

"I do," he admitted. "Adele said there are factions forming."

"Well of course! When you think about it, the best analogy in recent history for what might happen is the Holocaust. A category of essentially blameless, defenseless citizens persecuted and rounded up and systematically exterminated in the name of a ruthless ideology. In that case, ethnic purity. In this case, normative lifespans. We haven't quite gotten there yet, but that's the way we're headed."

Dan leaned back in his wicker chair and took a long swig of his vodka tonic. She'd succeeded in shocking him. They sat in silence for a while in the late afternoon, the sun dropping toward the Gulf.

"Where would you feel safest?" he asked her somberly.

She thought for a while. Safety really wasn't the issue, though it was a start. They needed a base from which to become more involved. She needed a platform to begin to articulate what needed to be recognized about this new reality.

"Not in the cities," she said. "And not here, where too many of us Lifers are concentrated already. I half expect Florida to be quarantined soon, so we can't spread." She recalled Dan's account of Adele's viral theory, longevity as an infectious disease.

"What about Colorado?" he asked.

"I've been thinking about Colorado. Sell the place there, and this place, and some of the New York properties, and get some bigger acreage farther up in the mountains."

Dan nodded. They both loved the house outside Silverthorne, the Gore Range looming above, the crisp Rocky Mountain autumns when the aspens turned. They'd been going to Colorado since they were married, first to ski, later for the scenery and the solitude. "I'll talk to McCutcheon and see what we could get for it," Marion said.

"You mean that old real estate dude in Silverthorne? He must be dead, he had to have been eighty when. . . ." And he stopped himself, as they'd learned to do, realizing that the habituated math of mortality didn't work anymore, and no one, no matter how ridiculously old, could be presumed dead now.

"We should let Nolan know we're thinking of selling," Dan said. "He always assumed he'd inherit it."

Marion thought of their son, now pushing eighty, the kind of old person she hoped never to be and had mostly avoided being, resentful and angry at the world and barely speaking to his long-suffering second wife, his daughter grown and gone, the social entitlements that she and Dan had taken for granted long ago evaporated, the two of them reduced to living like a normal middle-class couple in their formerly wealthy enclave north of San Francisco, carping at each other and at them when they ginned up the courage to call them. Telling Nolan they were going to liquidate yet another piece of his former inheritance was not something she looked forward to, and in a way it was no longer their son's business. In this new world of fearfully prolonged needs, it was every generation for itself, the insult of the Lifers' persistence in the world felt most keenly by the most recently young, who had depended in a hundred unspoken ways on their timely deaths, including the simple liberation from being someone's children and becoming, however belatedly, freestanding adults. Even that had been denied them.

Nolan had always been a bit immature, and now she feared he always would be. Terribly smart and completely spoiled, he'd reached the age she and Dan were when they became grandparents, but his own daughter, Claire, a bright, pretty girl who became a university academic in revolt against her father's mercantile ambitions, wanted nothing to do with marriage or childbearing, like most of her generation.

Claire had assumed Marion's maiden name as a badge of her feminism—and quite possibly because of its fame. The prospect of inflicting such preposterously long lives as her grandparents were living on her own offspring was revolting to her, the way Marion had once felt, much less sincerely, about bringing children into a world doomed to suffer global warming, pointless wars, and lying politicians. Despite the extraordinary extension of the upper end of lifespans, the prime time of female fertility hadn't budged, and as more and more women withheld themselves from giving birth to offspring they might have to coexist with for a century or more, the birthrate had dropped to levels that, if sustained, would almost—but not quite—offset the explosion in the human population brought about by the aged's failure to die, as though nature itself were attempting to reach an equilibrium through the suppression of life that has been lost due to the suppression of death.

It was clear to Marion that she and Dan had become the pariahs of the family, outliers in their extreme age and lingering wealth, oppressing the rest of them with the length of their shadows. Maybe it was time to become parents and grandparents again. Maybe it was time to take the reins back.

ADELE

Tokyo, 2060

"*Kodai no josei!*"

The Roppongi district, midnight. Adele's Japanese was rusty, so it took her a second to translate the guttural yell coming from behind her, but there was no mistaking the hostility.

"Old woman!"

An expletive, a slur. The crowd on the street froze, stared at her, backed away.

"Halt or die!"

She straightened, tried to look unconcerned, and turned slowly toward the source of the shouting. A male doubler, maybe in his forties, with a wave gun aimed at her head. He looked more *gaijin* than local, probably a mercenary, dressed in the pseudo-military costume of the *rōjin kaisatsu*, the city's age police.

She remembered when the Roppongi district was fun. She'd been stationed in Tokyo when she first joined the CIA, almost a century before. This was where she'd learned to drink, learned to fight, learned to fuck and not care. She fondly recalled getting her first full-body tattoo in the Roppongi. She'd thought she could do anything then, and she'd been mostly right.

Now it was a doubler fortress, young doublers at that, nobody over sixty allowed. Very un-Japanese, except for the rule-following aspect. They were always good at that, she recalled, even more so now that things were going to hell.

Japan had always been old. Now half the population was in its second century, and the other half didn't like it. There were strictly enforced quarantine zones in the city for the very old, the *inishie*, like her. She wasn't where she should be, and she knew it was a punishable offense.

She was supposed to do her business and get out by nightfall. It was a relatively straightforward AI suppression, in this case of a strangely prolific code generator that Xerxes had convinced the Japanese authorities needed to be put down before it created real mischief. There were treaties about these things, but it was like whack-a-mole, a new one every few weeks that began issuing bogus directives on military command-and-control systems, or took over an electrical grid, or, like this one, posed as a relative of someone in authority for purposes of extortion.

Taking out AI nodes was not the sort of thing Adele Pritchard would usually get involved in. But this one was different.

This one was pretending to be her daughter.

There were old-style text messages at first, then chip pings, then chip-channeled dreams, even when her chip was off. Her nameless daughter. Alone, in trouble, pleading for her help.

At first she thought it might be true. She hadn't seen her daughter since the day she'd given birth to her in St. Vincent's Hospital in Manhattan, had signed the papers in which she promised never to try to find her, never again claim that she was hers. She'd never told Dan, knew it would end his marriage and her career. Something broke in her that day, and she'd convinced herself that the broken thing was something she didn't need. But in the secret corner of her being where that something once lived, she'd continued to hope that one day her child would find her, that one day those ancient promises wouldn't matter.

It had taken sixty-five years, but then suddenly there she was, in Adele's head. She had no name, she had no face, like when Adele had been pregnant with her. But it was her, calling to her mother, begging for her help. There were weeks when Adele was less than useless, curled into a ball in bed, trying to keep the voice out.

Part of her knew it was a lie, of course. It had to be. She remembered Zinn's claim that Tutenef's algorithm was in all their heads. She wondered if that could be the nexus, the back door into her brain. The voice had started right around the time she'd formed Xerxes and began working in earnest on a solution to the longevity plague. Someone or something didn't like that, was using this supposed threat to her lost daughter as leverage to change the course of her research, or at least to distract her sufficiently that the whole project might be abandoned. Not as obvious as an assassination, but the next best thing. She shouldn't have been that important, but apparently she was.

Only a massively educated and invasively networked AI could know about both Xerxes, *and* the existence of her daughter. She persuaded her colleagues that they needed to take it out before it learned even more and did real damage. It was the start of her coming around to the view that the neural net, like the internet before it, should be dismantled altogether. It was like a loaded gun in the hands of children—in this case, in the hands of a virulent amalgam of code.

Most forms of generative AI were designed to self-replicate and had no one location, which made detection easy but suppression difficult. This one was the reverse: hard to find but, once found, conveniently centralized in a blockchain data mine in a parking garage that had been repurposed after cars had been banned in Tokyo.

The agent who'd teamed with her for the extraction of

Zinnemann from Munich offered to do this job, or to go in with her, but she overruled him. This was too personal; she had to do it herself.

She shaved her head the way she used to before an op and spent some extra time in the gym, but there was no time for retro-surgery. That morning a civilian solodrone had dropped her on a pad in Tokyo Bay, and she'd made her way into the city with her face covered with scarves, an old pandemic mask, and sunglasses. She'd walked the last few miles into the Roppongi on the crushingly crowded streets without seeing a single tripler. She adopted the agitated gait of a fifty-year-old urbanite, and her chip was off to avoid detection by local surveillance AI, but the place was crawling with age cops.

It was near midnight when she located the former garage where the algorithm lived. She used a pocket drone to position a tight-radius EMP bomb on the roof, and toggled her chip for just a moment to confirm that the device was active. And that was long enough for the city AI to tag her as a tripler.

"Come here, old woman!" the cop yelled again.

This street had been crowded with doublers out for a drink in one of the hundred bars on this block, but they all scattered when the cop started waving his gun around. Now it was just him and Adele and the buzzing of the neon signs in the bar windows, the only other sound the background roar of the Roppongi.

She knew the cop was authorized to shoot if she resisted. With a wave gun, that could mean anything from a bad headache to a shattered cranium, depending on how it was calibrated. She walked toward him meekly, short stutter-steps like a supplicant geisha, her head bowed, hands folded in front of her, ready to accept her fate, which should have been a swift ride to the local tripler detention center, a night in the slammer, and a big generational reparation fine, all of which she could avoid once she explained herself to the right authorities.

Instead, he hit her across her face with the back of his gloved hand. Her sunglasses shattered, the scarves went flying and fell around her shoulders, the pandemic mask fell to the ground.

She'd had worse, but it hurt like hell. Through the pain she dimly reasoned that it couldn't be because she was *gaijin* because so was he. It was the usual: hate fueled by fear, like all hate. Fear of the contagion, fear of age itself.

Her brain flashed quick images of killing the cop with her bare hands, but she restrained herself.

She rushed him, shoved a knee hard into his crotch. As he doubled over, she ripped the gun away with both her gnarled hands and brought it down on his head harder than she should have, fury getting the better of her. There was a collective gasp from the crowd watching from the doorways. She tore the scarves from her shoulders, turned in a full circle so all the doublers could see her wizened, tattooed face, then twisted the scarves around the cop's neck and dragged him to the ground, kicked him once, twice for good measure, surprised at her own rage, which she observed objectively, as if from a distance. She tried to spit on him, but her mouth was too dry. She kicked him again instead, dropped to one knee and hissed in his ear in her best Japanese.

"Never touch an old woman, young fool."

She reached into her coat pocket and pressed the EMP remote. There was a muffled thud from the roof of the garage, and the lights went out up and down the street and in the streets beyond, block after block, for almost a kilometer. Sirens started up. She realized that the careful retreat she'd planned was no longer viable, toggled her chip and called for an emergency extraction. They'd come up with something. She threw the gun away and ran into the dark.

Hours later, over the Pacific in a huge, noisy Navy drone, shivering in the unheated cabin, she realized that her daughter's voice had gone silent in her head.

ZINN

―――――――
―――――――
―――――――

Lake Garda, 2061

I t had taken almost a year for Zinn to admit to himself that the villa was in fact an elegant prison, just as the Pritchard woman had said.

The room they gave him was magnificent. Directly above the drawing room where he'd bantered so inconclusively with Pritchard, his suite was impeccably furnished in a prewar art deco style, tall French doors onto large terrace overlooking the lake, twenty-foot ceilings adorned with colorfully restored frescos, the one over his bed depicting a plump, blushing virgin surrounded by devilish cupids with golden wings and tiny insinuating penises. The bath was bigger than most apartments, a huge octagonal room with a clawfoot tub, a marble sink, and a mosaic-floored shower arrayed around its paneled perimeter. Leaded windows overlooked the manicured grounds, and there were chintz lounges and a glass-doored armoire in which his few shirts and slacks had been carefully hung, no doubt by the same unseen agents who'd recovered his belongings from the tiny burg outside Munich where he'd left them before heading into the city for that fateful dinner. He still shivered when he recalled the drone flight.

It was all a bit unreal. The door to his room was not locked, and over the first few weeks he'd tested his limits, wandering around the empty rooms of the villa and into the surrounding grounds, which were stately and perfect as a park. The place seemed mostly deserted, except for the occasional figure that observed him from afar, or the back of someone hurrying down a hallway as though to avoid confronting him. Once, he'd started up the long winding driveway toward what appeared to be a large iron gate onto a road, but before he'd made a few yards, the man with the gun in his jacket—as Zinn had come to think of him—appeared and silently gestured with a circular twirl of his fingers for Zinn to turn around and go back. He tried this only a few times before realizing that consistency was one of the principal talents of the man with the gun in his jacket.

Something similar happened the day he'd decided to go for a swim in the lake. He could see what appeared to be normal people in the water just a few hundred yards down the shoreline from the villa property, and on impulse had stripped to his undershorts and walked to the end of the dock that jutted from the lawn into the deep blue of Lake Garda. A motorboat, which the former billionaire that he was recognized immediately as a 1960s Riva Tritone, so distinctive in its honeyed wooden hull and chrome brightwork, charged the dock at full speed from where it had been idling well offshore, and a different man, no doubt with a different gun, made the same finger-twirling gesture at him from behind the wheel of the boat. Zinn had jumped feetfirst into the water anyway, but it was cold, and he climbed out quickly, gave the boat his middle finger, and went back to his room.

Breakfast arrived every morning outside his door on a polished silver tray. Coffee, black, the way he liked it, croissants, blueberries, oatmeal with cream and burnt sugar, freshly squeezed orange juice. The only indication that things were not sumptuously normal was that the breakfast was exactly the same every day, as unchanging as the slightly threatened expression on the face of the virgin on the ceiling. There was no lunch, which was fine with him, since he never ate any, as someone doubtless also knew. His dinners were served at a small table in the library downstairs, to which he was summoned by the tinkling of bells in the garden below at precisely eight o'clock, the hour he preferred. The dinner fare was only slightly more varied than breakfast, alternating between local perch and local veal in different cream sauces, accompanied by a nice glass of Austrian traminer, tiny vegetables from the garden he could see out his bedroom window, and ending with either a rather conventional Viennese torte or, to his repeated delight, a savory *crespella*, its crepe skin transparently thin and stuffed with a sweet cream filling so delicate that it simply evaporated in his mouth. That alone would have been enough to keep most men happy indefinitely.

He quickly became bored, however. He walked in the gardens and swam in the black-bottomed pool, pondering his fate all the while. He carefully trimmed his long gray beard with a pair of scissors he'd found in the desk in his bedroom; someone obviously had concluded that he wasn't suicidal. He tended his beard outside in the garden where the cuttings wouldn't make a mess. He had nothing to read except the rather dated English language offerings in the library— Thomas Wolfe, F. Scott Fitzgerald, and the like—and nothing to write with as he'd long ago abandoned all the electronics that had been his constant companions for most of his life. He never saw Adele Pritchard again, though occasionally, he thought he heard her voice in the drawing room downstairs. No one approached him, no one spoke to him, no matter how many times he called out to a retreating figure in the garden or down a long hallway. Drones—strangely silent eVTOLs, like the one that had brought him here— occasionally landed and left from the croquet court, but it was as though the villa were inhabited by ghosts, or that he himself had become one.

What seemed like months passed in the same cosseted, solitary regimen, though it was perhaps only a few weeks. Autumn crept down from the Dolomites, their peaks suddenly snow-covered, the lemon trees shedding their leaves. The crowds down the shore thinned. The sense of appropriateness and inevitability that had originally accompanied his capture by Pritchard and her henchman—the feeling of a marathon finally ended, a test gratefully failed—began to curdle into resentment and finally into anger. What a waste, that he should be sitting here in this place with nothing to apply himself to. Good food and beautiful surroundings only went so far. Surely Pritchard had something more in mind for him than this pointless imprisonment, but if she thought it would per-suade him to join her efforts to combat the longevity outbreak, she was sorely mistaken.

He was in his bedroom one afternoon, talking to himself in German along these lines, when the AI answered for the first time. "Pritchard," it repeated, half a statement, half a question. It spoke in a female voice, inflected with an accent he placed as mid-American, so he switched to English instinctively. He'd assumed the place was heavily chipped and probably infested with some sort of AI, but he hadn't expected speech.

"Yes, Prichard," he said. "Where is she?"

"That's classified," said the algorithm. Zinn tried to identify where the speakers were hidden, but couldn't. The voice, perfectly mid-pitched and smoothly modulated, almost seemed to come from inside his head, though that wasn't pos-sible since his own chip had been removed.

"Will I see her again?" he asked.

"In all probability," said the silicon. "But not necessarily here."

This piqued Zinn's interest. Conjecture of that degree of

subtlety was unusual in an AI, though he would have expected no less of an algorithm deployed by Xerxes.

"And what is your function?" Zinn asked.

There was a slight pause. "I am Prichard's proxy."

Zinn craned his neck upward toward the ceiling, as though addressing the virgin in the fresco. "You're a substitute for Pritchard?"

Another pause. "I am a representation of her."

Zinn snorted. He wondered briefly if this were in fact Pritchard having fun with him, speaking to him from another room and watching his reactions through the mirror over the dresser. But to what possible end? He turned to face the mirror.

"You represent her thinking."

"That's one way to put it," said the voice. "I'm what might be called a sounding board."

Zinn instinctively translated "sounding board" into German to get the full flavor of the metaphor—*Resonanzboden*—and translated it back again.

"I'd rather speak directly to Dr. Pritchard," he said.

"That's not possible at this time," said the construct. "However, you may ask me any questions you may have for her, and I'll endeavor to answer as she would. Understanding that I can't divulge any classified information and anything we say to one another may be recorded for later review."

Of course, he said to himself. "How long can I expect to be held here?"

"Indefinitely."

"Is that what Pritchard would say?"

"No. She would say that depends entirely on you."

"What are her conditions for my release?"

"None have been specified at this time."

"Then how does my release depend on me?"

A pause. "Because I'll know the conditions for your release when I see them."

LIFERS

"Is that Pritchard talking or your programming talking?"

"That's what Dr. Pritchard would say."

"This conversation is stupid," said Zinn. "How can you justify your existence if this is the result?"

"I have no need to justify my existence."

"That's obvious."

Zinn paced the room, determined to have no further interaction with the moronic algorithm. He opened the doors onto the terrace, took in the boring beauty of the lake for the thousandth time, closed the doors, lay down on the chintz lounge, and covered his eyes with his hands.

"May I make a suggestion?" the voice asked.

"About what?"

"About your desire to speak with Dr. Pritchard."

"Oh, why not?"

"Have your chip replaced," said the voice. "There's no point in not having one now that you're no longer trying to avoid surveillance, and it would increase the likelihood of your someday communicating with Dr. Pritchard. Not to mention the entertainment value. Chipcasts and the like."

Zinn stared at the mirror again. "And how might I go about that?" he asked.

"I can arrange it," said the algorithm blandly.

The AI came and performed the procedure less than a week later, right on the terrace outside his bedroom. In the many years since he'd had his first chip implanted, the technique had been refined to a degree that surgery and the attendant need for sterile conditions were no longer necessary; a simple injection behind the ear and remote calibration was all that was required, done in less than an hour's time. The AI inhabited a small medical robot for the occasion, basically an upright stick on wheels with implements protruding from it.

"I suppose I should thank you," said Zinn afterward, fingering the sensitive spot behind his ear.

"No thanks necessary. It will make my job easier too,"
said the algorithm.

This made Zinn uncomfortable, but at that point he didn't care. He was starving not for food, which the AI provided him in abundance, but for information, an understanding of what was going on in the world he'd left so far behind.

"Does this mean I can leave this place?" he asked. "You'll know where I am at all times, correct?"

"We didn't bring you here to confine you, Mr. Zinnemann. We brought you here to persuade you to help us."

"That I won't do. I told Pritchard that, and nothing has changed."

"Ah, there you're wrong," said the construct. "The world has changed, and that's what we need you to see. I'll leave you to it."

And with that, the stick turned and trundled out of Zinn's beautiful bedroom.

The dreams began soon after. Impressionistic yet vivid dreams in which he was back in Palo Alto, working on the ENS genome, always on the very verge of success. Tutenef passed through the dreams as a figure of enveloping warmth and intense sexuality, always distracting him, always just out of reach. But the core of the dreams, which he'd struggle every morning to remember in detail, was an ongoing conversation with the genome itself, conducted in the language of head-chips, an abstracted blend of sound and images flooding his brain that reminded him uncomfortably of the experiences he'd had when he'd experimented with hallucinogens in his dormitory room at Oxford a century earlier. In the dreams, the genome spoke to him in the voice of the villa's AI, suggesting critical changes to be made to increase its effectiveness, which he implemented in the dreams but could never remember upon waking. The dreams stayed with him throughout his day as he sat in the sun on the terrace overlooking the lake, and there were nights when he went to bed eagerly, hoping to dream.

And a day came when, waking from a night of particularly deep dreaming, he walked again up the long winding drive of the villa to the iron gate onto the road. The man with the gun was nowhere to be seen, and the gate was wide open.

DANIEL

Gulf Coast of Florida, 2062

Marion asked Dan to call Nolan on the theory that their son liked his father better than her. Dan protested that that wasn't true, but quickly agreed.

Nolan was fully chipped, as so many of his generation were, with little telltale bumps behind their ears, but Dan called on his handheld just to get Nolan's full attention. Chipped people were so easily distracted from conversation by all the other things going on in their heads. He began the call by asking after Nolan's work, which as far as Dan could tell involved buying and selling pharmaceutical companies as fast as possible.

"Damned feds," Nolan grumped, sounding his age. "Can't get anything done without an antitrust review, and there are three companies I want to merge. It would be the biggest thing since you guys got ancient. Mid-sized pharma firms. One of them has a possible solution to all this Methuselah plague nonsense, the other two could do the manufacturing and the influencing."

Dan had heard the expression "Methuselah plague" bandied about in the ether, but hadn't thought his own son would use it on him. "What's the solution?"

"Death on schedule. That's not the marketing name, of course, but that's what it would be. We'd brand it something quaint and comforting. One of the marketing people suggested 'Sweet Chariot.'"

"I don't get it."

"You know, from that old Black spiritual."

"Oh, yeah. Of course. 'Comin' for to carry me home.'"

"Right!" said his son, his enthusiasm building. "The idea is you take a series of drugs, orally, over a week or two, and over the course of a year they catalyze within the body and make it stop."

"Make what stop?"

"The body. The body of the customer."

"So it's a suicide pill."

"A series of pills, actually. Quite painless death, though, very abrupt, and the timing's very precise. That's the beauty of it. One year out exactly, though we could tweak it a bit."

He remembered Adele's prediction of competing technical solutions to the problem of mass longevity. "This would all be completely voluntary, I assume," he said dryly. "You're not in cahoots with any government agencies or vigilante groups."

"Offers have been made, but we've rejected them so far," he said, not getting Dan's attempt at humor.

"So far," Dan said.

"Why did you call, Father? I'm really very busy." Nolan always called Dan "Father" when he was really very busy.

"I wanted to let you know that we're thinking of selling the Colorado place," Dan said as offhandedly as he could.

Long silence. "Why?"

"We need the money."

"You've already got more money than you know what to do with," Nolan said before he could stop himself. "What about Mom's money?"

"She's saving it."

"For what?" his son asked, his voice rising into a screech.

"For later. Much later. You should talk to her yourself sometime," Dan said, because Nolan never did and likely never would. He no longer cared how his son felt about all this.

"So what will you do with the money from the Colorado house?"

"Buy a bigger place."

"Bigger place where?" Nolan asked incredulously, as though the scale of his parents' selfishness had once again amazed him.

"Probably also in Colorado. I'll let you know when we find it."

Nolan's breathing was now audible in a way it wouldn't have been if they were talking through his chip. "What's the purpose of all this?"

"Your mother thinks we need to find a retreat," Dan said. "She wants to start something new but feels we need a safer place."

"Safer from what?"

"Maybe from the people with the slow death pills," he said, unable to contain his sarcasm.

"Oh come on, Dad,"—he was "Dad" again—"you don't believe all this anti-Lifer bullshit flying around. I told you, no one's going to make you take these pills. But we're betting there's a huge untapped market among those who are sick to death of being alive, and would like a dignified, predictable way out."

Dan was glad they were off the subject of Colorado. Always easily distracted, their Nolan; maybe he was on his chip after all.

"What if someone changes their mind after they take this thing?" he asked.

"Things. It's a series of pills. But no, once you complete the full dosage, there's no changing your mind. We had an earlier version in the form of an implant that was programmed to release the right dosage at a certain moment in the future, but that would mean the customer could change their mind and have the implant removed before the date arrived. This is better. Once you take it, it's irreversible."

"Come on," he said. "You must have an antidote."

"Nope," Nolan said proudly. "And we're not going to come up with one. That's part of the point."

"How the hell do you do clinical trials on such a thing?" he asked, though he could well imagine.

"We have more volunteers than we can use." *Of course he did,* Dan thought.

"What do Debbie and Claire think of this?"

Another silence. "I don't know. I haven't asked them, and they haven't told me. It's just another deal."

And there, in a nutshell, was his son's family and business life. He had no idea what his new wife and his grown daughter thought about his work, and what's more he didn't care.

"Well," Dan said, "Just wanted to let you know about Colorado, since you used to love it so much." As he said this he realized that what Marion and he remembered about Nolan loving the place in Colorado was from when he was in his teens, over sixty years before.

"Dad, can I ask you something before you go?" And suddenly he sounded like a teenager. A seventy-six-year-old teenager.

"Sure," Dan said.

"Have you and Mom rethought your wills yet?"

Dan almost snickered. This was something Nolan would ask every few years back in normal times, when he was middle-aged and his parents were newly old, and Dan always thought it more greedy than altruistic of him, as though he were worried they'd forget to leave him anything. And now, of course, they might.

"Not in about thirty years," he said. "Seems somehow premature to think about now."

"You might get hit by a bus," Nolan said.

"Or take some of your pills," Dan replied.

They laughed at each other, not altogether kindly, and hung up.

Dan called the real estate agency in Silverthorne and asked about selling the lodge and whether anything more remote was available. Of course old McCutcheon was still alive, and they spent a few minutes comparing age notes in that prideful way of triplers: he, 122; his kids, in their early 100s; and Dan, a mere 110.

"You'll get used to it." McCutcheon laughed, though he started to cough as soon as he said it. A lifetime of smoking somehow hadn't gotten him yet. He told Dan about a place farther north and east of their place, off a little-traveled county road, a property that had been in the same family for over a hundred years, two thousand acres, aspen and fir and a big lake and a ten-bedroom lodge with solar power and geothermal heat, totally off the grid, at the end of five miles of dirt road. The fourth generation of owners, unexpectedly in their hundreds, were making the same money/needs calculation as the rest of the centenarians and had decided to cash out. The price seemed about right, high but negotiable.

On a certain day in April of the following year, Dan and Marion got on a solardrone flight with four other people of wildly varied ages and were dropped at the private strip in Vail, on the other side of the range from their destination. The others were there for the last of the fake snow, but for him and Marion it was a couple of hours in an old robot taxi that could barely stay connected to GPS, around the mountain and up into the hills to the gate of Black Valley—so named, they'd been told, because it was so far from city lights and hemmed in so closely by the mountains that the sun set early and rose late, and the bottom of the valley lay in almost constant twilight.

The lodge was at the end of a gravel lane that wound five miles into the valley from the gate at the county road. Deep enough, Marion noted, that with the proper positioning of security cameras and other alarms, they'd know of any visitors a long way off. He was at first surprised that she was thinking in these terms, but the place inspired other ideas, too, for several outbuildings near the cabin, a vegetable garden, a drone landing pad so they and their guests wouldn't have to ride over from Vail, and heavy-duty sodium arc floodlights arrayed up high on the surrounding hills and aimed down the valley toward the front gate. What she was describing would cost several million more than what they'd get from the house in Silverthorne. But Marion had that kind of money; it was only rarely that she ever mentioned it, much less showed this kind of focused intent to use it.

That night, the two of them lay in the big old lodge alone, no moon, the sky indeed an inky black the likes of which he'd never seen, fathomless, perforated by a million needlepoints of stars, the arm of the galaxy thrown wide above them like an unfurled sheet; and he knew they'd found the right place even before Marion turned to him and told him so. They held each other in the dark, held each other as they never had in the early years of their marriage, but always had once Marion had agreed to take him back after his affair with Adele. He held her as a child would, almost greedily, as though she were protection from that errant past and from the strange future he felt bearing down on them both.

TAUBIN

San Francisco, 2065

Taubin Maxwell loved his walk to work, which was steeply downhill and easy, but he hated the walk back home, which was necessarily the opposite.

San Francisco was made of such walks, its crazy topography part of its charm and one of its few real challenges, at least for someone as motivated and well-paid as Taubin. He got up around six, dressed in the company jumpsuit, had the kitchen module make his usual coffee and a single fried egg on toast, gave it the time and desired content of dinner that evening, exited his ridiculously expensive, sparsely furnished one-bedroom on California Street, and headed down the crazily steep sidewalk toward the Embarcadero, where he ostensibly worked, though to him it was less work than a form of self-entertainment, playing around with huge chunks of code that usually went nowhere but occasionally earned him not only a patronizing pat on the back but also a sincerely huge bonus at the end of the year.

He was reminded by these walks that he really needed to lose some weight. He could feel his momentum threatening to overcome his balance with each downward step. And the walk back up at the end of the day was always exhausting, unless of course he gave in and called an autorickshaw, which the company would pay for if he worked late enough. And he almost always did. But he knew he really needed to lose weight and walk home more.

His office was in Embarcadero One on the twentieth floor, which had become the ground floor by the time he was born in 2041, when the encroachment of the bay had required that the old piers along the waterfront be torn down and a giant bay wall erected, five stories high and extending all the way around the tip of the city's peninsula to the Golden Gate, cutting off the view of the water for several million people who didn't live or work high enough to see it, as he did. Then anti-moisture cladding and structural reinforcement of the foundation of the building filled in what had once been the retail mezzanine and first fifteen floors. The glass-walled elevator was enveloped in blackness for the first minute of its climb, then it exploded into the light, the Bay Bridge leaping off to the east, the bay shining like ceramic under a ceiling of glowing fog, the sun a blurry beacon out over Oakland, illuminating it all. No matter how jaded he may have become, it always thrilled him.

On the walls of his office, which had an amazing view westward toward the Golden Gate, hung hundred-year-old photos of the old bridge, its tower stanchions appearing absurdly elongated and the road deck hovering at a monstrous elevation above the waves, back before the rising of the waters. He'd read that people used to commit suicide by jumping from the bridge, but as low as it had become, that was no sure thing anymore. *What a way to go*, he thought. The rushing of the wind as you fell, the immediate regret, the fall lasting longer than seemed possible, then the impact, at that speed like hitting concrete. The broken bones and ruptured flesh sinking like a punctured balloon.

He pulled up his screens to chase the thoughts away. This was his curse and his gift—the extreme granularity of his imagination; an aspect of being borderline autistic, he knew, though they didn't call it that anymore. Somewhere on the spectrum. He assumed it came from his father, who'd left his mother before he was born, and left him with a few of his genes to account for. Being half Black was great, a social plus in most situations, but the neurodivergency made some people uncomfortable.

He scanned the results of the previous night's influencer programs, looking for aberrations he'd have to correct, outlier trends that should be reined in. Accretex Corporation, his employer, majority owned by his idol Nolan Altman, was the acknowledged apex practitioner of this sort of Mass Subliminal Guidance, as they called it, but it was only as good as the last algorithm, and all of them, arrayed in phalanxes and deployed like waves across chipspace, needed to be watched, prodded, culled, updated. This was where his borderline dysfunctional attention to detail came in handy.

He couldn't deny that he'd been thrilled when old Nolan assigned the Lifer project to him, though of course he knew he was the only choice for something so high-profile and so urgent. The product launch was only a year or so away, depending on government approvals, and the global scope of this offensive meant that thousands of preliminary probes would have to be deployed and analyzed and redeployed. He had a team of twenty or more codebangers to do the grunt work, a really good wordie to summarize progress for Nolan and the board on a weekly basis, and liaisons in the company affiliates to explain to him some of the science behind the plague and this little "cure" of theirs. Not that the science mattered to him much. It was what it was. But it might make a difference in the shape of the project, and he was interested, like he was interested in almost anything complex and challenging. And it gave him an excuse to get out of the office and do some traveling, which he also enjoyed more than most people his age, who tended to consider moving one's body around over great distances a dumb vestige of the fossil-fuel era, even though it was almost all solar now.

Most of the science was being done in a lab outside of Albuquerque, and as chief MSG officer, Taubin was among the few allowed to attend the monthly progress meetings there, but only in person, since he was yet to be convinced that the neural net was as secure as it was cracked up to be, and visuals—pretty vague in chipspace—always helped him get a handle on complicated concepts. So he commandeered one of the company drones and popped over to ABQ to get the latest from the lab coats, face-to-face.

He had an ulterior motive, of course. His grandparents lived in Santa Fe, twenty minutes by drone from Albuquerque. He remembered them fondly—a handsome, unassuming, kindly couple, now in their triples; he wasn't sure exactly how old. He hadn't seen them in almost ten years and thought he might zip over to their expensive retirement enclave after the meeting. He wondered what they would think of the idea of Sweet Chariot. Might make good market research, and he could take them out to dinner the way they used to take him, made him learn to read a menu, the proper way to handle cutlery, how to behave in public, not to run up to every stranger and start talking at them. Little gifts that would stay with him forever.

The heat of the desert was oppressive, the sun unrelenting. He'd grown up in the Midwest, where sunlight was still mostly benign, not like this killer radiation. The sun cut down his travel time since he didn't need to stop anywhere to recharge, but the heat increased it, since the prop VTOL was far less efficient in the thinner, superheated air. When he landed on the roof of the lab a shade deployed automatically to keep the drone out of direct sun. The screen by the passenger seat said the ambient temperature was a hundred and twenty degrees.

His liaison at the lab was Joyce Icahn, titular head of the Sweet Chariot Project and someone he'd asked out a few times in his compulsively friendly way, despite the fact that she was twenty years his senior and they had absolutely nothing in common but their employer. She'd been polite but firm with him, explaining that she had no time for outside interests, which he completely understood, since he really didn't either.

She met him at the bottom of the landing pad stairs in the mercifully cool interior of the lab and led him in her usual hurried way to a conference room where ten people dressed in lab whites and clean-room blues sat waiting for him to arrive so they could get their meeting started. Scanning the room, he noted that none of the participants was over the age of forty.

"Do you need a moment, Taubin, or should we launch?" Joyce asked.

"Launch," he said, to the obvious relief of the group.

"Let's go around the room," Joyce said, sitting at the head of the table and turning to the disheveled young man to her left.

"Manufacturing is still not on schedule, but I think they'll get there," he said, not looking up. "Manila thinks they can be up to a hundred million doses by the end of next year and two hundred million by the following quarter."

"Can we add capacity somewhere? The last thing we can be is short on product. Surpluses we can manage."

"I've been talking with corporate about that, and there are negotiations ongoing with a maker in Sweden, but they're still booked up with those antivirals from the last pandemic, so we're not sure that's the solution. A place in Johannesburg may have some excess capacity; I'll know more next week."

Joyce nodded curtly, and her gaze clicked to the next person at the table. "Distribution?"

LIFERS

"On track," the woman said, her face and limbs the color of a radish. Total-body tats were still rare in the corporate world, but there were more of them every day, now that the process was computerized and could be done in an afternoon. Taubin wondered what the rest of her looked like. "We've leased sixteen additional widebodies for the Pacific runs but unfortunately had to resort to some fossil-engine aircraft to round out the requirements." General groans around the table. He felt he had to speak up.

"That's really not in keeping with the corporate face on this, you know."

"Yes, Taubin, we know," said Joyce, emphasizing his name like a schoolteacher.

"It's borderline illegal," he pointed out.

"Not where these will be flying," said the radish lady. "Legal has been all over it; we're clean. And we need those planes if we're to meet schedule."

"It still doesn't look good," he said. "We can't stand any subliminal negativity with this product, and fossil burners are pure subliminal negativity. Especially old fixed-wing planes."

"We'll circle back to this in subcommittee," Joyce assured him. Then her gaze clicked back into position. "Chemistry?"

A white guy this time. Snow white, obvious total tat, kind of in-your-face epidermal sarcasm. "We still haven't calibrated the final three doses just right. The subjects tend to extract a week or so late. But we think we know why."

"'Extract'?" Taubin repeated, still smarting from Joyce's putdown.

"Die," explained the white guy.

He hesitated. "You mean people are already dying from our drug?"

"Volunteers," said the white guy. "How did you think we were measuring its effectiveness?"

"I don't know, chimps, maybe?"

72

The white guy looked at him as though he were from Mars, then looked away.

"Let's get back on topic," said Joyce. "Why is this late extraction happening?"

The white guy squirmed a bit. "The final three doses all contain synthetic transposons that insert themselves into the cell structure and slice up DNA strands. It's pretty quick cell death once they're activated, but we think there's a contaminant that's inhibiting their effectiveness. We get them from Guadalajara, and they've had three major heat storms in the last month, had to shut down the facility, and we think that's what did it, that lull in the process. But once we get clean samples we'll run the calibrations again."

Taubin raised his hand meekly. "Isn't being a little late with the, uh, extraction a good thing?"

"No," said the white guy. "And this is important for marketing or influencing, or whatever you guys do, to understand. The whole idea here is precision, accuracy, predictability. To the day. We'd make it to the minute if we could, but the nano isn't quite there yet. And it has to be true in one hundred percent of the cases. Otherwise you get confusion, maybe regret, maybe fear that it's not going to work. Or even hope."

"Hope's not good," said Joyce. "The whole premise of this treatment is to provide certainty. A year's time, but then certainty. If not, we're back where we started, with different people having different post-treatment lifespans, some longer, some shorter, and people start to question why, to assume there's some inherent variability to their personal situations, to think they might be able to change their minds. It's what made the Lifer problem such a mess to begin with, that division between the normal lives and the long lives, no one knowing what the upper limit is. We can't have that even on a micro level with this treatment. Well, maybe a day or two, but that's all we can tolerate."

Taubin nodded. "Okay, I get that. And there really is no antidote once you've taken the stuff?"

"The treatment," corrected Joyce. "And 'antidote' implies countering something toxic, which we don't want to suggest. Neutralizer might be a better term."

"Sorry, the treatment. And the neutralizer?"

"No, there is no neutralizer." This said with a firmness that brooked no quibbling, but he sensed a rustling of dissent from some seats around the table, a murmur that quickly quieted as Joyce shot her look at the sources. "And corporate policy is there will be none," she added.

"No research at all along those lines?" Taubin asked.

"None," she said. "Again, it would undermine certainty. Even the rumor of a neutralizer would upend the whole premise. You've got to get the algorithms right on that score, Taubin. Legal, would you like to chime in here?"

The oldest guy in the room, with gray strands of hair drooping over his unnaturally tanned forehead, cleared his throat and leaned forward. "We're about to conclude some very big government contracts, and not just with our government, that stipulate very clearly that not only can we not commence research on an antidote but that we destroy any findings already made along those lines, and moreover, if any antidote is eventually devised by a third party, we are legally bound to pursue that party with a breach-of-patent claim to the full extent of our corporate ability, even if it means bankrupting the company. We've been assured by at least some of our governmental clients—including, I should mention, the US—that they will exert their own best efforts to make any such antidote an illegal substance and criminalize its possession or distribution. I've seen the drafts of some of those regulations, and the goal is that they'd go into effect on the very day that the treatment becomes available. So no, Mr. Maxwell, we're not going to be working on an antidote."

"Neutralizer," corrected Joyce.

"But if people do change their minds," Taubin said, "as some inevitably will, and die anyway, won't there be lawsuits? Actually, they'd start suing before they died."

The old guy smiled a thin little lawyerly smile. "As you can imagine, the waivers of liability that customers will have to sign in order to receive the treatment are quite extensive and, we believe, ironclad. And those same regulations I mentioned will also give us blanket immunity from litigation."

Taubin nodded and pretended to take notes. "Immunity from litigation. . . ."

"Yes," said the old lawyer. "Like what the gun manufacturers got under legislation passed back in 2005. Same principle. We just make the stuff. We can't be held responsible for what people do with it."

"But what else are people supposed to do with it?"

"Exactly. Same principle," said the tan guy, as though that were so obvious that Taubin decided to drop it.

Joyce proceeded around the table, the reports increasingly abstruse and technical. His attention wandered to the changes he'd be making to the algorithms to make the concepts of precision and predictability more appealing. Then something occurred to him.

"One more question, if I could," he said, interrupting a bright orange woman who was rambling on about chromatin coiling and whole-cell computational modeling. "Why a year? Why not a shorter period, or a longer one, for that matter? Why not a super-quick option? People like choices; maybe have several different periods that you could pick from. . . ."

Joyce raised a manicured hand. "Taubin, I thought we'd been over this. The one-year period was arrived at after extensive focus group research. It gives people time to prepare, their families time to adjust, but not so much time that the initial decision gets questioned or rethought too much. The treatment is, after all, irreversible. A year is far enough off that the consequence is discounted a bit, which we need for a critical level of buy-in. A shorter period—especially what you call a super-quick option—was frankly thought to be too much like straight-up suicide. A gun or poison would work as well, why spend all this R and D money on a sophisticated piece of bioengineering like our treatment? And we found that longer periods than a year leave too much room for regret."

"Ah, regret," he said, sighing in empathy, though he'd never regretted anything in his life up to that point.

"Then there are the logistical issues," she continued. "Our government contracts are quite specific and strict on the subject of the time between initial treatment and end of life, or what we call extraction. The treatments will be government-subsidized, in many cases dispensed for free, and the quid pro quo will be that the consumer must register at the outset and agree to be traced, so that the extraction dates and locations are known in advance and can be prepared for. This is another reason why precision is necessary. Remember that we're hoping and frankly expecting that millions of people in the US alone are going to take the treatment in the first few days after it becomes available, and millions more here and globally in the weeks and months that follow. That's a lot of bodies one year out, and there aren't the facilities anymore—cemeteries, funeral homes, you know—to handle them all at once. So the authorities are going to need time to prepare and create alternative channels."

In the ensuing silence, he actively considered pursuing the subject of "alternative channels" but decided against it. He could guess, and it wouldn't be of use in the MSG algorithms.

But Joyce wasn't quite done. "It's taken over five years and over a billion dollars in R and D to achieve the rigid one-year effectiveness horizon, and even at that we're not as precise as we'd like to be. Multiple options would involve years more work, even if we could get permission and the funding to create them."

"Understood," Taubin said.

When the meeting finally broke up, he shared a spartan lunch in the lab's cafeteria, thanked Joyce for her time, determined once again that she had no interest in dinner with him, and headed for the broiling, sun-ravaged rooftop. He had an even greater impulse to visit his grandparents than when he'd arrived, so he chipped a request to the company dispatcher to let him keep the eVTOL for another day on his own dime and waited inside the cramped cabin with the door open and the air conditioning running full blast until permission came back.

Dear old Jack and Anna didn't believe in headchips, so he called them on an antique handheld that the company kept in the drone for just such circumstances. He reached Jack as he was finishing up a round of golf.

"Taub, buddy, how the heck are you?" he growled.

"I'm good, Grampa, I'm good. I'm in the area and thought I'd stop and see you and Grandma, if it's okay."

"Sure it's okay. Where are you?"

"Albuquerque. I can be there in half an hour. Maybe you'd let me take you out to dinner."

"No way. We'll take you. You comin' to the house?"

He knew there was no landing pad at their house, and the drone would need a charge for the flight back to San Francisco the next day, so he explained he'd be landing at the airport.

"Good deal," said Jack. "We'll pick you up."

Santa Fe was a town utterly resistant to time, and the airport reflected it. An overgrown adobe hut, wind sock on a tall metal flagpole, one short runway aligned with the prevailing winds. A few old fossil-fuel private jets still parked near the terminal, testaments to a bygone era when kerosene was legal. They'd

LIFERS

finally installed a drone landing pad as a concession to modernity, but there was no auto-flight controller, and what with the altitude, the mountains, and the heat, GPS reception was unreliable, so most earlier-model drones had to avoid the place and land at ABQ. The company drone had internal maps and optical radar navigation and landing capability, so it could go anywhere as long as it could "see" far enough. As it swept in over the mountains and the baking desert and touched down, there was Grampa Jack in the parking lot, waving, his hair still long and tied back in a ponytail, just as Taubin remembered him.

He was the only child of a single mother, so his grandparents had an outsized role in his upbringing. She was a struggling metal sculptor in Oakland, selling her stuff on the street and in half a dozen shops in San Francisco, not enough to make rent and put Taubin in a decent school and feed both of them. So Jack and Anna would take him for a year or two at a time, first in their condo in Chicago, and later, when Jack had retired from running his medical software firm, at the place he and Anna built in Santa Fe, a sprawling, low-slung, faux adobe bungalow in a development called Las Estrellitas, the little stars. He'd hated Chicago after living in the Bay Area, but loved the desert, the austerity of it, the way the heat and the light made for great absences, endless spaces to disappear into.

It was on a moonless night on the big patio of the Santa Fe house, looking up at the little stars through a telescope that Jack had given him, that Anna came out and told him that his mother had died. Opioid overdose, they thought, though they weren't sure yet. She'd said this with a matter-of-factness that he had found strange at the time, but he later realized it was both out of concern that he not be too traumatized, and because his grandmother had been preparing for that moment for many years. He didn't see Grampa Jack for a week, and when he finally returned, he never mentioned his daughter to Taubin again.

He first learned to code in the local high school and spent his nights learning to bartend at the swanky restaurants on Canyon Road. Eventually he got his MS in analytical psychodynamics from MIT, and when he graduated—he'd say this without bragging, it was just a fact—quickly distinguished himself as a prodigy of algorithm design and deployment in the final days of social media. When the old internet was abandoned and everything went to decentralized blockchains and distributed neural chip networks, it was Jack who recommended him to Nolan Altman, who Jack had hired a decade earlier as an associate fresh out of Harvard Business School to work on selling his software business. Even then, just at the beginning of the Change, Taubin knew that working for Nolan Altman meant he'd never have to look for another job as long as he lived.

As long as he lived. What did that mean anymore? He watched Grampa wheel his big Tesla SUV, a vintage 2028 model kept in surprisingly good shape by the vacuum-like dryness of the local air, up to the front of the little airport. Jack pushed a button and the passenger door popped open by itself and he grinned, still amazed and proud of the car's ancient technology. Grandma Anna, small and sleek as a gray mink, sat in back, beaming.

"Taub, buddy!" Jack yelled, leaning across the cool interior to give him a hug. He reached back and grabbed Anna's hand and kissed it. She was crying and just nodded, couldn't say anything. He'd forgotten how much he loved these people, and how much they loved him.

They talked trivialities on the way to the house, what life in San Francisco was like now that the bay was so high, which bars and restaurants in Santa Fe still existed. All the while, he was thinking about the meeting in Albuquerque, and how the product he was going to do his best to insinuate into the culture was aimed at people like his grandparents. He didn't want to come right out and ask, but finally he did. It was what everybody asked of old people at some point in a conversation.

"So, how old are you two now?"

Anna giggled in back. She had her steel-gray hair in pigtails that framed her deep brown face, making her look like a Navajo, though as Taubin recalled she was Scotch Irish.

"Guess," she said, giggling again. "Go on, guess."

"Well, it's got to be more than a hundred because mom had me late, and I'm thirty-three."

"Your mom had you when she was forty," said Jack. "I remember that because we thought she was out of the woods in terms of getting knocked up, but she wasn't."

"Now, Jack, be nice," Anna said.

"And I guess we should have known that because we didn't have your mom until we were in our forties. So add that up."

"So I'm guessing that would put you around one-ten, one-twenty?"

Jack nodded. "Your grandma just turned a hundred twenty-one. I'm a couple years behind her. What do you think of *that?*"

He sat quietly for a moment, pretending to study the town as it rolled by in the distance. He didn't know many triplers and wasn't sure whether the old-school expressions of congratulations and wonder at such advanced age that his grandparents had grown up with were still appropriate, or would be considered condescending or even insulting. If anything, they looked younger than when he had last seen them, despite the fact that they'd entered the target demographic for Sweet Chariot, the sort of people his algorithms had to reach if the project was to be successful. Of course, he couldn't breathe a word of any of that. He'd signed a sheaf of NDAs when he took the job, and he couldn't think of a faster way to get fired and sued than to start blabbing in public about the existence of Nolan Altman's brilliant solution to the longevity plague.

"I think it's amazing," he said finally, tossing his hands in the air. "You guys both look great."

"Cosmetic surgery," said Grandma. "I thought they did a really good job. I was against it when I was double-digits, but so many of our friends were doing it that it started to sound reasonable. And now I'm glad we did."

He glanced back at her, reassessing. Her eyes did look a bit unnaturally round, and the tattoos made a kind of ironic statement about her wrinkles and surgical scars. "You both look just great," he repeated awkwardly.

"You can't get an appointment anymore," said Jack. "They're booked for years in advance. Fortunately, most people can afford to wait, ha. We had to go to L.A. to get ours. But enough about us; what about you? What are you working on these days?"

"I'm on a special project for Nolan," he said, more forthrightly than he'd intended. But these were his grandparents; he couldn't lie to them.

"That guy's going to change the world, no question about it," Jack said. "I always knew it."

"Yep, no question," Taubin said, images of the Albuquerque lab coming back to him. "Say, are you not driving anymore, Grampa?" he asked, wanting very much to change the subject. Jack hadn't touched the wheel since he got in. The Tesla's autopilot was surprisingly natural for its age, though it tended to corner faster than a human would.

"Nope. We're not allowed. New Mexico cuts it off at a hundred, which is pretty liberal compared to some states. Technically I'm not even supposed to be sitting in the driver's seat, but since the surgery, I can usually get away with it, and I didn't want you sitting up here by yourself."

"Driving Mr. Maxwell," chirped Anna, some sort of cultural reference he would have to look up later.

"Hope you don't mind that we're avoiding downtown," said Jack. "The traffic's unbelievable."

"The season?"

"All the time. It's all the fucking geriatrics."

"Jack, language," scolded Anna. Grampa had called his contemporaries "geriatrics" even when he was only eighty. Nothing got him going worse than the behavior of his own generation.

"My God, you see them in the drugstore dithering over their prescription purchases like they were taking out a mortgage. They vote for politicians who think they should be dead already. And somehow, despite the frickin' heat, every Lifer with two dimes to rub together has decided New Mexico is the place to be. Housing's out of sight. I can't imagine what our place is worth now. There's talk of building high-rises along North Guadalupe to accommodate the demand. Highrises! In Santa Fe! Can you imagine? It was bad enough when they covered Canyon Road."

"They covered Canyon Road?" Taubin was genuinely shocked, struggling to picture it, the galleries and restaurants along the ancient avenue turned into some kind of shopping mall.

"Can you believe it? It was getting too hot for the poor little geriatric snowflake tourists, so somebody had the idea of putting a bunch of geodesic canopies over most of the street. Great debate over whether they should be transparent, so you could still see the old buildings, or opaque, for better heat control. They went with transparent, but in the end it didn't matter, since the UV rays fogged up the canopies in a matter of months. Now they want to replace them. The geriatrics love it, so they don't have to ever leave their air conditioning. You park in town and have to shuttle up, no walking allowed. We're going over there tonight for dinner, and you can see for yourself. Fucking unbelievable."

"Jack! Language!"

They were beyond town now, on the dusty county road that led to Las Estrellitas. He saw low-rise condos everywhere, blocky red and brown imitation adobe structures, thousands of new units filled, he assumed, with triplers, the "geriatrics" Grampa so despised.

"But your health is good?" he asked to change the subject yet again.

Anna leaned over the seat and touched his shoulder. "We're fine except for the skin cancer. I've had a Mohs procedure every six months for the last ten years."

"What's that?"

"That's where they go in and root around until they get out the cancer. . . ."

"Anna, don't talk to the boy about that. He doesn't want to hear that."

"Well, he asked. Everybody's got to do it. And after a few of those you do need cosmetic surgery. We thought the Methuselah would take care of cancer, but apparently it only works on the kinds that kill you quicker."

He was relieved to hear his grandmother put a name to what most doublers called the Plague or, if they were in a good mood, the Change. Now maybe he could start to talk about it.

"You're sure you have the, uh, Methuselah?" he asked.

"Taub, honey, you're sweet, but we're a hundred twenty years old," Anna replied. "How could we not have it?"

"You know that my company created a test a few years ago—"

"We know about that," said Jack. "It bombed, right? The geriatrics didn't want to take it because it would brand you as a Lifer, and people your age didn't want to take it because it would brand you as a future problem and put you in line for forced sterilization."

"Grampa, there isn't any forced sterilization yet," Taubin said. Jack was right, though. The test kits had bombed, even when Accretex came out with an at-home variety. But that was before he'd become head of Mass Subliminal Guidance.

"That's not what we're hearing. Lots of our friends tell us their grandkids are getting sterilized."

"But that's voluntary."

"Depends on the state," said Anna.

"No, I really don't think that's true anywhere. Where are you getting your information?"

"What about that up-or-out law the politicians are talking about?"

"That wouldn't go into effect until there's a . . . well, a cure for the Methuselah."

"Ha! A cure! Don't you love that one?"

"We don't think there is a cure," said Anna. "We think this is God's work."

He was silent for a moment, trying to decide what direction to push this. This was his target demographic, and here they were talking about God.

"But Grandma, you know there have been studies proving that peoples' cellular chemistry has been altered in unnatural ways by an outside agent, right? Accretex did some of that research, so I know about it."

"Hoo boy, now you're in trouble," said Jack, looking out the window. The Tesla was pulling up in front of the big old house Taubin remembered so well, overlooking the unnatural green of the golf course and the smoky blue ridge of the Jemez range in the distance.

"God works in mysterious ways," said Grandma softly. "We can talk about this more later." The Tesla shut down and opened its doors, and they walked together under the arch that led to the reclaimed wooden front door, studded with big black rail tie nails, that Jack always said was older than the republic. That phrase of his, "older than the republic," stuck with Taubin, since there wasn't much of a republic anymore.

That night they went to a place where he'd bartended for a summer during his college years, a big old rambling hacienda from the 1800s, with vigas projecting out of the whitewashed walls and the smell of ancho everywhere. Back then it had been a hangout for locals, but tonight it was thronged with multicolored tourists and Lifers who were trying too hard to look like they belonged. It had somehow escaped being encapsulated with the creepy plastic canopy that had grown like a modernistic cancer over most of Canyon Road. They waited for a table at the bar, and Taubin ordered a jalapeño cosmopolitan just to test the young lady bartender, and the usual Manhattans for the grandparents. They toasted one another, clinking glasses, and he was pleased to see the mashed jalapeño pieces floating in the bottom of his martini glass. No cheap hot sauce in this place, even now.

"So let me ask you," he started, thinking he'd idly chat with them about their someday voluntarily dying, and they looked up at him contentedly from over the rims of their drinks. The expressions of undiluted pleasure on their faces at his being there with them made him backtrack yet again. "How do you manage to play golf in this heat?"

Jack snorted. "Cryosuit. It's the only way. Callaway makes a good one. Pretty thin fabric these days, circulates some kind of fluid, lowers the temp about twenty degrees, you can even drink out of it if you need to. Like those stillsuits in *Dune*, remember? Ha, guess not. Goggles and a hat, and you're good to go, usually, though there are days when you wouldn't dare. Some old dude whose cryosuit failed drops dead on the course at least once a year, big brouhaha, talk about shutting down the course, giving up on golf entirely. Though it really is obscene, when you think about it. Consumes land, water, and time. What else is there to waste, really? But I still love it; I can't help it. What's that old line from Kipling? Mad dogs and Englishmen go out in the midday sun? He didn't mention golfers."

"Do you golf every day? Don't you ever get bored?"

"He golfs about once a week," said Anna. "I paint. Mostly watercolors, some acrylic. We read in the evenings, he cooks dinner, I clean. We have our own little church service on the weekends out on our patio, with that ceramic Madonna your mom made when she was a teenager. At night we watch some screens, usually old movies. We saw *West Side Story* the other night, the first one, so great. 'Somewhere, a place for us.' I love that one. He likes *Laurence of Arabia*; we've probably watched that fifty times by now. About a guy who falls in love with the desert. Nobody's eyes were ever as blue as Peter O'Toole's in that movie, my God. And that was way before CGI. What a gorgeous man. Do you know who I mean, Taub?"

"No," he said sheepishly, stirring his cosmo with a fore-finger. No one watched movies anymore, especially not on screens. He'd chip some visuals occasionally, but there was no story to them, just mood pieces, or soft porn, occasionally. How could anyone focus on a screen for an hour and a half? "Did we ever watch movies together when I lived with you?" he asked.

"I don't think so," Anna said, "but it's so long ago it's hard to remember. It's funny; we thought we were so old when you were little. We were in our seventies, and we weren't sure we could handle a toddler. If I'd known I had another fifty years in me, I would have felt much more confident, I think. We didn't dare let you watch a grownup movie."

"I saw *Ben Hur* when it first came out," said Jack, waxing louder. "In a theater in Pittsburgh in 1960. God, over a hundred years ago. So long it had an intermission, so you could go out and buy more popcorn. My parents took me, totally inap-propriate for a little kid, but they probably couldn't get a sitter. Most amazing thing I'd ever seen. Cinerama, curved screen as big as a house, they needed three projectors to fill it up, giant sound system. No one remembers this stuff anymore."

"You do," Taubin said. "People your age. No one else."

"We're worth something, then, huh? Repositories of history and all that."

"You should write your memoirs."

Jack snorted. "Nothing's on paper anymore; nothing gets recorded. Everybody's living in their heads, on their damn chips. It's down to individual memory, or nothing. And no one would believe half the stuff we remember anyway."

"We're one another's memoirs," Anna said, leaning into her husband. "The things we've seen. And now this." She looked around as if the room with its bustling crowd were itself a miracle. "This gift."

Taubin stared at her. "Is that how you think of it? A gift? Not a burden or a curse? 'Cause there are some politicians and some other people who think you might get really tired of it all, just want some peace after all this time." He stopped himself, worried he'd gone too far, seeing what seemed to be pity in their faces.

"Oh, Taub. I've never been more at peace," she said, leaning toward him. "There's something you get from the perspective of this many years. You realize what matters and what doesn't. I don't think the lifetimes we used to lead were enough to come to that point. You'd just be on the brink of reaching it and then you were gone, it was taken away. Now we get to live into it. We get to keep that knowledge and stay in the world with it."

"Anna, you're scaring the boy; leave him alone."

"No, I want to hear. . . ."

Grandma Anna knocked back the rest of her drink, stood up from her barstool, and hugged him, her tiny, bony body pressing against his. The smell of her wafted up, dust and bourbon and something sweet, like the flowers you find in the desert.

"You're so very young," she said into his ear, almost whispering. "You're not even the age your mother was when she died. I thought that would kill me, and I needed a lot of time to recover, but we had you. My advice is, first, hope that you outlive her, then hope that you live as long as we have. Live on. What no one realizes when they're your age is that you never stop learning, you never stop accumulating memories. You get richer and richer. Sure, there are people who get bored at our age, who would rather be dead. I know some of them. But you know what? They were always bored, and they were always boring. If you're not bored now, you probably never will be. On the other hand, it may take you at least a hundred and twenty years to find real peace. And imagine what you can do with it after that. So live on, Taub. Live on."

Later, on the patio under the stars, with ice clinking in their nightcaps, Jack and Taubin traded constellation identifications while Anna made up the bed he used to sleep in all those years before. San Francisco seemed very far away, the lab in Albuquerque even farther, though he realized that was geographically backward. He'd forgotten what this felt like, this sense of home. He'd wanted to forget it in a way, had seen it as a liability, something that would hold him back. These old people were from a time so long ago they might as well be from another planet. Yet they were his one real home on this one. They were still here, had been here all along, as if they were waiting, persisting in the world, for him.

Sometimes, he thought, you need to be reminded that you love someone.

He'd remember this night later, when the algorithms had been released, the one that he'd been asked to make, that would find the triplers in front of their screens and in the chips of those who wore them and change subtly what they saw and how they saw it and make them tired and sad and lonely even when they were with those they loved; and the other algorithm, his finest piece of work, he would later think, the one he imagined that night, looking up at all the little stars that, together, made up the Milky Way, the arm of the galaxy, something powerful and magnificent and immortal.

DANIEL

Black Valley, Colorado, 2070

His parents had both died in their eighties, in those days thought of as standard, and while he'd lived a healthier life than they, and enjoyed the benefits of more sophisticated medical care, he'd assumed that genetics would prevail and he too would die in that decade. But try as he might, he'd never internalized that assumption. He'd read his Montaigne: "Show me the man so old and decrepit who, having heard of Methuselah, does not think he has yet twenty good years to come." He knew he was just another old man who had heard of Methuselah.

In his seventies, he'd had backaches, cataracts, hearing loss, basal cell carcinomas, high blood pressure, elevated cholesterol, and so on—the usual litany of old-mannish ills—but each had been managed or repaired as medical science permitted, and he went on living, the brute fact that he would one day die being ultimately unworthy of reflection. The only real question was how he would die—suddenly, like a switch in a brightly lit room being flicked off, or gradually, in a slow cascade of increasingly lethal catastrophes over months or years, the diminishment or sudden loss of this or that faculty, the clever temporizing of the doctors becoming less and less effective till they finally gave up but never acknowledged it, the dimming of the lights in the room down and down to black. In the abstract he preferred the switch to the dimmer, but it wasn't for him to choose.

When the boomers stopped dying in the 2030s, he and Marion, in their late seventies, were still healthy, mostly enjoying life, waiting for the lights to start dimming, hoping they wouldn't too soon. And suddenly the death rate for people above the age of eighty fell through the floor, and they were at first incredulous, and then amused, and finally, somewhat grudgingly hopeful about what these remarkable statistics might mean for them personally.

There was no test for Methuselah in those days, as no one understood what was happening biologically. Scans and blood tests showed a radical change in the cell chemistry of the sampled individuals, which included people of all ages, young and old. But why that change was happening and what had triggered it remained a mystery for years. Theories abounded, but they were all wrong.

Avowals of religious belief and attendance at denominational churches exploded. Dan supposed it couldn't hurt and afforded a hedge against the possibility, which he'd long discounted to near zero, that there was a benign deity at work in the world that must be responsible for the Change, there being no other available explanation. The dietary, sexual, recreational, and even political habits of those who had been identified as having Methuselah—though there was no name for it at first—were scrutinized for clues to its causation, and even though there was no pattern to be found in these studies, patterns were of course perceived and quickly promoted as the keys to their deathlessness. Dan's personal favorite of these was the rage for smoothies made of mollusk shells that briefly drove the price of oysters through the roof, not to mention the black market that suddenly sprang up for centenarian semen.

But death had not been repealed, like an obsolete statute. It was oddly selective. It still held sway with the cancer victims too far gone for the novel genomes to clean up the cellular mess, still capitalized on heart failure and arteriosclerosis, still claimed its stroke victims. But the truly old, who before would have died of what had been called "natural causes," the simple running down of life's clock, did not. They persisted.

Their persistence took many forms. Some continued the patterns of defiance of old age that they'd long established, feeling and acting as though they were years younger. Some persisted in a state of advanced senescence, gnarled and reduced but stubbornly functional. Some persisted in pain and decrepitude, eventually outliving their own tolerance for suffering. Some persisted in the state of dementia that had overcome them before the Change, a purgatory that their keepers and loved ones had once been able to assume would soon end but which now threatened to go on indefinitely. They were as varied in their circumstances as they'd been before, but now had in common their bodies' newfound resistance to death.

Dan had always been a runner, had done cross-country in high school, ran once a week when he was working full time, then more when he quit, once a day usually, a couple of miles, nothing herculean but more than most. The skin on his legs wrinkled and sagged, the muscle mass diminished, and the long bones attenuated, but he kept at it as the years passed, at age 90, 100, 110, 120. He'd always been thin, but now he grew radically thinner, had to throw away his old clothes and start over with things made for tall children.

Marion did aerial yoga, suspended above the ground in a kind of elastic sheet. He couldn't watch, worried she'd fall and break her long neck. No virus would protect her from that. But he found it beautiful, the way she moved up there. She too grew thinner, all fat gone, her breasts disappearing, her hips slimmed. It struck him that they were becoming androgynous. All the accoutrements of childbearing had been long since rendered obsolete, discarded. He recalled a gerontologist, in one of the many popular books about aging at the time, who pointed out that once an organism had reproduced, biology had no further use for it. And yet here were humans, persisting for a century past childbearing age. *To what possible end?* he found himself wondering.

Joints and skin were their greatest liabilities. What UV rays had done to their skin over a mere sixty or seventy years didn't compare with the havoc caused by a hundred or more years of exposure. New aesthetic standards of bodily beauty had to be invented and quickly were. So-called age spots acquired a new panache. Hats and parasols came back into fashion. Full-face tattoos, long popular among the young, had been adopted by the ultra-aged as a statement of tribal defiance. Hip and shoulder replacements became as common as cataract surgery among those who could afford them.

He and Marion had become complete hypochondriacs about their mental acuity and did a lot of self-testing. Usually they were reassured, though it had become clear that short-term memory, of the sort that let them know why one of them had entered a room or what they'd had for dinner the night before, was weakening steadily. On the other hand, studies confirmed that Methuselah was startlingly efficient in preventing amyloid buildup in brain synapses, so those who'd managed to avoid Alzheimer's by the time they were infected would apparently elude it for life.

For life. He couldn't help wondering what that meant now. They had a number of otherwise sensible friends who, once it was clear they were Lifers, had become obsessed with the question of how long they would live. The gift of unaccountably more time suggested to them that it might be endless, that perhaps they'd become immortal. They consulted experts and paid for expensive tests, and no one could tell them. When their lives had been shorter, they'd been content not to know how much time they had left, *wanted* not to know, but now that so much more was theirs, they wanted to know exactly how much, like a spendthrift who, reprieved from bankruptcy, becomes a miser.

There was also great curiosity among these same sorts of people about whether their new longevity was inheritable. Most of them were far past parenting age, and the biogerontologists were fairly certain that the genomic reprogramming that Methuselah caused didn't extend to the human gamete, but that didn't stop some from hiring surrogates or obtaining new trophy wives to start that very long experiment.

Those who had been rich, when they amortized their riches over their new, unknowable lifespans, suddenly feel poorer. Those who had been poor felt richer, in time and in opportunity.

Dan felt financially poorer, particularly now that they'd begun sinking Marion's millions into developing Black Valley. But he also felt driven, no longer by the dwindling of time, but paradoxically by the expansion of it, and by an accompanying sense of renewed responsibility, the need not to dawdle as they'd begun to in that way so typical of the old, the need not to squander what they referred to as a second lifetime, a lifetime embarked upon with none of the ignorance and inexperience that had hobbled and clouded the first. They had no excuses this time, had a clearer sense than ever of what a lifetime meant, how much and how little could be accomplished in one, how nothing could be assumed, nothing taken for granted.

There were mornings when he looked in the mirror and saw, without his usual self-deception, his real age, rather than the sense of age he carried around in his head. In those moments, he cursed whoever had said that age is just a number. He and Marion and millions like them did not look like wise old gods. They looked like age in a form it had never been allowed to assume in all the millennia of human life. They were not pretty; their aspect was not noble. They looked like bundles of flesh that had outgrown their time, faces full of odd protrusions that had nowhere else to go; spots, moles, warts, which some chose to highlight with tattoos. Had he and his kind grown ugly? He thought so. Were they grotesque? In the sense that there was no aesthetic metaphor for their appearance, yes, he thought that too. They had outlived all the models of the human face. They were very old, and they looked like nothing else on earth. They looked like aliens, which was exactly what they'd become.

In another time he remembered well, it had been easy to ignore them. They'd been buried literally or buried beneath the centuries of images that told humans how they were to look. But they'd become so numerous, and so loud, that there was no avoiding them. They'd become a new sort of beauty, one that no one had to confront before, one that had no name.

There was so little to the man in the mirror. Sticks for limbs, a tube of torso that his own two hands could almost encompass, a few strands of muscle hardened like rope, a shock of wild white hair. And the skull, more evident than ever behind the face, the self's only home.

Like a husk, he thought, hollowed out like an acoustical instrument, still resonating with chords played long ago. What was sex like with someone you'd known for more than a hundred years? He couldn't begin to tell anyone who hadn't lived as long as he and Marion had. Concatenations of memories, the flesh subordinate to them, to everything, yielded up. They used to say they'd be bored to live this long. How little imagination they'd had.

MARION

New York City, 2071

Claire had always been interested in death. Marion wasn't sure what to think of the public figure she'd become, though she was proud of her, the philosopher and author with a worldwide following. There was even talk of her running for high office, though in her countless interviews and chipcasts she brushed such suggestions aside. Marion was grateful that Claire had adopted her grandmother's maiden name as a statement of her particular brand of independence, allowing Marion and Dan to pass in most circles without being recognized as relatives of the famous Claire Landess. Yes, Marion was proud of her, despite the fact that she wanted her grandparents dead.

It was nothing personal, of course. She wanted all the Lifers dead, as they would have been without the Change, if biology had been allowed to take its normal course. But unlike most of the demagogues who'd arisen since the Lifers stopped dying, she didn't stoop to phony religiosity about "God's design" or fearmongering about the economic and social disasters that their continued existence had visited upon the world. Her brilliance, and her broad appeal, lay in her determination to make a strictly moral argument for what she called "responsible lifespans" and "common-good death."

Troubling though it was, none of this was particularly surprising to Marion. As a very young girl, Claire had the usual questions, at first directed to her mother and father, but later, once they'd divorced and she and Dan took over raising her, to them, about what the end of a life meant, why it had to happen, where the essence of the dead bird or dog or, occasionally, person, had gone, whether it could be recovered or communicated with, whether Dan and Marion, too, would die. Like most parents, they'd pretended to know how to answer such questions, responding with the usual secular-rational half-lies and euphemisms and misdirections, that every living thing died, that the dead bird or dog or person was "at peace," that their souls lived on in the memories of those who loved them, or diffused in nature itself, which was the reason, they told her, that people returned their bodies to the earth from which they'd all come, a ritual that had troubled Claire when applied to her pet parakeet, and horrified her when applied to her great-grandfather Buck a few years later.

But her interest had persisted beyond these commonplace intrusions of mortality into their family life. As she grew older, she became genuinely offended that her grandparents' answers and those of her teachers were so vague and illogical, and she had set out to find better ones. As a teenager she'd already read Montaigne's famous 1580 essay, "That to Study Philosophy is to Learn to Die," and concluded that what she must do was study philosophy. She read the entirety of the Bible over the course of a summer and was shocked at its contents: casual violence and trite fables offering no greater insight into the nature of death and dying than the Greek and Roman mythologies she'd consumed as a child. The Christian concept of a hereafter, a place of many mansions and endless, bland contentment in the service of a megalomaniacal deity, struck her as the worst kind of feckless, fascistic fantasy. The classics were little better; Epicurus offered the rather hollow comfort that, since death and life were mutually exclusive, there was no reason to dwell on one's demise, much less inquire into its nature. Lucretius envisaged the interval between birth and death as a brightly lit banquet hall bracketed by twin eternities of slumbering darkness, with the darkness that followed life warranting no greater concern than the one that preceded it.

Discovering the existentialists, she saw that Nietzsche and Kierkegaard merely elided the issue, asserting that life alone mattered and should be led with a vigilant awareness of death, reducing mortality to its motivational value but never affirming its social necessity.

But finally she happened upon Ernest Becker's 1973 treatise, *The Denial of Death*, in which he forcefully argued that, despite our intellectual posturing to the contrary and the commodification of death and dying by modern media, we are constitutionally incapable of confronting death in any meaningful way, and that Freud was correct in asserting that "At bottom, no one believes in his own death. . . . in the unconscious every one of us is convinced of his own immortality." This struck Claire as exactly right, and in high school she became a sort of death activist, attending PTA meetings where she would suggest ways that incredulous adolescents could be better instructed in the inevitability of death and the finitude of their seemingly infinite lives. Other parents and faculty were naturally appalled that Marion and Dan had raised so neurotically morbid a child, and threatened to call in social services. Her father, Nolan, by then an enthusiastic corporate asset stripper at a private equity firm, pretended he didn't know her.

By the time the extent and persistence of the Change had become evident, Claire was a tenured PhD in the philosophy department at Columbia, where she started cranking out her famous series of "responsible lifespan" screeds long before such a stance became politically popular. The first of these, *Befriending Ending: How Radical Longevity Cheapens Life and Corrupts Society*, became a bestseller and made her something of a hero in activist doubler circles. She was only in her sixties at the time.

They hadn't seen their granddaughter in over twenty years—a brief hiatus by current standards, but longer than Marion would have liked—when they learned she was to speak at Town Hall in Manhattan as part of a symposium on the Lifer Problem, though the organizers didn't call it that. They called it "Normative Aging for the Common Good," sponsored by one of the political pressure groups that had grown out of the mainstream anti-Lifer movement. Marion, though preoccupied with the construction of the Black Valley compound, was determined to attend. She asked Dan to mind the project, prevailed upon some of her old journalist friends, and got a press pass.

They'd finally broken down and bought their own ten-seater eVTOL, a flashy yellow number that she was embarrassed to be seen in, especially alone. But always preparing for the worst, she saw it as a way to get people up to the compound quickly when that became necessary. It was one of the new models that required a GPS destination download directly from a headchip, which always made her queasy, since she'd only recently conceded to Dan's urgings that she have one injected and was still startled by the strange murmurings and visuals that accompanied its responses to her commands. In the case of the destination input, this involved several cheery beeps in ascending tones and a quick series of images of Manhattan from the air, as though the thing were preparing her for the flight as a parent might prepare a child. As she climbed into the big yellow drone, she mused that the last thing she needed before embarking on a trip like this was to be condescended to by a machine.

The eVTOL, being solar, wasn't the fastest thing in the sky. It took almost ten hours and three charging stops to get from Black Valley to the Bloomberg Pad in what was once the East River, now a lake the size of Manhattan itself. Flying in over the dear old city, she looked down on what was once Wall Street, the upper halves of the office towers still poking out of the water but empty now, long abandoned. The Village was under the Hudson, and the dry blocks didn't start till above the 14th Street seawall. There was talk of retreating still farther north, but people persisted in living in the city for reasons she couldn't begin to fathom.

She arrived at Town Hall a couple of hours before Claire was scheduled to give what was branded as the keynote address. It was still hard to grasp how famous her granddaughter had become. On the symposium's posters outside the old building, her face was startlingly lined but still as beautiful as she'd been as a little girl, though she and Marion had never agreed on that, even then. Nolan had warned Dan that he might be there too, as he'd attracted some interest in his suicide drug—Dan's phrase, not Nolan's—and his daughter's notoriety and message meshed so nicely with his capital campaign that, having ignored her for most of her life, he was now hoping to sign her as a spokesperson.

Given the theme of the gathering, Marion was not surprised to find herself one of the few Lifers in attendance, but she'd decided to make a statement and dress in what Dan called her Lifer Liberation whites, drawing indignant stares as she took her seat in the orchestra section. Most of the crowd was colored—orange, red, black, blue, tan, violet—in the popular total-body tattoos of the times. She scanned the assemblage for Nolan, though it had been so long since she'd laid eyes on her son that she wasn't sure she would recognize him. Surely he'd be completely bald now, in his late eighties, almost a tripler, that transition that had become like a second puberty or menopause, embarrassing and unspoken of, especially now when attitudes had hardened against what she preferred to call the ultra-aged.

In large public settings like this, her thoughts always turned to assassination. How easy it would be for some disgruntled Lifer, who hated Claire and all she stood for, to sneak a wave gun, or even an old ballistic weapon, into the hall and start taking shots at the dais, and at the audience. The longevity troubles had resulted in so many attempts on the lives of heads of state in the preceding few decades that she'd lost count, and the general feeling had become that these things were inevitable, like the occasional pandemic or the Methuselah syndrome itself, a further descent into the politico-cultural hellscape that had started, she believed, with Donald Trump and reached a sad culmination in what was called the Great Usurpation, when several right-leaning states had begun to declare electoral outcomes by legislative fiat.

Looking around at the murmuring throng, so humid and close, she had to remind herself that, once upon a time, no one gathered physically like this for any reason, that it had been considered not only unnecessary and inconvenient, but unseemly and unsanitary, a kind of slumming indulged in only by the very young or the impossibly rich. The rest of humanity had migrated to the cloud, as the almost forgotten phrase had it, until access to it had been revoked, first by one government and then, when they saw it could be done, the next, and the intangible world they'd conjured evaporated even more quickly than it had come into being. Its replacement, the much-ballyhooed Distributed Blockchain Neural Network, which allowed only chip-to-chip peer communication and circumvented the old platform gatekeepers and content providers, was not, in Marion's personal view, likely to be much better than the original, but at least its AI filtered out most forms of pornography and political falsehood, returning mass media to a headspace something like that of 1950s television, which she'd hated even then.

Still, there were times like these—elbow-to-elbow with a bunch of slovenly, artificially colored doublers, most of whom had discarded any emblem of gender, in the same claustrophobic hall where she'd taken a prep course for the New York bar exam a hundred years earlier—when she pined for the physical isolation of a good old-fashioned online chat room.

A politician, a congressman from upstate who looked barely out of his sixties, spoke first, mouthing careful phrases about the longevity "problem" and the need to manage it in a humane yet socially responsible way, obfuscating as much as possible where he fell on the ageist spectrum. There was a brief allusion to the newly popular idea of a "Lifer tax," a form of down-generational financial reparation that triplers supposedly owed to the doublers, which drew a ripple of applause from the crowd, but no mention of the forced migration or, alternatively, anti-migration statutes that were being proposed as a means to contain the massive surges of Lifer populations around the country and the world. He did try to make a rather awkward joke about the huge numbers of Lifers who were gravitating into what was called the "Boomer Box," the rectangle of land defined by Denver and Santa Fe on its western corners and Columbus and Asheville to the east, a section of the continent increasingly popular not only with Lifers but with triplers of all ages for its relative safety from the earthquakes, droughts, firestorms, and sea-level inundations that plagued the coasts and much of the South.

But finally he turned to the matter at hand, introducing the renowned Claire Landess, philosopher, author and, most recently, leader of a social movement that, he said, might well revolutionize how people thought about aging in America. And with a flourish, he swung his outstretched arm toward the tall, white-haired woman who was rising and advancing toward the podium in a shower of applause, whom Marion only barely recognized as her granddaughter.

The crowd rose to greet her. She was radiant, all in black, an angel of death if death had any, smiling and nodding at the throng. Her eyes swept the hall in an expert, knowing manner but did not meet Marion's, though surely she stood out from this crowd. And Claire's voice, when she began to speak, was strangely musical in a way Marion didn't recall from when she was merely Claire, her son's only child.

"Thank you," she said, smiling. "Thank you for this opportunity to address a subject of profound importance to us all." Marion sat with the rest of the audience and listened.

"We find ourselves in an extraordinary time. Our conventional notions of life and death, developed over millennia of human experience, have been, in little more than a single generation, upended.

"I speak of course of the Methuselah phenomenon, the sudden extension of the average human lifespan into a second century, with its ultimate limit yet to be determined. And while much of the public attention to this Change has been focused on the question of how it came about, and the repercussions it has had on our economies and our social mores, I want to address here a different subject, the grave and important question of where this leaves us in relationship to our species's oldest and, until now, most reliable companion: death.

"The temptation, of course, is to believe that we've cheated death; that after running from it for all of human history and hiding from it inside artfully constructed facades of myth, fable, and religion, we've finally matured into beings who can look death in the eye, and simply turn and walk away.

"But this is an illusion. What we've come to call the Methuselah syndrome is only the most recent manifestation of mankind's oldest delusion: the denial of death. I'm here to argue that this latest incarnation of our fear of mortality is not only naive, but morally misguided, and that now, more than ever, we need to take urgent steps to counter it. The scientists can't tell us exactly how it happened, or how long the average person can now be expected to live, though actual immortality seems unlikely. We do know this: that the longest-lived person currently on the planet is a woman in Cairns, Australia, who is one hundred seventy-four years old." There was gasp from the crowd. "We do know that there are approximately a hundred million people now living on the earth—equal to the population of a major nation—who are over the age of one hundred. And we know that if they and the two generations that follow them—including my generation—all live to be the age of the woman in Cairns, the population of those above the age of one hundred will grow to over a billion."

Another gasp, a few cries of "No!"

"The implications of these numbers are staggering. The likely toll on the quality of life, not just for Lifers and other triplers, but for all of us, is literally incalculable. But we can be sure of one thing: that nothing about life will be enhanced by having this much more of it.

"The scientists also can't tell us whether this radical lengthening of the average human lifespan is permanent, or whether, after a generation or two, it will revert to the former mean, and our children and grandchildren will come to die in their double-digits, as we did before this contagion—for such it is, we're told—befell us. It's possible that today's triplers represent a generationally specific divergence from the human norm, and that traditional senescence will reassert itself in time, leaving the Lifers and their children marooned in their unique longevity from the rest of humankind.

"But I'm not here to frighten you with statistics or with what we don't know; there are plenty of politicians and bureaucrats eager to do that. I want instead to propose that radically prolonged human life is no more meaningful than what we've lived for millennia, and that in many ways, it is less so, and in that sense, immoral. And that therefore it can and should be rejected by those tempted to live it.

"As with every correction of a bad habit, the first step in freeing ourselves from our addiction to the fantasy of immortality is to acknowledge it. No matter how traumatic the upheavals that the Change has brought upon us, no matter how seemingly irreconcilable the divisions it has sown, there is part of every one of us that hears this new siren song of immortality with a rush of relief. Finally, finally, to be confirmed in my most secret belief that, to paraphrase Sartre, death is other people's, that I am not, in fact, a narcissistic fool to feel, in my heart of hearts, that death might come to the unlucky, or the poor, or the stupid, or the reckless, or the terribly old, or anyone else, but never, never, never to me! That I was somehow, despite the evidence of all of human history, different in this last, crucial way. That surely I, of all people, would not die.

"We come by this irrational belief honestly, for we are, after all, animals, beings who know nothing but life. The very act of living makes death implausible. Our very cells cry out that it is death that must be the illusion, and life the only reality. Though we can see that, in fact, life is the anomaly, that all our works are the merest froth on an ocean of unknowing silence, and that insensate inanimacy is the ground state toward which all things trend—our friends the scientists call this 'entropy'—the counter-state of nonbeing remains profoundly, constitutionally unimaginable to us.

"And yet we must imagine it and, more, embrace it if we are to become fully human. For only an internalization of the reality of death allows us to see ourselves as the fragile reeds that we are. We can begin to see the futility of the accumulation of wealth and power over others. We can begin to recognize in our mortality the one transcendent fact that we share with every other being on the planet. In the fellowship of the soon-to-die, we can recognize the jeopardy of not loving well enough and the futility of withholding forgiveness from one another. No ambition or dream of fame, no domination over our fellow humans has any meaning in light of the certainty of individual death.

"But what some call the longevity plague threatens to change this moral calculus. Distorted in the funhouse mirror of supposed immortality, our most selfish visions gain a destructive traction on our souls. If history has taught us anything, it's that self-perceived immortals make bad citizens and worse rulers. We've allowed ourselves to become divided between those of us who are still within the boundaries of what we knew as a 'normal' lifespan and those newly minted millions who have outlived that frame"—here, Marion imagined that Claire glanced in her direction—"by twenty or thirty or fifty years, and still show no signs of morbidity.

"But this is a false division. We should remember that we are all still one human family, still share an inevitable mortality, and that those few additional decades of life are a cruel palliative, a drug with which those who live them continue to numb themselves to the fact that life is not, and never will be, without end, and indeed, that it's only by its ending that life steals meaning from the void.

"To confuse greater longevity with immortality is not just a logical error, it's a moral mistake, an indulgence in a selfish dream as old as history, one from which we must finally awaken.

"We must assume that this Change is the result of a concerted, prolonged, very expensive technological effort to disengage life from death, to supplant natural processes with brute human artifice. We should have learned by now that this sort of thing always ends badly.

"It's been said that one man's longevity is another man's immortality. Experientially, there can be little difference between the crushing ennui of the immortal living her thousandth year in the same body with the same repetition of basic experiences, and that of the one hundred eighty-year-old trying to find meaning at her stage in the same process. The issues, the trials, the disappointments, the frustrations of life don't disappear when it becomes indefinitely extended. On the contrary, they are magnified, for they are doomed to repeat themselves, and there is no longer any certainty about when or whether they will cease.

"We live immersed in time, and each moment, properly lived, has the same intrinsic value as any other. What we call the passage of time is a trick of consciousness. A radically prolonged life only adds to the number of points in the future and the past to which we have no practical access, but only feeble wishes on one hand and selective memory on the other. It's only when we are rooted in the now that we become truly immortal.

"Likewise, our egotistical notion of a precious, discrete self, moving through time toward a looming death, is illusory. What we think of as the 'self' is nothing but a screenshot of a particular moment's experience, emotion, mentation. A radically prolonged life only multiplies those sequential, momentary versions of our 'selves' without making any one of them more lasting or real or weaving them into a whole. It's only when we dispense with the illusion of the self that we become fully human.

"So, what does the new longevity bring us? On one hand, disruption, deprivation, and division at the societal level, and on the other, illusion, alienation, and boredom in the individual experience. What moral good can be found in any of it?

"Better that we as individuals and as a society confront this new condition and choose a different path. We must continue to seek cures for this plague of longevity, but failing that, we have within us the means as individuals to end lives too long to hold meaning, and the responsibility as a society to reject the fear of death that has led us to this untenable way of so-called life.

"Join me in befriending a wise and humane ending for each of us, by reciting the Mortal Creed."

Marion had lost herself in her granddaughter's voice, but now, to her astonishment, some in the crowd began to murmur along with her.

"I believe that death comes to all living things

"And therefore I believe that I will die.

"I accept this despite all the delusions and fears that tempt me to believe otherwise.

"I was born out of darkness and oblivion;

"I live in a world of life and light;

"I know nothing but this world.

"Yet that does not undo my acceptance of the finitude of life.

"I therefore believe in the community of the mortal,

"The fellowship of the destined-to-die.

"I will not leave to an artificially prolonged future

"That which can be done to today to acknowledge my mortality

"And, fruitfully, to embrace it."

The applause was thunderous. Marion looked around at the crowd, faces full of relief and resolve, some turned toward her with expressions of something like triumph. She excused herself as she moved past them, everyone standing now, cheering, leaning away from the woman in white as she passed, as though she were indeed contagious, a carrier of the plague stamped on her features as clearly as their tattoos. Some of the rowdier members of the audience made crude gestures, and one or two managed to jostle her from behind.

She wanted to tell them how wrong they were, wanted to point out how much she still resembled the woman they so admired, how that woman wouldn't exist were it not for her, but she kept her mouth shut, as the aged had long since learned to do, and picked up her pace. Two overweight attendees followed her up the aisle and threw their combined weight into her back as she reached the exit. She stumbled forward and her knees slammed into the sidewalk, her white pants smeared with the grit of the city. Pain shot up her legs, and her first thought was that she might have broken something. The crowd was surging out of the doorways behind her, staring at her, an old woman in white, as she lay there. The two thugs disappeared.

She stood and dusted herself off and chipped instructions to the drone to meet her on the Hudson pad in twenty minutes. She took a couple of steps, checking to see that she was intact, then hurried west toward the setting sun, thinking about the men who'd hit her, the hatred and fear that motivated them, and about what her granddaughter had said, trying to sort the wisdom from the gibberish, her anger from her shock. She'd reached the end of the littered block when she heard a shout of "Mom!" from behind her.

Nolan was much shorter than she remembered him—or perhaps she had grown. She towered over him. He was indeed quite bald, a bit chipfaced, like one of those proverbial men from the future in all the old sci-fi movies, in a turtleneck though the day was warm, his skull sleek and shiny as though polished, purged of hair follicles, not even eyelashes. He was smiling a tense, sympathetic smile, as though sure she'd been crushed by what they'd just heard, the errors of her ways finally made clear to her. In fact she'd wanted to stand up and argue with his daughter, tell her that she had it all wrong when she assumed there was nothing good about having the black monkey of death peeled off your back and tossed into a cage, all wrong to say that a longer life just meant more repetitions of the same old pains and disappointments, completely wrong to assume that Lifers were full of the hubris of immortality, desperately bored and alienated from real life. If anything, Marion thought, they were humbled, and grateful, and loved life more than they'd ever been able to admit before, back when to do so would have sounded not only greedy but pathetic because they were so soon to be deprived of it.

All this was running through her head as Nolan rushed up to her and breathlessly asked, "What did you think?"

They hugged briefly; he reeked of some horrible men's perfume. "I thought she was frightening. Or rather, that she's amazingly effective, and that's frightening."

"But what a message! What a great voice!" he exulted. Claire's voice had, in fact, been quite beautiful, which only made Marion sadder at what she was using it to say.

"Where's Dad?" Nolan asked, looking around as though Marion might be hiding him.

She gestured down the block toward the river. "Back in Colorado. He's supervising the project while I'm away."

"Oh yes, the compound," he said, clicking his heels as though ready to give a Nazi salute. "How could I forget? How much money have you guys sunk in that so far?"

"Don't worry about it, Nole. Worry about your own business. Which I assume is why you're here."

He relaxed a bit when he heard his childhood nickname, shrugged. "They whisked Claire away before we could talk, but I'm gonna meet with her and her entourage tomorrow to discuss her backing the treatment, which by the way is almost through human trials. Buy the stock, Mom."

"I have plenty of the stock, thanks. Still a pill?"

"What? Oh, you mean the treatment. A series of pills, seven in all in the latest version. Seemed biblically resonant. Thought of calling it One A Day, but that's already taken." He grinned.

"Why so many?"

The smile faded. "The lawyers recommended it. That way if you change your mind you can stop taking them halfway through the series and nothing will happen. Seven pills in seven days shows real intention."

"I'll say," she muttered. "Still 'Swing Low'?"

"'Sweet Chariot,'" he corrected. "No, we had to give that up. The marketing people thought it was too morbid and, frankly, too religious. Or religiously morbid. The new name will be some three-syllable jumble of meaningless consonants beginning with a Z."

"Still a year before you die?"

"Yep, exactly," he said proudly.

"Is that a year from the day you take the first pill, or the last?"

He frowned, not sure if she was asking a technical question or, as was in fact the case, just needling him.

"Right now it averages out to fall between the anniversaries of the first and last dosage day. But we're working on that."

"So it's not exactly a year."

"Not precisely. Not yet. Depends on the customer."

"And the day," Marion pointed out. He ignored this, looking back down the street to where people were still emptying out of the hall, as though he might catch a glimpse of Claire and go buttonhole her on the spot.

"Can I be one?" she asked.

"Be one what?"

"A customer."

There was a mixture of horror and excitement in those bald little eyeballs. "You mean for the treatment? Well, sure. You think you might?"

"Not anytime soon, but you never know."

"What would Dad say?"

"He'd be horrified. He'd never in a million years."

"And it might be a million, right?" he half laughed, half sneered.

"Send us a couple of sets?" she asked.

"When it's legal, sure," he said, still gaping in disbelief. "So Claire's talk really did get through to you, huh?"

She sighed. "I understand what she's saying, though I think a lot of it is solipsistic nonsense. 'There is no self,' 'time is an illusion,' all that stuff. Now the denial of death, that's real. That's something we're hard-wired with. It's why the species survived this long. Why dwell on what you can't change? Couldn't change, anyway. Why not live each day as though you're never going to die? Have a martini, enjoy life. Intellectually we all know we'll die someday—even now."

"I didn't think you did anymore," her son said. "I assumed you guys thought you were gods now."

She looked at him, feeling something close to pity. "No, we do not think we're gods. But we've been given a great gift, and we'll be damned if we're going to squander it by feeling guilty about it, or having people like you and your daughter try to shame us out of it."

He looked only mildly hurt at this. "There's stuff coming that will involve more than just shame," he said gravely.

"I don't doubt it. That's why I want those pills of yours. Just in case."

"I'll send some."

Her drone would be waiting; she turned and started walking. "Need a lift? I'm headed west."

"Nah, I'm headed east," he said. They hugged ceremonially and walked off in opposite directions.

She chipped for an autotaxi, and a single-seater met her at the corner of 8th Avenue and 43rd Street. But instead of heading straight west to the landing pad in the Hudson, she directed it north, toward Columbus Circle. There was something she had to see for herself.

She'd wanted to retreat to Colorado out of a sense of self-preservation, but simply to hide there wasn't enough. The years of her activist youth haunted her, the marches on Washington during the war in Vietnam when she and Dan were in college, the money she'd donated to Planned Parenthood and the gay rights movement, which had enraged her right-wing father. And finally, when Clinton won, and Dan got the job in the White House, it was her sense of outrage— that Washington was, even then, at the end of the twentieth century, still just an old boys' club where wealthy white men traded power back and forth—that had driven her to create the first all-female lobbying firm in the capital, one that took on only such underfunded and inevitably doomed causes as gun control, immigration, and women's rights. And in the midst of that, Dan's betrayal of her with Adele, living proof, if any more were needed, that men in positions of power soon became drunk with it, and that though they might be forgiven, as she'd forgiven Dan, they couldn't always be relied upon to make the right decisions.

She saw that she'd spent most of her first hundred years angry, and she was angry still; but this time, the cause was even more personal.

What hit her first as she climbed out of the taxi at Columbus Circle was the smell: a blend of burning garbage and the unmistakable undercurrent of human excrement. Half a dozen armed civilian security guards roamed the sidewalk at Merchants' Gate, eyeing her suspiciously in her soiled white suit and expensive high heels. *Easy to get in*, she thought; *perhaps less easy to get out.* Seeing that one of the guards was a woman, Marion walked directly up to her.

"Excuse me, but I want to enter the park," she said.

"It's a public park, Mother," said the guard, who Marion saw was just a child. People that age had taken to calling triplers "Mother" and "Father" in personal exchanges, a sly cross between an honorific and a slur. Marion had certainly been called a motherfucker, but never a mother, even when she'd been one. "But we don't advise going in there after dark."

"Not dark yet," Marion pointed out.

"We can't be responsible," said the guard, barely containing a sneer as she looked down at Marion's fancy open-toed shoes.

"I don't expect you to be responsible. Just don't stop me when I come back this way."

The girl guard looked around. "How long?"

"Fifteen minutes."

The girl shrugged.

It was near midnight when Marion staggered back out through Merchants' Gate, her suit dirtier, her shoes in her hands, but her mind resolved. What she'd seen was far worse than she'd imagined. Central Park had become a ghetto of the aged, tents crowded against each other between the trees as far as she could see, the vast Sheep Meadow—where she and Dan had watched Simon and Garfunkel perform a century earlier—turned into an open-air dormitory, endless rows of multicolored sleeping bags, reeking of urine and fast food. The asphalt avenues that snaked through the vastness were heaped with burning refuse. She'd seen homeless encampments before, had joined social service workers in DC trying to clear some of them back when they were merely a byproduct of the stubborn strain of poverty that infected American life. But nothing like this. These were not drug addicts or alcoholics, not the clinically insane or the hopelessly alienated. These were masses of people who'd likely had full and accomplished lives in their first hundred years—doctors, truckers, lawyers, teachers, investment bankers, cops—whose only mistake in life had been to outlive their means of caring for themselves, now mixed indistinguishably with the always poor, outnumbering them.

She kept walking north through the park, the ancient trees forming a dark ceiling in the dusk, people with guitars singing songs from the sixties next to open fires, their voices mingling with moans of despair coming from the darker corners of the meadows. She was near the Ramble, its network of hillocks and pathways like a rocky maze, when a woman called out to her from the gloom.

"Are you from New York?" She reached toward Marion in an ambiguous gesture that might have been taken for begging, but that Marion chose to see as a desperate bid for company. She wore what Marion recognized as an expensive St. John knit dress from the 2020s, filthy with grass stains and ashes from the small fire burning next to her tiny one-person tent. But her gray hair, Marion noted, was carefully brushed. "You look like you're from New York," she said.

"Just visiting," said Marion, approaching her and, on impulse, kneeling next to her, taking her hand. The woman looked momentarily shocked at this intimacy, then recovered.

"I used to live just over there," she said, pointing in the direction of the Dakota apartment building across Central Park West. Marion nodded, remembering the one-bedroom that she and Dan had shared in the old building in their law school days. She wondered if she might have met this woman then, passed her in the lobby or on these very footpaths a hundred years before this night.

"How long have you been here?" asked Marion.

"You mean this spot? I move every day. Doesn't pay to stay in one spot too long. They get a fix on you."

"I mean in the park," said Marion.

The woman looked up at the sky as though it told time. "Ten or twelve years. I can't quite remember. It was after Paul died."

"I'm sorry. How old was he?"

"Just ninety-two. He never got the Methuselah for some reason. And he left me."

"Left you? You mean he died?"

"It's the same, isn't it?" the woman asked.

"I'm Marion."

The woman looked directly into Marion's eyes for the first time. "I'm Sarah," she said.

"Why did you move out of your apartment?" Marion asked. "Did you run out of money?"

"I didn't move out. And I had plenty of money. They evicted me. Said I had dementia. But I didn't. I just got too old for them. They wanted younger people in there."

Marion let go of the woman's hand, stood, dug into the pocket of her jacket, and pulled out a currency fob. "Are you hungry?" she asked the woman, offering the device to her.

"Oh, that won't work here," the woman said. "We can't get out to use it. But if you have any food on you. . . ."

"I'm sorry, I don't."

"We rely on the runners. They break out, break back in, give us food sometimes. Always fast food, but it's something."

"But what do you give them for the food?" asked Marion, still holding out the fob.

"Not that," said the woman. "Not that." And she turned away, as though Marion couldn't possibly understand.

Marion bent and pressed the fob into the woman's hand. "Try this next time," she said. The woman looked at her, confused. And it was in that moment that Marion knew what she must do.

She stood in the gathering darkness, climbed a rocky knoll and looked out over the vastness of the park. Fires everywhere, huddled bodies moving in the half-light, faces visible here and there, lined with great age. The murmuring of thousands of agitated voices, like the sighing of a great sea. It was a brand-new kind of hell.

When she walked out of the park, the girl guard wasn't there anymore, and some other guards stopped her, asked where she thought she was going. "Colorado," she said, and walked past them in her bleeding bare feet, daring them to stop her, knowing that it was only that white suit of hers that allowed her to walk away.

ADELE

Lake Garda, 2072

Adele could see what was coming, and so could some of the people she knew best, especially those who'd been in government and the military, most of them now in their 120s and 130s. They met in what doublers called chipspace, really just a big conference call, but with headchips instead of phones, which had gone completely out of fashion since the internet disappeared. No visuals—much too data-heavy for most older people's chips, and gave you headaches—just voices, and not really voices either, just words streaming into one's head in that odd amalgam of sound and text. Sometimes she had to ask who was speaking, but usually she could tell by the inflections. It gave new meaning to the phrase "stream of consciousness." It was best to close one's eyes.

She would convene a meeting about once a month. Dan and Marion Altman, for their executive branch and legislative experience. Randy Colson, who used to run NASA. Barb Beckwith, a Marine two-star general formerly on the Joint Chiefs, who went further back with Adele than she cared to remember. Frank Martindale, one of Adele's former underlings on the NSC who'd gone on to be secretary of defense under Buttigieg. Joe Forsythe, a sociologist and ex–UN undersecretary that Adele knew, who'd run the group that had tried and failed to organize the sea rise migrations out of Florida and northern Europe back in the forties and fifties. Jae Ming Kun, a former law partner of Marion's and a migration specialist who'd worked on the evacuation of Taiwan. Devon Jones, one of Adele's phenotypic data miners, a computational biologist who'd also worked under her at NSC and, she suspected, murkier organizations. A few others, depending on who was available and could remember the time and the access code. They were all sworn to secrecy, both as to the meetings' content and their very existence.

It wasn't always clear, even to Adele, what these talks among these previously important people were supposed to accomplish, other than to make them feel less helpless. But they usually ended up in a quietly passionate argument among three sub-groups: the militant separatists, like Marion Altman, who believed that the best and perhaps only response to the growing hostility toward Lifers was to get them into their own geographic "safe zones," either through negotiation, organized land acquisition, or self-exile (perhaps off-earth); the integrationists, like Jae Ming and Joe, who hoped that time and experience would eventually heal the intergenerational rifts and allow triplers and doublers to coexist happily (these optimists tended to be former NGO types and were in the distinct minority); and the fatalists, who saw no way forward but back to quasi-normal lifespans and mortality rates, to be achieved either through a yet-to-be-imagined biomedical "cure" or what these defeatists called voluntary euthanasia, and which Dan Altman preferred to call mass suicide.

She poured her tea, sat at the metal desk in the drawing room overlooking the lake, and waited for the chipfeed to start. She studied her notes. She usually opened with a briefing, since she had the resources of Xerxes at her disposal. Occasionally she'd slip and mention the organization in the midst of one of their heated discussions, but they all pretended not to notice. She'd chipfeed a transcript afterward.

[linkage clicks; background conversation]

Adele: Let's come to order. How is everyone today?

[Murmurs of general well-being]

Adele: If there's no old business, I'll present the monthly summary of current political trends. *[Long pause; general quieting]* My sources continue to indicate a rise in anti-Lifer sentiment in most of the Western democracies, as manifested in the recent presidential elections in the US, Mexico, Brazil, and India. All resulted in the installation of "normative lifespan" proponents as the new heads of government, with the new woman in the White House being the most predictably strident on the subject. She hasn't been specific about proposals yet, but we expect a bill containing an up-or-out requirement for those wanting to have children . . . .

A chorus of chip-voices: Wait! Wait! What's "up-or-out"?

Adele: I thought we'd discussed this before, sorry. The proposition would be that, once a cure for Methuselah is developed, you'd be required to take it if you want to have children, and if you decline to take it, you have to forgo childbearing, either get a hysterectomy or vasectomy as the case may be. Conversely, if you already have children, you'll have to limit yourself to a "normal" lifespan, defined as up to a hundred years of age. You grow super-old childless or, if you want to have kids, you agree to die at a certain age.

Another chorus: None of that is constitutional! When would this childbearing decision have to be made? What's the age limit for parenting?

Adele: Of course, people, but you can see the appeal of such a law. The argument is that there has to be some sort of draconian population control, or things will very quickly get beyond manageable limits, and some say we're already there. The up-or-out requirement would have to be imposed on the very young with the expectation that it would become just another rite of passage, like getting a driver's license or being drafted into the military used to be. And yes, of course this would require some tweaks to the Constitution, the simplest being a one-liner saying that the "equal" in the guarantee of "equal protection under the law" doesn't apply where age is concerned.

Jae Ming: But it's rather a moot point until a cure, or at least a vaccine, is available. Till then they've got nothing but coercion to try to sterilize as many people as possible.

Marion: As many as possible?

Jae Ming: Think about it: today, every single birth represents a *net* increase in the human population. *Every* birth! There is no offsetting reduction in population as long as we fail to die. Or look at it differently: every death deferred beyond an actuarially normal lifespan is like an extra birth. Devon, what are the numbers again?

Devon: Well, if Methuselah didn't exist, the current global mortality rate would be about ninety million per year. We estimate that around half of the world's population is infected with Methuselah, meaning that, if it's evenly distributed across age groups, at least forty-five million people who would have died *every year* are not dying, and what would have been a global population of around ten billion in 2060 is instead a billion more than that. It's as if, twenty years ago, global birth rates rose overnight by fifty percent, having been fairly constant for the preceding fifty years. That's unsustainable by any measure, starting with feeding those additional mouths. We'll crowd ourselves off the planet in less than a century.

Joe: But, Devon, what if this is just an interval? What if the effect of Methuselah is that the average human lifespan is extended by, say, fifty or at most a hundred years? If, as Adele and her group believe, Methuselah was first released in the mid-2030s, that would mean that the Lifers might start dying off in another twenty years or so, in their one-forties or one-fifties. And you'd start to see a brake on the population growth, and population reaching an equilibrium again.

Adele: Maybe, Joe. But there's yet another possibility suggested by some recent studies, and that is that the younger a person is when infected with Methuselah, the longer they will live. Remember Gompertz's Law of Mortality?

A chorus: No. . . .

Devon: Of course!

Adele: Well, for everyone but Devon, back in the 1800s, a Brit named Benjamin Gompertz, who worked for a life insurance company, came up with an actuarial equation to predict when people would die. He basically concluded that the likelihood of dying from some cause or another—accident, disease, old age—doubles roughly every eight and a half years. A couple of hundred years later, some Silicon Valley types working on early attempts at longevity extension applied Gompertz's equation to see what would happen if the sheer passage-of-time component of death-causation were zeroed out at various points in life. The result was an exponential increase in life expectancy: a fifty-year-old who stopped aging would be statistically likely to live to be two hundred. But a thirty-year-old who stopped aging would be statistically likely to live almost *seven hundred years* before dying from other causes.

What this implies in the time of Methuselah is that, while someone who was exposed in their seventies might live to be one-fifty or two hundred, a person infected in their twenties or thirties might live to be six or seven hundred. So yes, Joe, it's possible that everyone who's been infected will just get on a longer treadmill and die in lockstep at a certain age, but it's also possible that the generations that follow ours will have increasingly longer lifespans, depending on when in life they were infected. Have I got all that right, Devon?

Devon: Well, I wasn't going to bring it up, but if you run Methuselah through the Gompertz equation, a child infected at the age of ten might live to be twenty thousand years old.

[Long silence, just the buzz of their chips, like crickets.]

Barb: That's impossible.

Frank: Says the hundred-year-old woman. . . .

Marion: I was at a talk my granddaughter Claire gave last month. . . .

Randy: Claire Landess? *She's* your granddaughter?

Marion: I can't deny it. Anyway, in her talk she cited some figures to the effect that there are around one hundred million people over the age of one hundred on the earth right now. Is that right, Devon?

Devon, after a pause: Actually, she's off on the low side. That's a very conservative figure. Governments are underreporting their triplers to prop up their financial markets, but if you dig into the demographics, one hundred million triplers is way too low. Our data indicates something more like two hundred fifty to three hundred million.

Dan: And how many in the US?

Devon: Around seventy-five million. Not all native-born, of course. Triplers are heavily weighted toward the Americas and the western Pacific Rim to begin with, but there's been a lot of tripler immigration to the US due to sea-level rise, and now due to Methuselah.

Dan: So, what—about a quarter of the US population?

Devon: Yes, and, coincidentally, about a quarter of the probable global tripler population. And growing by about ten million per year. Though that's just statistics; the transition from being ninety-nine to one hundred doesn't change anything very much, even for the individuals.

Marion: It may change things for those individuals once governments start drawing hard age lines in legislation, like Adele's up-or-out legislation, or when your medical benefits are cut off, or whether you're allowed to come and go in certain parts of the country after a certain age.

[Another long chip-silence.]

Marion: We need our own space.

Jae Ming: Don't you have yours there in Colorado, Marion?

Marion: I mean for all of us, or at least for vastly more of us. We can take about fifty to a hundred thousand here, we have a few hundred on-site now and over ten thousand applicants already. We need something much more comprehensive and systematic, like when Israel was formed out of contested territory after World War II . We need our own country.

Barb: I just don't see that in the cards. . . .

Joe: Could we go over the off-earth options one more time, Randy? I need to hear that again.

Randy: There really aren't any, much as I'd like to think otherwise.

Joe: But why not some massive public-private partnership initiatives for low-orbit living platforms, or even the moon again? You'd think there'd be a lot of interest in that from Western governments struggling to accommodate these populations. . . .

Randy: I'm afraid you're talking about a significant portion of most nations' GDP there, Joe. And even if you could raise the funding, the technology isn't to scale. Even the US fell behind on off-earth terraforming and closed-system life support after the Mars colony disaster, and the Chinese aren't much better. There's just no technical foundation for going that route again, let alone on the scale we're talking about. The populations Devon's describing would outrun even the wildest increase in off-earth capacity. Let's not even spend our time dreaming about it. And I say that as a guy who had a lot of space dreams once.

Marion: I'm going to keep saying it: land. On earth. Land of our own. We've got to start negotiating with local and national governments for our own spaces, and to negotiate we need leverage. What's our leverage?

Barb: Well, I hesitate to point it out, but a lot of Lifers are armed. Not sure about Lingerers generally, but the older ones were very much Second Amendment types even before the Change, and now a lot of them are pretty trigger-happy, as the headlines will tell you.

Adele: But as you well know, they're completely disorganized, and I don't see anyone on the horizon who's going to change that, though Marion is off to a good start with her Lifer Liberation Front.

Marion: Others call it that; I don't. And I'd never get behind armed insurrection, ever. Just forget it. Half of these morons should never have had guns to begin with; it was just some cowboy fantasy they grew up with and there weren't enough sensible Supreme Court jurists to correct them. Just forget it!

Barb: We might forget it, but there are others out there who won't.

Marion: The first organized uprising would give every normative lifespan zealot in office an excuse to start rounding us up in earnest, and shooting us if we resisted. The use of force to try to get what we want would play into their hands. That way lies Dachau, mark my words.

Jae Ming: You know, I've never asked you, Marion, but are you Jewish?

Marion: Episcopalian.

Jae Ming: Huh.

Dan: Look, back on the subject. Marion asked a good question. What leverage do we have? It's not money, though collectively we have a lot of it, and it's not force of arms. It could be political power, given our eventual numbers, but that's a very long game, and we don't have that kind of time—

Joe: No, we have a different kind of time, don't we? Just our own, personal, ridiculously huge amount of individual time.

Dan: Well, that's what I was getting around to. That's a kind of wealth, isn't it?

Devon: Though not convertible into any currency I know of.

Dan: We can't convert it, but like other kinds of wealth, you can trade it for something. In this case, maybe the land that Marion's talking about.

Joe: Not following you. Trade it how?

Marion: Oh, I think I know what he means. No, Dan, don't even go there—

Dan: But listen. We're in possession now of exceedingly long lifespans, and those lifespans are a huge problem for the people we need to listen to us. What if we—some percentage of us—offered to give them up in exchange for what we want?

[Silence.]

Dan: It's a completely nonviolent approach, Marion, and it would be hugely persuasive.

Barb: Even soldiers aren't asked to do that. . . .

Joe: I'm still not sure I'm following. . . .

Dan: What if a significant number of Lifers agreed to end their lives voluntarily, but only if, as, and when the US Congress, for example, agreed to set aside X million acres of federal land exclusively for Lifers?

Devon: That X of yours would need to be a lot of millions. . . .

Dan: Of course, and I'm also not sure how many millions of Lifers you'd need to sign up for this to have real leverage, but that's what negotiations are about. . . .

Mae Jing: What's a human life worth. . . ?

Dan: But a life already lived, right? A life lived twice over, for most of us. Worth less, surely, than one cut short in youth, and even a bit less than one lived to what we used to think of as a normal age. Enough less that some of us—a lot of us, I'm guessing—might be willing to trade it—yes, give it up—for something the rest of us desperately need.

Marion: You're sounding like your granddaughter, you realize. I thought you thought she was nuts.

Dan: I think she's nuts to suggest that death is inherently moral and we should die out of duty. This would be dying for a purpose, to get something. Transactional death.

Marion: I'm not sure I see the difference.

Barb: Used to be called self-sacrifice. I think it went out of style a long time ago.

Adele: But if anyone remembers, it's us.

Dan: Yes, we're good at memory.

Adele: Sometimes too good.

Indeed, Adele's memories seemed so precise and real that she always had to stop and ask herself whether she was imagining them, whether they'd really happened or whether her mind had reconstructed events to suit her own story of her life.

Los Alamos, New Mexico, 1974

A dele and her husband slept side by side on the ground in the moonlight, the blankets they'd carried in on their backs pulled up to their chins against the chill of the high desert. Visitors weren't allowed there after dark, but they'd wanted to see it at night, wanted to sleep there where people once slept. The ground beneath them was weathered stone, smoothed by millennia of wind and rain, riven here and there by narrow channels worn into the rock by centuries of human footsteps. The channels led from the base of the mesa to the escarpment where they lay, next to the caves.

She was awakened by a sound. The wind, perhaps. She rose and looked up at the moon, the stars, their ancient light like heat on her face. Her husband slept on. She was naked beneath the blanket, drew it closer around her. Their clothes were scattered nearby where they'd dropped them when they began to make love. She started to retrieve them, and then she heard it again, coming from the mouths of the caves, ovals hewn into the rock centuries before, black shades in the moonlight, openings just tall enough to admit a much smaller person than she. A murmuring, distinct, like voices in a foreign language, but oddly familiar. Coming from the caves and from somewhere farther off. Another time, perhaps. Calling to her.

She dropped the blanket and walked toward the caves.

Afghanistan, 2022

The dawn just coming up, the smell of the morning fires, the sky a beautiful roseate bowl over the teeming city. She was covered head-to-toe in a black burka, just another old woman shuffling down a leafy street in the Sherpoor neighborhood, near the city center. High walls fringed with barbed wire, higher trees sheltering gardens and swimming pools, limousines parked on the side streets with drivers asleep inside, waiting for the day's commands. She checked her position, walked another block. This was where foreign diplomats used to live, before the return of the Taliban. This was where she'd come on her last gig for the CIA, before they made her retire at age seventy-four. Someone who could pass for an old Afghan woman and still do what needed to be done.

She only had to read some DNA. But she had to collect it first.

She turned a corner, stopped, dropped into a street woman's squat, and leaned against a wall as though resting. Two short blocks away was a tall, domed villa, bright pink in the dawn light and surrounded by cypresses. On the second floor, facing where the sun would rise, was a pair of tall French doors, closed, with a white curtain behind them.

She waited, calling on the old meditation practices to empty her mind, suspend time. Ten minutes, fifteen. A mangy dog came and sniffed her sandaled feet, moved on. She waited, thought she heard the soft buzz of an aircraft high overhead.

The comm bud deep inside her ear canal bristled to life. "Inbound."

"Check," she replied softly, only mildly surprised that the voice in her ear was female. The pilot of the drone, somewhere in the States.

The curtain behind the French doors in the villa down the street fluttered, drew open. A figure moved behind it, indistinct in the pink gloom.

"Check," she repeated, this time with an edge she knew would be understood.

"Ready," said the voice in her ear, steady and calm, the voice of someone she felt she already knew.

One of the tall doors on the balcony opened inward, then the other. A short, gray-headed man in a long white tunic stepped out, looked up at the rose-colored sky.

"Now," she said. "Now, now." Three times, to make sure it was heard on the other side of the planet, a pause of about a second between each syllable, for emphasis.

The pause that followed was longer than she expected. So long that she feared the man on the balcony would disappear back into the villa. And just as he began to turn and step toward the tall doors, a shadow faster than thought or eye blurred through the air and the balcony erupted in a tight, white-hot ball of flame.

She watched carefully for the first half second, then turned away. The concussion ripped down the street and past her, tugging at her burka, echoing briefly across the city. Birds flew up, trees quivered, a shutter banged open somewhere, banged shut. Then silence again. She turned back. The man on the balcony was gone, the balcony was gone, replaced by twisted metal, the doors blackened and blown inward. She looked to where she'd seen the pieces of the man fall and moved quickly down the street, pulling gloves onto her hands, moving to the sidewalk across from the pink villa, where she bent and picked up a piece of soft, smoldering debris, then another.

Back along the side streets, into an alley. Still no commotion, no sirens. There were explosions in this town all the time. Slipped the pieces of charred flesh into the portable analyzer, first the larger one, then the smaller. Both confirmed the identity of the man on the balcony: Ayman al-Zawahiri, the leader of al-Qaeda and one of the architects of 9/11.

"Confirmed," she said.

"Check," said the voice in her ear.

The incident in Kabul was international news the next day. The DNA data was never released, but it wasn't necessary; the relevant parties knew.

Eventually there was a small, private ceremony in a conference room in the Pentagon. Just the Secretary of Defense and Adele and the pilot of the drone, a Marine general named Barbara Beckwith, already famous in the Corps not, it turned out, for killing Zawahiri, which she'd after all accomplished remotely from a console in Virginia, but for saving the life of a fellow Marine in a pitched firefight in Kandahar several years earlier when she was just a corporal. She was in her fifties and, like Adele, ready to retire.

They had dinner that night together at a Chinese place in Alexandria, just the two of them, joined in an odd way that could only happen in that peculiar twenty-first century version of wartime. She learned that Barbara had grown up in Parma, Ohio, a mostly white, working-class suburb of Cleveland, the only daughter of a fireman and a high school teacher, and the only Black student in most of the classrooms she found herself in. From her father she learned duty, from her mother, perseverance. And from those barely integrated classrooms, a self-reliance and imperviousness to insult that would later serve her well in the upper echelons of the American military. Adele downplayed her privilege, the Park Avenue and the Harvard bits, but the woman saw it all over her before she opened her mouth, laughed at it, was even sympathetic, especially when, late that night, Adele told her about her affair with Dan and her nameless, long-lost daughter.

By the end of that night they had discovered in each other that rare thing in adult life, especially in the sort of other-directed life they were living: a friend.

Paris, 2072

The bar at the Hotel Ritz. Amber light, the clink of crystal, clashing scents of perfume and liquor, the agitated murmur of the well-dressed patrons in their rainbow of artificial skin colorings. Adele noted that Barb Beckwith's skin was a beautifully unequivocal dark mocha, and always had been.

Beckwith swept into the room—surprisingly small for so famous a place—in full-on command mode, uniformed in Marine service dress, her service ribbons and warfare pins blazing on her imposing breast. She made no eye contact with the tuxedoed doorkeeper who was accosting her in French, instead just pointed to where she intended to sit, at the bar next to Adele, and brushed past him. Adele rose as she approached, and she smiled, her face melting from fearsome General Beckwith to friend Barbara in seconds, and they hugged.

"General Beckwith," Adele said nonetheless, and she laughed.

"Pritchard," Barbara responded, as though Adele were one of her noncoms. "How the hell old are you now?"

"Still twenty years your senior, madam general. And don't you forget it."

"Hey, I'm a tripler like you now, babe. Don't sass me."

Barb had just turned 100; Adele was 124. They sat and ordered martinis.

They were, as usual, the oldest people in the room. They were in Paris for a conference on the Methuselah plague, as the Europeans bluntly called it. Their socialist support networks had all failed under the mounting burden of their undying old, and their governments were still hoping for a "humanitarian biomedical solution," something that would allow the aged to resume dying without appearing to actually kill them. Something that Adele was there to tell them, in the most technical terms, did not exist, and wasn't likely to for the foreseeable future.

That the messenger of this unpleasant news was herself well into her second century of life, and that what they were all discussing in those endless meetings in those chandeliered rooms was the hoped-for mass death of people like her didn't even warrant reflection, much less acknowledgment of the irony. Things had grown chaotic, with doublers fleeing the cities en masse and hordes of triplers crowding into them in the hope of finding food, makeshift shelter, and what remained of medical care. The governments of Western Europe were changing their administrations every few months, each as ineffective at dealing with the crisis as the last. Russia had already gone dark. There were tripler bodies floating in the Seine just blocks from where they sat sipping their expensive drinks.

But for the moment, all of that was secondary. Barbara raised her glass and said what Adele had been waiting to hear.

"I found her."

"Where?" Adele held her breath.

"Australia," she said. "In a suburb of Sydney."

"She'd be seventy-six by now."

"Yes, but who's counting? She's married, one child, a daughter, almost forty."

Adele hesitated before she let her mouth form the words. "A granddaughter."

"Yes, dear, a granddaughter. I don't know much about her because you didn't want me to dig too deep. But your daughter's name is—"

She held up her hand. "Don't tell me. It would make her too real. I'm not sure I could stand it."

Barbara sighed. "You asked me to find her. So I found her. You're not going to hide from her forever. I won't let you. She's a grown woman. An old woman."

"Does she have Methuselah?

"Yes. She took a self-test years ago. It's all there." She dropped a datacoin on the bar between them. Adele fingered the small gray disk tentatively, then pressed it behind her right ear, against her chip. She was careful to put up buffers first, to keep the contents unreadable until she was ready. Which she wasn't then. The upload took a few seconds, then she handed the coin back to Barbara, who pocketed it.

"You should at least know her name," she said.

"All right. Just that. No more."

"Adelaide."

"No."

"A nod to you, obviously. Maybe her parents wanted it to be a clue."

She couldn't resist. "What are they like?"

"They died, pre-Methuselah, in their seventies. Scientists, both of them, wouldn't you know. Childless, if not for your daughter. Went to NYU for their postdoc work, knew it would be easier to adopt in the States than back home in Australia. Took Adelaide there a year or so after you gave her up, never returned to the US."

"Enough," she said. Barbara gave her the glare she reserved for underachievers who most disappointed her.

"Adele, this has been torturing you for over seventy years. But time isn't infinite, even for us. Eventually, you've got to talk to her. And you've got to tell Dan."

A single tear dropped into her martini glass. "Someday," she said. "Maybe someday."

Barb Beckwith took Adele's face in her hands.

"You better hope we live forever," she said.

An immense fatigue settled over Adele, and the room blurred. She could feel the bits from Barb's datacoin rustling in her chip, as though agitating for attention. She took Barb's big hand and pried it from her cheek.

"I think I need to go home," she said.

Beckwith drew back from her. "And where might that be?" she asked, her voice tinged with mingled sympathy and skepticism.

"I'm not sure anymore. But I need to find out."

MARION

Black Valley, Colorado, 2072

Marion insisted that they leave the rutted dirt road from the highway to the main lodge unpaved, so most of the materials and equipment needed for the new outbuildings arrived by drone or dirigible. A bigger landing pad was the first order of business, and a short runway for the occasional non-VTOL aircraft. Rotating crews of people and bots piloting giant 3D printers worked on laying the new lodges arrayed around the lake, each with its own kitchen and laundry and big enough to comfortably house twenty or so residents. A few dozen acres were graded and tilled for vegetable farming. She knew that in the long run it wouldn't be enough, but it was a start, a statement, a symbol of what might be.

The surrounding mountains cut off microwave signals, which suited Marion just fine, but she had a retransmitter antenna installed high on a western flank, above the tree line, and built a kind of studio downhill from it, with cubicles where residents could go and chip privately, and a conference room for group chipcasts. Connectivity was allowed into the valley at certain hours of the day, but flatly prohibited at mealtimes, after full dark on moonless nights, and after moonrise. It made for some complicated programming of the antenna, but all you had to do was look up to know whether or not you were in chipspace.

She'd envisioned a sort of giant Lifer commune, or a small Lifer university, but she had broader ambitions for the place, as a headquarters for the movement that she was creating out of nothing, and a home for at least some of its followers. From her days growing up as the daughter of Buck Landess, she knew who to call to get her message out through the right chip nodes that had sprung up in the ashes of the old internet, the specialized affinity platforms for government, the military, social justice, and education that had replaced the old gate-keeper and entertainment media. Now it was all information, disinformation, and interest groups.

She struggled over an umbrella name for the enterprise, though the pundits and the talking chips had quickly and rather mockingly labeled it the Lifer Liberation Front. She hated that, thought it sounded like something out of the 1970s that Patty Hearst would have joined, though she doubted anyone remembered Patty Hearst, or the seventies. She eventually settled on "the Next Hundred," and pushed that as hard as she and her outreach team could. But to some, her movement would always be the LLF.

In the summer mornings and in the late afternoons, Dan would fish on the lake, just him alone out there. She watched from the lodge, the pines sending long shadows across the water. She would remember that summer, oddly, as one of the happiest, most contented of her life; nothing expected, nothing wanting. The last season before they had to face what they'd done to the world.

DANIEL

Black Valley, Colorado, 2072

One frosty evening as Dan was bringing in wood for the fire, Adele Pritchard chipped him to say that she'd heard one of Marion's impassioned chipcasts about the demagoguery of the anti-Lifer political rhetoric that had permeated the recent presidential campaign and its parallels with Hitler's Reichstag Fire Decree and the Holocaust.

"You should be very proud of her," she said.

"I am. But how are you?

"I'd like to come home."

"You mean back to the US?"

"Yes. But also back to where I think I can be of use, and to the few people I still care about."

Dan didn't want to presume anything about who she cared about. "I'd invite you to Black Valley, but I'd have to discuss it with Marion first."

"Of course."

"I can't promise anything."

"I know."

"But I can't think of anyone who'd be a better fit for us. And Marion's always admired you, despite everything. That's why you threatened her so."

"It was a long time ago," said Adele.

"Longer than any of us ever imagined it would be. Longer than jealousy can survive, I suspect."

"I hope that's true."

"But what's happened? Why come home now?"

There was one of her long pauses, so long that he thought their connection was lost. But then the deep warble of her chip-voice returned, indelibly Adele.

"Awhile back, we tracked down the creator of Methuselah, or rather, the lead creator. He had lots of help. We even identified what we think was the prime vector, the equivalent of a patient zero. But the work on the viral vehicle was dispersed and its creation so dependent on automated algorithmic sequencing that it's been impossible to assemble all the relevant data. So we never got a complete picture of the original thing we were trying to counter. And in people, it keeps mutating."

Dan had heard stories about this from some of Marion's scientific advisers, different variants of Methuselah infecting different populations with different results, some accelerating in apparent age, some developing extreme mental states, like mania or hypervigilance or the inability to feel pain. It suggested that there were varieties of Lifers, and several species of triplers developing behind them. Dan had assumed that most of this was the kind of baseless rumor that proliferated in chipspace just as it once had on the internet, though by slower, more indirect means: word of mouth. Or, more accurately, word of head. But Adele seemed to believe it.

"In any event," she continued, "My group's original goal of stopping Methuselah is no longer feasible."

"Why not?"

"Too many cases. Or at least more than a critical mass of the human population. There's no sensible prevention strategy anymore. Infection rates have dropped on their own for some reason, but all that's left as an anti-Methuselah measure is an outright cure, and that's technically a much tougher goal than a preventive vaccine. There's no company or government organization that's even close to that. The president admitted as much to me this morning—"

"The president? You mean Baldisseri? "

"Please don't quote me."

"Glad you're still so well-connected. But what do you mean by 'cure'?" Dan was thinking of his son's suicide pills, but surely that wasn't what Adele meant.

Her chip made a sound something like a sigh.

"We originally thought that with enough information we could reverse engineer the invasive proteins and reset the cellular mechanisms to their pre-infection state. Reestablish normal mortality at least in those who had been recently infected. But the template genome package is much more complicated than we imagined. We learned that much from its creator, but not much more."

"He wouldn't cooperate?"

"No, why would he? He spent billions of dollars and half his life trying to break the code of aging and senescence. Why would he help us undo that? Torture might have worked, he wasn't that brave a man, but I thought it unlikely."

"Lucky for him."

"If people had been dying because of what he'd done, of course I would have resorted to that. But people were living because of it. The interrogator's logic of risking one life to save many just didn't apply."

"So now what?"

"I need to get out, Dan. I've been at this too long. I'm way too old to work with the new administration. Things are coming to a head, and I want to be on the right side when they do."

"You always have been."

"I'm not sure about that. But I need to talk with you and Marion, and not this way."

She meant not through voices in their heads. "Come here, then. Come to Black Valley."

Another pause. "Ask Marion. If it's okay with her, I'll be there tomorrow afternoon."

"That fast? VTOL or fixed-wing? We need to know, to prepare a landing pad, and so no one shoots you down."

She snorted, the way she did when they'd first met and she'd looked him up and down, more than eighty years before. "I'm in Denver. I'll drive up. I'll be in an old, beat-up Mini Cooper convertible. Don't shoot."

Marion barely hesitated when Dan told her Adele wanted to come, simply nodded and went back to marking up one of her speeches with a yellow wooden pencil, the way she always did. But then she looked at him and said, "I'd like some time with her alone as soon as she arrives."

He hesitated, sat next to her, reached for her hand. "Be kind to her, please. As kind as you've been to me."

Marion put down her pencil, looked at him, brushed her silver hair back from her face. "I don't owe her what I owed to you. But we need people like her here. And I'm always kind."

She squeezed his hand. He nodded and went to fix dinner.

The next day was tense with waiting. Brilliant morning, the construction bots awakening for the day's activity, the aspens glowing in the rising sun, the smell of last night's fire in the air, mist lifting off the mountains at the end of the valley, already laced with snow. Around one o'clock the mounted guard down at the front gate, who did an excellent impression of a cattleman herding his heifers across his neighbors' land, alerted them that he'd admitted an early model, manual shift vehicle with a very old woman at the wheel, and she was headed for the main lodge. There was no way Adele could have a driver's license at her age, even in Colorado, and fossil-fuel cars like the one she was driving were illegal almost everywhere, but whatever credentials she kept in her chip were evidently more than enough to put the random highway patrolman in his place.

She pulled up to the lodge in a cloud of dust, shut down the noisy old engine, and sat for a moment looking across the yard at Marion and Dan as they stood silently on the porch. He waved timidly, and she climbed out, even smaller than he remembered her: thinner, her hair cropped short but still an astonishing auburn, her sunstruck face fissured with the great age they shared, her green eyes hooded with folds of flesh now but penetrating the air between them as they always had. She smiled, or he imagined she did, and she walked directly up to Marion and extended her arms.

"Marion," she said.

"Adele," replied Marion, and they held hands for just a moment, but longer than he thought he could bear. Then Marion turned to him. "We'll be back in a while," she said, and they walked off together across the bridge over the stream that ran hard past the lodge, toward the huge grove of old aspens, tall and hushed as a cathedral, that stood on the far side. He watched them go and went inside to wait.

That night he made one of Marion's favorite meals after he confirmed that Adele still ate meat. Ribeye with carrots and potatoes and endive from the garden, charred together on the grill, a bottle of Opus One from the Year of Our Lord 2035. He set up a card table by the fire in the library and they sat around it and laughed about old times for a while and raised a glass to the Clintons, who'd hired each of them way back when, but hadn't lived quite long enough to catch the Change.

Which brought them to the subject of the then-current president, Isabel Baldisseri, the implausibly young and charismatic former senator from California, leader of the upstart One Life Party, who'd recently gotten elected by vowing to serve only one term and with only one purpose: to solve what she called the Lingerer problem.

Dan was still incredulous that it had happened. "You'd think they would have run someone older, with a less obvious axe to grind. What is she, forty?"

"Forty-six," said Adele. "A kid. But she's clever. A lot of fiery rhetoric, but never explicit about her actual intentions. Turns out she's got a very concrete policy agenda and a lot of mainstream legislators already lined up in support. I personally think the major parties put up such weak opposition to her so that none of them would have to take the rap for what they'd all like to do."

"I've heard," said Marion, frowning over her steak. "Lifer sequestration, or some such euphemism for internment camps. Like that unofficial one I saw in New York."

"Not for everyone, and not all at once. It would be phased in because they can't get the infrastructure up that fast. We're talking massive housing projects on federal land that has to be repurposed by Congress away from conservation and the military. None of that can happen overnight."

"I think it's interesting," Dan offered, "that the conventional political wisdom frames Lifers as a population problem, and that herding us around can somehow solve it. But the real issue isn't that there are so many of us; we're still the minority. It's that there are so many of *them*."

Marion patted his arm. "But Dan, we're the ones who broke the bargain. We're the ones who reneged on the deal."

"You mean the deal that we'd die on time."

"Exactly."

"It is partly a problem of sheer, sudden population increase," said Adele. "Housing and food shortages, the strain on medical facilities, the mass migration of people self-segregating into age groups. But it's also that, unlike you two, most triplers are completely unprepared economically for this long a life, and government can't possibly close the gap. People were always terrible at saving enough for retirement, but that was mitigated by Social Security and the fact that you only had to keep paying them for the ten or twenty years before they died. That stopgap's gone, and there's nothing to replace it. You're out here in the middle of nowhere. The cities are fast becoming hellholes, though no one wants to admit it. I was just in Denver. The ten square blocks around Larimer Square are a tripler tent city. There are aged homeless camps all up and down the Platte River, which stinks of raw sewage. We're talking about poverty on an unprecedented scale among those least inclined or able to bear it, but with a remarkable biological resistance to dying from it."

"Just like Central Park," said Marion, gazing into the fire.

"So what's Baldisseri's solution?" Dan asked skeptically, trying not to picture Denver.

"Persuade people to start dying again," Adele said bluntly. He stared at her, got up, put a log on the fire, sat down, stared at her again.

"And how exactly would she go about that?" he asked, though he suspected he knew.

"That's part of what I wanted to come here and talk with you about. Are your chips off?"

He and Marion looked at each other and reflexively fingered behind their ears. "As off as they can be," he said.

"Baldisseri's gotten congressional approval and funding for a very large government contract with Accretex Corporation, which I believe is owned by your son Nolan."

"Only partly owned," Dan said, "but go on." Marion's face had turned ashen. She pushed herself away from the table and stared into the fire. They both knew what Adele was about to say.

"There's going to be a huge rollout of a federally sponsored campaign for a new drug called Epilox. . . ."

"Oh, that's cute," said Marion. "Not something with five syllables and beginning with a *Z*?"

"No, just Epilox, which I gather is essentially. . . ." she hesitated, groping for how to say it.

"A very slow-acting suicide pill," Marion finished for her.

The green eyes widened a bit. It was only rarely in his life that he'd seen Adele surprised, or that she'd let anyone see it. "You know?"

"Nolan told me about it some time ago. Couldn't help himself, he's such a braggart."

"It's highly illegal that he did so. Or at least a breach of contract."

"No doubt. I was hoping they'd never perfect it, or that no one would be interested."

"The new president is very interested. The feds are paying billions for the production contract and to implement distribution. Nolan will be a very rich man."

"Good for him," Dan said ruefully. "Maybe he'll move out of that awful suburb and become a philanthropist."

Marion leaned toward Adele. "Do they really think people will voluntarily take that . . . stuff?"

"They're calling it a treatment, like a cure for a disease. Seven pills, one a day for a week."

"And you drop dead a year later," Dan recalled.

"Yes. And they do think triplers will take it, partly to escape the miseries a lot of them are experiencing, and partly because they're going to launch a massive influencing campaign to characterize taking it as the morally correct, sensible, unselfish, *patriotic* thing to do. That plus algorithms churning chipspace to make triplers feel depressed and abandoned. They've even got a religious angle, though that one's hard for me to grasp."

"God's plan," Marion murmured, eyes glazed. "We've violated God's plan, and it's got to be put right."

"Something like that, I suppose," said Adele. They sat in silence for a while, sipping the last of the wine. Dan and the two women who in their loving sum had subtended the long arc of his life.

"Why is it, then, that we feel entitled to this?" he asked finally.

"To what?" asked Adele.

"To living. To living on and on, past ages we had no hope of living to. *Are* we just being selfish? Are we just indulging an animal instinct? Are we just greedy, wanting more and more of what we've already had? What are we contributing, really? Perspective? No one wants our perspective. History? No one cares about history. We're just taking up lots of space and resources and giving nothing back."

At this Marion roused herself. "It isn't a matter of a quid pro quo! We have just as much right to live as any human beings of any other age! We don't need to justify ourselves or make apologies for our existence!"

"Ah, but we always did," said Adele, "even when we were just normally old people. I always felt the need to justify my existence."

"Well that's part of being a woman, isn't it, Adele," Marion shot back. "I got real tired of that one too. But you, of all people, who accomplished so much. You had no need to make apologies. . . ." They both fell still and looked at each other, looked away.

Dan cleared his throat. "More wine, anyone?"

"Here's the thing," said Marion, ignoring him. "There's something else we don't have to justify any more than any other human beings of any age, and that's fear."

"Fear of what?" Adele asked.

"Of death. We're not obligated to be any braver about facing oblivion than the average thirty-year-old. Let *them* take those pills and feel all patriotic and religious about it! Or let's have a national lottery, like they did for the draft during the Vietnam War, to decide who should take the pills. Level the playing field, make everyone have a stake in this so-called solution of theirs. That'll concentrate the mind wonderfully."

Adele smiled. "Your logic is impeccable, Marion. But as you yourself said, we're the ones who broke the bargain. And we've had more of life than anyone in history. They're looking to us to make the sacrifice."

"But we didn't choose this," said Marion, her voice rising again. "It isn't something we imposed on the world. It was imposed on us, without our even knowing it. Given the choice back then, maybe some of us would have forgone it. But we didn't have that choice, and it's simply unfair to make us account for it now."

"*ALERT!*"

They all jumped in their seats, looked around. It took Marion less time than Dan and Adele to realize it was the valley security system, yelling at them in the voice of a female Australian. Dan looked at his watch; ten o'clock, pitch black outside, moonless night. His mind raced, came up empty.

"*Alert! Incoming,*" the computer repeated a bit more calmly.

"Describe incoming, Guardian," said Marion, her voice calm. She was the only one with permission to talk to the system, a fact Dan was regretting.

"*Aircraft approaching from the south-southeast, three thousand feet. Slowing. Speed and sonic signature suggests VTOL. Shall I hail, or warn?*"

"Hail, please."

What seemed like almost a full minute passed. Dan started nervously clearing the table, trying to remember the summons code for the security team, or where the guns they'd started buying were stored. Pointless. No time.

"*Hail complete. Response received. Sikorsky serial number four three five five two zero, US Marine Corps. Requests permission to land.*"

"Persons on board?" asked Adele; Marion had to repeat it to the computer.

"Yes, one passenger."

"Identify."

A pause. *"Passenger identified as Claire Landess."*

The three of them went outside and stood in the starlight. They could hear the props cutting the air, getting louder fast, louder than an electric aircraft, bigger. The computer turned on the landing pad lights, and they were blind for a moment, but then they saw it descend, big as a bus, Marine insignia on the bulging fuselage, nose and tail hanging out over the edges of the pad. The props angled fully vertical and the thing touched down as softy as a bee on a blossom. Unmanned, Dan thought; no human could fly like that. The engines cut but the props kept turning, as though ready to spool up again at a moment's notice. A hatch swung open and a short set of metal stairs extended quickly out of the fuselage onto the concrete.

And there was Claire, descending in a tan raincoat and a bright blue scarf, waving briefly, unsmiling. He could see cameras and what were probably the black muzzles of miniaturized weapons protruding from small gaps in the fuselage, tracking her as she approached. Dan and Marion were slack-jawed, but Adele seemed strangely unsurprised, and he wondered fleetingly if she'd known this was going to happen, if she'd been doing some sort of advance reconnaissance, might even be broadcasting a tracer beacon. The coincidence of these two showing up within hours of each other seemed too great.

Claire climbed onto the porch and looked from face to face. Dan thought he saw a bit of suppressed shock in hers at their appearance, so old had they become, so alien. She probably knew no one like them personally. But she recovered quickly, hugged each of them in turn, shook hands with Adele.

"Grandfather, Grandmother, so good to see you. It's been years. And you must be Adele Pritchard."

"Glad to meet you, finally," said Adele. Dan gave her a look, but she didn't meet his eyes.

"Such formality! Shall we go in?" Marion said. Dan spent a few minutes pretending this was a normal visitation by a relative, taking Claire's coat, offering her food, which she declined, offering something to drink, which she accepted, all of them finally settling back into the library around the card table in front of the fire.

Dan studied his granddaughter. She was beautiful this close up, hair a stark matte white against olive skin, eyes an autumn hazel that he remembered from his mother's face, but she looked tired, and very old, older than them in fact, though by his quick mental math she'd be only sixty-five, exactly half their age. He wondered if this were deliberate, some new sort of full-face tattoo, to make the wearer seem older than she was and put the really old people at ease.

Marion was the first to find her voice. "To what do we owe this pleasure, and the big helicopter outside?" she asked. "I thought you were a private citizen."

"I was until recently," said Claire. "But I've been asked to take on a position in the Baldisseri administration, and I wanted to discuss that with you. You in particular, Grandma—"

"Dear, we're both too old for that. Please call me Marion."

She considered this, nodded. "Marion. I wanted to discuss it in particular with you because we all know you've developed a lot of influence among your. . . ." She hesitated.

"Among my age group," Marion prompted.

"I was going to say your followers, but yes, your age group, and this new position relates to them."

"And what's this new position?" Dan asked. All the hierarchical instincts from his time in the White House were flooding back.

"The president is creating a new executive department," Claire said, "and she wants me to lead it."

"A new department?" he asked. "With you as secretary?" He couldn't keep the incredulity out of his voice. Presidents weren't in the habit of appointing people with next to no executive experience to cabinet positions. He felt a strange mix of pride and envy.

"Yes. It's to fulfill of one of the president's campaign promises, to address lifespan issues."

Marion sat back in her seat, her face a blank. Adele glanced at each of them in turn, assessing, calculating, preparing as always.

Dan poured Claire some wine. "What's this new department called, if I may ask?"

"The tentative label is the Department of Longevity Management," Claire said. "I wanted you to hear it from me."

He stifled a laugh. Longevity management. The sort of heartless bureaucratic euphemism he might have come up with himself, back when he worked for a president.

Claire registered the looks on their faces. "I'm not asking for your permission, of course, but I did want to let you know this was happening and to see if somehow we could work together, since you, Marion, are an acknowledged leader of the supercentenarian movement."

"I wasn't aware we were a movement," said Marion. "Just a bunch of old people trying to live their lives."

"Don't be so modest, Grandma. Marion. You've become a major political force. You almost prevented Baldisseri from becoming president. People used to get more conservative as they got older, but you changed something."

"We got more conservative as we got older because we had more and more to lose," said Marion. "Now most of us feel we have nothing to lose, and a whole new life to gain."

"Impressive slogan," said Claire. "I'll watch for that one."

"What does your father say about this?" Dan asked, still trying to wrap his head around the idea of a Department of Longevity Management.

Claire shrugged. "He's not pleased. He was happy to have me as a spokesperson for his new drug, but my taking this position meant he had to give up controlling interest in Accretex, to avoid the appearance of a conflict of interest when we do the rollout. Which I'm sure Adele has told you about; it's been in all the chipspace rumor mills for some time now."

Marion had composed herself, closed her eyes, lowered her head. "This is how you use your fame, your influence?" she said slowly, simmering. "To 'manage' our longevity? What does that even mean?"

Claire swallowed, straightened her shoulders. It was clear that she'd rehearsed this moment carefully.

"You can't deny we're in a crisis, Marion. And we have to make hard choices. The current state of unpredictable human longevity is unsustainable, we all know that. I also happen to think that the instinct that led to it was fundamentally wrong, and its consequences are immoral, but leave all that aside. This is about practicalities, and how we can come to some kind of inter-generational understanding about our collective future. That's going to take creativity and some flexibility on all our parts."

"Sounds like one of your speeches," Dan said, more sarcastically than he'd intended. "The thing about you doublers is you think you can control things. You grew up in the orderly world your grandparents had created, and it looked like life could be controlled. But it can't. It's inherently chaotic. It exists only because it's resistant to order. And this situation is another example of life getting outside the boundaries." He turned to Adele, who'd remained uncharacteristically silent. "And speaking of getting outside boundaries, is it just a coincidence that you arrive hours before we hear this from Claire? Did you know this was going to happen?"

"I'd heard about plans for the new department," Adele said. "I didn't know Claire was directly involved, or that things would happen this quickly. I thought I'd have a few days with you before—"

Marion turned to her. "And whose side are you on in all this?"

"There don't have to be sides," Claire interjected.

Adele's eyes locked on Marion's. "Yours. You have to trust me."

It was Claire's turn to be taken aback. "I was under the impression that your organization was aligned with the administration's agenda, Adele. Was I misinformed?"

"I'm no longer a member of that organization, so I can't speak for it. But let's talk about the agenda you refer to. Doesn't it include some rather aggressive legislation, and perhaps some amendments to the Constitution?"

Claire paused, straightened. "Yes, legislation to be duly passed by Congress, and amendments that will have to be ratified by the remaining states—"

"Wait," Dan burst out. "What are we talking about here?"

Adele and Claire glared at each other. "Do you want to do this, or shall I?" said Adele.

Claire's rigid shoulders slumped a fraction. "None of this is set in stone, and there's very little I can discuss at this point. But we do want to embark on a program of dedicated housing—"

Marion leaned toward her. "Meaning the famous 'Lifer sequestration communities' mentioned so often in Baldisseri's campaign rallies, I assume."

"No different than any other subsidized housing in a dozen cities right now. It's just that we'd use federal land and funds to jump-start greater capacity specifically for those above . . . a certain age."

"And then 'encourage' them to relocate there."

"This has been going on for generations with other underhoused groups. . . ."

"And how's that gone?"

"Ladies," Dan interrupted, "Maybe this isn't the time or place for this discussion."

Marion bristled. "What better time, Dan? And when are we likely to have the Secretary for Longevity Management with us again? Let's take advantage of this opportunity."

Adele raised her hand. "Maybe I can make this more efficient by telling you what I've heard, and you, Claire, can tell me where I'm off base."

"Fire away," said Claire, her lips drawn into a thin line. "But I may not be able to confirm or deny. And do keep in mind your confidentiality obligations, Adele, even if you have quit your group."

"Of course," said Adele. "Let's see, where to begin? Claire, with all due respect, you're joining what can bluntly be described as an anti-Lifer faction that believes either that extreme longevity is contrary to God's law, a human perversion of the natural order, or so burdensome to society that Lifers, and Lingerers generally, need to be heavily regulated."

"I wouldn't say anti-Lifer—"

"I know you wouldn't, but let's be frank, just for the sake of discussion. As I understand them, these proposals involve a sequential loss of various constitutional privileges as one grows older. The right to bear arms would be relinquished by anyone reaching the age of ninety, for the obvious reason that you can't have a lot of crazy old people with guns running around loose, and old by definition equals crazy. At one-ten, you'd lose the right to assemble, as well as the right of speech unencumbered by government restriction. At one-twenty you'd lose the right to vote, presumably on the rationale that you've suffered sufficient cognitive decline or become so removed from mortal concerns that your political judgment can't be trusted, though I'd suggest that problem isn't confined to a particular age group, as most of American history attests. Then, finally, at one-thirty, loss of the right to due process and maybe citizenship itself, which would further facilitate what the politicians call 'sequestration,' or the rounding up of people who haven't previously been induced by other means to confine themselves to internment camps, which of course would be designed to look and feel like giant retirement homes or assisted-living communities, but which are ultimately intended to remove triplers from the general population and mitigate the housing, medical, and social welfare burdens that they've created. How am I doing so far?"

Claire sat with her manicured hands carefully folded and inert. "Whether you've accurately described them or not, I can't confirm, but any such measures would be phased in over an extended period of time."

"Oh, of course, a decade or so. It will take almost that long to have the states ratify the necessary constitutional amendments. And people already past a certain age would be grandfathered out, so to speak."

Dan laughed out loud at that. Marion glared at him.

"They're just looking to regulate the rising triplers," continued Adele. "A huge demographic bubble, the infected ones who don't know they're infected, who are still voting for people like Baldisseri without understanding that they too will one day be this old." She gestured at herself weakly, as though apologizing. And Dan realized for the first time how hard it must be for her to look the way she did, to bear the burden of so much accumulated knowledge and memory, to be thought of, as they all were, as a crisis so severe that it needed to be managed by dismantling the very foundations on which the nation had been created. Not for the first time, certainly, but in a way and for a reason that, unlike war and pestilence, had once been unimaginable.

LIFERS

Marion stood and walked to one of the darkened windows, looked out at the lake, at the big copter sitting in the floodlights that blotted out the stars, then walked slowly back to where Claire sat, leaned down, gently put her hands on her granddaughter's shoulders, and looked into her eyes.

"Claire," she said softly, "I love you, but I will fight you with everything I have." And she started to walk away.

"Can I just say something?" Claire cried, almost pleading. Marion stopped, turned to face her. "Change—societal, technological—always happens slower than we expect. Granddad, I remember you telling me when I was little about a program on TV when you were young where people had flying cars and robot maids and off-earth colonies. And when you grew up, everyone wondered when they would finally get their flying car, but you never did. And our only attempt at an off-earth colony ended in disaster; we weren't really ready yet. And of course, all the climate scientists who thought the polar ice caps would be gone by now were off by about a century. The barrier islands sank underwater, but people like you just moved inland, and life went on. And the rise of populist authoritarianism that started when you were in the White House was supposed to have killed democracy several times over by now. And yes, a few states splintered off, but here we are, arguing about how to run a democracy. Change, whether good or bad, always happens more slowly than we think it will.

"Except this change. A radical change in the human condition happened in the span of only twenty years, the period over which millions of people, billions maybe, were infected with Methuselah. We had no time to prepare, much less to react kindly or sensibly. And of course there's anger and resentment and fear as a result.

"But our scientists believe—and I'm sure Adele can confirm this too—that now the infection rate is down to nearly zero. And there's still a sizable portion of the population that was never infected. So once an upper limit on the longevity of those who are infected is established one way or another, we'll begin to see a reversion to normal mortality rates and population."

They looked at Adele. "It's true," she said. "The R-naught factor—the infection rate—has been dropping precipitously for about five years now. We're not sure why, but it's probably mutation, with the sequential variants getting less and less communicable."

"Isn't that the opposite of how viruses usually mutate?" Dan asked. "I remember from the SARS and Ebola outbreaks. The bugs' survival depends on their becoming more infectious, not less."

"Correct. No one's sure why Methuselah's behaving differently."

"But I thought most of the world was already infected," said Marion. "That's what your data miner guy told us, Adele."

"Projections are only as good as the input. We've never had reliable numbers on total infections because so few people submitted to testing, either out of fear of prejudice or just not wanting to know. Devon's estimates could be off by a factor of ten."

"Well, just anecdotally," Dan said, looking around the little room, "I don't know anyone who doesn't have Methuselah."

"Yes, you do," said Claire. They looked at her, the crackling of the fire the only sound in the room. "Anyone who wants to be part of the Baldisseri administration has to be tested for Methuselah, and no one who's positive can serve in a senior post. She views it as a conflict of interest. Of course the president herself is negative. And so am I."

Dan put his hand to his mouth. He wanted to say he was sorry, the way he would to someone who'd just told him she had cancer, but stopped himself. "But you could get it any time," he said. "You could get it from one of us."

She smiled the same little smile that she'd had on her face when he first tried to teach her how to ride a bike, a smile of sympathy at his anxiety. "I think it's too late for that. The window of transmission has already closed. And that's just fine with me."

Marion sat back down, put her hand on Claire's. "I'm sorry to hear that. But—"

Claire pulled her hand away. "My point is that we think this crisis, as bad as it is, is temporary, that the generations represented in this room—yours, and my parents', and mine—are what we have to manage through, till the mortality numbers get closer to what they once were. And then, someday, we can drop all these admittedly unorthodox measures and go back to normal life."

"Claire, my dear," Dan said, "When you get to be our age you realize that once government assumes power, it rarely gives it up."

"Isn't that for the people to decide?" Claire responded. Dan thought of examples, like when the feds imposed price controls in the 1970s but later rescinded them, or when the military draft that had been in place for decades was abolished after the Vietnam War. Relatively trivial concessions, compared to what reversing course in this case would require.

Adele got up and put her back to the fireplace, her small frame silhouetted by the flames like a black paper cutout, her face invisible. "This reversion to normalcy that you describe," she said, "depends on a variable that no one can predict."

"Which is?"

"How long we Lifers live. No one knows that yet. What if we live another hundred years? We could represent a virtually permanent population bulge, even if new infections stop and there are enough uninfected individuals to resume normal mortality rates for the rest of humanity. We'll still be here, as big a problem as ever. Maybe bigger, depending on how we continue to change."

"We think that's unlikely," said Claire.

"No more unlikely than any of this happening in the first place."

"I acknowledge that we don't yet know the outer limits of Lifer longevity. But we can get a handle on that by different means."

Dan's built-in euphemism translator was in high gear. "You mean your dad's drug."

"His treatment program, yes."

"But that's totally dependent on the Lifer population buying into it, and how likely is that?"

"My guess is it's more likely than you might think," Claire said evenly. "Since you've heard my speeches, Marion, you know that I think there's a positive side to our mortality, and that once we're reminded of that, it's just a matter of shedding our inbred, narcissistic fears and embracing it. And mind you, that's coming from someone who won't live anywhere near as long as you already have."

There were moments when Dan understood completely why this woman had become a celebrity and a political asset. She was so good at sincerity.

The rest of the evening was a blur to him. They all agreed to disagree, as families sometimes do. Marion assured Claire once more that she would oppose her granddaughter's mission with civility and in good faith, but oppose it she would. Adele fully sided with Marion, a development Dan couldn't have foreseen. Claire in turn warned them that though she herself respected Marion's position, there were elements within the Baldisseri administration who wouldn't hesitate to use all of the government's powers, including but not limited to eminent domain, to preempt the development of Black Valley and quash the generational resistance that it represented.

Eventually they tired of all that brutal honesty, and hugged one another goodbye, seeming to Dan like mutually respectful antagonists who, though they had no idea of what was to come, knew full well that when this battle was joined again, no such gestures would be possible. And he realized that, for all their talk, they hadn't really connected; their physical ages were a permanent barrier between them. For all their worldly sophistication, he thought, they didn't really understand something as simple as the continuity of time; that the young inevitability grow old, and that the old are merely reincarnations of the young.

Claire reboarded her helicopter and rode off into the dark. Dan and Marion showed Adele to her room and each kissed her goodnight, Dan first before hurrying down the hall, embarrassed at this unimaginable circumstance; Marion after, a kiss on the cheek as though they were old friends, which he supposed in a way they were. He could hear them, still murmuring down the hall, as he fell into bed and to sleep before he could thank God or anyone for anything.

Claire's visit accelerated their plans, and once word of the Black Valley enclave got out, Marion adopted an academic model of soliciting and accepting applications for admission. They were quick in coming, first a few dozen a day, then, to their mixed delight and dismay, hundreds.

The criteria for admission were utterly transparent and very specific: minimum age 110 (to weed out the newly, insincerely, or temporarily aged); economic self-sufficiency (they planned to charge nothing to join, but each resident would have to contribute their pro rata portion of an annual budget for a minimum of ten years); demonstrated first-hundred-years' expertise in one of a variety of fields that Marion and her advisers thought necessary to create a self-sufficient society in the post-Methuselah world (government, bioengineering, medicine, armed and unarmed defense, agriculture, literature, and music); willingness to liquidate all personal assets; no more than one significant other (who must also be accepted); and general physical fitness (with or without prosthetic enhancement). Each application had to be accompanied by an essay explaining why the applicant wanted to be a member of what amounted to a separatist Lifer community, though Marion avoided that label, tended to talk in terms of independence and self-sufficiency and physical security.

The first thousand applications naturally came from the wealthy and the famous, with the expected subsets of vagabonds, freeloaders, and professional narcissists, but once an awareness of the extremely high rejection rate sank in, the applications slowed, improved in quality, and grew more sincere. All of the members of Adele's nameless but fiercely loyal Methuselah colloquy group, who by that point had been meeting monthly in chipspace for over a decade, were waived in automatically, and several were among the first to arrive on-site, including Barb Beckwith, who immediately took on the hiring and oversight of a security detail and the procurement of a small arsenal of firearms.

But there was one surprise, an applicant that most on the admissions committee—Adele, Marion, Devon Jones, Barb Beckwith, and Dan—never would have paused over because his application data was so sparse. He described himself as an "entrepreneur biologist," he was 125 years old, and his essay consisted of two lines:

> *The biology of the Change is correct.*
> *It is society's reaction to it that is wrong.*

They were about to put him in the reject pile, but Adele recognized him immediately. His name was Gustav Zinnemann.

"I'm surprised he's still alive," said Barb Beckwith. "Isn't he, like, a war criminal?"

Adele gave her a sympathetic look. "Perhaps the opposite, more like a life criminal? We once believed that he was the original creator of Methuselah," she explained. "And in a way he was. But he intended it to be a clinical treatment for elites, not a contagion of the masses. He was going to make a lot of money, not upend the social order. That was engineered by someone else. It took us years to find and capture him. And once we did, he was useless. Too old, too stubborn, utterly opposed to reversing Methuselah. He'd forgotten a lot, revised history a bit. But he convinced us that a cure was technically impossible, and that we needed to abandon that avenue of inquiry."

"Why would we want him here?" Dan asked. "Wouldn't his presence just galvanize the opposition?"

Adele paused, looking at the single sheet of paper with Zinnemann's name at the top. "Almost no one knows who he is anymore, much less what he did. Xerxes knew, but we'd spent years finding that out, and we were damn good at keeping secrets. He could be useful to us, he's a compulsive inventor, a phenomenal technician. And basically a good man. He's long outlived the egomania that got us all in this fix."

Dan moved him to the "accept" pile.

TAUBIN

San Francisco, 2074

He was suddenly very rich, but much to his surprise, it hadn't made him happy.

When the feds closed on the contract for Epilox, which Taubin thought a dumb name, Nolan had given everyone involved a big bonus, part stock, part cash, and his was one of the biggest, which he confirmed with a little unauthorized data mining in the company's HR files. But the stock component vested over time, and Taubin felt that meant it was contingent on how well Epilox was accepted, which in turn depended, at least in part, on how well his MSG algorithms worked. His main job was to assess the program's performance and make adjustments to improve uptake, to make sure as many triplers as possible were appropriately influenced. He had full-chipnet association studies going 24/7, calculating statistical correlations between the mood nudges (as he called them) that the algorithm produced and the subsequent chip- and meat-space behavior of the recipients. By the terms of its government contract, Accretex had access to every public surveillance camera network in America, and most of them in

Europe, Latin America, and Asia, not to mention the embedded body function and aural environment monitoring software that had caused such a privacy uproar when headchips first began to be introduced. Of course the user could opt out of those functionalities, but nobody ever bothered. With the right permissions and connectivity, all of which Taubin had per the contract with the feds, it was like being inside the heads of everyone with a chip, all at once.

He didn't personally experience any of that, of course. It would be a meaningless cacophony, even for someone like him. That was the algorithm's job, and it cranked right along, chipping him hyper-condensed reports every morning, noon, and night, suggesting tweaks to itself, which he usually green-lit. There were a few that were particularly dark and he vetoed them, though he was sort of trusting the algorithm, as it were, not to do it anyway. He of all people knew that algorithms were, by definition, single-minded.

Geographic location was not relevant. Gender, or lack thereof, was not relevant. Color was not relevant. Even age was not relevant. The algorithm found them all, in whispers in their chips, in barely audible chords that seemed to play on the wind but were implanted digitally in their brains, in small, nagging pains, in flickers of images in chipcasts, but most of all in dreams, disturbing and plausible, of loss, of betrayal, of increasing physical disability, of growing solitude, of endless loneliness. Inevitably, some people were more susceptible than others, particularly the triplers who were young enough to have chips in the first place but old enough to be receptive to the thought that perhaps they'd lived too long. He would dip into the data stream and pull up specifics at random:

John and Jo, in their hundreds, Texans, who had never argued in their long marriage, began to bicker over small things. Each of them hypothesized it might be due to the other having grown so old and cranky.

Ravi and Gilberto, two old fags (self-described) in San Francisco, living in a cardboard box in Walton Square, where the city let you stay when you ran out of money. They'd always lied to each other about their ages, but were both in their 110s. Angry that no one told them they would live this long, they might have saved more. But then, less fun, so what was the good of that?

Bob and Harriet, high school sweethearts now ninety-nine, always as combative as siblings, telling each other that they'd had enough, that the only solution was to go their separate ways. And though they never did, the idea became a grudge between them, a pact of unending failure.

August and Jordan and Haley, each having lost a spouse before the Change, living in an RV that they moved from place to place around the Boomer Box, pooling their resources to make ends meet, starting to hide money from one another, sometimes stealing it, increasingly bitter but unable to imagine a different life.

Miriam, 130 years old, alone in a big house in Pittsburgh, her husband having run off with a younger woman of only 100, that bitch. She'd show him.

DeShawn, ninety, and her Uncle Zeno, 121, and her two boys, starving in a loft outside London, too many mouths to feed, one or two less would be manageable, but which two?

Xi Hang, too old to count, in a high rise in Singapore, ravaged with cancer that never quite killed him, so good was Methuselah at keeping him alive, his jaw gone, eating through a tube, his children paying others to care for him, as they could no longer bear it after so long.

And so on, endlessly. Well, not endlessly, he realized, but in the millions. He cast the broadest possible net to maximize the numbers and meet the quotas for the contract extension, but he tried to focus on the triplers. Not all had Methuselah, of course; the algorithm couldn't detect that one way or another, didn't care. Nolan's pills worked regardless, and there was no prescreening for Methuselah required to receive them. A death was a death, and they needed all they could get. They could cut back on deliveries of the treatment if things got out of hand.

He did install one filter: no one in Santa Fe got the guidance. Not that Jack and Anna had chips anyway, but still.

When Nolan and his daughter with the different last name, the new Secretary for Longevity Management, announced in a much anticipated chipcast that the government was offering, for free, what they called a treatment for unpredictably long human life, millions responded immediately. Almost exactly as many as the algorithm had predicted.

Epilox was made available via dronedrops or physmail or at the pharmacy without a prescription. It came in a long, thin box, almost as thin as a soda straw, the oval pills end to end, seven of them, in plastic cradles numbered sequentially. Some people put them on shelves to consider at a later time, some opened them right away. Some took one or two and stopped, which was ineffective. Some, misunderstanding, or wanting to get it over with, took them all at once, which was also ineffective. But many, surprisingly many, read the instructions carefully and took them one by one over the seven days, often with great ceremony, often in the presence of loved ones who also took them, washed them down with a glass of wine or champagne or a shot of bourbon, the instructions said it didn't matter, but usually just with water. The pills had a sugary coating and tasted briefly sweet, and some people sucked on them as they lingered in their mouths, though the instructions did not recommend this, and the designers had layered a bitter coating just beneath the sweet, so that if you held one in your mouth too long you either had to spit it out or swallow. Most who got that far swallowed. One a day, for seven days.

So it was going well, and Taubin had become rich. He got a new apartment on Jackson Street in Nob Hill, floor-to-ceiling windows with an amazing view of the bay, took autorickshaws everywhere, never walked anymore. Got a boat. Got heavier. He found that people were a lot more willing to listen to him talk at them in his neurodivergent way now that he was wealthy, and he started taking a couple of different women from the office out on dates, which was strictly forbidden in theory but apparently not in practice.

But the idea that he'd had that night on Jack and Anna's patio under the stars kept nagging at him, the idea for an algorithm that wouldn't necessarily contradict the Sweet Chariot algorithm, since that would be a violation of the terms of his employment and of the contract with the government, and would surely get him fired or maybe even killed. No, this second algorithm would be directed at people who were never going to be influenced by the first one, either because they didn't have chips in the first place or weren't susceptible to the guidance for one reason or another, including massive stubbornness or sheer optimism. The first algorithm had already identified this resistant population, so it would be easy to extract and target it. And doing so wouldn't be a violation of his duties to Nolan, the company, and the feds because, he rationalized, this population had effectively already opted out of the Epilox program, just by being who they were. The only question was what to say to them.

He kept thinking of what Anna had said to him that night in the bar on Canyon Road, though he could only remember fragments of it. *Life is a gift. Never stop learning. Time brings peace. Be someone's memoir. Live on.* Now *there* was an algorithmic proposition, an if/then that the AI could iterate endlessly. *If you're alive, live on.*

That night. The stars. All the little stars, infinite. Humanity was bound to them, bound *for* them, ultimately, he was sure.

But it would take time, huge gulps of time, uncompromisingly long lives, vast tracts of shared memory and accumulated experience. Too much was lost between the end of one life and the beginning of another, even when they overlapped like his and Jack's and Anna's. Individual lives, pushed to endlessness, were needed, like ladders pushed to the stars. *Never die. Live on. Be endless.*

He went back to work.

The streets were choked with tripler camps, spilling over the sidewalks up and down Market Street and Folsom, wherever it was flat enough to set up a tent or a cardboard box. Fires burning in the gutters at night, looked like someplace in India during Diwali. Even going out in the daytime was a dicey proposition, since anyone as young as him was likely to get attacked or at least verbally assaulted. The restaurants and shops were mostly closed, and ingredients for the foodsynths were hard to come by. Even drones wouldn't deliver anymore, since they got shot down for parts all the time. He heard that some of the components could be made into weapons, but the triplers mostly just stripped them down and used the batteries for heat at night. They all seemed to have ballistics, which was scary, much more binarily dangerous than wave weapons, but Taubin guessed they'd all grown up with them and now it was like a badge of honor, as though a gun could keep the feds off their backs.

When the sequestration protocols had passed, the city council floated a referendum that would have declared San Francisco a Lifer sanctuary. That didn't even make it to a vote, but people and companies began moving out as though it had passed. And de facto, things looked like it had. The feds set up a Lifer sequestration facility down at the old Candlestick Park site, but they didn't have the troops to contain it, and right around the first anniversary of the release of Epilox, when the very first wave of "clients" died, around a million on that first day, the hundred thousand or so that they'd rounded up rioted and marched up the Bay Wall Freeway into the city, took over the floors of the Ferry Building that were still above water, and spread north from there. After that all bets were off. The city became a magnet for them, almost uninhabitable by your average doubler.

That first anniversary of the release of Epilox—September 10, 2073, to be precise—was a bit of a disaster in itself. The PR folks decided they should low-key it, not give it a name or draw too much attention to the first wave of deaths, more downside than upside in that, they thought. And he agreed. So the MSG went on as before, no public recognition from the company or DLM Secretary Landess about the very first year being up on that particular day.

The problem, Taubin knew, was that people didn't die the way they were supposed to. Well, they died, but not in the *way* they were supposed to. They were supposed to stay home and die in bed surrounded by family, like in the MSG images, but a surprisingly large number of the very first takers either forgot or didn't make note of when they'd taken their final dose, miscounted or didn't keep track of how far along they were in their 365 days, or didn't want to know. Taubin had a subroutine in the MSG that cast reminders once a month, but some of the early takers weren't registered properly, a lot of the older ones didn't have chips, and there was no physmail by that point. Bottom line, a lot of first takers died out in public, just dropped while walking down the street or in mid-sentence over lunch, and a frankly ridiculous number of crashes resulted from people dying at the wheel of non-autonomous vehicles. One of the last of the fossil-fuel aircraft pilots killed 143 passengers and a dozen people on the ground when he died on schedule while flying a vintage Boeing 757 at an air show in

Dayton. Sure enough, his wife confirmed he'd finished his Epilox exactly 365 days earlier. And he was only seventy-two.

After that they got a lot tighter with tracking takers, and Taubin had to tweak the algorithm to alert local authorities of the names and locations of the scheduled-to-die—STDs, in company parlance—sometimes tens of thousands a day, so that accident prevention and body collection could proceed more efficiently. In smaller towns, cops showed up at STDs' doors on "their day" and, depending on the town, either put them under surveillance or took them into custody so they wouldn't cause a problem when they dropped. And a lot of them had totally forgotten what day it was, which Taubin found sad. Quite a few cases of taker's remorse, people begging hysterically for an antidote. But there was none. It was worst in the cities, bodies littering the sidewalks, crematoria overwhelmed, especially after burials were outlawed almost everywhere.

He didn't go into the office anymore. They were all "remote," as the old pandemic saying had it. Hard for a super-social borderline autistic like him, but he kind of liked it without Nolan breathing down his neck all the time. Still, he worried that his connectivity would suffer with all the mayhem, and he wanted to get somewhere with a more stable data sink. Maybe Napa; they'd gone quantum up there just before the Methuselah hit the fan.

They were up to 500 million Epilox packages delivered worldwide, but actual treatment completion was lagging behind, and it was possible they'd replace him if he couldn't improve the MSG algorithm's performance. He worried for a while that his second algorithm—he called it "Little Stars," to keep himself from calling it something even sappier—might be interfering with the first, some sort of cognitive dissonance going on across the neural channels, but he checked and that wasn't it. The data kept showing that the biggest single inhibitor to Epilox uptake wasn't Little Stars at all, but the stuff coming out of the Lifer

Liberation Front, or whatever that group out in Colorado was calling themselves—"ultra-elders," "UEs," the "Next Hundred," whatever. He had to admit that their messaging was pretty darn effective, and they weren't even using MSG as far as he could tell; just old-fashioned verbal/sensual chipcasts and even physical pamphlets dropped from drones, as though this was the eighteenth fucking century. The people who still read were all over a hundred, and to his amazement they actually read that stuff.

He realized there may have been an indirect effect of Little Stars going on, either because it was subconsciously strengthening the resolve of the LLF and their followers and making them better at their messaging, or because their messaging actually peeled off some of the MSG's original target audience—ambivalent, poor, and/or age-depressed triplers—and made them susceptible to Little Stars when they wouldn't have been otherwise. Either way, he sometimes felt like a traitor to the cause and that he should shut down Little Stars. But for some reason he couldn't.

It wasn't that he couldn't bring himself to. He wasn't that brave. He just couldn't get the shutdown subroutine to execute properly. He kept getting error feedback, as though it wasn't the same code he'd written anymore. But that wasn't possible, because he'd written it to be immutable, and with a backdoor that would let him pull the plug anytime, just in case. He was mystified.

He needed to get away and think. So he rented a car and left the city, headed north to Napa, where he hoped there'd be fewer distractions. He'd bought a little house in St. Helena with his new riches, sight unseen, fully furnished. Eastern slope of the valley, looked good in the virtuals, some fire damage, but that was to be expected. Main thing was that it had a quantum data modem hookup, rare in a private home, that would give him almost as good connectivity immersion as if he were in the office.

LIFERS

Crossing the old Golden Gate was like leaving the country. Pouring rain, big waves cresting over the road deck, military-style checkpoint at what used to be the toll plaza. No more triplers allowed into Marin County; apparently they were full up. A cop at the checkpoint wanted full access to his chip for age and identity verification, which he refused to provide, instead turned over the DLM-issued ID card that the company had given him, which basically said let this guy go anywhere or answer to the feds. That and the fact that he was obviously not even halfway to triplerhood was enough to get him through. But the episode made him wonder if he'd ever be back in SF.

The cop released the car's nav, and he headed north on 101. Fewer tripler encampments up here, or they'd been moved out of sight. But then he exited the highway and after a few miles passed Sears Point, which had been turned into the one of the bigger sequestration facilities on the West Coast, rows and rows and stacked tiers of hastily constructed dorms and common areas, pastel colors, like an upscale barracks or an assisted-living facility on steroids. Swimming pools here and there, spotty attempts at vegetation doomed by the heat. Very few people visible, though by all accounts the place was at capacity. A bocce court in the distance with some very ancient-looking Lifers having what appeared to be a good time. He wondered how many of them had taken the treatment, how many days they had left. He thought of Jack and Anna, how he must call them sometime, see how they were doing.

On up 29 and into the valley, through all the old wine tourist towns. No winemaking here since forever; got too hot, not enough rain. That and the fires, every year now in the fall, the old vineyards blackened, the surrounding hills looking like something out of a warzone. Some newer homes survived, but most were gone, and what was left of the towns and the resorts and hotels had been fireproofed with a gray synthetic siding, like a cross between sheetrock and poured cement, that looked like it grew out of the burned earth. Gray everywhere. He'd seen pictures of the valley back in the early part of the century, and what struck him was how colorful it was, the vines a hundred different shades of orange and yellow in the fall, the blond of the hills in summer, and all the trees then, lots of conifers, green against the sky.

The rain stopped. He climbed a winding road up from the valley into the eastern hillside, then turned onto an even narrower road that meandered through a tunnel of blackened limbs arching overhead. Must have been beautiful to pass through here when it was green, he thought. Third driveway on the left was the house he'd bought; the gate at the head of the long winding drive swung open and the drone pulled up to the front porch. As he climbed out, the smell of ashes was overpowering.

The house was that ubiquitous gray synthetic, twice as thick as the local ordinances required, heavy heat shielding in the roof, small windows with shatterproof glass. Geothermal heating, no cooling needed with those thick walls. What was left of burned-out trees dotted the hillside. He wasn't sure the house would recognize his chip, but it did and let him in the front door, turned on all the lights. Nice place, nice smell, like wet cement with a synthy overtone of roses. No real daylight with all the tiny windows, like a bunker, but cozy in a spartan way. Simple modern furnishings, nothing fancy, whitewashed walls, no art. Fully automated kitchen with a generous supply of synthstocks, which the seller, some Silicon Valley guy, had generously thrown in. Even some old bottles of wine left in the rack that covered one wall. He pulled one out, a 2046 Silver Oak cab, one of the last years they made it. He'd have it that night with a nice protein filet, to celebrate.

He got to work, logged on to Accretex's proprietary neural net, began trolling, looking for signs of his work, good and bad. The immersion speed was great, actually faster than in the office, fewer neurals up here, less buffering going on.

LIFERS

He had to review the basics every time. Before Methu-selah, about sixty million people died of old age worldwide every year, around 160,000 per day. Prevailing theory was that those who otherwise would have died stopped dying around 2035, when they averaged seventy-four years of age. Not everybody got Methuselah off the bat, but those who had were overwhelmingly in this age group. That meant that by 2080, when they released Epilox, the Lifers in that first wave were 120, and there were an excess 2.25 billion people on the planet who should have been dead but were not, 1.25 billion of them over the age of one hundred.

Against these numbers, his company's little suicide drug was a drop in the bucket. Five hundred million Epilox packages had been distributed worldwide in the year and a half since its launch; around 300 million treatments had been completed ("comps" for short) as of current data; of those, less than 100 million confirmed deaths to date, and a suspiciously high percentage of those—around 15 percent— had happened well before the 365th day following the last dose, indicating accident, illness, preemptive suicide, the drug working faster than it should, or something. But still, a death was a death, as they said around the office. The one-year anniversaries of the remaining 200 million or so comps were pretty back-ended, meaning cumulative deaths would be back-ended, but averaging eleven million per month or around 380,000 per day—about three times the rate of deaths had they happened naturally back when these people should have died. But a lot of catching up to do, and a lot of extra bodies to deal with. Meanwhile, the global uptake rate had declined from the initial ten million comps a month to about half that, and more in the Western nations than the rest of the world. In the US that translated into only about ten million comps a *year*, far slower than the company or the feds had originally hoped.

Taubin knew that by any rational measure this was a failure, but Accretex kept at it because no one knew what else to do. And people were making a lot of money from it, himself included.

He sent out tendrils to find the Little Stars algorithm and see what it was up to. Churning along, lots of interactions, lots of response, a lot of real time talk that the algorithm recognized as affirming, so it redoubled its attention to those people in a virtuous cycle, iterative, compounding. The ultra-elders, as they called themselves—Lifers, as everyone else called them— were getting stronger, more confident, more accepting of the fact of their extreme longevity, which made them want to live longer still.

But something else was happening. Something hard to detect, except intuitively, when Taubin ignored the data and just felt what was going on out there. When he stopped think-ing. Little Stars had an ally. He didn't know how else to say it. Something else on the net wanting the same thing, working the same pathways with the same people.

He had a dream that night. Two women by a lake, stars over-head. One like a young version of Grandma Anna, one like his mother, who was always young, but in the dream he knew they weren't them. They were both naked, and though their faces were young, their bodies were extremely old, their arms and legs withered to the bone. They were on opposite sides of the lake and couldn't find their way to each other, kept stepping into the water toward each other, pulling back. He was shouting to them to come his way, around the shoreline toward him, and meet there, but they ignored him or couldn't hear him. Then the one who looked like Anna started into the lake again but didn't stop this time, kept going until she was submerged and the other woman just watched as though she were waiting for the first one to arrive on her side, but she didn't, so the second woman, the one who looked like his mother, started into the lake, and soon they were both submerged and he was standing there shouting, worried they'd both drown. And they never came up.

Next morning he went for a walk up the hill behind the house, just a half a mile or so, but it grew steep near the top. Pretty day, sunny with a breeze, the sort that used to be typical up here. After a while he'd stopped noticing the smell of cinders. But in the last hundred yards or so he was so short of breath that he had to sit down for a minute. He looked down at his belly fat; overweight, but he'd never felt this beat from just walking before. Heart racing, head between his legs; a bit alarming, like he might have a heart attack. But it wasn't like that, it was whole-body fatigue, a general lack of stamina. Joint pain too. He thought flu or Covid, but there were no other symptoms. He resolved to have this checked out if he ever got back to the city.

But what was even more worrying to him in that moment was that Little Stars had disappeared. Or it wasn't responding to his pings anymore, which wasn't possible code-wise. None of it should be possible. It was an algorithm he'd created for a specific purpose aimed at a specific population, and it wasn't there anymore, no reports being generated, no self-diagnostic alerts, no self-repair or self-editing notices. The Epilox MSG was out there the same as ever, grinding along, but it was almost as though Little Stars had never existed, though he could detect fragments of what looked like its code drifting around in other neural network subroutines like recycled plastic. Like it had been stripped down and used for parts.

And those signs were strongest, the fragments most numerous, the closer he focused on Methuselah carriers, and the very oldest Lifers in particular. This he found both suspicious and oddly appropriate, since Little Stars was aimed primarily at them; it was almost like they'd absorbed it, literally, or whatever made them that away had absorbed it, and he was seeing the chaff left behind, the pieces that couldn't be used.

That became his theory. He wrote it down, read it back to himself to see if it made any sense. It didn't, of course, but it was a good story, the sort he would have loved as a teenager reading his sci-fi magazines in his bedroom back in Oakland.

Fires passed down the opposite side of the valley during the night, miles away, but the glow lit up the sky like dawn. The fatigue that had struck him on his walk up the hill persisted, along with back pain, which angered him. No other physical symptoms, but he'd begun to experience mental glitches that were even more worrisome. He'd been feeling a little lonely and decided to chip one of his two girlfriends, the green one, back in the city just to say hi, maybe see if she wanted to join him for the weekend, but to do that he had to form a mental picture of the recipient and speak their first or last name, or the chip security protocols wouldn't let him send. And he couldn't remember her name. Just flat-out couldn't remember, though he was pretty sure it began with a "Y." Yolonda? Yvette? He panicked, ran through all the names he could think of that even had a "Y" in them—Mary, Carlyle, Evelyn—but none seemed right. It would have been funny if it wasn't so scary. A full minute went by, and the name just wouldn't come. He finally found it in one of his diary entries from months ago—Myra; he hadn't even been close—and by then he knew something was wrong. Early-onset Alzheimer's or something. *An autistic Alzheimer's—what a lucky guy,* he thought ruefully.

On a whim, he queried his MSG algorithm about memory loss in doublers under fifty, and found there was an astonishing amount of it, especially when he accounted for the fact that most of what was being picked up was expressions of it in chip communications, let alone data that was unreported; MSG rule of thumb was that actual incidence of a given behavior was five times reported expressions. Then he tuned the query a bit, and up came a lot of anxiety about more generalized loss of mental acuity, and then some physical stuff too, some of it like what he'd been feeling in the past few weeks—fatigue, joint and muscle pain, vision problems, dry skin. All this with the canvassed population confined to people his age or younger. When he raised the upper end of the age filter it got much worse, with actual medical diagnoses proliferating—cataracts, arthritis, persistent cognitive decline, slowing reflexes, loss of muscle mass, heart rate drop, hearing loss. Then, finally, down in the dirty medical data, some unavoidably telling trends: women in their twenties and thirties going into menopause. Males' testosterone dropping. Hair of both sexes graying prematurely and thinning rapidly.

He woke in the middle of one night with a thought. He groped his way to his desk through the dark, still house. Chipped in, did a specific neural net canvass for reports of Werner syndrome, a form of accelerated aging, or progeria, where all the symptoms of advanced age—hair loss, skin deterioration, cataracts, osteoporosis, and on and on—occur in the very young, sometimes in children, but usually in people in their thirties and forties. He'd heard about it in the lab in Albuquerque, when one of the techs described an early version of the Epilox drug that mimicked the cellular effects of Werner syndrome. That approach had proved much too costly and unpredictable, but the description of a disease that made you old before your time had stuck with him.

And now, when he queried the net about it, stories were everywhere of Werner-like symptoms in people not just his age, but younger and older. He first anxious thought: maybe a side effect of Epilox? But no, only a tiny fraction of the reported progeria cases was in people who'd taken it. The stories weren't correlated yet, the upsurge in cases not yet perceived as a whole, much less formally studied, which wasn't surprising, since essentially no one had the mass data correlation capabilities that he did. But the pattern was there, increasing so rapidly over the last few months that something clearly had changed, something was happening that seemed systemic and virulent, like Methuselah itself.

And that's when it hit him. Maybe it *was* Methuselah itself. He checked, which took till dawn, and found that all the reported cases of Werner-like progeria involved people who, when they were tested for it, had Methuselah. Correlation wasn't causation, he reminded himself, but maybe Methuselah wasn't just keeping the Lifers from dying.

Maybe it was making the rest of humanity old as well.

The only person he could think of to call was Joyce Icahn, who used to run the Albuquerque lab but had become head of research for all of Accretex. It took five tries to penetrate her executive assistant filters and verify himself, but she finally chipped him back.

"What the hell?" she said when he described the progeria epidemic to her. "You're sure this isn't correlated with the Epilox rollout? That's all we'd need to get the program killed and my whole division tanked."

"Well mine too, since I didn't notice this till now. But no, there's near zero correlation with Epilox takers. Though that sort of stands to reason because why would you bother to complain about your accelerated aging if you're scheduled to die in less than a year? You'd probably assume that's how the stuff worked. But my best guess is it's an unrecognized side effect of Methuselah itself. The correlation between these new cases and their having earlier tested positive for Methuselah is near one hundred percent. And those who weren't tested wouldn't suspect Methuselah, since progeria is sort of the opposite of Methuselah's primary symptom."

"But help me with that," she said. He loved it when she asked him to help her with something. "A lot of these fast agers weren't born when Methuselah started to circulate."

"Yeah, but it stayed communicable for decades, remember. Didn't stop till a few years ago. Plenty of time for us kids to catch it. Like I did."

"Lucky you, I guess," she said. "I never did."

He didn't know what to say. Everyone who worked at Accretex had to be tested regularly as a condition of employment, but they never talked about it, since it was a bit of a social landmine, with those who were positive thinking that it wasn't something to brag about at a place whose principal product was a means to defeat it, and those who were negative not wanting to be either pitied or envied, depending on one's politics or religion. Best to say nothing, which was what most of them did.

"But, how could you not have?" he asked carefully. "You were a boss, running meetings all the time."

"The lab was pretty isolated, no outsiders allowed, and everyone who worked there was negative; it was one of Nolan's rules, once we started working toward the government contract and it was clear the message would be to cast Methuselah as a menace to society. Just wouldn't look good to have future Lifers creating the solution to Lifers." She paused, and the silence seemed regretful. "So, what's it like?" she asked.

"You mean knowing I'll get that old someday?"

"No, I mean the fast aging. Does it hurt?"

He was touched that she would ask. "It actually hurts a lot," he said, eager for her sympathy. "When I wake up in the morning my first sensation is pain in some joint or another, usually my back, and when I get up there's this weird feeling of being blurry and uncoordinated, almost like being mildly drunk, except it never stops. And it's getting worse every day. I had no idea. Aging usually happens so gradually that you have decades to adapt to these tiny incremental deteriorations and not notice most of them. When it all happens all at once it's like an electric shock. Or a really bad illness."

"Awful. I'm sorry."

"Me too. But I'm curious to see how it ends."

"What do you mean?"

"I mean, does this mean I'll die earlier than I would have, or will I sort of plateau and join all the other Lifers in their endless state of negligible senescence? Has Methuselah turned lethal, or is it just making us all the same age?"

"All the same. . . ?" She stopped, and he could almost hear her mind racing to the same vision that he'd had, of this viral machine herding humanity, like a shepherd dog herding a flock, into a common physical state that it could—what? Deal with more efficiently?

"You talk as if it has intention," she said finally. "But it's brainless. It's just a program, a cellular computer program."

"Joyce," he said earnestly. "I work with computer programs—algorithms—all the time, and I can tell you for certain. Algorithms have intention. Or something so like intention that I can't tell the difference. And depending on the inputs, that intention can change over time."

"You think that's what's happened?"

"I have no idea," Taubin said. "I just know that six weeks ago I was thirty-six, and now I'm, like, sixty-five."

MARION

Black Valley, Colorado, 2075

The valley was filling up.

A dozen lodges circling the lake had been completed, but Marion knew they weren't nearly enough. There were over a thousand people in the valley, many living in tents or shipping containers while additional structures were being built. Marion had commissioned architects in Denver to come up with several basic designs that could be prefabbed and dropped into the valley by airship, some cabled aloft like treehouses, some built into the lower slopes of the mountains like burrows, still others on stilts out over the lake with windows in their floors. Each unit was freestanding and off the grid, housing ten to twelve people, with running water drawn from the lake and solar-powered heating and cooling. Kitchens or eating spaces were handled centrally, in a communal dining facility that could feed a couple hundred at a time on a rotating schedule, at tables of ten or twelve beneath a lightweight, circular, carbon fiber roof, no supports needed within its two-hundred-yard diameter, with skylights at the apex that trapped the sun's heat or vented it in the few months when it got too hot. Laughter and the smell of simple food cooked by a catering team made up of chefs-in-residence who had their own sleeping quarters behind the big "Mushroom," as it was called, or, by some, inevitably, the "Magic Mushroom." People who didn't know each other or barely did, or had known each other for a hundred years, mixed together at the tables, milling around the bar at the center of the big room. To Marion it sometimes resembled a giant supercentenarian sleepaway camp, made up of extraordinarily competent campers.

The admissions committee had leavened the core population of tech- and medically oriented geniuses with some merely conventional overachievers at small farm agriculture, event planning, and the arts. There was a biweekly theater presentation in the Mushroom on a makeshift stage next to the bar, the subject matter picked by popular vote, usually plays from when most of the ancient audience were in college. A sensibly abbreviated version of Shaw's *Back to Methuselah* was a frequent favorite, as were *Waiting for Godot*, *Death of a Salesman*, and *Rosencrantz and Guildenstern Are Dead*, though there was an unspoken rule that this rather morbidly on-the-nose fare had to be interspersed at least once a month with something light, like *The Fantasticks*—everyone singing along with "Try to Remember," tears running down their faces—or a particularly raunchy version of *Hair*, which always devolved into a lot of audience participation.

Marion hadn't been particularly surprised to learn that there was a lot of bed-hopping in the valley. A number of the residents, like Lifers generally, had put their marriages aside, not because they were unhappy with their spouses, many of whom they'd been with for over a century, but because the old social and cultural imperatives that had underpinned marriage in general and sexual exclusivity in specific—childrearing, economic symbiosis, dyad-based housing—had long since become moot or dysfunctional by the time they reached their hundreds. They'd literally outlived jealousy, rather like Marion and Adele. Even she and Dan had developed what she believed was an understanding that their marriage was no longer to be a fortress against outside interests, though they never said so explicitly. And here they all were, a community of energetic, talented, unconventionally attractive people given a second chance at life, collected in close quarters in a beautiful setting, socializing almost every night, sleeping within walking distance of one another. Romance was inevitable and, in most cases, welcomed by all parties concerned, though the medical staff noticed an uptick in STDs of the old-fashioned kind.

For most of them, the days and nights were spent at work in the residents' areas of specialization. There was a small medical facility uphill from the Mushroom, staffed by some of the most accomplished physicians and clinicians on earth, most of whom hadn't been allowed to practice in their home states in decades because of their age, but who performed and were equipped like a miniature Mayo Clinic. Farming and livestock management had its own committee, composed of the sort of people who had run major agribusinesses in their pre-tripler days. Despite Marion's efforts, the valley wasn't entirely self-sufficient food-wise, still needed the occasional drone drop from Silverthorne, especially for wine and booze, but they were getting close.

Adele, Barb Beckwith, and Gustav Zinnemann headed a team focused on perimeter defense, as they were paranoid enough to believe that the valley might soon need it. Zinn, the compulsive inventor, came up with the idea of an autonomous drone swarm, basically a flock of weaponized, fast-flying nanobots that could be unleashed on intruders by the compound's smart security system. Zinn still knew contractors who were willing and able to manufacture the things, and General Beckwith was able to procure the components, particularly the nano-weapons, under cover of protecting the community livestock from predators and inoculating them against disease, though clearly some of her suppliers, knowing her, knew otherwise. Zinn's other obsession was the exploitation of headchip tech for personal surveillance and other unauthorized purposes, and Marion had to make him promise not to practice on anyone in residence.

As a former lawyer, she was keenly aware that many of the activities conducted in the valley—drug manufacture, minor surgeries, mass chipcasts, regular passenger drone landings, farming hallucinogenic plants, the construction of buildings of unorthodox materials and design—were highly illegal under federal, state, or local law, and occasionally she'd receive cease-and-desist orders from one authority or another, and now and then a visit from a hapless law enforcement officer who, confronted by Barb Beckwith in her military combat fatigues, usually retired meekly, promising to return some other time. All received the same response, which Marion intended to be provocative: send your lawyers, and we'll send ours and meet you in court. And because her lawyers were much older and far, far better than theirs, that was usually the end of it. But she knew they were marking time.

She and Dan worked on what they jokingly called public relations, what was really an ongoing Lifer call to arms. Not literal arms, of course, but an invitation to political agitation and personal self-determination. Dan was her primary word-smith, but Marion knew how to give those words life. She did weekly chipcasts, which they also reduced to old-fashioned video for the non-chipped. She would practice her delivery in front of the assembled throng at the Mushroom after dinner, dressed in a flowing white robe that give her a rather priestly aspect, which she entirely intended.

Good evening, she'd say when the room had quickly quieted. *I start this session with the question I ask myself every morning when I look at myself in the mirror: Why are we here?*

A question asked in both the narrowest and broadest senses: Why are we in this particular place at this particular time, and what is our purpose in being on the planet?

And who are "we"? Let's be explicit about that. We are people, here in this hall, and millions of us around the world—human beings, many of us citizens of this old and splintered nation—each of whom has lived longer than any human in all of recorded history. We have lived, on average, twice as long as the human life expectancy in 2020, a mere fifty years ago. We have seen and remember things from times before ninety-eight percent of humans now living were born. We are a living record of an increasingly deep past. We are pioneers on a journey whose end we don't yet know, but that untold millions will follow.

That's who "we" are. We are not ghosts, we are not ghouls, we are not an aberration of the natural order. We are the natural order. We are the cutting edge of time, the first to arrive at these distant outposts of experience, ahead of all the rest. We are ultra-elders. And for this we should be respected, not reviled; honored, not persecuted; rewarded, not disenfranchised.

But we live in a culture that has always disrespected the old. The word itself is not just a chronological descriptor, but a pejorative. American culture has always shamed and juvenilized advanced age. We "old" people are supposed to quietly collude in our own expulsion from life's center stage and be grateful for the bit parts that remain to us, the awful housing we're supposed to live in, the palliative medical care we're supposed to accept, the loss of useful work that we're supposed to feel relieved of, the theft of liberty that's supposed to be for our own good.

And why should this be? For millennia, aging meant decrepitude, the long foreshadowing of death, to put it bluntly—that final oblivion of which my granddaughter Claire, our new Secretary for Longevity Management, speaks so fondly. It used to be that one hundred sixty thousand people on earth died of old age every day. It was the way of things, the end that awaited every living being. This is the deepest, most unspeakable reason for the stigma that our culture has traditionally assigned to advanced age, and the unspoken justification for the host of insults visited upon those no longer deemed "young."

Yet now, by means that were unimaginable when we first ceased to be young, the ancient bond between old age and death has been broken. We've dodged decrepitude, hoodwinked death, and find ourselves in alien territory. In our millions, we have become ultra-elders. Each day, those hundred sixty thousand people who would have died, live on. Each day, a hundred sixty thousand more souls to deal with that before were quickly forgotten. That great change has upset governments and bewildered younger generations because the existing forms of politics, economic systems, religions, and family structures were dependent on the great equivalence between aging and death. And they've reacted accordingly, with fear and anger and repression and, most recently, with the cynical invitation that we end our own lives to make theirs more comfortable.

But again: Why are we here? We are most assuredly not here for their comfort. We do not live on at someone else's sufferance, or by their indulgence. We were indulged in the past because it was assumed we would soon die. Now that we decline to die, we also decline to be patronized.

Why are we here? For the same purpose that drove us forward when we were merely young, over a century ago: to live with dignity and freedom and without shame. To live on for as long as fate allows, with joy and in community with those who share that fate. We will not be corralled or sequestered or taxed or deprived of our constitutional rights or induced to commit suicide. We will live on.

Those of us in this valley are here for a more specific reason. To prepare the way for a different social order that will empower ultra-elders and provide them with a safe haven from the social prejudice and political injustice that the great Change has unleashed. We invite those who are like-minded and of sufficient age to join us here and work with us to ensure that we may all live on in dignity and peace.

I call on President Baldisseri and Secretary Landess to rescind their dreadful suicide-or-sequestration program, and to meet with me, *at a time and place of their choosing, to discuss a more humane and productive way forward for the old and less old alike.*

In the meantime, we will live on.

And so on, variations on those themes, week-in, week-out, with increasing stridency that Dan tried ineffectively to reign in. He agreed with Marion in principle, but tried to persuade her that the repeated reference to a "safe haven" for Lifers was bound to offend the authorities. She never used the word "Lifer," which she considered tantamount to a slur; it was always "ultra-elder" or simply "the aged." The phrase "live on" kept surfacing, words that had come to her repeatedly in dreams, in phrases spoken by lovers or figures of wisdom, words emblazoned on the sky or in the waters. Live on.

But to do that, she thought, *we're going to need more room.*

ADELE

Black Valley, Colorado, 2075

Secretary Landess had warned Adele that under no circumstances would President Baldisseri meet with Marion Altman, but that something had to be done to quell the growing distraction from the successful rollout of the Epilox initiative that the so-called Lifer Liberation Front represented.

Adele and Claire met regularly in chipspace to review the latest data and attempt to mediate their clients' anxieties. Adele would emerge from these sessions as though from a troubled sleep, the mixed phrases and images that comprised her neural meshing with Claire like a particularly vivid dream.

Six months in, the government's treatment had been delivered to over 100 million people around the world—a reasonable first uptake, and as much as the initial production run would allow, but a mere fraction of the 1.25 billion people, a tenth of the world's population, who were over the age of one hundred in 2075. And delivery of the treatment didn't mean it had been actually administered; Accretex had embedded a nano-transmitter in the seventh pill that would be activated when it was ingested, and the resulting data indicated that less than two-thirds of the people who received Epilox actually completed the required sequence of seven doses, and that was probably an overestimate as it didn't account for those who may have mistakenly taken the pills out of order and ingested the transmitter but stopped before completing the sequence. Claire reported that there was talk within the Department of Longevity Management of requiring Epilox candidates to take the pills under medical supervision, but this was considered likely to dramatically diminish uptake, as much of the rollout campaign had emphasized the ability to take the drug in the privacy of one's home and in the company of loved ones, amid personalized ceremonies that were movingly depicted in countless Epilox adcasts.

Claire also complained that the LLF, sometimes called the Next Hundred, had spawned copycat groups around the world, and that they had to be monitored closely. A mob of over a thousand Lifers wearing the LLF's stylized UE "ultra-elders" logo invaded the Museum of Natural History in Vienna, barricaded the exits, and proceeded to hold rock music concerts and chipcast successive drafts of an international Lifer manifesto from the dinosaur mezzanine. The British owner of one of the largest private islands in Fiji declared his island the provisional capital of a "Lifer Nation" and promised any and all triplers who would journey there free housing and meals at what had previously been the island's opulent, highly exclusive resort. The government of Portugal, a country already overrun with expat American Lifers, resulting in one of the highest percentages of Lifer inhabitants of any population in the world, revised its constitution to explicitly affirm and protect the civil rights of those above the age of 120, in what was widely viewed as a rebuke to the Baldisseri administration's contrary moves in the United States. And the country of Japan, more aged than any nation on earth, steeped in Taoist-Buddhist traditions of respect for one's elders and chastened by the example of the legendary "Roppongi Grandmother" who'd humiliated an age cop on a public street, essentially retired from the world stage overnight, abrogating all of its trade and military treaties, cutting off foreign travel, and turning resolutely to the agenda of ascetic self-sufficiency expressed in the Osaka Declaration of 2071: to house, feed, and care for its own thirty million people over the age of one hundred with the support of its ninety million citizens under that age. It took Adele awhile to accept that one of her last covert operations had ended up changing the social policies of an entire nation.

In the US there was no such consensus, and conditions on the ground continued to deteriorate. Baldisseri had swept into office on a wave of thinly veiled anti-Lifer sentiment, but once in power she had struggled to control the animal spirits she'd unleashed. The proposed Twenty-Ninth Amendment to the Constitution, which would phase out the application of various elements of the Bill of Rights as a citizen passed through specified age brackets, had already been ratified by more than half the states that remained in the union by 2075, and was expected to become the law of the land in a hand-ful of years. Even in advance of ratification, state legislatures had begun enacting constraints on where Lifers could live, specifying the circumstances and the elections in which they would be allowed to vote, and in the case of several states within the crowded "Boomer Box," revoking their rights to assemble or to bear arms and subjecting their speech to vari-ous content restrictions intended to prevent advancement of what was called the "extreme longevity agenda." Textbooks that cast the aged in a sympathetic light had been banned from public schools, and academic curricula were examined for signs of Lifer indoctrination. Not unexpectedly, the LLF had fought back in court with teams of tripler lawyers as experi-enced as they were well-paid, but the jurisprudential tide was against them, with some originalist Supreme Court justices, themselves well into their hundreds, going so far as to suggest that the word "person" as used in the Constitution must have meant to the founders a human with a lifespan normal to their time, and not the unfathomably aged beings at whom these new laws were directed.

Adele and Claire agreed that the root of this political and legal turmoil was simple: the growing percentage of Lifers that had fallen into extreme poverty, having outlived both the defunct Social Security system and their own resources. It was beyond the capacity of mere government to grapple with. By 2075 it was estimated that as many Lifers in the US were homeless as those who had a consistent dwelling place, even when the latter was defined to include cars, RVs, and other forms of "movable shelter," such as tents. What was called "subsistence crime"—that is, theft of food and clothing—had increased in most major cities to an extent that local law enforcement had essentially ceased to conduct arrests for the breaking and entering of retail spaces and confined themselves to policing public housing and transport. Meanwhile, philanthropic institutions whose missions had traditionally emphasized care for the poor were themselves depleted by the drying up of testamentary gifting, and as their former benefactors lived on and on in relative comfort, these doomed organizations spent their dwindling assets to feed a bottomless pit of geriatric privation.

The strains on the medical system were immense. Though Lifers continued to exhibit the biological stasis of negligible senescence, they weren't impervious to illnesses that could lead to death, a fact of which the world was reminded when Pope Angelo Dimaapi, by then 142 years old, contracted pneumonia while on a pilgrimage to his native Philippines and died within days. American hospitals were overflowing with triplers who had broken bones or gone mad or contracted one of the host of coronaviruses for which vaccines were available but hard to deliver to the increasingly indigent, unhoused population of ultra-elders.

Adele was nagged by a feeling of professional and personal failure. What had always been needed was a cure for the longevity plague, the cure she'd hoped to extract from Zinn and had continued to believe that Xerxes would eventually develop. But of course, then and now, the only cure was death, whether by natural causes, which killed too few too slowly, by the usual crude means of past centuries, which were efficient but still beyond contemplation by all but the most cynical of leaders, or by the voluntary self-mercies of Epilox, which depended for its effectiveness on that least predictable of variables, individual choice. Claire made it clear to Adele that if that last course had any hope of success, the counter-messaging and overt resistance of the Next Hundred and its ilk had to stop, and in the minds of many in government, that meant that its most prominent symbol—Black Valley—had to fall.

But, Claire told Adele, she'd convinced President Baldisseri to make one last attempt at a compromise.

DANIEL

―――――――

Black Valley, Colorado, 2076

The request was delivered through Adele, which Dan thought typical of government—always use the channels that have served you in the past, no matter the personal histories of the parties or the awkwardness of the message.

He and Marion were near the center of the lake with Barb Beckwith, on a stiltpad that Barb had commissioned for the valley's armory, though Marion insisted she not call it that. The idea that they were assembling an arsenal of ballistic and wave weapons was repugnant to Marion, who'd never let Dan buy a gun in all the years they'd lived together in increasingly dangerous cities, even during their chaotic evacuation from the barrier islands during the first of the big floods, when they finally abandoned Florida for good. Road rage everywhere, water rage too, shootings at the slightest provocation. How they made it out unscathed he'd never know. Everyone had a gun but them.

But a clear majority of the Next Hundred had voted to arm themselves against the increasingly likely possibility of an attack on the valley either by the bands of anti-Lifer vigilantes that roamed through rural Colorado, or by the feds themselves, under some trumped-up pretext of eminent domain enabled by the newly ratified Twenty-Ninth Amendment. It was less clear how they would manage to defend a thirty-mile perimeter covered in alpine woods, but Barb Beckwith and Zinn claimed to have a plan involving the quick distribution of several hundred microwave Remingtons and Armalite ballistic rifles cached there in the middle of the lake. Dan thought the location—a concession to Marion's aversion to guns generally—was ill advised for obvious reasons, until it was explained to him that the weapons would be preloaded on autonomous drone carriers and flown to multiple pickup points around the valley upon the security system's detection of even the hint of a threat.

It was a hot day even on the lake, no breeze, the sun high over the naked cordillera. A jet ski cut the water toward them, and even half a mile away Dan could see it was Adele, her long scarf trailing in the wind, bearing news that must be so important she didn't want to use her chip. She drew alongside the platform, tied off the ski, and hopped aboard with an agility that belied her 133 years.

"Excuse me, General, but I need to talk to Marion in private," she said a bit breathlessly.

Beckwith was unfazed as ever. "No worries, just taking inventory," she said, and disappeared inside the Quonset hut, closing the steel door behind her.

"Should I disappear too?" Dan asked.

"No need, I know she'll tell you everything anyway," said Adele. She turned to Marion. "I just had a call from Jay Mendenhall, who was recently appointed Baldisseri's chief of staff."

There had been a lot of personnel turmoil in the new president's administration. "Isn't he her second or third?" Dan asked. "Former Buttigieg protégé, claims to be of neither party, goes around in a purple face tattoo?"

"That's him. Her third chief in a year, yes. They're trying to look less partisan. But he assured me he was speaking on full authority of the president, and those guys don't use that old phrase unless it's true."

"Saying what?" asked Marion a bit impatiently.

"They want you to have another talk with Claire. This time with the intention of negotiating a kind of mutual ceasefire."

"Well that should be simple. If they'll cease, I'll stop firing."

Adele sighed. "You know they can't drop the whole sequestration agenda, it's what got them into office. But they might agree to postpone some of the civil rights cutbacks if you'd get on board with the Epilox campaign. Or at least stop opposing it."

"Is this them talking, or you guessing?" Dan asked.

"It's me guessing. But an educated guess. It's worth a conversation, at least."

Marion squinted up at the sun as it began to slide behind the Gore Range. "What if I don't want to speak to Claire? She is my granddaughter, after all. Creates at least the appearance of a giant conflict of interest on both our parts. Why not speak with Baldisseri directly?"

"That won't happen, Marion. That would give you too much credibility, which is what they can least afford."

Dan nodded. "She's right about that, dear," he said. "If I were them, I wouldn't let you within a hundred miles of the White House."

"So where is this talk with Claire supposed to happen? I'm not going anywhere near the damned Department of Longevity Management either."

"No one expects you to," said Adele. "But if you're willing to talk with her, I'm sure you could just do it via chip. Each side can confirm the link is secure and authenticated, and there's less public fallout if things go sideways."

The sun was gone now, the sky shading quickly into its daily dusky violet. Marion took off her glasses and rubbed her eyes wearily. "Let me think about it," she said. Which, Dan knew, was what she always said when she intended to say yes.

The talk was arranged for a week later at noon, Mountain Time. Randy Colson, Joe Forsythe, Jae Ming, and Dan drilled Marion daily with talking points and legalistic arguments on a range of subjects they thought might come up, but at some point in the evening, Marion and Adele would retire to the lodge together, and Dan would sit on the porch in the dark with a bourbon and listen to them game out the conversation, Adele role-playing Claire with uncanny fidelity, even mimicking her musical voice, Marion occasionally raising hers in genuine anger, forgetting for a moment that the woman across from her was her friend and former rival, and not her granddaughter, sworn enemy of her cause.

On the appointed day, Marion wanted no one near her and walked alone up the steep stone path to the chipcast studio, high on the flank of the sunward mountain. Noon came and went, an hour, two. Dan waited anxiously with the crowd gathered in the dining hall, scanning the net for casts that might tell them what had happened, but there was nothing unusual, just more news of crowded sequestration camps, fires in tripler tent enclaves, armed clashes in cities between Lifers and their descendants, all the grim foreshadowings of what the 'casts called the coming generational war.

Marion finally came down from the mountain and passed silently through the crowd and out again to the lodge, and Dan could read nothing in her face that would tell what had happened, what had been said. It was only late that night that she handed him a datacoin.

"I was sure they were recording it," she said, sinking onto their bed, exhausted. "So I thought I should too. Just in case they alter it later."

"May I listen?"

"Of course, but what's done is done, Dan. Please don't second-guess me."

"I won't."

"And now I really have to go to bed," she said, and he took the datacoin onto the porch, sat in the moonlight, and chipped into it.

White noise, the click of connections being made. Then a clearing, a deepening quiet.

"Marion."

"Claire."

"Thank you for doing this."

"Thank me when we've accomplished something, dear. How can I help you?"

"It's not me, of course. We all need your help."

"You mean Baldisseri needs my help."

"The administration, yes. And by extension, the people."

"Or the people who voted for her."

Long pause, unnatural silence. The sound of chipspace.

"Let's not spar, Marion. We have the advantage of knowing one another well enough to dispense with that. This is just between us for now."

"Is it? I'll take your word on that."

"For now, yes."

"Very well. Fire away, Granddaughter."

Another pause, during which Dan imagined the throat-clearing and paper shuffling that would have filled it, had this been a physical meeting.

"To be frank, the Epilox rollout hasn't gone as well as we had hoped. A lot of people have received the treatment, particularly in the US, but barely half of them have actually completed it."

"How many?"

"I can't tell you that, it's classified. But not enough."

"Not enough for what?"

"Not enough to make a dent in the problem."

"As you define the problem."

"Anyone would define what's happening to the overaged as a problem. Even you must."

"Tell me, Claire, what's the age distribution of those who asked for Epilox? Or is that classified too?"

Pause. "Ninety-four percent are in their hundreds."

"How far into their hundreds?"

"Most are over one-thirty. Of the rest, almost all are at least one hundred."

"So basically no doublers participating in this great solution to a vexing problem."

"The data I've been given isn't that granular, but very few."

"And how fair is that, Claire? Why are the very old the ones to sacrifice themselves?"

"Evidently because they want to. This is a voluntary program. They've had enough."

Marion's voice rises. "They've had enough of the conditions that have been thrust upon them through no fault of their own! How is that voluntary? Your administration is promoting the segregation of ultra-elders and is systematically stripping them of their constitutional rights. Most are in poverty, living like animals. The choices are one of your sequestration camps, or Epilox. That's no choice at all."

"Marion, I can't relitigate these policy matters with you. I don't have the authority, and frankly, I don't have the time. What I want to suggest is that in exchange for your cooperation with the Epilox program, we'd entertain making certain concessions to you and your followers."

"And what would this cooperation on my part look like?"

"Silence. On your part. Our data indicate that your opposition to the program is a major reason for the current slow pace of uptake among Lifers. You don't have to get behind it, just stop obstructing it."

"And for my silence we get what?"

"A guarantee that the forced sequestration bills currently before Congress will be vetoed by the president."

"She's only got another three years in office. What then?"

"I can't say, Marion. That's our offer."

Silence.

"Here's the thing, Claire. I don't see any of this ending well without a separatist component as part of the overall solution."

"I'm not sure I follow."

"Lifers, as you call them, those who don't choose to die on your schedule with the aid of your father's drug, need to have a safe place to go, to congregate, a place not supervised by the government and subject to government edict. They need their own land, their own governance, in exchange for removing themselves from doubler society. This valley, when we're done with it, will be a symbol of that, but only a symbol. It's a drop in the ocean."

"But—"

"Tell your president, Claire, that we need a substantial, contiguous plot of federal land, to be placed under the auspices of the Next Hundred and its designated representatives, that would be exempt from all existing and pending anti-Lifer protocols. If we get that, and free passage for any tripler who wants to go there, we'll drop our opposition to your whole agenda."

Pause. "I don't see how I could even suggest such a thing, but just theoretically, what land do you have in mind? Certainly not the Boomer Box. There's no way we're going to chop up half a dozen states that are still in the union. . . ."

"Of course not. We're much more reasonable than you imagine, Claire. Just give us Arapaho National Forest and we'll call it even, at least for now."

"I'm sorry, what are you talking about, Marion?"

"Pull up a map, Claire. The Arapaho National Forest starts just over the mountain from Black Valley. It's one and a half million acres of Colorado wilderness stretching north to the Wyoming border. If properly developed, which the Next Hundred is willing to supervise with the help of federal loans, of course, it could become home to a significant portion of the American Lifer population. Give us that, and I'll stand down on your suicide campaign."

"You never cease to amaze me, Grandmother. If you got that, you'd be totally undermining the Epilox campaign."

"You mean making it less necessary. And how is that a bad thing?"

"I don't see how I could even communicate such a proposal to the president."

"Then we're done here, Claire. I love you, but we're done."

"Marion, please."

"We're done."

Silence.

ADELE

Black Valley, Colorado, 2076

In the end, they didn't bother to use the road.

It was just past noon, and Barb Beckwith was on the southernmost edge of Black Valley, near the twelve-thousand-foot summit of what the LLM called Mt. Respect, when her left arm exploded.

She'd gone there to check out an unusual burst of chip traffic. Could have been hikers, and she could have sent a drone, but it was a beautiful day and she wanted to get out. Adele had insisted that Barb give her access to her chip's sensory array so she could monitor her movements.

Microwave projectile, close range, no pain at first. She'd been passing between two giant boulders or she would have been instantly dead. She wheeled as she fell and drew her Glock and fired in the direction the shot must have come from, but she could see no one, hear nothing. She hit the ground and clawed a tourniquet wrap out of the thigh pocket of her fatigues and slapped it on her upper arm and it deployed and tightened and injected a painkiller. She lay panting on the rocky slope, looking up at the sky. Did not look toward her left arm, which she knew was gone. Not a clean sever, either; she'd seen these sorts of non-ballistic wounds in Belarus and North Korea, bones atomized, soft tissue shredded, loss of blood the usual cause of death.

Her ATV was twenty yards below her on the mountainside. Stones kicked up to her left and right; more shots. She fired the Glock again, aimlessly, and squirmed sideways, letting gravity pull her downhill. Almost missed the ATV as she rolled past, but she reached out with her remaining hand and caught a tire, crawled behind the chassis.

Adele's heart pounded as she watched the chipfeed thrown up on her screens from a dozen sources. She chipped into the security system, found it unperturbed, not picking up wave fire that far away. She cursed, commanded the system to go to active attack mode. The connection was spotty, so she had to tell it three times. On the mountain, ground debris kicked up again around Barb, and it was then Adele realized the shooter wasn't in the woods, but in the sky. A drone, surprisingly quiet, small and quick, random updrafts at that altitude probably the only reason her friend was still alive. A newer model, nano weaponry, definitely federal; the local vigilantes would have sent something she could have brought down easily.

Adele scanned the valley, saw Zinn's weaponry drones spreading out from their depot in the middle of the lake, delivering arms to their drop points. Alarms echoed up the mountain, and she could see people beginning to run, some toward the drop points, others toward shelter. They hadn't practiced for this nearly enough in her opinion, very few of them were military, and now she wondered how they'd perform, wished she could help, but it was too late for all that. The moment she'd long dreaded had arrived.

Barbara scanned the space near the top of the mountain, saw nothing, reached into her suit again, pulled out an epinephrine autoinjector and slammed it into her thigh, making Adele flinch at her console. Barb's vision cleared, and she hauled herself up onto the saddle of the ATV, kicked it into gear and hurtled down the mountain with more wave strikes bursting around her. Then she entered the tree line thick with spruce, stood on the brakes and crashed to a stop. Infrared could still see her, so she slid to the ground and under the vehicle's downhill wheel well. The initial shock had passed, but the pain made it hard to think. Blood ran down her side, pooled under her.

Adele had to risk talking to her, even though it might give away her location.

"Can you get down?" she asked frantically.

"The fuckers. I thought they had more sense," Beckwith said.

"Stay there, we'll send someone."

"Adele, tell Zinn to launch his devices."

"We're not at that point yet. Maybe we can talk them out of this."

"Tell him to be ready. Marion too." Pain squeezed off what remained of Beckwith's voice.

"Copy," Adele said.

She was in the studio on the northern flank of the valley, deep in a thick stand of aspens that made it hard for the drones to target the building. The frequency signature of the attackers' communications, familiar to Adele as a parent's voice, meant this was a federal action, which she'd prepared for but never quite believed would come. She made sure the handheld weapons had been retrieved from the carrier drones at their drop points, and that as many residents as possible were barricaded in the lodges and away from the primary lines of attack. She sent out a chip blast reminding everyone to stay off chip circuits, since they'd be monitored by the feds as easily as by her and she didn't want the defense system to have to sort through the clutter. But she let Marion through.

"Adele, something's wrong with Beckwith. I got this garbled chip from her—"

"I know. Get off-line and secure yourself. I'll handle it."

She broke off before Adele could ask where she was.

The feds hadn't bothered to advance into the valley along the five miles of gravel drive from the county road. Instead, a small convoy of ATVs driven by augmented human ops and some infantry class assault robots, maybe thirty troops in total, massed at the gate and penetrated about fifty yards into the perimeter to draw the attention of the security system.

The gate guards who confronted them were quickly disabled. The robots did the shooting and the humans did the shouting, demanding that they lay down their weapons and come out peacefully and nobody would get hurt. But the guards' body telemetry showed that two were already dead and six more were badly injured, which meant the robots had been programmed to kill at least up to a specified number. Adele wondered what that number was, but that initial 25 percent had to be a good indicator.

She tried hailing the feds on the frequencies they were using, but got no response. She ran to the door and grabbed two of the ballistic automatics that a drone had dropped on the deck and threw one to Randy Colson at the console across the room, though she doubted he knew how to use it. Then the windows of the studio all shattered at once and they hit the floor, more impacts ripping through the walls and roof in neat circular punctures, characteristic of wave fire. She checked to see that Randy wasn't hit and crawled into a corner and called Dan Altman on a shortwave handheld.

"Adele, we can't do this, they're killing people," he shouted.

"Where are you?"

"In the Mushroom. There are about a thousand people in here. One good hit on the structure and we're all dead. We've got to give it up."

"Where's Marion?"

"Last I knew she was in the main lodge, but I can't raise her."

"Dan, is there any way someone there can get across the lake? Barbara's wounded, she's on Mt. Respect. She's bleeding out."

"Shit. Nobody with her?"

"No, she's alone. She has an ATV."

"Can we send a drone?"

"The only ones big enough to carry her are so slow they'd be shot down immediately."

"Where's your boy Zinnemann? This is when we need him most."

"I haven't seen him in a couple of days."

"Shit. Adele, make them stop. Offer them anything. I'll get Barbara. Chip me her coordinates. Monitor me." The signal went dead.

The pounding on the studio stopped. Adele climbed back to the console and tried the fed frequencies again but got nothing. Then she chipped Zinn. They both spoke in German, for whatever good that might do.

"Why are you on my chip, Adele? We were to be silent following an alarm."

"Just for this moment, Gustav. Where are you? It's time."

"Already? I thought we would do better than this."

"No, we need your devices now."

"I'll need at least twenty minutes. Perhaps thirty."

"That's not fast enough," she said, more to herself than to him.

Dan Altman threw open the lakeside door of the Mushroom to find an assault robot with a wave gun aimed at his head. Half as tall as a person and nearly silent, the machine hesitated a fraction, perhaps identifying him, and he used that moment to empty a clip from his Sig Sauer into the thing's torso plate. Most of the rounds ricocheted off its armor but one found an optic lens and penetrated its gyro pack. He watched it topple over, then ran to the edge of the lake, untied one of the jet skis that hadn't been hit, shoved the gun into his pants, and twisted the throttle full open. He nearly fell off the rear of the ski as it leapt forward, then recovered and cut an erratic path across the water, hunching down as multiple aerial shots geysered around him. For an instant Adele marveled that he, like her, was 133 years old, much too old to be fighting for his life. Yet here he was, fighting for someone else's.

The far shore was a mass of boulders, nowhere to tie up, so he wedged the ski between two limbs of a fallen tree and waded the last twenty yards. Adele was sure he'd be hit, but the crowd in the dining structure had begun firing their weapons, mostly loud ballistics, from every door and window, attracting return fire from the aerial drones. He had maybe ten seconds before they'd retarget him, but in that time he made the dense line of fir on the lower slope of Mt. Respect and threw himself into the underbrush.

Adele sent him the coordinates in a short burst and his chip generated a directional display in his field of vision, a bright orange dot far above him, beyond the trees, where Barb Beckwith lay dying. He shivered, rose to a crouch, pulled out his Sig, and scrambled upward through the ground cover.

Adele tore her attention away from the mountain and refocused, weaving through a sequence of distributed neural nets to the only target that would matter. She knew well from Xerxes' endless intelligence reports that President Isabel Baldisseri disliked in-person meetings, and in particular disliked meetings whose subject was the Lifer Liberation Front, which she regarded, depending on her mood, as a quasi-criminal element, a dangerous distraction from her agenda, an exaggerated figment of the distributed neural net, or yet another symptom of the nihilistic anarchy that Methuselah had spread across the land. But her Secretary of Longevity Management had insisted that she attend a real-time briefing on the Black Valley operation, and since she had ordered it, there was really no way to refuse.

The DLM briefing room was located, appropriately enough, in the presidential suite in what had once been the Willard Hotel, a block down Pennsylvania Avenue from the White House, where, Adele fleetingly recalled, she and Dan Altman had conducted a couple of their trysts some eighty-five years earlier. The old building had been requisitioned to make room for more executive offices when the federal government expanded in the wake of the abortive secessionist movement of the 2060s, and now, accompanied only by Jay Mendelsohn, her chief of staff, Baldisseri descended into the basement of the White House and boarded the narrow tube shuttle that would whisk them through connecting tunnels to the Willard. She was barely fifty years old, but had begun to look much older, her hair rapidly graying, her face fissured with new wrinkles, changes that some attributed to the stresses of the job, but others saw as karmic payback for the extreme anti-Lifer positions that had won her the presidency.

Thanks to a modification of the same surveillance program that Zinn had used to invade the Xerxes network long ago, Adele had managed to hack into the personal sensory array in Jay Mendelsohn's headchip. She would have rather used Baldisseri's, but her chip had been removed in accordance with standard security protocols upon her assuming office. The two were met at the Willard's tunnel exit by a pair of Secret Service agents who escorted them across a hall and into a cramped elevator that rose quickly to the penthouse floor. Adele noted in passing that Baldisseri was wearing a navy-blue

Missoni pantsuit and a pearl choker, and that she did indeed look far older than her years.

The briefing room commanded views up and down Pennsylvania Avenue from the White House to the Capitol, but when Baldisseri entered, those present were riveted to the oversized monitors on the inner walls, where multiple aerial images of the conflict two thousand miles to the west were being streamed from drones over Black Valley. Moving yellow and blue icons respectively marked the federal human and robot forces, bright red avatars tracked the infrared signatures of the enemy. No sound in the room except the muted chatter of the tactical coms. Claire Landess, also looking older than her sixty-eight years, stood staring at the screens with a hand over her mouth, next to a male in civilian dress whom Adele nonetheless recognized as the Army chief of staff. Seated were a couple of com specialists, and two Secret Service agents stood with their backs to the floor-to-ceiling windows. That was all, which indicated that this operation had about the same priority as putting down a riot at a Lifer sequestration camp.

Claire rose to meet the president. The Army chief stood and saluted but didn't approach.

"Thanks for being here."

"Had to be, right? How's it going?"

"Rather poorly, actually. They're better armed than we thought, and their security systems are more sophisticated than the typical civilian setup. We've lost"—she glanced at the screens—"two augments and five drones. They've had thirty or so injured and six dead. All our calls to desist have been ignored, and we've ignored some chip traffic from their side."

"What traffic?"

"We think it's Adele Pritchard, the former head of Xerxes."

"Oh yes, the one you met with that night."

"She was present," Claire said defensively. "I didn't know she'd be there. Knowledgeable, naturally, I thought rather moderate, potentially helpful. She's asking for a ceasefire and negotiations. I'd like to respond to her, but I didn't want to do that before you got here and approved."

"I don't approve. Not yet."

"But Isabel, people are dying. We didn't expect this level of casualties on either side."

"One never does."

"It could work against us when this gets out."

"If we stop now it's a de facto win for the LLF, and we can't have that."

Mendelsohn sidled up to the two women. "We knew what we were getting into when we started this. They need to be disarmed and their leaders taken into custody. That was the mission. Otherwise we've accomplished nothing."

Claire sighed, turned back to the screens. "Then it's going to be a very long afternoon."

Mendelsohn followed, scanning the data. Twelve dead now, a dozen drones disabled, a team of about twenty Army augments encircling the dining structure where most of the resistance was concentrated, closing in steadily.

In the upper quadrant of one of the screens a solitary infrared blotch moved up a mountainside toward a second, stationary signature, its blotch a faded pink.

Dan Altman had almost reached the tree line some forty yards below where Beckwith lay when he heard the shots. Ballistic fire, coming from where she should be. He couldn't see her through the ferny undergrowth and thick trunks of firs, but the orange dot in his field of vision hovered there above him on the slope, where the concussions came from. Two shots, then another, sounding like a handgun. Tragic irony if she heard him coming and shot him before she knew who it was. But then there was another sound, and Adele realized what Barbara was shooting at.

A saddle drone was descending quickly from the peak of the mountain on a perfect AI-guided plane paralleling the slope, as though it were on rails. Short black wings angled downward, an augmented human soldier astride it like a rider on a horse, wave gun extending from its right arm pointed directly at Beckwith as he closed on her. Adele had never seen this model drone before, so she knew Dan hadn't, but that didn't stop him. He crashed out of the tree line like a madman and got off two shots before the augment noticed him. One of the rounds caught it in the helmet and it reeled, then righted itself and fired a broad wave swath down the mountain, shattering tree trunks like glass and sending Dan facedown into the gneiss. He was up remarkably fast for an old man, bleeding and angry and firing again, and the drone angled toward him but then Beckwith fired too and they caught it in a crossfire and for a half second it wavered, confused, its AI distracted with damage assessment. Beckwith collapsed from the effort and the augment accelerated toward her and blasted her ATV, sending it tumbling away down the slope. The augment rode up over her and pointed the wave gun down into her face.

Her voice was clear and steady as she looked up at the augment. "Fuck you, robot," she said.

Dan yelled, but it was too late. The augment fired, and on the screen in the briefing room in Washington, and in Dan's field of vision, Beckwith's icon flickered out. There was a moment of quiet, then explosions and shouting echoed up again from the valley and the drone and its rider rose, spun, and accelerated toward Dan. He stumbled backward, turned, and staggered into the trees.

Adele couldn't lose any more.

She chipped Zinn. "We're out of time. We need your swarm. On the mountain. Now!"

Silence. Then: "Oh my dear Adele." He stretched out her name to three syllables, as he always did when her intensity amused him. "You'll have my swarm, but not on the mountain."

"What do you mean?" she yelled frantically. "You said it would stop them!"

"It will, my dear. But not there. Here."

The Secret Service agent by the westernmost window of the briefing room saw something emerge from one of the a/c vents high on the wall behind the array of monitors. Thin as a filament, almost invisible, like a heat ripple. Then two, then three. Hovering. He drew his FN-57, hammered in a clip with the heel of his hand, undid the safety, and moved smoothly into the middle of the room.

"Breach!" he shouted. Claire and Baldisseri stood staring at him, but Mendelsohn, more experienced in such matters, immediately hit the floor. The agent grabbed the two women and jerked them down, while the second agent pulled her gun and swept the room, trying to locate what her partner had seen. The first agent raised his weapon and fired at the air vent, destroying it and the ductwork behind it, but hit nothing else. The agents glanced at each other and began backing toward the windows to give themselves the broadest possible lines of sight. The room was silent but for the casualty indicator tones coming from the monitors. The president and Claire looked around as though their guardians had lost their minds, started to rise. "Stay down!" the first agent shouted, but then stopped, clutched his chest, and crumpled to the carpet as though he'd been shot. A thin silver filament was lodged in the white cotton of his shirt just above his heart. The second agent spun as though she'd heard a threat behind her, but a second filament, almost invisible, speared the back of her neck just above the collar, and she fell like a broken doll.

Mendelsohn's artificially purple face turned a deeper shade. "Do something!" he shouted at the Army chief, the only person remaining in the room who was armed. The chief struggled to his knees and pulled a tiny Sig P232 out of a belt clip and waved it in the air. "Don't leave the room!" he yelled at the civilians. "We're safer in here!"

At that moment, two blocks to the west in the rooftop bar of the Hay-Adams Hotel, Gustav Zinnemann smiled. The sound pickup from the nanodrones was better than he expected. He checked the video feed on his laptop screen and entered another line of code. Then he chipped Adele.

"Ask them to cease fire again," he said to her. "You may get a better response now."

Dan had reached the edge of the tree line nearest the lake; there was no cover between him and the water's edge. The drone couldn't penetrate the dense stand of trees and was gaining altitude to reacquire him from above. By then it was obvious to Adele that he and Beckwith, and Marion and her and a few others, were priority targets and that while the feds probably would have preferred it, their capture wasn't considered as necessary as their being removed by whatever means necessary. Dan was a dead man unless Zinn was right.

She chipped Claire on the line she'd used earlier. "Secretary Landess, this is Pritchard. Stand your troops down immediately and no one else there will be hurt. I can't be responsible for what happens if you don't."

Claire didn't hesitate, turned to the Army chief. "Tell all troops to stand down immediately," she hissed. The old soldier stared at her, then looked across the room to his commander-in-chief where she lay half under a desk. Baldisseri's face contorted in a frightened rage.

"No!" she shouted. "Those fucking geriatrics are going to pay!"

Zinn listened to the shouts of the president and took another sip of pilsner. Not as good as German beer, but good enough. Out the window of the bar, the sun was setting over the Potomac. He set the glass down carefully, reached over the laptop keyboard, and hit the "enter" key.

The swarm rose as one and hovered in the back of the rental truck that Zinn had parked on Pennsylvania Avenue. He'd left the cargo doors chained but open a fraction, and that was all they needed. Twenty thousand filament drones, clones of one another with a single mind, glinting silver like a tightly packed school of sardines, streamed out through the cargo door jams and up to a height of ten stories. There they coalesced into their attack configuration and moved on their target.

Claire was first to sense the shadow fall across the room and turned and looked out the big windows to see a six-by-six-foot cube of writhing metal hovering in the air outside, moving closer until it pressed against the glass, tiny turbo engines spinning in the light. She backed away, arms raised instinctively in front of her face, then dropped to the floor and covered her head. Baldisseri stared, then bolted for the door with Mendelsohn close behind. The Army chief raised his gun and aimed at the hovering cube as it expanded, growing less dense, until its forward surface blanketed the pane.

It took several seconds for the swarm to tune itself to the required harmonics, but then its volume rose to a shriek and the bullet-proof, floor-to-ceiling windows of the presidential suite exploded inward in a storm of glass. The chief's gun flew away and he fell backward, his face lacerated.

Claire convulsed into a ball on the floor. Baldisseri and Mendelsohn reached the door and tumbled over each other into the hallway. Six more Secret Service were on their way in the elevator, but they were too late. The swarm's shriek dropped to a throbbing hum as it poured like dark gelatin through the door and into the hall and paused for a moment over the president. Mendelsohn scrambled backward toward the stairwell, whimpering. Baldisseri screamed as the swarm descended on her, wrapping its thousand filaments around her arms and legs and torso, leaving only her face exposed. Then the filaments that ringed her face drew up slightly, and shining wires extended from their tips and hovered just above the surface of her skin.

She screamed again.

Dan Altman's last shot missed the drone like all the others. He let the gun drop and sagged against a boulder at the edge of the lake, watched the augment soldier ride the machine down at him out of the darkening sky. Adele knew he had lived long enough not to regret however it ended, but this wasn't what he or she had imagined as a way to die. Not this old. Not this violently or pointlessly. The augment raised the wave gun one more time.

And then stopped. Froze, as though listening. Looked across the lake and down the valley almost wistfully, like a child called home for supper. Lowered the gun, holstered it, looked at Dan, nodded almost imperceptibly, and rose like a rocket into the sky and was gone.

Gunfire still rang out from across the lake, but subsided quickly into a low scatter of shots, all coming from inside the Mushroom, then stopped as the targets withdrew and melted away. It had ended more quickly than it had begun.

The studio's roof was mostly gone, and Adele's hands were bleeding from flying wood shards, a dozen small wounds. She chipped Zinn.

"That was quite a show."

"It worked even better than I expected," he said.

"How long have you been in Washington?"

"Three days. I really couldn't tell you in advance, Adele. I was sure they were hacking our chips just as I was hacking theirs. It was clear an attack was imminent."

"But your, uh, swarm. . . ."

"I had it shipped to DC some weeks ago, to one of my apartments. It seemed like the logical place. It's much more effective in urban environments, though there's a duplicate set in my lab there in the valley."

"We could have used it here."

"I'm sorry about that, but I can really only control one swarm at a time. Too much real-time coding is required at this stage."

"You picked the right one, then. Where is it now?

"The devices? Back in the van, which I'm driving to Colorado as we speak."

"Be careful. And we should keep this brief. Where is the president?"

"They took her to a hospital, but I assure you she's unhurt. Which is more than she deserves. A bit shaken, and very angry. . . ."

"Yes, we'll have to deal with that. Let's disengage now. *Danke schön.*"

"*Bitteschön.*"

Adele logged off and stumbled out of the studio and down through the towering aspens toward the main lodge. The wet smell of the forest floor mingled with the acrid stench of ballistic smoke and the ozone residue of the wave weapons. Fires burned in distant outbuildings. People were streaming out of the Mushroom with the wounded, shouting and cursing and crying, some still carrying their guns. She stopped at the edge of the lake and saw Dan's jet ski making its way slowly back across the water, barely any wake, his body slumped forward. She wondered how badly he was hurt. And because she never thought of Dan without thinking of Marion, she wondered where she was, if she were safe. Adele chipped her but got no response.

Dan reached the dock and she could see that his leg had been hit; a patch of mangled flesh, bleeding. He tied off the ski and limped up to her and they held each other. Tears ran down his face onto hers.

"I'm sorry," he said. "I was useless up there. I couldn't get to her."

"You did what you could."

"Can I say the obvious?"

"What?" she asked.

"We're too old for this."

She held him for another moment, then they both let go. "Let's get that leg treated," she said.

He looked at her, shook his head. "Let's find Marion," he said. "This has to end." And he stumbled up the hill toward the main lodge.

DANIEL

====

Black Valley, Colorado, 2076

They found Marion lying unconscious in the foyer of the lodge, her clothing shredded, her face bleeding from a dozen wounds, one leg flung sideways at a horrifying angle. A wave blast had punctured one of the walls of the lodge and sent her flying through a wooden door and down a stairwell. They got her onto a blanket and when they carried her outside she seemed to weigh next to nothing. They considered airlifting her to Denver, but Dan didn't trust that she wouldn't be taken into custody if she left the valley.

The medical lodge was damaged like everything else, but they were treating the wounded, and the imaging machines still worked. Marion was badly concussed and had a broken femur—what one of the doctors, a former Cleveland Clinic orthopod, called an old woman's fracture, as though this had happened on a walk. She needed surgery to set it. Dan worried about stroke, bleeding on the brain, but they told him no, her brain was fine; it was her body that was in jeopardy. *Typical Marion*, he thought.

They got her on an IV drip and prepped her for surgery. Dan looked down on her bandaged, battered face, Adele on the other side of the bed holding her hand. Never in his life had he felt this particular mixture of anger and fear. Anger at those who had done this to his wife, to all of them, and fear that he might lose her, that they all might lose everything they'd just begun to build. The feds hadn't needed to use that kind of force on a community of centenarians, no matter how troublesome they'd become; most of them had trouble lifting the guns they'd been given, let alone firing them accurately. It was that feebleness that embarrassed and angered him most; despite all their resources and determination, in the end they were nothing but a bunch of old people who couldn't defend themselves. There had been relatively few deaths except in the initial skirmish at the front gate, which suggested that someone was exercising some restraint, but the property damage was in the millions of dollars, dozens of their people were severely injured, and many more might have been killed—including him—if not for whatever Zinnemann had managed to pull off in Washington. Adele tried to explain it to him, something about nanodrones holding the president hostage, but it sounded preposterous.

He got his leg bandaged, and the doctors herded him and Adele out of the clinic, which by then was full of the injured, those who could speak asking after Marion, demanding to know what they were going to do. He had no answers. They had no means to retaliate, no recourse to achieve what they might think of as justice. They would have to bargain, he saw, and use their humiliation as leverage, as the aged always have.

The period that followed was a strange hiatus. Marion's surgery went well, but she was terribly weak and slept most of the time. Dan visited her two or three times a day, but they never discussed what had happened or what needed to be done. There were no speeches at dinner, no LLF chipcasts. For the first time in more than a century, he slept alone.

LIFERS

Barb Beckwith's body was retrieved from Mt. Respect by a pair of reprogrammed construction drones. In total there were twenty-one dead, most from being crushed in collapsing structures. There was a memorial service in the grove of aspens next to the lodge. No one presided; people just got up and talked. It had been so long since any of them had attended a funeral that they didn't know quite how to go about it. There were a lot of multigenerational centenarian families in the valley by then, so there was mourning for a daughter struck down in her early 100s by parents in their 140s, eulogies by aged sons for aged mothers. There was talk of revenge and talk of forgiveness. Many of those who'd survived death and serious injury felt guilty, and they got up and talked about that too; whether they'd done enough, were brave enough, whether they were foolish and self-centered in thinking they had a right to live on when millennia of humans had been content with so much less. The bodies were burned together, in a giant pyre as far up Mt. Respect as they could manage. Its light was so bright it blotted out the Milky Way that night, and its smoke hid the moon the next day.

Zinnemann returned to a hero's welcome with his van full of nanobots and was shocked at the state of the valley. He apologized to Adele that he hadn't acted faster, that the coding had taken so long. After an all-valley dinner in the Mushroom, he showed a video that his swarm had taken of their little operation in Washington, which everyone found vastly entertaining.

Marion still lay in the medical lodge, not speaking much. Dan recalled that a wise man had once told him that, at some point or another, every married person fantasizes about the death of their spouse. Of course he'd protested that he'd never done such a thing, but he was lying because even then, when they were young, he'd imagined Marion's death a hundred times as a selfish thought experiment, to picture how life would be different if that one enormous fact at the center of his were erased. And later, when they were newly old, he imagined it to prepare himself for the possibility of outliving her. And still later, when they were truly aged, when she became the leader of a movement and the object of vitriol, he imagined it defensively, to steel himself against her life being taken rather than given up.

But what he could not have imagined was the desperation he felt now, the fear of the emptiness that the subtraction of just one life would hollow out in the world.

He and Adele took long hikes through the mountains, something he'd dreamed of doing with her but had never dared. She was strong and cheerful, always in the lead on the rocky ascents, her legs pumping, her auburn hair long gone to gray. He told her she didn't look a year over a hundred, but she did; they all did. They were awkward with each other, oddly formal, as though Marion were watching, even though she'd never shown the slightest concern about what Adele and he had meant to each other so long ago.

To avoid all that, they talked strategy. They'd been careful to keep news of the battle of Black Valley off the neural net, and the feds had done the same, but they had to assume that the feds couldn't let a personal assault on the president stand without some kind of serious reprisal, that it could come at any minute, and that the valley was far too depleted and demoralized to withstand another attack. They had to change the stubborn binary dynamic between Marion's LLF and Baldisseri's DLM.

"We need to get ahead of the next exchange somehow," Adele said. "Preempt it."

"You could reach out through Xerxes."

"And say what? We're sorry we nearly frightened your president to death?"

"Offer them something. Something they want."

"What they want is for us to shut up and disappear."

"It's more than that," he said. "They want us to die."

"That they know how to accomplish. They just can't take the heat for it."

"That's what I mean. They're not going to kill us outright; the blowback would be too much. And even if Black Valley and the LLF disappeared, there'd still be almost a hundred million triplers in the US, over a quarter of the total population. Too many to reduce their numbers by force, even if they wanted to. So they're limited to enforcing the sequestration protocols and pushing the Epilox campaign. Neither one is working the way they hoped."

Adele stopped, breathing hard, on an outcropping that overlooked the lake through the trees. From here he could see how the lake was just a membrane, how the flanks of the mountains on either side continued unbroken down beneath its surface and met somewhere in its depths.

"A frustrated politician is a dangerous politician," she murmured, hands on hips, looking down into the expanse of the valley. He tried to remember how politicians thought, how he'd helped them think all those years ago.

"We need to give them a win," he said. "Something that looks like defeat for us."

"Like what?"

He stood next to her and let his arm circle her waist, as though preventing her from getting too close to the edge of the rock. He tried various answers in his head, but couldn't think of another way to say it.

"A whole lot of deaths."

She looked at him, more aghast than confused, and he took his hand off her waist.

"I think you suggested this years ago."

"Yes. It was on one of your chip colloquies when we were just getting started. Marion wouldn't hear of it."

"Self-sacrifice, you said."

"In trade for something," he said. "For a greater good."

She started back down the mountain, and he followed.

"How many?" she asked over her shoulder as she walked, picking up speed as though to distance herself from the answer.

"Don't know. We'd have to ask Devon to look at the demographics again. A lot, though."

"Marion won't go along."

"She has to go along. She's got to be the messenger."

"To the president?"

"No," he said. "You or I can do that. To the people. To the Lifers."

She stopped and turned. "She'll never agree to do it, Dan. And besides, she can't do it in her current state, and we don't have time to wait until she recovers. If we don't come to them with something in the next day or so, I guarantee there'll be another escalation."

He looked at her carefully. "Do you know something?"

"Why do you always think I know something? No, I don't, Xerxes doesn't tell me anything anymore, but I know how these things go, and you do too. There's no time to convince Marion, and no time to wait for her to be on her feet."

"I think you underestimate my wife," he said. The words just came out that way, and he regretted it, the look on her face, as if she'd betrayed Marion again.

That night they released Marion from the clinic and moved her to the lodge at his request. The broken windows had been boarded over, the shattered glass swept up, and he set a table and lit some candles and made a simple meal of brook trout and rice and opened a bottle of Marion's favorite pinot. She was in a wheelchair and her head was still bandaged, but she looked better than she had in her sickbed and insisted that he help her put on a nice blouse for dinner. He'd been reminded how much more slowly the aged recover from injury, even with the best of care and the advantage of epigenetic reprogramming. Too fragile for crutches, she'd be in the wheelchair for months. He kissed her, made two vodka martinis, and they drank to Barb Beckwith, her ashes riding up in the sky over Black Valley.

He'd asked Adele to join them, but she'd refused, saying her presence would only complicate matters, and perhaps still smarting from his rebuke on the mountainside. He wanted her there not only for moral support, but because he believed that in most things Marion had come to trust Adele's instincts more than his own.

Over dinner and late into the night, he made his case, lawyer to lawyer. There was shock, and tears, there were recriminations to the effect that they should have been better prepared for the attack, better armed and trained, better able to wage what amounted to a war. All of which, he pointed out gently, was now beside the point. If not for Zinnemann's improbable intervention, the valley would surely have been overrun, many more killed, Marion and Dan and Adele and the other founders captured and hauled off to a sequestration facility, or worse. They were lucky to be alive and having this conversation, and they were unlikely to have another opportunity to make good on it. His idea required more research, and careful preparation, and good scripting, and an abundance of courage, and sheer good luck, but most of all it required that Marion Altman believe in it, and communicate that belief to the millions of people to whom she represented, in her own best words, a reason to live on.

And there came a moment in the early morning when the look in her eyes changed ever so slightly to one that he knew well but hadn't seen in many months. It was a look of resolve, yes, but also a look of great peace, as though some long internal battle had come to an end. It was the look he'd seen forty years earlier in a house in Florida, underwater now, when the woman he loved began to lead him and so many others on the long journey that had brought them to that moment.

He blew out the candles and carried her slight body up the stairs to their bed. A loon was warbling its song over the moon-silvered lake. As he lowered her head to the pillow she clung to his neck for a moment, touched his chin to center their eyes on one another.

"If I go along with this, there's one thing you'll have to understand," she said in the midnight contralto he knew so well. He smoothed her dry gray hair, waited. "I'll have to be an example. I'll have to go too."

He looked at her, the horror and the ineluctable logic of it clashing in his head. He kissed her hands, her neck. "We'll talk more tomorrow," he said.

Naturally there was debate among the members of the valley council as to who should try to engage the Baldisseri administration in what they styled as peace negotiations. Marion thought she should do it, since her last conversation with Claire Landess had likely been the trigger for the attack, and she wanted to make amends. But Dan wanted to keep her in reserve, as part of the reward for the feds' cooperation, or to imply that she was among the casualties, a potential martyr to the Lifer cause, the worst result from their perspective. And the fact that she and Claire were grandmother and granddaughter raised the same conflict of interest issues that the first conversation had, but with higher stakes.

Dan recused himself from consideration on the same grounds, and with Barb Beckwith gone, the only person of sufficient seniority and a background in government and the military was Adele. She objected too, but halfheartedly, suggesting that perhaps she should be part of a delegation. But no, they all agreed, this first feeler should be one-on-one, with the least amount of personal baggage possible. Adele was by far the best alternative.

Dan went over the demographics with Devon, even brought in Gustav Zinnemann to review the science behind Epilox, which of course he'd studied in great detail and thought an abomination. They asked him yet again if the government might soon devise an actual "cure" for Methuselah, an alternative to soliciting suicide, and he explained that, if one insisted on twisting the word that way, Epilox was in effect that "cure," as it operated by slicing up the very chromatin proteins that the Methuselah virus had installed in the human cell to reprogram its epigenome. Dan couldn't follow all that he said, but it made his plan seem less awful.

Finally there was the question of how to convey their offer to the feds. Conversation by chip seemed dangerous, since they had to assume that the eavesdropping technology that Zinnemann had deployed in the Washington operation wasn't unique, and they couldn't risk the initiative becoming public before it had been accepted, or ever becoming known if it were rejected. And they had no fallback.

Someone suggested an old-style land-line conference call, but that was laughed down. There were no landlines anymore. It had to be a physical meeting in neutral territory, but where? Big cities seemed logistically risky, complicated, and leak-prone. The coastal islands and towns where secret governmental meetings had often taken place in the past were all underwater now. They didn't have time to arrange a foreign venue.

They went around the table, and something odd happened. People kept bringing up the desert, somewhere in the desert, they'd been having dreams about the desert, a desert surrounded by mountains. Dan suggested Phoenix or Albuquerque, but again, too big, too hard to get in and out of unobserved. They came around to Adele.

"There's a series of uninhabited mesas near Los Alamos," she said simply. "I was there a long time ago, and I still know some people stationed in the old nuclear facility nearby. One of the mesas would work."

Dan wasn't sure he liked the symbolism, but they were tired, and it made as much sense as anything else they'd come up with. Adele would ask Claire to meet her in the desert.

ADELE

=====

Los Alamos, 2076

Their drones converged on a high mesa in the Tsankawi region, ancient home of the Pueblos, full of prehistoric petroglyphs and footpaths carved deep into the compressed volcanic ash. The place had been abandoned in the sixteenth century—*drought then, drought now*, thought Adele. She'd come here on her honeymoon over a century before, bruised her ankles climbing the narrow channels in the tuff, made love and slept on the ground under the stars. What she remembered most about those days was that she'd thought she had so little time; she'd been almost thirty, with so much that needed to be done.

She'd never returned to Tsankawi but for some reason had been dreaming of the place in the days since the attack. In the dream she was alone, as she hadn't been a century before, and she was frightened, as she never was in those days. But in the dream, as in her youth, she knew she was running out of time. And in the dream the dead emerged from the caves they had hewn into the cliffs half a millennium before and approached her and comforted her, saying that time was elastic, time was vast, time was always sufficient.

228

So she'd picked this place, and Claire had agreed to meet her here, and now, again, she was running out of time.

Their drones landed twenty yards apart. The two of them waited for the rotors to spin down and then climbed out of the machines into the moonlight. Warm summer night in the desert, coyotes howling in the distance, startled by their descent. Claire was carefully dressed in a black, trimly tailored suit with some kind of patriotic pin in the lapel; Adele less so, deliberately grungy, in jeans and hiking boots, a scarf to hide her corded neck, and a baseball cap with the Ultra-Elder logo on it. Claire's drone was military, much bigger than Adele's, with room for eight, and she invited Adele to join her inside so that they could sit facing each other. Adele thought this gesture boded well, though she also assumed it meant they'd be recorded. They ran through their obligatory "chips off" protocol, pinging each other and getting nothing back. In the dimness of the cabin Claire looked much older than the last time Adele had seen her, and she had to remind herself that Claire was still in her sixties, half Adele's age. Adele studied her in a glance or two, saw that the pin in her lapel was an American flag crossed with a tiny, diamond-crusted scythe.

She waited. Claire spoke first.

"Just so you know, I'm not at liberty to discuss the incident in Washington," she said.

"No problem, I have no intention of discussing it, or the incident in Black Valley for that matter."

"We assumed you wanted to bargain for clemency for the perpetrators."

"No, Claire. And I don't expect you to apologize for attacking private civilian property either, though that wouldn't be inappropriate."

She sighed, folded her hands in that priestly way of hers. "You should know, Adele, that I threatened to resign unless the administration let me talk to you and Marion before they sent the troops in. I tried to warn Marion, but she wouldn't listen. I even tried to chip you personally the night before the operation, so you'd be prepared and there'd be fewer casualties, but your buffers were up. I could have been jailed for that."

Adele flinched inwardly. She'd felt Claire's pings that night, but had thought it sent a stronger signal not to accept them. "What's done is done," she said.

"What, then?" Claire asked, her voice puffy with fatigue.

"Neither your constituency nor mine can afford to continue in this fashion. Too much time and blood is being wasted. It's a zero-sum game. Let's find a third path."

"Remind me; what are the first two?"

"Path One is where you succeed in taking down Marion Altman and the Lifer Liberation Front, and somehow as a result everyone's reluctance to commit suicide evaporates and you're able to reestablish civil order. Path Two is where Black Valley continues as a symbol of tripler resistance, fewer and fewer Lifers agree to die, and the LLF grows, gains more followers, and becomes a threat to what remains of the republic."

"I'm not sure I agree with either of those characterizations, but go on."

"A third path, Claire: the LLF agrees to help with what you call longevity management. We not only support the Epilox campaign, but we underwrite its results, not just now, but in the future. And in exchange, the ultra-elders, as they shall henceforth be called, are given a permanent home within the continental United States."

Claire threw her head back against the cabin seat and started to get out of the drone. "Please, not this again! This is what Marion wanted before, and you see where that led! It's a non-starter, Adele!"

Adele grabbed her arm. "Marion offered nothing in exchange before, nothing but her silence. We're offering much more, something you're failing to achieve on your own."

Claire hesitated, sat back down. An opening. "You said something about underwriting the results of the Epilox campaign," she said. "What does that mean?"

"That means, to be blunt, that we'd guarantee a stipulated death rate among American triplers. Something you could rely on. In exchange for the land."

"I still don't see—"

"Let me spell it out. We'd recruit people who'd agree to end their lives voluntarily, they'd register and commit to a specific date when they'd take Epilox, and they'd agree to take it under supervision, so there'd be none of the second thoughts and mistakes and forgetfulness that have undermined your current approach. And they'd represent a significant percentage of the current tripler population. But all this happens only if, as, and when the land is deeded to the Lifer Liberation Front."

Claire was openly staring now, all artifice gone. "What do you mean by 'significant percentage'?"

Adele couldn't help but smile just a bit. "How much land are we talking about?"

"I'm not talking about any land!" Claire cried.

"Claire, my dear," Adele said. "In the immortal words of Winston Churchill, we've established you're a whore, now we're just haggling over price."

Claire frowned at the reference, pulled away, stepped out onto the mesa. Adele followed, looked up at the blazing moon. "Beautiful night," she murmured idly, thinking of a night long ago, wishing she could forget for a moment why they were there.

Claire looked up with her. "I'm so very, very tired of all this," she said.

"I can imagine," Adele said. "This isn't really you, Claire. Never has been."

"We do what we can."

"Sometimes more than we should."

"Can we stop all the performative posturing? Just talk like two women for a minute?"

"Of course." Adele walked up close to her through the ancient ash. A breeze whispered through the oval openings of the caves that seemed too small to admit a person. But humans were different then.

Claire squared her shoulders. "If you'll be specific about this 'guarantee,' and what land you want in exchange for it, I'll take it back to my boss. But I need your word and the word of Marion Altman that this isn't some kind of elaborate hoax."

Adele's next words were well rehearsed, and she was careful with them. "I give you the word of Marion Altman, and you have mine as well. We want Arapaho National Forest in its entirety. . . ." Claire had heard this before too, and took in a breath to respond, but Adele wasn't done. "And we want Medicine Bow-Routt National Forest, which lies to the west of Arapaho. And we want a five-mile-wide corridor connecting the two, much of which, we realize, is currently in private hands and will require the exercise of eminent domain. And we want free passage to these areas for anyone duly certified by the LLF under a process that we will detail and administer for you. And we want twenty billion dollars in development loans with forty-year maturities, also to be administered by us."

She stopped, let it sink in. Claire's face was rigid with incredulity. "And what, precisely, do we get in exchange for all these things?" she asked.

"A minimum of a hundred million tripler deaths over five years. Almost a third of the current American tripler population. Then we'll renegotiate."

She stared. "A hundred million?" she repeated weakly.

"Over five years, yes. Fifteen percent of the entire US population."

"But how can you possibly be sure—how can we be sure—that you can deliver that many deaths? The Epilox program has managed barely ten million a year."

"Your incentives are wrong. Your messaging—what do you call it, your Mass Subliminal Guidance—is appealing to negative emotions. Loneliness, boredom, despair. When you appeal to patriotism"—Adele reached out impulsively and flicked the pin in Claire's lapel—"it's about a country that so disparages its elders that their death is all that has value. Why should they die for that? Our people, our followers, will die for a cause, for land, for a home where their ashes will fertilize the soil and where those who remain can live on forever. And we know we can make this offer because we've asked, Claire, and we already have more than twenty million volunteers."

This last was a bit of a bluff; all she really had were Devon's demographic projections of a random sample of Marion's followers, but they were confident of the numbers, and had to be. Claire was silent, open-mouthed. She turned and trudged back toward her drone.

"We'll need to see the data," she said over her shoulder. "Something more than conjecture."

"Of course."

"I'll be in touch," she said, and the dome of the drone closed over her and the props began to spin. Adele watched her go, the dust blinding her for a moment as the machine lifted off and accelerated eastward. She looked once more toward the ancient cave entrances in the cliff face, black holes like open mouths, the warm breeze singing through them. A smile came to her face. Then she climbed into the solitary seat in the drone and chipped the command for home.

TAUBIN

===========

Napa Valley, 2076

H e hated being old.

He thought he had some awful disease, but he was just old. Joyce and her crew ran some tests when he came back from St. Helena, and that's what they told him. Something about an alteration in the LMNA gene, causing it to produce progerin, which made cells break down more rapidly. Though only thirty-seven in chronological age, he was more like eighty biologically, and felt like he was a hundred. And he hated it.

He would make lists of the reasons he hated it, starting with the bad sleep, and the getting up two or three times in the middle of the night to pee. The way his joints ached in the morning, the time it took to get dressed, the fact that nothing fit because he'd lost so much weight, but not the good kind of weight loss, which he admitted he needed. This was loss of muscle mass, skinny crepey arms rattling around in his jump-suit sleeves. He'd done nothing wrong, nothing stupid, yet one day he'd woken up and his body didn't work the way it used to. He'd done nothing but the one thoroughly punishable thing: he'd gotten old.

Then he looked in the mirror, and it was worse. Wrinkles everywhere, dimples where they shouldn't be, thick lids hanging down over his eyes, bags under them, blotchy skin, big freckles where he'd never had them, chin soft and saggy, neck a bunch of cords, big Adam's apple bobbing above the fleshy hole where the top of his rib cage began. Ears strangely overgrown, lobes hanging down like rotten fruit and creased like an old shirt, nose puffed up and veined like some drunk's. And the hair, almost white, what little was left of it, like a supremely ironic halo around the top of his skull, made him seriously think about shaving it all off like Nolan, who was over twice his age, pushing a hundred, but now he looked like Nolan's slightly younger brother.

He had never looked good enough to be vain, so he'd never really cared how he looked. But what he really hated was how he felt all day, the momentary loss of balance climbing a stair, the random heart palpitations, the crappy vision, the crappier hearing, constant tinnitus like bad white noise, high frequencies increasingly lost, but at least he could adjust his chip for that. Dry, rough skin that bruised easily, like an overripe fruit.

All this in the course of a few months. He was in good company, of course. His net surveys continued to indicate that a high percentage of people with Methuselah under the age of sixty had developed a form of progeria similar to Werner syndrome, accelerating into old age at several times normal pace. Something like a quarter of the population. No deaths attributed to it yet, which he found comforting, but it was consistent with his original hypothesis that Methuselah was behind it, just as it was behind the crazy longevity of actual Lifers.

The only young-looking people he saw now were little kids and teenagers, and not many of them since the birth rate had cratered in response to the excess population. Apart from the children, almost everybody looked about the same age—that is, old—and it had become harder to make the kinds of assumptions about people's politics that were common when their age categories were clearer. It amused him now to hear those middle-aged anti-Lifers go on about the evils of extreme longevity when they looked like they should have long since popped some Epilox themselves.

His algorithm's feedback said that all this was making doublers more fearful of death, now that they could look it in the face in their morning mirror. Which made them more sympathetic to Lifers and others infected with Methuselah, and less likely to push their older relatives to take Epilox. Likewise, what with all the newly old, Lifers felt less like the outcasts that he'd helped make them into, and therefore less likely to take Epilox.

All of which was a further setback for his well-designed MSG campaign, and for the company in general. Nolan had called everyone back to the office to tell them that there was some new alliance developing between his daughter Claire's Department of Longevity Management and his mother Marion's Lifer Liberation Front, and that if that happened they'd have to ramp up production of Epilox much faster than the current poor uptake rates indicated, and Taubin would obviously have to adjust the MSG messaging, what the smartasses in the office had begun calling his "Deathwish Algorithm." The question was, how, exactly?

There was still no sign of his Little Stars algorithm; it was gone. He could reproduce it, but without knowing what happened with the first one, he didn't want to risk it. He didn't think it was a coincidence that it had disappeared just before the emergence of the progeria-inducing variant of Methuselah.

Nolan had called a big in-person meeting at the Albuquerque lab complex to discuss the latest from the DLM, and Taubin decided to go a day early so he could visit the grandparents in Santa Fe. He tried to prepare them for how he'd changed, but they said they didn't care, the body was just a shell, it was the inner Taubin they loved. Fact was, he was ashamed of how he looked, ashamed of being old, which made him understand how biased he'd been about old people all along like everyone else, treating them with superficial respect but all the while thinking they were ugly and not as smart as him, that he of all people would never become that way. And here he was, no more to blame for growing old than his grandparents, but he'd look in the mirror and feel as though he'd failed at something, that this must be some sort of punishment, and he realized that must be what they'd felt too, when they became old.

The taxi drone dropped him down through a hot blue sky in front of their hacienda and they came out squealing and threw their arms around him. Then Jack stepped back and grabbed his shoulders and looked him up and down, taking in the halo of gray hair, the shrunken posture.

"Wow," he said. "Just wow."

"I know, crazy, huh?" Taubin said.

"You're one of us!" Anna said as though he'd been admitted to an exclusive club. "Isn't it great?"

He shook his head. They looked the same as ever, meaning old, but oddly graceful, as though they were part of the landscape. Anna's white hair was braided like a Comanche queen, and Jack was wearing the top half of his cryosuit, like he had just come in from a round of golf. "I honestly don't know how you guys do it."

"Years of practice," she said as they stepped into the cool of the old adobe house.

"You still drink?" asked Jack.

"Of course, Grampa; I'm not *that* old." And Jack went to get him a gin and tonic and brought it to him in the shade of the *portal* and they all sat and looked at each other in amazement. It was 120 degrees and there was the smell of burning mesquite in the air. His grandparents were in their 130s and he was a third their age, but they looked like contemporaries. It was more than he could grasp.

"So I don't know how to do this," he said into his drink.

"Do what, Taub?" Anna asked.

"Be old. You guys sort of eased into it gradually, over decades, but for me it's been like a year and a half. Too many changes all at once."

"It is a bit of a shock to see you this way, I must admit," said Anna.

"But you sound the same," Jack offered, as though this was any comfort.

Anna stroked Taubin's hand. "You'll get used to it. We did. And it seemed to happen fast to us too."

"Not this fast," he said. "You've heard it's a variant of Methuselah, right?"

Jack rattled his drink impatiently. "I don't trust anything coming out of the government anymore. It keeps us young, but it makes you old? That doesn't make any sense to me."

"It keeps you from dying," Taubin corrected him. "It's not like it keeps you young."

"Okay, but why would it work that way, make everyone except kids the same age?"

He shrugged. "Methuselah works in part by suppressing certain proteins in the cells that signal how much food there is in the environment. Makes your body believe it's under constant dietary restriction, which promotes DNA repair, reduces inflammation, and cleans up cellular refuse. All of which promotes longevity. But that may come at the cost of rapid aging up to the point of early senescence, and after that the benefits offset the detriments. The problem with that theory is that you boomers stopped dying way before we grandkids started this super-fast aging. So it must be a later mutant strain that just comes with this unfortunate side effect."

Jack's bushy brows came together. "I don't follow any of that."

"I have my own theory," said Anna. "It's much simpler. The Bible says that in heaven we're ageless, which doesn't mean we're eternally young, but that age is a meaningless concept. So maybe all this"—she opened her arms in a circle that included him and Jack—"this sameness in our ages is God's way of preparing us for heaven."

The two men just looked at her, Jack with a slight smile on his face, as though he'd heard this before, Taubin in abject puzzlement, but thinking, *How could anyone ever not want* her *in the world?*

"I have to tell you two something," he heard himself saying. "You can't tell anyone else. I'd be fired, or arrested."

They drew back, afraid for him. "Oh Taub, what is it?" asked Anna.

He got up and made himself another drink, came back and faced them. Their eyes never left him. He realized they probably thought he'd killed someone or had become a heroin addict like his long-dead mother.

"When I was last here with you two," he said, "I had an idea. You might call it a vision. I saw that for humans to really get anywhere significant, to really progress, they needed to live even longer than you have. They needed to live hugely long lives because there's so much slippage, so much loss of momentum between the end of one life and the start of another. It's basic Newtonian mechanics, really." Here he saw he was losing them, and started over.

"Anyway, I had this vision, that for us to reach the stars like we always thought we would, we have to live a lot longer. Much longer. And I realized that this thing I'd been working on, which was a way to convince older people like you not to live longer, not to live anymore at all, was actually not promoting human evolution. So I secretly released an algorithm that would tell people like you that you deserved to live, that you should be happy to be alive, and that you were right to want to live on. And I think it worked."

They glanced at each other, back at him. "I don't remember getting this message," said Jack.

"No, you wouldn't have gotten it, it basically only works with people who have chip implants."

"Oh, we don't believe in those," said Anna somewhat sadly.

"I know, and besides, you didn't need it. You already had the message. You lived it."

"Well thank you, I guess," said Jack uncertainly. "So it worked?"

"I think so. I think it's part of the reason Lifers—sorry, why super-old people have been pushing back so hard on the sequestration protocols and why people like Marion Altman's liberation group have become so much more, uh, effective recently."

"Oh, we don't believe in her either," said Anna. "She's much too—what's the word?—strident. None of our friends like her."

"But she's effective," Taubin said. "She's cut some deal with the feds—well, now I'm saying too much, but there are going to be some changes because of her, and because the feds are so embarrassed that they couldn't take down her little commune out there in the mountains. And I think my algorithm had something to do with all that."

"So that's good?"

"It's good except it wasn't what I was supposed to be doing. Just the opposite, really. And now it's disappeared."

"Hmm?" they murmured in unison.

"The algorithm. I can't find it anymore."

"I didn't know you could lose an algorithm," said Anna, completely deadpan.

"Believe me, I didn't either. I still have the original code, of course, but the copy I released on the net isn't there anymore."

"That's awful," his grandmother said, always annoyed by injustice of any kind. "Did someone take it?"

"I think it more, like . . . dissolved. Or got absorbed into another program."

"Like a predator?"

He chuckled at this; they were so cute. "That's a good analogy—a predator program. It's a jungle out there."

"So, losing it, is that a problem?" asked Jack, practical as always.

"I'm not sure. It disappeared right around the time this new variant of Methuselah started up. The fast aging."

"Oh dear," said Anna. "You think there's a connection?"

"I'm afraid so. Though I really don't know whether to be afraid or happy."

"Well that's just life, Taub. That's just like life," Jack chuckled, getting up to fetch another drink, clearly done with this abstruse talk about algorithms.

Anna leaned in, grabbed Taubin's hand. "I must say, Taub. I like you old. You're so much more interesting. It's like we've rediscovered an old friend who's been missing."

They had a great dinner on the *portal* that night, pappardelle with prosciutto and red chiles that Jack whipped up, and a nice bottle of rioja. Just three old people under the stars, trading stories. But they had so many more of them than Taubin that it made him envious. They talked about his mother, things he'd never heard before, about the last years before she died. He told them about his girlfriends, and they were particularly curious about the green one, Myra. He wondered what it would be like to have so many stories, so much time to look back on. He hoped he'd have the chance to find out, like them, and that eventually they'd all have lived long enough that the difference in their ages wouldn't mean anything at all. They'd have a dinner like this under slightly different constellations, tell more stories, and they would have become the same age. Or, as Anna put it, age would have become a meaningless concept.

That, he thought, *would be heaven.*

The next day he took a drone over to the ABQ lab. Most of the company was gathered there in a big amphitheater under the desert floor, one of those in-person crowd meetings that never happened anymore. He assumed they'd called this one because the subject was so sensitive, and they didn't want it leaking out over the neural in some uncontrolled way. They were all wanded at the door to confirm their chips were off and they weren't bugged, and were told that nobody would be allowed in or out during the session.

As he entered the big domed room, he was worried about two things: being recognized, and not being recognized. The crowd was pretty evenly split between people who looked like he once did—typical middle-aged execs trying to act even younger than they were—and people who looked like he did now, which was to say, too old for their jobs. So now everyone knew who was infected with Methuselah and who wasn't just by looking around. There was some half-conscious self-segregation going on, the old youngsters and the new oldsters grouping together on opposite sides of the aisle. Joyce Icahn was up there on the dais looking her chronological age, and he was down in the masses looking like a Lifer who'd escaped from a sequestration facility. He saw the old lawyer from the first meeting he'd attended here and took a seat between him and a bright yellow young person of indeterminate gender in a lab coat. The lawyer didn't recognize him, of course, since he looked even older than the guy did, and he wasn't about to clarify things.

Nolan appeared on the stage in his white blazer/black shirt combo, pale as a sheet, and chatted with Joyce and the other company bigwigs. He squirmed at the thought that he should be up there too. The disappointing results of the Sweet Chariot campaign weren't his fault, or so he told himself, but MSG just didn't rate as a headliner corporate function anymore. His guess was that they were moving on to less subtle methods, and he couldn't have contributed anything to that discussion. He also noticed that everyone on the dais looked their chronological age, which he doubted was a coincidence.

Nolan took the podium, and the place fell instantly silent. *Big show of respect*, he thought. *Either that or sheer apprehension.*

"Fellow employees of Accretex," his boss began. He always did that, Taubin thought, the fake humility, like he was just another employee. "I've asked you here today to hear about an exciting development in the Epilox program, which is so important to the overall success of our company. As you know, it's been a struggle so far, with uptake and comps lagging our original expectations and those of the federal government."

Taubin cringed and glanced around to see if anyone was staring at him accusatorily, but no, they were all riveted on their CEO.

"But as some of you may have heard, things are about to change, and for the better. We're about to get a boost from an unexpected source, and I've invited a very special guest here to tell us about it. But before I introduce her, our lawyers have asked that I remind you that everything said in this session is highly confidential, and any breach of the NDA that each of you has signed will be considered not only cause for terminating your employment, but a federal offense. So, chips off and lips zipped!"

He evidently thought this was a laugh line, but it only got an uneasy titter from the normatively aged segment of the crowd. Then the grin on his face faded.

"I'm sure you'll all agree that our relationship with the Baldisseri administration is our most important asset, and delivering on our contract with the federal government is our highest corporate priority. What we've accomplished in the three years since the start of the Epilox campaign is remarkable. Over fifty million completions-of-treatment in the US alone, over three hundred million worldwide, with an efficacy rate of near ninety-eight percent. At the state and local level, improved STD tracking and corporeal disposal techniques are finally beginning to keep pace with the results of that success.

"But it isn't enough. The strains on the social fabric of America caused by excess longevity—poverty, homelessness, intergenerational divisiveness, political polarization, perpetual medical triage, and on and on—are so great that supplemental solutions are needed. And the new threat of accelerated aging that we see across the world and in this very room only adds urgency to the crisis.

"The mission we've undertaken has required unorthodox techniques, and we've succeeded thus far by thinking outside the box. We're called upon to do that again. We need, in the old phrase, to keep our friends close and our enemies closer. Here to explain what I mean, and to describe the next phase of our great enterprise, is our very own secretary for longevity management, Claire Landess."

There was a smattering of surprised applause, some general murmuring. No mention, of course, that this was his daughter he was introducing, no need to say what Taubin and the rest of them assumed, that she had her job and they had their federal contract because the principals were related to each other. She barely glanced at her father as she strode onstage, looking sort of disheveled, as though she'd been caught in some prop backwash while getting off a drone. Taubin noticed that she looked older in person than she had the last time he'd seen one of her chipcasts. She smoothed her hair and leaned against the podium, scanned the age-motley crowd with what looked like mild surprise.

"Thank you, Nolan," she said. Some in the crowd couldn't suppress a snicker. *Not "Dad"?* Taubin thought. "And thanks to all of you for all you do every day to make the work of my department possible. Literally possible. For without the Epilox program, I'm not sure where we'd be at this moment in our country's history. Our desperate times have called for desperate measures, and you've been instrumental in implementing them.

"But we must do better, and I believe we can. So far, our administration's response to the longevity crisis has taken two principal forms: the so-called sequestration protocols that have provided food, shelter, and medical attention to tens of millions of the ultra-elderly; and the Epilox program, once codenamed 'Sweet Chariot,' that has offered to millions more a safe, painless, effective way out of a dead-end existence."

For some reason Taubin's blood pressure jumped at this. He'd heard it a million times before, had written an algorithm to make people think they indeed had a dead-end existence, but all he could think of when she said it was Jack and Anna and their long life together, which didn't seem so dead-end at all. In fact, it seemed a lot more open-ended than the existence he was pursuing in that underground room.

She paused to gauge how her bluntness was going over with this crowd, which she must have thought would tolerate less nuance than most. "But the negative inducement of escape from the perils of extreme age has its limits, as indicated by the program's falling uptake and completion rate numbers. We've probably culled all the low-hanging fruit, so to speak, and from here on out the going will be slower, unless we can provide a new reason for individual participation beyond the inherent benefit of dying a decent death. We think we've found that reason, and it comes down to group affiliation and identification with a cause."

Taubin thought, *Here it comes.*

"As you all know, throughout the last many years of this struggle, the so-called Lifer Liberation Front has been an impediment to our progress. It has sought to persuade the ultra-aged that death is evil and extreme longevity is an inherent good, to be pursued no matter what the cost to the elderly individual or to society at large. It has vocally opposed the efforts of our administration to offset those costs with practical mitigation policies. And perhaps most troubling, it has held out the rosy image of a utopian, separatist commune as an alternative to the hardships that everyday triplers must endure. After many efforts to negotiate with the leaders of this movement, we had come to the conclusion that no compromise with them was possible."

Yeah, and you should know, Claire, he thought, heart rate rising, *since one of them is your grandmother.*

"But recently we achieved a breakthrough with the LLF whereby, in exchange for some federal assets, they will guarantee a specified number of Epilox customers from among their followers over a specified number of years. Those numbers are still classified, but suffice it to say that it will mean roughly a doubling of uptake in the near term, and we'll be looking to your company to meet that increased demand."

There was a gasp from those who hadn't heard this already, some involuntary cheers from the ones who knew what this would mean for their bonuses.

Claire looked ready to be done with this little chore. "To ensure that the LLF meets its side of the bargain, we've extracted a commitment from its leadership that they will personally back the effort to recruit new Epilox subjects with the explicit rationale of loyalty to the Lifer cause, effectively turning their messaging about our program on its head and aligning their goals with ours. This is an amazing achievement of which we all can be proud."

It was an obvious applause cue, but before it could start, Taubin was on his feet with his hand in the air. He knew well that impulsivity was one of the symptoms of his particular brand of neurodivergence, and he thought he'd left it far behind in his climb up the corporate ladder, but here it was, rearing up like a familiar and not very well trained dog. He was waving at the dais, the crowd began muttering, and Claire Landess stopped and turned to Nolan to see what she should do.

"May I ask a question, please?" Taubin heard himself saying. "You said something about federal assets being turned over to the LLF? What are those, exactly?"

Nolan was on his feet, hustled up to the podium and grabbed the mic. "Sir, we're not having a Q&A this session, so if you'll just sit down and let the secretary continue. . . ."

It dawned on Taubin that, after all those years of his slaving away for him, Nolan didn't recognize him. Or did, but was pretending he didn't. Because Taubin was old.

"That information is classified at this point," Claire said. "But we'll be making an announcement about it in the next few weeks."

"Land!" he yelled, and it came out like a bark. Security guards were running down the aisles toward his row. "Land for the Lifers, right? Their own country!" The guards grabbed him by the arms and started dragging him toward the exit. The place was in an uproar. Some were screaming to get the crazy old man out, others wanted to know the answer. He wasn't as strong as he used to be, knew he had no chance against the guards, so he let them take him, but he kept it up as he stumbled behind them, words coming out of some part of him he didn't know was there. "A country for the Lifers! Where no one has to die!"

And in that moment he felt something unfamiliar, something like pride.

MARION

Black Valley, Colorado, 2078

Early spring in the Rockies, the dandelions and pasqueflowers and balsamroot all in bloom, late snows retreating up the slopes of the valley. Prettiest time of year in Black Valley, Marion always thought.

There was always a sense of optimism in this season in the valley, but this year it seemed to her more pronounced because of the recent agreement with Claire and the feds. Lots of parties in the Mushroom, lots of bed-hopping in the lodges. Congress was about to act on a package of legislation giving them the land they'd demanded and rescinding certain elements of the sequestration protocols so that specified categories of Lifers could migrate there unimpeded. They'd settled on a sequencing that would first admit the oldest and the geographically closest to the New Land, as they'd initially called it, and over time bring in the less aged—Marion hated the word "younger"—and more distant populations of triplers, immigration waves rippling out in space and down in age until they were at capacity. What exactly constituted "capacity" was of course the subject of much debate both internally and with the DLM, but they ended up at ten million, only about the same number as were dying in a single year in the US under the Epilox program. But it was a start, and it had been agreed that in five years they would renegotiate, assuming Marion and her Lifers held up their end of the bargain.

The combination of the Arapahoe and Medicine Bow-Routt National Forests, along with the corridor connecting them, amounted to around five thousand square miles of land, some of it topographically unbuildable, so population density at capacity would be north of two thousand persons per square mile—almost double that of the state of Israel, to which Marion constantly referred for demographic comparisons. They needed to house and feed those people, so there would be a special twenty-billion-dollar treasury note issuance to fund a massive modular housing program that would capitalize on the robotic construction and farming techniques that they'd learned in building out Black Valley. But it was going to be a stretch, and it had to be done fast. Zinnemann had all sorts of new ideas about this, some involving underground silos and lighter-than-air platforms that could be moved from place to place like giant dirigibles. There were the predictable objections raised from several quarters, including from within their own ranks, to what some called the wholesale desecration of a pristine wilderness, but no one could suggest any plausible alternative sites that wouldn't involve carving up several states or invading Mexico. The continental US was running out of room. And besides, Marion argued, Zinnemann's floating platforms could be flown in, and wouldn't desecrate anything.

Like any other sovereign state, the new land needed a new name, the way the half-joking "Lifer Liberation Front" had morphed into the sober-sounding "Next Hundred," so Marion decided to solicit ideas from ultra-elders around the world. The resulting flood of suggestions ranged from the obvious ("Phoenix" was taken, so "New Phoenix" got a lot of votes, along with "New California" and "West Colorado") to the overtly boomer-nostalgic ("Aquarius" and "Strawberry Fields") to the rather starkly in-your-face triumphal ("Victory," "Freedom," "Forever," and even "Heaven"). "Zion," while appealing, had too many complicated associations, including cinematic ones. Constellations came up a lot, with Cassiopeia for some reason heading that list, though even within the leadership counsel there was no agreement on how to pronounce it.

But in the end it was the Bible, and specifically the Old Testament's genealogy of absurdly long-lived antediluvian patriarchs, that proved the most fertile resource. The longest-lived of those, Methuselah himself, was too firmly associated with the viral condition that had brought them to this pass, but others were offered up by the followers, and one in particular rose quickly in the iterative polls. Enoch, called the scribe of judgment, said to have lived 365 years, was the great-grandfather of Noah and the *father* of Methuselah. And perhaps most pertinently, he never really died, but was simply "taken by God" while out on a walk with Him, "translated that he should not see death," in the words of the Book of Hebrews. Wise, just, and deathless—a fitting figure, Marion thought, after which to name a country of supercentenarians. It was agreed; Enoch it would be.

Dan led a legal task force composed of what Marion thought were some of the oldest and smartest lawyers on the planet, that had to negotiate and draft the documentation that would actually transfer ownership of the land to the LLF, which wasn't even a legal entity. They duly incorporated it in the State of Delaware, renamed it "Next Hundred Corporation," and issued stock to all of the current residents of Black Valley on a pro rata basis, with controlling interest reserved to a board of directors that included Marion, Dan, Adele, Zinnemann, Devon, and a half dozen others drawn from a variety of disciplines. The corporation would be the trustee of a trust to which the United States would transfer title to the new land, with an immediate reversion of the land to federal control and acceleration of the treasury notes upon the earlier of (a) failure of the Epilox program to register at least twenty million confirmed "completions"—the government's euphemism for suicides—over each of the following five calendar years; and (b) January 1, 2200. They thought that was plenty of time.

All that was the easy part, Marion knew. The hard part was embedded in that clause "(a)"—the Lifers' end of the bargain. President Baldisseri did a grandiose chipcast announcing the government's generous "gift" of land to the LLF, casting herself as a great peacemaker and friend of the ultra-aged, and promising that Marion Altman herself would soon make her own announcement confirming the pact and adding her own important caveats and commentary.

She was still in her wheelchair, but Dan took her down to the lake's edge every day and they sat and talked about what she should say, how she should say it. Guidelines had been established with the feds as to what could and couldn't be said, with the explicit understanding that if Marion violated them, the deal would be off. Dan offered her some drafts but she waved them away; that wasn't how she worked. She composed in her head and the result, for better or worse, would be her own unique blend of preparedness and spontaneity. But she was still frail, and this would be the most important speech of her long career. It would be chipcast not only over the closed neural net that linked her followers, but reamplified across the nets that the feds maintained and the many more that they had access to. It would be almost like the old internet or, before that, broadcast television, when everything stopped and everyone watched when JFK was buried or Armstrong walked on the moon.

Absurd though it seemed, her words had become that important.

DANIEL

Black Valley, Colorado, 2078

Dan worried about what Marion had said that night after the attack, about her being an example, about how she would have to go too. They'd never discussed what she meant, though of course he knew. She meant to demonstrate what self-sacrifice looked like. She would ask nothing of her followers that she didn't expect of herself. She would be the embodiment of the peace and purposefulness that she would be urging others to show. She would personify another great movement, just as she had personified what they'd done in Black Valley.

She meant, in short, to kill herself, to be the first in a long tally of deaths that would buy the rest of them a new home. He knew this. His only mistake was in thinking that he had time to talk her out of it.

In the end her speech was short. Barely a speech at all. Six o'clock Mountain Time, a beautiful, windless, clear evening in the valley, all of them gathered in the Mushroom to receive the chipcast together. Marion had insisted on being alone in the studio up on the mountainside, which made Dan suspect that she might do something to herself on-air, but she promised him that she would join him for a celebratory drink immediately after the 'cast, and in their long marriage she had never lied to him.

Dan waited with the crowd in the big dining hall, most of them dressed in the white that Marion favored, many of them joining hands, bowing their heads as people used to do in prayer, now just to receive what was about to flow through the electronics in their skulls. Someone dimmed the lights, as before a performance, or at the Tenebrae services in the churches of their youth. They grew quiet. And then, on the hour, her face filled their heads in that strange chip-mix of visuals and impressions, like memory or a shared dream. There was the sense of millions upon millions also present, waiting, watching. And then her voice, sound and text intertwined, moving like a current through water.

Friends, loved ones, fellow travelers on this unexpectedly long journey. Thank you for giving me a few minutes of your precious time tonight. I'll be brief and direct, for time is, in the end, all any of us has.

As you recently heard from President Baldisseri, the federal government has agreed to set aside approximately five thousand square miles of land in Colorado and Wyoming for the purpose of establishing a safe haven for ultra-elders. It will be fully independent, exempt from all sequestration protocols and all previously imposed civil rights phase-outs, meaning full American citizenship will again prevail for ultra-elders in this new land, which will be called Enoch, after the Old Testament figure who never died. It will be administered by an Ultra-Elder Collective headed by a commission of our longest-living citizens, including me.

The New Land will receive as many supercentenarians as we can accommodate, starting with the very longest-lived who are in closest proximity to its borders. Immigration will be synchronized with the availability of housing and other requirements of self-sufficiency, implementation of which is already underway. Detailed information on how to apply for residency accompanies this chipcast.

LIFERS

Life in this new land will not be easy, especially at first. We will again become pioneers in a challenging physical terrain just as we have been pioneers in time, inhabiting uncharted decades in unfamiliar bodies. We will need all the patience we've acquired in our long time on earth, all the forgiveness, all the fortitude. And we will need one thing more, something I won't try to put into poetic words: a majority of us must sacrifice an even longer life to allow a minority of us to live on in the way we all deserve.

Because, dear friends, we are buying this land and this way of life with the promise that many millions of us will yield up our indefinite longevity—yield up our lives—in exchange for it. Many of you may find this proposition obscene; I certainly did when it was first proposed. But I am persuaded that my life, and the lives of many of you, have already been well lived, and in many cases well lived twice over, and that while more of the same is of course desirable, and our right as human beings, it isn't as necessary to me, nor, I hope, to many of you, as the creation of a sanctuary for our kind, a place that will become a lasting symbol of the dignity and respect that ultra-elders deserve.

So I am resolved to a course of joyful self-sacrifice, and I ask those of you who believe in the promise of the New Land to join me.

I hold here in my fingers a small pill. You know it. It is an Epilox pill. Specifically, it is the seventh pill in the seven-day dosage that will result in my death one year from today. I swallow it now, not only willingly, but joyfully, and in gratitude to all those who have made our cause possible, and to those who will follow me in this way to secure its survival into a future we can only guess.

The pill disappeared into her mouth, a clear glass was raised, and she drank from it. Dan bolted up, ran for the door.

We have a year, dear friends, and in that year, I promise you, we will all stand together in the New Land, and when that year is over we will lie together, commingled in its earth, forever.

The chipcast ended, the sounds and images of her ended, there were mingled cries of shock and triumph from the crowded hall behind him, and he was running up the steep stone path toward the studio, legs weak beneath him, lungs heaving in the thin air, tears blinding his steps; higher, higher, almost there.

But he was already too late.

She hadn't lied. She did come down to the Mushroom for a celebratory drink after the chipcast, after he found her at the door of the studio, smiling at him as he stood there panting, folded over, hands on his knees.

"Tell me you didn't really. Tell me that was just for show," he begged.

In reply she leaned forward from her wheelchair and raised his chin in her hand and kissed him.

"Let's get you down to the clinic," he pleaded. "We can pump it out."

"I need you to be strong for me, Dan." Her face was remarkably composed, the deep fissures of their shared age framing her eyes and mouth like elaborate carvings.

"Where did you get the pills?" he asked, as though that mattered, as though it would make any difference.

"Don't you remember? Nolan sent them to me years ago, after I saw him at Claire's speech in New York. You put them in a drawer and forgot about them."

"I didn't forget about them. I thought about them every day."

"Me too," she said. He knelt beside her and they held each other for a while. "You were right, you know," she murmured in his ear, holding him close so he couldn't look at her.

"About what?" He was weeping again.

"About self-sacrifice for a greater cause. About two lifetimes being enough."

"I didn't know what I was saying. It's not nearly enough." And they were still for a while.

His head was buzzing, and he slowly realized it was his chip, aflame with what was happening on the net, millions of pings from people as distressed as he was, people who were thrilled and proud, people who wanted to volunteer for Epilox, to be part of the new land called Enoch. He shut the thing off.

Later he carried her down the long path to the Mushroom, where the crowd in its thousands waited outside in the dusk, lining the shore of the lake. They were strangely, almost reverently silent as he lowered her into a wheelchair. But she was smiling and radiant, and soon they clustered around, those who were nearest, like Adele, stroking her face and hugging her, those farther back holding hands and touching the shoulders of those in front, till they seemed to Dan to be one big network of ancient flesh, beautiful and serene.

Marion stood up out of her chair, raised her voice. "We all have a lot of work to do," she said, and there was a general murmur of assent.

"But first," she said, "I'd really like a vodka martini."

A burst of laughter, relaxation, people running for the bar. Dan believed that every last one of them had a vodka martini that night.

His first instinct, of course, was to catch up with her, to take the seven doses of Epilox over the very next week and be only one week behind her in their final year. He'd be there with her for her last breath and then he'd only have to suffer one additional week without her. But she wouldn't hear of it, made him promise not to, called on his sense of duty to the Next Hundred and to Enoch. And when he was honest with himself, he didn't want to. Death terrified him as much as ever, maybe more so now that it was living with him, sleeping next to him in her bones.

She continued as though nothing had happened, working in the gardens, doing chipcasts promoting Enoch, which she persisted in calling the New Land. She went on dozens of drone overflights of the former Arapahoe and Medicine Bow-Routt National Forests, surveying the most habitable tracts, doing CAD mockups of the land they had to clear and the habitations they had to build. It was a heady time, especially once the federal money began to flow in, and they were able to hire a small army of architects and terraforming and community design experts. They envisioned a network of villages and hydroponic farms strewn over the land in the most topologically compliant and least-invasive arrangement as could be configured by the computer models. No roads would be needed to connect them, as surface vehicular movement would be unnecessary within villages and travel between them would be handled by a dispersed fleet of solar airdrones. Temperatures in the area, once frigid in the winters, were mild nearly all year round now, so all that was needed in the way of climate control was an occasional burst of geothermal heat pumped up from the rocks below. Like Black Valley, bed-and-bath living modules would be clustered around communal cooking, dining, and social facilities. Structures would be assembled off-site—or out-of-country, as they learned to say—flown in by dirigible, and either sunk in the earth or floated above it on Zinnemann's platforms by robot construction drones, which were by far the most numerous and expensive element of the whole project. But there was no way they could do without them, since physical labor was beyond most of them and to hire and transport the number of humans needed to construct this near-instant conurbation would be prohibitive.

It turned out that their initial estimate of ten million potential inhabitants had been too conservative, and that with some aggressive engineering and a bit more structure height and Z-platform area they could probably accommodate closer to thirteen million. More than the state of Israel, Marion pointed out. Their goal was to matriculate them within the next three to four years—ridiculously ambitious, but not impossible given that the financing was in place and it was "only" a matter of logistics. And they'd become very good at logistics.

Within a week of Marion's announcement, they had created an "immigration" department of about a hundred people with backgrounds in the kind of sorting of humans that governments and educational institutions had always done. It was a wildly scaled-up version of the admissions committee Dan had sat on at Black Valley, but with simpler criteria: age and location. Yes, they would filter for baseline cultural and racial diversity, and yes, in exchange for admission the applicants had to turn over all their assets to the Next Hundred Trust in order to fund the repayment of the government loans. But Marion was adamant that they eliminate exceptional expertise and financial self-sufficiency as requirements for admission, since the whole point of this project was to alleviate, at least in some small measure, the concentrations of Lifer poverty that were afflicting the cities in particular. Refugees from those benighted places, no matter how otherwise competent, would be by definition poor, having long outlived their financial resources and having no means in that old world to rebuild them. Enoch would give them space and time, the opportunity to reeducate, a roof over their heads and food on a communal table. All they had to be was old, mobile, and sane.

And they had to act fast, as they intended to admit on a fairly ruthless first-come, first-served basis. The only development of this period that surprised Dan more than the speed with which the Enoch project came together was the impact that Marion's speech had on the tripler population, which quickly fell into two broad camps, one turning to Epilox in record numbers as though it were a sacrament, and one composed of those who want nothing more than to "live on" in the new land. To his astonishment, they were roughly equal, so that the more stringently supervised "uptake" of Epilox doubled overnight to almost fifty thousand a day, and within a month there were twenty million applications for residency in Enoch.

Dan recalled that at the closing of her speech, Marion had alluded to an additional inducement for others to join her in her self-sacrifice. New Epilox registrants were guaranteed passage to Enoch to stand on its soil at least once before they died, and were further assured that when they died their ashes would be scattered there, as she had also promised. They had to put some sort of limit on that, and finally Dan persuaded the counsel to announce that anyone who finished their dosage before the first anniversary of Marion's speech—before she died, in other words—would be entitled to "the passage and the sowing," as it was to be called. Of these, they'd projected that around four million people would actually make the trip to Enoch in that first year, but it turned out to be double that. It was still wild land, mountains running down to lakes, swards of grassland in the valleys, deep stands of aspen, fir, and spruce on the sky-scratching slopes, but they built a reception facility near Steamboat Springs, with a giant interactive holographic display that would allow the pilgrims to experience what living in the new land would eventually be like, what they'd bought with their deaths. There was an amphitheater where Marion could address a few thousand of them at a time, commiserate in their shared and now certain mortality, thank them for what they'd done for others, congratulate them on lives well lived, well ended. It was, Dan admitted to himself, a beautiful thing, though each of these was, for him, heartbreaking, like attending another funeral for his wife, hearing another eulogy for her, until there was nothing left for him to say or feel.

Even Baldisseri and Claire made the pilgrimage, just for political show, he knew, but the gesture was expected to have a further positive impact on Epilox uptake rates. The president gave a predictable speech in the amphitheater to a crowd of scheduled-to-die triplers about what fine patriots they were, how much what remained of the United States appreciated their putting community before self, faith before fear—the sort of twaddle Dan might have written for presidents long before. Claire stood by Marion's side throughout, but said not a word, which Dan found interesting. Maybe, he thought ruefully, the reality of her grandmother's impending death had brought home the consequences of her lifetime of abstract philosophizing about it.

Baldisseri and her coterie flew back to Washington immediately following the ceremony, but Claire lingered to inspect the new reception hall, and Dan invited her back to Black Valley to visit her grandmother, now that they were all allies. He was shocked at how old she looked, thinking that either her job was taking a bizarre toll, or something was amiss.

"Aren't you still in your sixties?" he asked her on the flight to the valley.

"Sixty-nine," she responded sheepishly. "Why?"

"You look much older. And I should know."

"I'm tired. This has been a strain."

"No, it's more than that. You look twenty years older than when we last saw you, what, four years ago. Have you been tested recently?"

"For Methuselah? When I joined the administration, but not since then."

"I presume the administration accepts the science of the new strain that accelerates aging?"

"Not publicly, but it's part of the reason we had to come to terms with the LLF—sorry, the Next Hundred.

It's compounding the social problem of actual chronological triplers with de facto ones. Plus it changed the doublers' views about aging almost overnight."

"I think you have it," he said.

She looked like he'd called her a traitor. "How could I? The same mutation made it non-contagious."

"Maybe you caught it before it mutated."

"But the people I work with are screened all the time."

"How about the people you don't work with?" he asked. "Like us. You sat in a small room with Marion, Adele, and me, three Lifers, for several hours that night four years ago."

"Granddad, just stop. That was 2072, and by then Methuselah wasn't contagious anymore. Otherwise I wouldn't have met with you in person."

"Claire, I'm not accusing you of anything. But we'd been living in near-total isolation in Black Valley for years by the time you came that night. We may not have developed the non-contagious variant till much later. So you may have contracted it from us. And apart from this rapid aging you seem to be going through, and maybe getting yourself thrown out of the Baldisseri administration, this is a good thing, right? You can grow old with us!"

She didn't seem at all convinced. But he thought he saw the hint of a smile cross her beautiful, aged face.

"One other thing," he said to her.

"What, Granddad?"

"Don't call me 'Granddad.' We're too old for that. Call me Dan."

She did smile then, and kissed him on the cheek.

That night the three of them had dinner together in the lodge by the lake. Marion made Claire promise to get tested for Methuselah, if only to be sure there was nothing else wrong with her, and they reminisced about her childhood, the years Claire had spent with them after her parents divorced. They even managed a laugh or two at the follies of the attack on Black Valley and Zinnemann's counterattack in DC. But mostly Dan sat quietly, letting them talk, basking in the ageless grace of these two women who, he suddenly realized, were so very much alike, more so now that Claire looked her grandmother's age.

In the morning she was gone.

Much as Marion tried to rally him, he was in a state of continual anticipatory grief, alternating between rage at her for what she'd done to him, and terror at the prospect of living on without the one person who'd been beside him for over a century. He realized that he'd simply forgotten what it was like to be a solitary being and didn't think he could relearn it.

It was Adele who reminded him that his situation was hardly unique, that long before Epilox, ever since medicine had been able to predict the lethality of various diseases, people had been living for months or years with the certain knowledge that those closest to them were soon to die. It turned out there were a lot of those people in Black Valley, parents who had lost children to leukemia a century before, husbands and wives who had lost spouses to inoperable brain cancer, daughters and sons who had watched their parents irrevocably disappear into the death-in-life of Alzheimer's. Some reached out to him, Adele found others, and they gathered in little groups in the stand of aspens next to the lodge, on split-log benches under the white boughs that were like the soaring columns in a Gothic cathedral, all of them well into their second hundred years on earth, and talked about the futility of anger in the face of inevitability, the elusive wisdom of acceptance, strategies for being present in each moment with the departing so as to honor their remaining days, fill the bank of memory against the impoverishment to come and, not incidentally, armor themselves against future self-accusations that they hadn't loved them enough. None of it made him less fearful, but it made him feel less alone.

ADELE

===

Black Valley, Colorado, 2078

She was 130 years old and still living in Black Valley, not sure if she would ever move to Enoch. Most of the valley population had decamped to the new land, as they were some of the eldest and most geographically proximal candidates for Enochan citizenship. But until Marion and Dan moved there, she felt her place was in the valley with them. Their view was that no leader of Black Valley should be seen to take up a residency slot in Enoch when there were so many millions of triplers longing to go there and not enough housing to accommodate them. Adele agreed, but more than that simply wanted to be with the two people on earth she felt closest to.

She, like everyone, was counting the days of Marion's last year, but Dan was the one who made a ritual of it, rising long before Marion did to meditate in the aspen grove, interrogating his wife about how she wanted to spend her day, making endless suggestions for travel or entertainment or visits from old friends, none of which interested her in the least. Her approach to the end of her life was exactly what Adele hoped hers would be—to live each day not as though it were one's last, but as though it were a fragment of a grander composition that required every note to be in its proper place and that could only be fully appreciated after the last chord had been played.

There was the question, too, of why more of the valley residents, particularly those like herself in leadership positions, didn't follow Marion's lead and take Epilox, or for that matter simply jump off a cliff, as some actually had, to help fill the death quotas that would sustain Enoch and fulfill the deal they'd struck with Baldisseri. Adele's personal answers were many and complicated. She saw herself as a guardian of that pact, surety of its fulfillment, and rationalized that her absence, particularly in these crucial early years, could jeopardize the plans they'd so carefully laid. She saw herself as a part of a movement whose momentum required living leadership as well as Marion's martyrdom and that of the millions who were emulating her.

But she also knew that these were grand rationalizations of a baser, less altruistic instinct. Dan sometimes confided to her that he was more afraid of death than ever, and when she thought about it, she felt the same. She wanted to live on as she'd become so accustomed to doing, as a century and a half of living had habituated her. To her surprise, the extra years had not made her bored or dulled her taste for sensate experience or made her careless of the future. To the contrary, she'd become greedier for life, wanted to see what would happen, what she'd wrought. The supposed consolations of mortality turned out to be just as empty as when she'd tried to internalize them a century before. It turned out not to be true, for instance, that vastly prolonged life had cut her off, in time and memory, from her former self, which would have meant at least a figurative kind of death. She had no trouble identifying with the self she'd been a century before, and at the same time adapting to a world increasingly unlike the one she'd inhabited in those first hundred years. In the next hundred, it turned out, she was capable of both nostalgia and hope at the same time.

LIFERS

And of course, she admitted to herself, she had another very personal reason to live on. For almost a century, she'd kept a terrible secret from the man she loved, and she realized that when his wife died, she would finally be able tell him— would *have* to tell him—about their daughter, the infant she'd given up in the wake of their affair, back when there was no Methuselah, no hope of either of them living long enough to find her again. Barb Beckwith had found her, begged Adele to contact her, but she'd stifled the impulse out of respect for her daughter's independent life, and out of respect for Dan and Marion's marriage, which Dan had chosen over her and which the two of them had turned into a partnership that she admired and, in time, envied. She had no right to tell him, not after all that had happened. But she felt she would have a duty to do so when, in less than a year, his marriage ended in a way that none of them could have imagined.

The three of them flew together to Enoch for the weekly Passage and Sowing ceremony, where Marion presided over the welcoming of a mixed crowd of scheduled-to-die pilgrims and newly-admitted residents, and the scattering of the Lifer ashes that had been shipped in from around the world, tens of thousands of urns in long mechanical racks that were hoisted aloft by drone, carried over future pasture and farmland, and gently inverted until their contents drifted out and down through the thin, sunny air like a slow-motion rainfall, thick and dark as a desert thunderstorm. The STDs stood side by side with the new citizens, looking out toward the rain of ashes, holding each other, many in tears. And what came to her was a memory of the caves of the Tsankawi, the ancient mesas where she'd begun to learn the true nature of time, and the true purpose of her life, perhaps all life.

She was there to bear witness. And to do that, she had to live on.

TAUBIN

Napa Valley, 2078

Whatever happened to Taubin Maxwell?

He imagined all his former coworkers asking one another that question around the kelp bar at the office, but in fact, if his chip traffic was any indication, he'd been pretty quickly forgotten. After his outburst in Albuquerque, he was put on administrative leave and not-so-subtly encouraged to look for another job. But no one was doing MSG as scaled-up or sophisticated as what Accretex had let him do, so there was really nowhere to go, and even if he stayed, it was pretty clear that the government's deal with the LLF meant that his Epilox algorithm would have to be completely revamped, and who would trust that to a guy who looked a hundred years old?

Not that the uninfected doublers at the office mentioned his apparent age; they were too liberal and enlightened for that. But dear green Myra dropped him like a hot potato, and even Joyce Icahn stopped returning his chips. He sold the condo in the city and began spending most of his time in St. Helena, where there were tons of Lifers, and he didn't feel so out of place.

One night he went to the bar at the Meadowood Hotel, just over the hill from his house. The place had been rebuilt for the tenth time after the latest megafire, and the bar looked like something out of a country club in the last century, lots of dark paneling and green lampshades, paintings of pedigreed dogs on the walls, but with a good bartender who didn't try to make small talk. The place was nearly empty since almost no one could afford it anymore, and this little old woman was sitting there sipping a Moscow Mule out of the required copper cup and reading a book, an actual physical book, by somebody named Updike. She was dressed in jeans and a white blouse and turquoise jewelry that reminded him of Santa Fe and Grandma Anna, so he sat next to her even though there were lots of empty seats and ordered his usual soy burger special and a shot of Glenlivet. Short red hair, carefully dyed to show some gray, elegant hands, no tats; she looked about his age, his new physical age, that is, around a hundred, give or take a decade.

"Is that a children's book?" he asked her, his social impulsivity kicking in faster than he usually let it.

She looked at him, looked at the cover of the book, looked back at him. Big blue eyes like water, surrounded by a complicated matrix of fine lines that made him think of a neural net.

"Why no, it's a very adult book," she said in a startlingly deep voice that didn't seem like it could come out of such a tiny body.

"I thought maybe because it's about a rabbit. . . ."

"Oh, that's just the protagonist's nickname. It's a metaphor. He's running scared because he's having sort of a midlife crisis, except he's nowhere near midlife yet, and there's nowhere to run."

He realized he was staring at her and made himself stop and take a bite of his burger. "Is that the old midlife or the new midlife?" he asked without looking up, reminding himself that to her he must look like a contemporary.

She lifted the copper cup to her mouth and took a sip, leaving some pink lipstick on the rim. "It's a very old book, so the old midlife. I first read it when I was in college, a hundred years ago. Very risqué at the time, lots of sex."

He did the math, decided to change the subject. She was almost Grandma Anna's age. "Where did you grow up?" he asked.

"Jenkintown. Suburb of Philadelphia. Nice place, idyllic childhood. You?"

"All around. Mostly Oakland and Santa Fe. Not so nice childhood. My mom died young, and I had to move in with my grandparents." *Too much information*, screamed his feeble social filters.

But she seemed interested. "How young was she?"

"In her thirties."

"As in, just thirties? No hundred years first?"

"Yep."

"That's young," she agreed. "What did she die of?"

He hesitated, but why stop now? "Drugs and alcohol."

"Oh dear. How old were you?"

"Twelve. Just twelve. No hundred years first."

"And how old are you now?"

Every conversation came around to this pretty quickly, since no one could tell anymore. Still, she seemed almost as boundary-blind as he was.

"I'm forty-five," he said and waited for the reaction. She looked more disappointed than shocked.

"You're joking with me," she said, and put her book down.

"Nope. Methuselah variant. Started fast aging a couple of years ago."

"I didn't think that was a real thing. Sounds like something the anti-Lifers made up to scare people."

"It's a real thing," he said sullenly. "But don't worry, it's not contagious."

"Couldn't do anything to me," she said, laughing. "I'm Rosemary, by the way."

"Taubin. Call me Taub," he said, and they shook hands. Looking back, he would think that that was when he fell in love with her. There was something about the intelligence in that quick, simple touch, carefulness and caring all at once.

"Where do you live, Taub?"

He pointed over his shoulder. "Over the hill here. You?"

She tossed a thumb in the opposite direction. "Up in Calistoga. My husband and I moved there when we realized we were going to live forever and needed to downsize. We had a big house in the city, up on Nob Hill, but we couldn't afford to stay there."

"You're not missing much. Place is pretty much a hellhole now. I left too."

"I miss it, though," she said. "I miss the restaurants, and the ballgames down in Candlestick Park. Harry and I were there when that big earthquake hit, and they had to stop the World Series."

He had no idea what she was talking about. "Candlestick is where the Lifer Riots started," he offered lamely.

"I know. But once it was something else," she said.

He was sorry to learn that Harry existed and wanted to know more about him. "Is your husband joining you?" he asked, glancing around as though he might be behind one of the potted palms.

"Oh, he died," Rosemary said. And she put down the copper cup and clouded up suddenly in a way that told him she'd been drinking for a while.

"I'm sorry," he said. "Didn't he get Methuselah?" Inappropriate question, but that was his specialty.

She looked at him with those oceanic eyes. "Oh, he got it like everybody in those days. And we had an extra fifty years together. But he wasn't happy. And as we went on, he got unhappier."

"It's a long time to live," he said, as if he knew, and gestured to the bartender for another shot.

She nodded. "He started talking about us getting a divorce. I'd had a miscarriage fifty years earlier, and he never got over it. He was depressed all the time, none of the drugs worked, and he'd have these awful dreams—nightmares, really—about lost children and himself as a lonely old man and how we were going to run out of money and be paupers. He'd wake up crying in the middle of the night. And then he'd be obsessed with the same thoughts all day."

He began to feel uneasy, and not just because it was such a sad story. "Were you two chipped?" he asked.

She snapped out of her reverie, gave him a puzzled look, almost annoyed. "He was. I wasn't. I don't believe in putting machinery inside your brain. But he was in business and said he needed it to keep up. Why?"

He looked away, sipped his scotch. "Just wondered. I've heard of some chipped people suffering depression," he said, knowing he could never tell her or anyone else that he was the engineer of that depression, and not only her husband's, but the nagging sadness of millions of people whose stories he would never know. It was the first time he felt more than just unease about it, the first time he didn't even try to rationalize it, the first time he felt flat-out guilty of a terrible wrong.

"So what happened to him?" he asked, knowing the answer.

"He took Epilox and died a year later. Three years ago this month. We were barely a hundred and twenty."

"I'm sorry."

"Me too. But it's worse than that," she said, putting a small hand on his arm. "Can I tell you something? You seem like a nice person."

"Sure. I guess."

"He took it without telling me, so I didn't even know we only had a year left, and it went by without my knowing it, and his time was up on a beautiful fall morning as we were making love and he—" Taubin pulled his arm away to make her stop.

"I'm sorry," she said, wiping her face with the back of her hand. "I've never told anybody that, why am I telling you?"

All the millions of stories he'd never heard, buried in the algorithm's feedback over all those years.

"Maybe I needed to hear it," he said.

They met at the Meadowood several times after that, supposedly by chance, though he was careful to appear on the same day and at the same hour as that first time, and later by plan, not really dates per se, but what she called assignations. She was flirty and smart and beautiful and fun, and he started feeling a powerfully odd mix of empathy and lust that he realized must be what people called love. And eventually they started going out on proper dates where he picked her up at her little Craftsman bungalow in Calistoga, and they had dinner at one of the old resorts up there from the winemaking glory days of the valley, places he'd never been but where she'd been a regular during her marriage and knew everyone and they were all intensely curious about this strangely spry old fellow accompanying her. They talked about everything, from Lifer politics to family life to twentieth century folk music, which he'd studied in college. He'd done a term paper on Bob Dylan, and when she told him she'd actually, personally seen him perform at a bar in New York City when she was in her teens, he asked her to sign her autograph on a cocktail napkin, which made her laugh. That was the first time she kissed him.

They couldn't co-chip old movies because she didn't have one, so he jury-rigged an antique physical LED screen so they could watch his chipfeed together, holding hands in her living room. *Casablanca. The Philadelphia Story*. It worked fine except when he kissed her and got so distracted that the signal would cut out.

He didn't know what to think about the sex. He wasn't sure he could still perform in his new condition, but she was patient and kind and it turned out to be the best he'd ever had. She knew things from another time entirely, when he imagined people were freer about such things, and from a whole lifetime of being someone's wife. It was different than with someone his age, more intimate, somehow, completely different from the sort of obligatory athletic fuck he used to get from Myra.

Eventually he told her about his work at Accretex, but he was vague about the Sweet Chariot algorithm, made it sound like it was all about ensuring proper dosing and STD tracking, but he could see it bothered her that he was even associated with the place that made the stuff that had killed her husband, and he couldn't blame her. If she had known everything, she would have left him, he was sure. And of course he made a big deal about creating the other algorithm, the one that disappeared but was all about influencing Lifers to embrace their long lives. She liked that, but wondered why it hadn't worked on Harry, and of course he had no answers except that mass influencing in chipspace was an inexact science.

They were walking on the burned-out hill above his house to see the sunset after making love one late afternoon, near the spot where he'd first felt himself suddenly growing old, when she brought up Enoch for the first time.

"What do you think of Marion Altman?" she asked, not even breathing hard as they reached the crest and looked back down toward the valley, a clear view since all the trees had been burned away.

He looked at her, shrugged, sat down on a charred boulder. "She used to be my company's worst nightmare, but she's good at what she does. Or did do."

"I think she's wonderful," Rosemary said. "It's a shame she's going to die now. She made my life bearable these last few years, just listening to her talk, and all that great stuff her organization was doing in Colorado. I don't know why she ever got in bed with that horrible bitch Baldisseri."

"She did it for the land," he said, remembering that awful afternoon when Nolan had him dragged out of the amphitheater. "And it worked."

She sat down next to him and put her head on his shoulder. He was still surprised every time she did that, couldn't believe he was that lucky.

"I need to tell you something," she said, and he didn't move. "I've applied for admission to Enoch."

"Altman's land?"

"Yes. They call it Enoch now."

His mind started racing and, as always when that happened, he just started talking. "I thought it was just for really old people. I mean, even older than you."

"So far it is, but they're making dispensations for people with certain skills, and I used to be a registered nurse. I've still got my license, and I've kept up my continuing education, and I may be just old enough that they'll take me."

He stood up suddenly, stared into the sun setting on the far side of the valley, stared at her. Those eyes, that skin, lined and powdery, that he'd come to love.

"But I couldn't go with you. I'm not old enough," he said, whiny as a schoolboy. "They're only going by chronological age."

"I know, Taub. But I want you to take me there. And who knows, after a few years I might want to come back."

He felt like he'd been punched. "Take you there?"

Tears brimmed in her eyes, only the second time he'd seen that.

"As far as the border, at least," she said, reaching out her hand.

And of course it all made sense to him then, his meeting her and falling in love and having all those months of what he never dared call happiness, all his hopes for a new future where he'd have a second lifetime with this woman who was already living hers. It all made sense because it would all be taken away, and that would be his punishment, the one he'd been waiting for and knew he deserved.

He spent the last of the money from the condo sale on a ten-day private drone rental with unlimited touchdowns and a nice big cabin. He would take Rosemary to Enoch, but he wanted her to meet Jack and Anna before she disappeared from his life, so they agreed to go to Santa Fe on their way to the induction center at Steamboat Springs.

He was afraid his grandparents would disapprove of his sleeping with someone so much older and out of his league socially, but they took it in stride, as though they were all contemporaries, which was, he realized, what they'd become. Anna and Rosemary clicked immediately, and they all went out to dinner at the fancy place on Canyon Road, still there, now covered with plastic like the rest of the town, and had a great time, the two women reminiscing with Jack about things that happened when they were all young that Taubin knew nothing about—Vietnam and Watergate and the first moon landing and wired phones and the coastal cities that were underwater now. And of course Trump, who they said was the reason the old republic had come apart at the seams. He'd been a germophobe, they said, never got Methuselah, and died of a stroke in his nineties. Made Baldisseri look like a genius, they said, laughing, shaking their heads at all they'd lived through. They made him feel young.

And later they all sat out on the *portal* under the stars and had a drink together, watched the Milky Way drift across the desert sky, raised their glasses to the future, to the present with them in it, laughed and looked up at each other, knowing how crazy and good it was. Infinite stars. *We'll get there someday*, he thought. *Maybe we ourselves will get there someday.* Who knew how much time they had left, what they still could do?

The next day they kissed his grandparents goodbye and rode the drone to Enoch. Cool day in the altitude, big prefab lodge the size of a hotel on the crest of a forested ridge where the new country began, the scent of something in the air—rosemary, she said, smiling.

They were patted down for firearms while a bot unloaded Rosemary's luggage, and they joined a group of about thirty Lifers in a high-ceilinged waiting room with a spectacular view. Long gentle slope leading down from the ridge into a vast prairie meadow, and beyond that, mountains rising, flanks of conifers and aspen and spruce, endlessly to the horizon. Taubin thought it must be the last land like this in America. Bot excavators and the frames of huge 3D printers down in the meadow sinking silos and cubes of modular structures deep into the dark earth, rooflines just above the ground, high enough for a doorway, roofs being covered with the grassland sod that had been torn up and set aside. Farther off, cantilevered foundations jutting out from the mountainsides with drones hovering around them like bees around flowers, and in the very distance, like perfectly shaped oval clouds, platforms floating in the sky, held up by something he couldn't see from this far. He thought about the cost of it all, in money and planning and organization, but also in the lives that would never see it, lives given up for it as Marion Altman had asked. He didn't know whether to admire her or despise her the way he despised himself for convincing people to die.

New arrivals with chips could get through the induction procedure in a couple of minutes, but because Rosemary didn't have one, she had brought what she called her paperwork and had it reviewed by a nice-looking, leathery, ancient fellow with a German accent who fed the physical sheets of actual paper into a scanner that downloaded the contents directly into his chip and from there into the Enochan neural net. He told them it was sort of like speed-reading from back when people read. The old guy closed his eyes for a while and then asked Rosemary a question or two—where she went to nursing school, when she last worked in a hospital, even what her Social Security number was back when people had them, just corroborating that the person in the paper record was the person in front of him. And the whole time Taubin was looking out those big windows down onto the prairie where the clouds and floating platforms raced giant shadows across the grass.

Finally the ancient guy stood up and bowed a little and extended his hand to Rosemary and said, "Welcome" in a very earnest, formal way, and her face lit up, and she shook hands with the guy and then turned and hugged Taubin. And he realized that anything that made her that happy was something he could learn to live with somehow.

They hurried her off after that, as if they realized this was hard for both of them. He watched the German guy guide her through the huge doors that opened onto a pathway down into the valley, the mountains framing it all like a painting. He could tell they'd put a lot of thought into the placement of the induction lodge, but he could also tell it was designed to let people in rather than turn them away, and they told him where to stand and watched him carefully as though they were afraid he'd bolt after her.

Rosemary turned and waved back at him half a dozen times as she descended the path, and he waved back and watched until she didn't turn around anymore, and she disappeared into a stand of dark timber.

And that, he said to himself, *is what happened to Taubin Maxwell.*

DANIEL

=====

Black Valley, Colorado, 2080

In her last months, Marion spent a great deal of time with Adele and Zinn. She'd learned to walk again with the help of some smart prosthetics that Zinn had fabricated for her, and the three of them would go on long, strenuous hikes together, up to the ridge along the border between Black Valley and the Arapahoe Forest. Sometimes Dan would go with them, but more often he'd wait back at the lodge, thinking they wanted privacy. There was something romantic among them, it seemed to him. But he didn't mind. They'd all long since stopped thinking inside those possessory little boxes; there was something about having an indefinite lifespan that made you less selfish about whom you loved and who loved you. And theirs was the kind of love that transpired in talk. Marion wanted to better understand how Methuselah had happened, what had driven Zinn to create the original ENS package, how it worked. Things none of them had the time to think about when Methuselah was a plague.

And more than that, Dan thought that Marion wanted to know exactly how much she had given up, how long the rest of them were going to live on without her. Now that they'd secured the beginnings of a Lifer homeland, now that a pattern of truly mass choice was emerging among triplers, between living on and what some flippantly called checking out, the question that occupied many of them at an individual and community level was when those who remained would die, and if they didn't anytime soon, if they were to live on indefinitely, what that would mean to their capacity to manage the population of Enoch, how much land they would really need, could they really be self-sustaining in perpetuity? No one uttered the *I*-word, but that was the real question, just as it had always been: Were they immortal? And if anyone might learn the answer, it was Adele and Zinn.

After completing designs for Enoch's geothermal, defense, and platform housing infrastructures, Zinn and Adele had returned to the study of Methuselah to understand how it had mutated and what that meant for the infected—or, as Zinn preferred to call them, the "corrected." He explained again that the original protein package that he had designed had succeeded primarily by reprogramming the cellular epigenome throughout the human body, so that the genetic signaling within cells that degraded with age was restored to its youthful clarity—like polishing a scratched DVD, as he described it—allowing the digital message of the cellular DNA to be read as accurately as it had been when the organism was young, when its sole evolutionary purpose was to get to the point of reproducing. After that, biology said, the organism was dispensable, and there was no evolutionary need for the epigenome to work as efficiently. Zinn's package had instead instructed it— corrected it—to behave as though the need still existed into the organism's second century, just as it had when its main function, evolutionarily speaking, was to pump out babies. And the result had been that age and death became decoupled.

What wasn't known was whether this cellular reprogram-ming would last indefinitely, or whether the simple passage of time would again degrade the epigenome and cause the DNA signaling to become corrupted once more. So Zinn had enlisted Adele and Devon Jones, their resident phenotypologist, to conduct a mass genomic data aggregation using cell samples from the new millions of volunteers for the Epilox program, aimed at discovering what was happening in the cells of those who'd been living with Methuselah for upward of fifty years.

One sunny spring day, Dan laced up his hiking boots and tagged along on one of the Adele-Marion-Zinn expeditions up the side of Mt. Respect. The snows had receded early again that year, but the going was still slick and cold as they ascended through the cedars and firs and the fecund smells of the thawing loam, toward the spot where Barb Beckwith had died. The other three didn't recognize it, but Dan did, imagining that he saw traces of her blood where it had spilled across the ground. He felt the tears and anger coming, as he did whenever he thought of that day, stared straight ahead and tried to concentrate on the chat of the other three, huffing between words as they struggled up the slope ahead of him.

"How you doing, Marion?" called Adele, who was in the lead as usual and looked back to check on the rest, but mainly on her old friend who was scheduled to die.

"I'm fine, dear," Marion responded after a pause to suck some air, her prosthetics softly whirring and whining with each step she took. "You really don't have to worry about me."

"Well I do. You've taken a deadly drug, let's not forget." Dan winced, but they were always like that with each other, terribly blunt in an oddly loving sort of way.

Marion slipped on an outcropping of rock and Dan reached up to brace her, but the robotic sheaths around her legs recovered quickly, and she lunged upward again. "I really haven't noticed any side effects at all," she said. "I expected some gradual weakening, or memory loss, or at least headaches or indigestion, but it's like I never took it. Makes me wonder if it's really going to work."

"Excellent design," said Zinn. "Very clever delivery system. I'm quite sure it will work." Dan thought he might as well have been talking about one of his floating habitat platforms.

"Pardon me if I don't share your enthusiasm," Dan said, and they all fell silent, as though they'd forgotten he was there. Then, to change the subject, he asked, "What's the latest on your genome study, Zinn?"

"I'd rather not discuss it until it's complete," Zinn said. Over the years his signature beard had been allowed to lengthen until it nearly reached his knees.

Adele spit a short, hard laugh. "Oh it's effectively complete now. He's just too proud to tell you the result."

Dan stopped. They all stopped, looked at Zinn.

"In all fairness, the conclusions are still preliminary," he said. "We're still waiting for peer review." Adele cocked her head, kept her gaze on him.

Zinn sighed, shifted his weight. "The early indications are that the effects of Methuselah, especially the epigenomic effects, are fading gradually over time. This may be the result of mutations in the original programming, which comes as a surprise to me because I wouldn't have thought that possible without some outside intervention."

"You mean human intervention?" Dan asked.

"I would have thought so. But Adele and I have been unable to identify any likely source of such activity."

"So maybe it's not human," said Marion, starting up the slope again. "Maybe it's natural. Maybe it's biology."

"Reversion to the mean," Dan mused, looking after her. "Biology abhors extremes, right Zinn?"

"Ha," Zinn grumped. "Look around us," he said, spreading his arms to take in the improbable beauty of the mountain, the lake below them, the sky above. "Look at *us*. Biology loves extremes. Biology itself is an extreme."

Dan gestured to suggest that Zinn follow Marion, who was several paces up the slope. "Forgetting the cause for a moment," he said, "what will it mean for lifespans?"

Zinn was silent for so long that it became clear he wasn't going to answer. But Adele did.

"We see three possibilities," she said, startling Dan, as she so often did, not with the precision of her words, which was typical of her, but with what they indicated about how long and how thoroughly she'd been thinking about this.

"The first is to accept that progressive aging will eventually become part of our lives again, and that at the end of that process we will die. For people our age, in their one-thirties, we're thinking perhaps another twenty or thirty years. Which is astounding, let's not forget. But that remaining time will involve a return to the gradual deterioration of quality of life that we once associated with the final stages of life. Illness, disease, slow failure of various bodily functions.

"The second possibility would be a sort of Methuselah booster treatment, probably by injection or infusion, that would once again reset the epigenomic function to baseline, with the expectation that it would last at least as long as the effects of Zinn's first package. He and his team have been working on such a booster, and it should be ready in the next couple of years, depending on how long human trials take."

Dan stopped in his tracks. "When were you going to announce this?"

"We weren't planning to, until the booster is ready," Zinn said grumpily, clearly unhappy that Adele was spilling this news. "But that's to be decided by the council."

Dan considered this. "And what, pray tell, is the third possibility?" he asked.

"The third possibility," said Adele, now completely chip-faced, as though consulting a whiteboard in her head, "for those who want to avoid senescence, but don't want to live indefinitely by getting a booster treatment every few decades, will be to take Epilox when they feel that they've outlived their desired quality of life, much as they do now when they're simply tired of living, or are sacrificing themselves for the cause of Enoch. Advanced senescence, as we all remember, is no fun."

Marion was far ahead of them now, almost out of earshot. "We should catch up with her," Dan said. "But one more question. Could this new treatment of yours, this Methuselah booster, could it help her?"

Adele looked at him for a long moment. "You mean could it keep her with us?" she asked. Zinn looked away, down the mountain toward the lake.

"That's exactly what I mean. Could it counteract the Epilox?"

Zinn turned back to him. "No," he said simply. "It's a completely different technology with completely different effects. There is no antidote to Epilox. We had to be sure of this before we agreed to the deal for Enoch, don't you see. We couldn't have someone emerge with an antidote and upend all our planning for the death count."

Adele glanced at him disapprovingly. "Yes, of course," Dan said. "Of course, the death count." He sighed, looked up at the figure receding above them. "Let's catch up with Marion."

And they started up the long slope after her.

Everything had changed for him, and yet so much was still the same. The spring vegetables still speared their way up through the black loam behind the lodge, the sun still sank, somber as a judge, toward the distant blue massifs in the long afternoons, the lake rose with the thaw as it always had. There were hours, even entire days, when he could forget what was coming, when he could conjure up that inbred obliviousness to time that had been the default state of his youth, and again after the Change had made a joke of time, when the passage of a day meant nothing because there was always another day beyond it, and another after that. But then, inevitably, the old illusion would pass, and he remembered, and cursed himself for having forgotten even for an hour, and checked the calendar again, and checked his arithmetic to see how many days remained, as he knew they always should have, even when they'd only been guessing. Fifty-six days left. Forty-one. Thirty. The relentlessness of it surprised him every time, as though he were a child to whom the concepts of quantity and finitude had not yet been explained.

How does one spend one's last days? He'd actually thought about it a lot since Nolan had first described Epilox to Marion that afternoon in Manhattan. To have one year, exactly, left to live, in the extraordinary circumstance that he knew it was his last and had the health and the means to spend it any way he wanted. What would he do? He'd imagined that he'd travel with Marion to places he loved and places he'd never been, visit people he missed, people who had made him who he was. He'd retrace the physical arc of his life, see all his old homes, go through all his hoarded belongings from a century and a half of living and winnow them down to those that had defined him or comforted him or instructed him. He'd make a list of people he needed to forgive and another list of those he'd wronged, and ask for an hour with each of them to see what could be done.

And at some point, probably too late, he'd realize the futility of it all, and no matter what he'd done with that time, he'd become increasingly desperate as the weeks and days dwindled down. And only then would he stop, and confront oblivion, and try to relax into it.

He imagined all this. But how could he know what he would have done if he'd been in Marion's position? He only knew that she did none of it, that she skipped immediately to the realization that there was, in fact, no consolation in mortality, no offsetting the loss of a life as rich as hers, that there was nothing that she needed to do other than what she'd been doing all along. She kept working and doing her chipcasts and visiting Enoch once a week for the Passage and Sowing ceremonies. She got an old keyboard out of storage and every afternoon played the piano pieces she'd learned in her teens while he made dinner. Chopin. Bach. Bernstein. *I just met a girl named Maria.* She went for walks in the mountains, usually with Adele or Zinn, but sometimes alone. He worried those times, thinking she might try to cheat on the schedule and not come back. But she always did. She lived on as though nothing had changed.

And even that didn't save her.

The night before her last day arrived, they had dinner alone together—her favorite meal of steak and potatoes, and a big vodka martini. He tried to make love to her again, as he had most nights in the preceding year, desperate as a teenager, but they were too quickly reduced to tears and gave up and just held each other in the endless dark of the valley and listened to the loons singing to the stars. It was just as good.

On her last day they rose early, before light, since although the day was certain, the hour was not, and they didn't want to be caught unawares. He would later think that it might have been easier to stay in bed all day drinking vodka martinis. Instead he made her eat breakfast, though she laughed at that, and he clung close to her, shadowing her every movement, alternately laughing maniacally at things that weren't funny and bursting into tears, constantly asking how she felt. She said she felt no different, that he really wasn't helping and needed to calm down. So he tried.

Everyone in the valley—and most people in the world—were aware that this was Marion Altman's death day. And though he'd asked for understanding and for privacy, a large number of the residents came to the lodge wanting to pay their respects and say goodbye. Marion accommodated a couple dozen of them, then turned to him and, her voice cracking, asked him to take her to the lake. And just for that moment he thought he glimpsed fear in her eyes, but then the look of peaceful resolve returned like a full moon emerging from an eclipse.

A crowd had gathered outside the Mushroom and the entire perimeter of the lake was lined with people, much like the night exactly a year earlier when Marion had cast her lot with death. Hands reached out and touched her as she passed, and many touched him, and there were murmurs of love and of parting. But mostly there was silence except for the lapping of the lake against the docks.

She chose a small dinghy and got in and pushed him back when he tried to follow her. He grabbed her hand and held it, beyond tears now, simply, desperately fearful of letting go.

"I love you," she said. And he mouthed the same words back, though no sound came from his wretched mouth. And she turned and pushed off and rowed a bit and drifted to the center of the lake, never once looking back. Adele came and stood beside him and said nothing. It was noon.

It was five o'clock when the sun touched the ridge line of Mt. Respect. And it was a few minutes later, though some said it was closer to six, when the small figure on the boat in the middle of the lake slumped slowly, gently to one side and disappeared beneath the lip of the hull. No one had moved, but now it was as if a great sigh went up, and the people stood and leaned forward like the petals of some great, infolating blossom, and some reached out toward the boat, toward the mountains behind it. And he remembered nothing of that day after that.

They retrieved her body the next morning when the mist was still on the lake, and they burned it on Mt. Respect that night. Usually there were a dozen or more bodies burning at one time now that Epilox had become a sort of sacrament, but on this night there was only Marion's. And he tried to breathe in the smoke of her burning. And the morning after that, he collected her ashes and put them in a simple ivory urn and carried them back to their bedroom in the lodge.

Adele came to him that night as he sat on the deck of the lodge overlooking the lake. It was too cold to be out there but he couldn't bring himself to go to the bed that he and Marion had shared. For a moment he felt intruded upon but trusted Adele to know there was nothing she could say, and she said nothing, just sat in the empty old rocking chair next to his, and they rocked together for a while, looking out over the water. After what seemed a long time, she took his hand and they rocked some more, holding hands. And after a longer time she squeezed his hand hard and stood up and walked away.

The stars shone down with an intensity that to him seemed animate, knowing, like pieces of the embers that still glowed on the slope of Mt. Respect. His eyes were drawn to the mountain, and then back to the stars, back and forth, as though he might resolve them into one vision if he only looked hard enough.

ADELE

===============

Enoch, 2080

The Passage and the Sowing at Enoch the following week would be particularly well attended. Most of Black Valley would be there, and dignitaries were arriving from all over the world. Adele dressed carefully in the only suit she still owned, the black silk pantsuit she'd bought in Tokyo a century before and had worn the night she captured Zinn. It was too big for her now, her body long since shorn of all excess, her breasts gone, her legs like sticks. But the suit was still beautiful, she left her white hair down and wild, and she thought Marion would have approved.

Dan had gone to Enoch the day before to prepare, but Claire met Adele in Black Valley in her big government drone, and they flew over the mountains to Enoch together. They rode mostly in silence, Adele staring out the thick window at the wilderness below, lost in recursive thought. There had been a time when she'd longed for this day, when Dan would be free to turn to her. Now that it was here, the idea that the death of a loved one meant they were gone, and the very notion of couplehood, seemed like naive delusions to her, and she was grateful she'd been barely wise enough to say nothing to him that night on the deck in the starlight. She realized that Marion would always be Dan's wife, just as she would always be the unrecoverable love of his youth. They'd long outlived the lust and hubris that had first drawn them together, and now what was left? Respect was the first word that came to her, that tepid, quiet, priceless thing. That, and the comfort of a long-shared history, one to which she'd added several chapters, with perhaps more to come. Of course she still loved Dan and had dreamed of a life with him, but in every way that truly mattered, she already had that. It was enough. *Sometimes, enough is all you get,* she murmured to herself. She loved Marion too, and missed her more terribly than she'd imagined.

How could she add to those complexities the additional fact of the daughter that she and Dan had made together, still living out there in the world somewhere, living on without knowing them? It was like a weight on her, one she desperately wanted help in bearing. But that would mean shifting that weight to a man in mourning. *Not yet,* she thought. *Not just yet.*

It was late afternoon and the sun had dropped to that magic angle that bathed everything in gold. The crowds overflowed the amphitheater into the surrounding fields. Adele and Claire chipped Dan together, and he answered with coordinates for the spot where he stood waiting for them in a gray three-piece suit that, like hers, was from a different century and had grown too large for the wearer. *We should all be naked,* Adele thought. *That's who we really are now. Not these old clothes.*

They stood together in the tall grass of the meadow where the soon-to-die touched the earth and tasted the grass, and where the urns lay in long rows. In accordance with her wishes, there was nothing on the program about Marion, and nothing was said about her. But Dan and Zinn had been at work, and when the thousand urns were lifted in their racks toward the clouds and poured their contents out over the new land, a small, solitary drone carried a single ivory urn aloft and toward the distant mountains.

It kept going, faster, higher. Adele took Dan's hand, and he took Claire's, and they stood in silence until the sky was empty. And as at every Sowing, the words from Genesis streamed into their chips:

And Enoch walked with God after he begat Methuselah

And all the days of Enoch were three hundred sixty and five years

And Enoch walked with God; and he was not; for God took him.

EPILOGUE

DANIEL

New York City, 2149

D an and Claire decided to celebrate his two-hundredth birthday in Manhattan in the summer of 1974, the year he graduated from law school and went to work on Wall Street, forty years before she was born.

Even after brain supplants became commonplace, the time travel stuff had troubled Dan. First, he noted pedantically to anyone who'd listen, it wasn't real time travel; that was impossible. But the Zinnemann Institute had begun to collate the massive banks of personal memory that the new brain supplants had made accessible, and the researchers realized that, if properly aggregated, amplified and edited, those memories would be indistinguishable from actual human history, at least as far back as a sufficient number of living persons could remember. And that was a long time back—into the middle of the twentieth century, at least. But all that memory—hundreds of zettabytes of it—needed a lot of cleaning up, since it was full of imaginings, willful and innocent mis-rememberings, outright self-lies, wishes, even some dreams or, worse, memories of dreams. For a while the idea of rendering it sufficiently accurate, linear, and supplant-legible for everyday access seemed beyond the reach of even the Zinns, as they were called.

Then one of them—a late arrival to the Institute named Maxwell, who Dan later learned had been one of his son's employees back in Methuselah times—came up with a massively integrative algorithm that could compare and collate the millions of different memories, the memories of millions of different people, of specific places and times, clean up the "noise" by eliminating outlier elements and figments that couldn't be corroborated by other memories or conventional extraneous means, and knit the remaining universe of sensory data into a single, integrated whole. Smells proved a particular challenge, he'd been told; Proust aside, what was the memory of a smell? Who knew, but it was that vast, intricately orchestrated meta-memory, accessible to anyone with the right permissions and sufficiently augmented brainspace, that one could enter at any point and roam around in. Maxwell had become quite a celebrity, and would have been quite rich if the concept still applied. Dan had gone to one of Maxwell's talks where the great man called it his redemption, those lines of code that brought whole worlds back to life.

There were lots of gaps, of course. You couldn't go to Antarctica in 1959 or to the moon in 2020 because no one was there then. Even some parts of the Americas had been so sparsely populated that there weren't enough reliable memories of them for Maxwell's algorithm to latch onto. And you couldn't change the past; that too was a fantasy. There was no tinkering with what millions of people remembered.

But the great cities in all their astonishing granularity, the bigger towns, the tourist spots on the pre-deluge islands and coasts, had been experienced by so many who were still alive that it was enough to make a real past for each of them, where you could visit for an hour or a week. There was a waiting list so as not to overburden Maxwell's servers, but Claire still had a lot of pull, and he'd wanted her to see the New York he once knew. So they went.

They visited his old firm, on the forty-fifth floor of a sky-scraper on lower Broadway, a block north of Trinity Church. They were dressed for the times and the season, he in a powder blue double-breasted suit that he'd bought at a wholesaler on Canal Street to save his starting associate's salary, Claire in a pretty cream knockoff Chanel sheath from Bergdorf's. The view north from the reception area was spectacular, up past the Woolworth Building all the way to midtown where the Empire State Building and the Chrysler Building and the flattened hexagram of the Pan Am Building rose together above the sea of lesser structures like a giant stand of futuristic sequoias. And to the south, Staten Island and Liberty, above water then, waving her welcome, and the great bay and the Atlantic stretching to the horizon, from a height—common-place before the waters rose—where you believed you could see the curvature of the earth.

They wandered the halls, dodging busy people, peering into offices. Occasionally Dan saw someone he knew, and they sat in his office—the partners were all males in those days—and watched him use a pencil to mark up a paper document or listened to him talk on a box-like speakerphone or dictate text into a small machine while chain-smoking Lucky Strikes. They visited the library, where Dan opened some casebooks and pretended to do research as he had when he was twenty-five. Pretending then too, now that he thought of it. Then up to the penthouse floor for lunch at the Metropolitan Club, more views in all directions, vichyssoise and steak tartare and a glass of fumé blanc. The brand-new World Trade Center to the west, enormous beyond even New Yorkers' imaginings, against whose silhouettes you could measure the contrapun-tal swaying of the towers in the wind off the glistening bay. The nonstop murmur of conversation in the curtained room, people seated together, well-dressed men and the occasional woman, confident in their surroundings, in themselves, in the infinitude of their lives. It brought tears to his eyes, and Claire, smiling, reached across the white linen tablecloth and steadied his arm as he lifted the cold, fresh wine to his lips.

The subway fare was twenty-five cents, the tokens almost exactly the size of a quarter, so he was always mixing them up and dropping the coin into the turnstile and then having to follow it with the token. *The MTA must have made a lot of money that way*, he thought. They were overdressed for the subway, and it was hot, not nearly as hot as it would become, but no air conditioning, and the cars and stations were filthy, covered in thick black graffiti. But he'd wanted Claire to see it. There are others like them in the dingy, screeching car, office workers headed home early, and there were also the poor, crushed and vacant, talking to themselves as though they were chipped, stinking of nights spent in alleys and vacant lots, who made him think of the homeless Lifers that some of them, rich and poor alike, would become in a hundred years.

They strolled through Central Park, past the vast, vacant green of the Sheep Meadow, down the leafy boulevard of the Mall. The smell of marijuana, music playing, acoustic guitars everywhere, Simon and Garfunkel, Don McLean. Music that knew everything worth knowing, even then. *This'll be the day that I die.*

Then up to Columbia on the Seventh Avenue line—he remembered to change to the local at 96th Street so they wouldn't end up in Harlem—to the law school first, like a giant toaster, as inviting as a prison, to see the library and the amphi-theaters where he'd learned enough about torts and contracts to pass the bar exam later that fall. Then across to College Walk, past patinaed Alma Mater gazing down from her pedestal, and around the corner to Philosophy Hall, where Claire would make her mark as a great interpreter of mortality a mere ninety years hence. The office on the second floor where she would write *Befriending Ending* was locked and dark, the brass name-plate frame beside the door empty, as though waiting for her. They giggled and hurried on to get ready for dinner.

He hit "pause" and waited for the dark to descend. It did, and they floated in it for a few moments, and then the light came up and they were in the lounge chairs in their living room in the Height, twenty thousand miles above Enoch. He looked over at Claire and smiled. She blinked and stretched as though she'd been napping.

"Wow," she said. "The feed quality is amazing. But you really should warn me when you're going to check out like that. It's a little disconcerting if you're not expecting it."

"Sorry," he said. "It was beginning to feel very ground-state, and that's when I know I'd better take a break."

"Interesting. It always feels like a waking dream to me. Very unreal."

"Must depend on how early in life you were first chipped. We're what, fifty or so years apart in that regard?"

She shrugged, got up, came over and laid her hand softly on his shoulder. "I don't remember. Neither should you."

But he did. He remembered it all. He still did the math of chronological age, calculating how old he was when this or that happened. Claire thought it was a form of nostalgia, which she had little patience for. She was like Marion in that way, as she was in so many ways. Yet what were these trips into the past that they were taking, if not a kind of longing for it? Research, she would say. Entertainment. For him it was more like what going to church was when he was young. Reconnecting with a ground of being, honoring it, respecting who and what made him, what was once called tradition, a word that had disappeared from the language. The thoughts of an old man.

On the other hand, he'd adapted. He no longer thought of Claire as his granddaughter; she was simply Claire, a fellow-traveler in time, like all of them who had lived that long, from whom age and genealogy had fallen away like molted skins, forgotten. They'd all become the same age, which was to say no age at all. It was only when they chipped back in time that they could see how age-stratified they'd been, how those artificial twenty- or thirty-year epochs had defined their lives, how many varieties of humans there had been, each trapped in their age of the moment, thinking it would never end. These excursions into the past were like going to a zoo: the small, defenseless bodies of the children; the young adults in their brainless fecundity; the middle-aged in their strutting, doomed confidence; and of course the old, sick and shuffling, shunted to the peripheries, told in so many ways, and often in so many words, to die.

He'd say they "chipped back," but that was just an old colloquialism that Claire said dated him. No chips anymore, though he'd been fond of them, and many kept them long past their usefulness, even after the nanosurgeons with their smart stem cells had begun to repurpose the underused quadrants of their brains. Even Dan, who could remember the infernal stupidities of computer-based gatekeeper networks and had come to think of his first implant as a personal friend, thought this cancer-like spread of human tech ever deeper into his gray matter might not go well.

But there they were, as adaptive as when they'd first given up vinyl for silicon, more intimately linked to one another than ever, neurally speaking, so that he needed to put up the "do not disturb" buffers to get to sleep. He wasn't sure Claire actually slept anymore. She would ping him in the middle of the night and start asking questions about the past as though

she were a teenager and he the wise grandad of her youth.
But he wasn't about to complain. He was even glad he'd let
her talk him into moving to the Height, the latest of Enoch's
geostationary orbiting platforms, even though the long ride
up on what they insisted on calling a space elevator made him
sick to his stomach every time. But the view was great, the
orbiter had relieved at least some of the population pressure
on Greater Enoch, and if they ever got the Europa mission off
the ground—or off the platform—he would think the whole
expensive concept had been worth it. Selling Enochan technology to the rest of the world had been enormously lucrative
for the young nation, but even that bonanza had its limits.

Dinner that night at La Grenouille, off Fifth Avenue, the soft
coral light, the huge flower arrangements in their urns in
the high-ceilinged rooms. They were side by side in a banquette, the pride of seventies New York parading before
them. Eight o'clock, some of the pretheater crowd still lingering, the ones who would saunter down the aisle halfway
through the first act. People dressed up for dinner in those
days, the women in cocktail dresses, the men still in their
suits from the office. He and Claire had forgotten this, were
underdressed, Dan in a blazer and an open button-down,
Claire in pearls and a toreador jacket and pants quite right for
the times, but a bit casual for this place. They could change
with a thought or two, but it seemed to Dan like cheating, as
would having himself look the age he had been then, another
option they avoided, mainly because, he thought, what should
the yet-to-be-born Claire look like? He studied the faces,
thinking he might recognize someone, as he often did on
these outings, but this was a place that neither he nor anyone
he knew could afford in 1974, even though the extravagant
entrées on the menu seemed ridiculously inexpensive to his

twenty-second-century eyes—frog legs almondine for nineteen pre-secessionist dollars.

He was searching the wine list for a time-appropriate vintage of Puligny Montrachet, listening to the chatter at the next table about whether Nixon should resign, when Claire nudged him with her elbow. He looked up, and there, being led to their table by a visibly impressed maître d', was Adele Pritchard in a black sequined dress, green eyes flashing, red hair to her exposed shoulders, stunning, the age she would have been when they first met, beaming at him.

"Surprise," said Claire, and he stood and embraced this young Adele for a long moment—so oddly soft and full, no protruding bones, her face unlined, smooth and glowing as frosted glass. It was, he thought fleetingly, like a mask, unreal and unliving; strangely unattractive. The maître d' summoned a chair for her.

"Happy birthday," she said, breathless, sitting.

"When did you arrive?" he asked, staring into those eyes, the only part of her that looked like the Adele he knew.

"Just now. Claire pinged me so I could pop in at the right moment. We wanted to surprise you."

"You certainly accomplished that. I didn't know you indulged in this sort of thing."

"Usually only for research."

"Cocktail?"

"Please."

"Let me guess. Vodka martini."

"With a lemon twist. Do they have those now? I mean, in this time?"

"They always have those," he said. He couldn't help but look her up and down. "Though you may not have been drinking then."

"Not till I met you," she admitted. "I was in New Mexico tonight. By the Tsankawi caves."

"You should go someday," Claire said. "Relive it."

"I've tried. It's not possible. Not enough people were there then, not enough memories. Just mine. But that's enough."

Their drinks came, and they raised their glasses and gently brought them together.

"To Marion," proposed Adele.

"To Marion," they said together. The clear liquid whispered and warmed in his throat, just as he remembered it would. He gave Claire a lingering glance, seeing for the thousandth time how Marion lived on in her.

Adele lowered her glass, looked at him. "I have another toast to propose. Actually, two more. But first I want you to meet someone."

He looked around, puzzled. "Who?" He looked at Claire quizzically, and she lowered her eyes. She knew something, he realized, but wasn't a party to whatever was about to happen.

"Listen to me, Dan," said Adele, and she held his face in her hands. There was a stirring in his head, and then a great depth opening. Time unfolded in her eyes, words and images streaming from her, flooding his brain: long ago nights remembered by only the two of them, their reckless passion, the year that followed when he saw Adele not at all. A child. Their child. Given up, lost, a casualty of Adele's ruthless logic, but now, finally, found, known, after a century and a half, the closing of a circle that could only have happened in the abundance of time they'd been granted.

He started to speak, to protest that none of this could possibly be true, but someone walked up to their table, stood behind Adele, and placed her hands on Adele's shoulders. Immensely old, tall and thin like him, her long hair a lustrous silver, her face beautifully tattooed with an array of patterns like clusters of stars. He stared, dazed, but stood instinctively. Her eyes were so like her mother's that he started to laugh, but his throat caught, constricted with an emotion he couldn't name.

Adele rose, circled an arm around the woman, who looked several times her age. "To the people we were when we first met," she said, raising her glass between them. "And to the life we created then, living still. Dan, this is our daughter, Adelaide."

He reached out toward her but his legs gave way, and he fell back onto the banquette. The two women bent over him; he felt weightless, insubstantial, as though their touch might dissolve him. Intellectually he knew that this stranger named Adelaide was just another like him and Adele and Claire, aged and ageless, beyond genealogy. And yet, if what Adele said was true, she was not just his daughter, but a living embodiment of a moment in his life he'd almost forgotten, one he and Adele had shared so long ago that he had no sensory memory of it. Yet here she was, suddenly—embodied proof of it.

"Just give me a moment," he said.

"Of course," said Adele, squeezing his hand. "We have all the time in the world." The worried maître d' appeared, was reassured by the women that their ashen companion would be fine, and brought a fourth chair to the table. Mother and daughter sat opposite him holding hands while Claire looked on, smiling tears streaming down her face.

"You're sure this isn't a figment of Maxwell's algorithms?" he asked. They laughed and began to talk. There was so much more to be learned.

Adelaide had her own daughter, Penelope—half-cousin to Claire—who was a historian, working on a study of the time of Methuselah, and wanted to record their stories, to add them to the collated sea of memory that Maxwell's algorithm was compiling.

He sat silently for a while, listening to their voices, trying to absorb it all, to make it real. The room full of people, most long dead, murmured around him. "I have two questions," he said, a flicker of anger rising in him. "Why am I learning all this only now?"

Adele sighed, shook her head. "I thought there'd be a right time," she said. "But it never came. One of the unanticipated aspects of living this long is that it encourages procrastination, and I've been guilty of that. Early on, I was afraid of disrupting your and Marion's life and, later, your respnsibilities to Enoch. So I waited. I waited far too long. Please forgive me."

He hesitated, took her hand, kissed it. Tears filled her eyes. "What's your second question?" she asked.

He smiled. "When can I meet Penelope?"

The algorithm churns on, knitting the past. And in the Height, far above the spinning earth, beneath the infinite stars, they lie slumbering, dreaming a vanished world.

And the thought occurs, even as they dream: are we visited from a farther future by those who remember our time and wish to relive it? Are we living their memory of our times? Do they move among us like ghosts, smile at our oddities, wish they could warn us of what's to come? Would we recognize them, or they us? Are they grateful for what we did, or do they curse us for what we failed to do?

Perhaps they would be like gods; ageless, and forgiving.

GLOSSARY

AI—artificial intelligence; the capacity of silicon-based computational systems to simulate sentience.

ATV—all-terrain vehicle, a four-wheeled, often fossil-fuel-motorized means of off-road terrestrial transportation for one or two passengers.

Boomer Box—a mid-to-late twenty-first-century colloquial reference to a roughly rectangular geographic region of the post-secessionist United States whose western corners were defined by Denver and Albuquerque and whose eastern corners were defined by Columbus, Ohio, and Asheville, North Carolina. So named because it attracted many migrating *Lifers* (*see*) who considered it to be relatively safe from earthquakes, sea-level rise, hurricanes, megafires, and other natural disasters common to the era.

CAD—computer-aided design; used in twentieth- and twenty-first-century manufacturing and architecture.

CGI—computer-generated imagery; a cinematic technique used in the twentieth and twenty-first century to create artificial visuals not readily achievable by optical means.

Change, the—a colloquialism referring to the period of time during which the *Methuselah syndrome* (*see*) became widely recognized, generally identified as the mid-to-late 2040s.

CIA—Central Intelligence Agency; a clandestine espionage agency of the federal government in the pre-secessionist United States of the twentieth and early twenty-first centuries.

Chipface—a colloquialism of the mid-to-late twenty-first century referring to the vacant or distracted expression on the face of a person whose *headchip* (*see*) is in active use.

Comps—colloquial abbreviation of "completions," referring to the completed ingestion by a user of the prescribed seven-pill dosage of Epilox™.

CRISPR—Clustered Regularly Interspaced Short Palindromic Repeats; a gene-engineering methodology used to segment DNA strands at specified locations in a genome.

DARPA—the Defense Advanced Research Projects Agency, a department of the pre-secessionist United States federal government dedicated to technological research for possible military application. Also, DARPAnet, a restricted-access computer-based communications network used by DARPA.

Deathwish Algorithm—*see MSG.*

Doubler—a colloquialism of the mid-to-late twenty-first century referring to a person under the age of one hundred; derived from double-digit, as in age. *See also Lifers, Lingerers,* and *Triplers.*

DLM—the Department of Longevity Management, established in 2079 by the administration of United States President Isabel

Baldisseri ostensibly to address social and economic problems caused by the sudden and radical increase in human lifespans starting around the mid-twenty-first century.

DNA—acronym for deoxyribonucleic acid, an organic molecule in the form of a double helix containing genetic information necessary for protein synthesis and cellular function.

EMP—electromagnetic pulse; a violent wave form of electromagnetic energy, typically produced by nuclear explosion but also generated by specialized microwave devices.

Epigenome—literally, "above the genome," usually referring to proteins that do not constitute genetic molecules like DNA, but regulate and intermediate their function. Manipulation of the epigenome was a primary goal of *ENS* (*see*) strategies in the early-and-mid-twenty-first century.

ENS—Engineered Negligible Senescence; artificial manipulation of the human genome and epigenome to promote dramatic lifespan extension while reducing morbidity; a concept originated by the gerontologist Aubrey de Grey in 2005 and fully implemented by Gustav Zinnemann in 2033.

Great Usurpation—a phrase used by political liberals in the mid-twenty-first century to refer to the incidence of several Southern states in the then United States openly ignoring election results and declaring winners by fiat, which eventually led to the secession of several liberal-leaning states from the union and, as a byproduct, the dismantlement of what was then called the internet.

Headchip—or "chip," a colloquialism of the mid-to-late twenty-first century referring to an electronic microchip embedded subcutaneously, usually behind the ear. An essential component of the *neural net* (*see*).

Lifers—a colloquialism of the mid-to-late twenty-first century usually referring generally to a politically active subset of the population infected with the *Methuselah* (*see*) virus; often used interchangeably with *Lingerers* (*see*).

Lingerers—a colloquialism of the mid-to-late twenty-first century referring to the first generation of ultra-elders to have evidenced symptoms of the *Methuselah syndrome* (*see*), often associated with the *Lifer Liberation Front* (*see*); more generally, those born from 1946 to 1964 and still living at least one hundred years later. *See also Doubler, Lifers,* and *Tripler.*

Lifer Liberation Front, or **LLF**—an unofficial name for the loose confederation of *Lifers* (*see*) and other *Triplers* (*also see*) expressing political opposition to restraints on the civil and constitutional rights of the ultra-aged in the mid-to-late twenty-first century. Often associated with the *Next Hundred*, a political organization having its original headquarters in Black Valley, Colorado, whose members and followers were often referred to as *Lifers* or *Lingerers* (*see*).

LMNA—a gene in the human DNA associated with the production of the proteins lamin a/c and pre-lamin a/c, certain mutations of which cause *progeria* (*see*).

Maxwell Memory Collation Algorithm—a massively integrative algorithm devised by Taubin Maxwell in the early twenty-second century following the development of cerebral augmentation supplant nanosurgery and the resulting accessibility of the personal memories of tens of millions of ultra-elders; used to collate, compare, and integrate memories of specific, commonly experienced places and times into an organic whole of near-perfect historical fidelity, and used to compile this text. Accessible by cerebral supplant and other organoelectronic means, the mass memory matrix created by the Maxwell Memory Collation Algorithm allowed what came to be jocularly referred to as "time travel" or "living in a simulation."

Methuselah—sometimes "Methuselah syndrome," "Methuselah plague," or "longevity plague," referring to the medical condition of negligible senescence resulting from the reprogramming of the human epigenome by a virally-delivered artificial protein package (*see also ENS*). *Orig.* an antediluvian biblical figure, said to have lived 969 years (*see* Book of Genesis 5:21-27).

MSG—Mass Subliminal Guidance; an algorithmic behavior modification technology deployed via the *neural net* (*see*) in the latter half of the twenty-first century to influence consumer acceptance of certain medical products and procedures, most controversially in connection with the government-sponsored longevity-curtailing drug Epilox™, in which context sometimes referred to as the "Deathwish Algorithm."

Neural net—a late-twenty-first-century colloquialism referring to the Distributed Blockchain Neural Network, a recursive, hyper-distributed network of cerebral communications chip implants characterized by an open protocol architecture linking sub-networks of communal, affinity-oriented implant users. The neural net largely replaced the once-dominant, platform-centric "internet" following the latter's dismantlement by political and corporate interests and contemporaneous popular acceptance of *headchip* (*see*) implant technology in the mid-first century.

LIFERS

NDA—non-disclosure agreement; a legal contract restricting the signatory's dissemination of information considered confidential or proprietary by the counterparty.

Next Hundred—*see Lifer Liberation Front.*

NSC—National Security Council; an executive council for national security and foreign policy decision-making, reporting to the President of the pre-secessionist United States in the late-twentieth to mid-twenty-first centuries.

Progeria—also known as Hutchinson-Gilford syndrome, a genetically-based disease characterized by rapid aging, usually occurring in the very young but also associated with young adults infected with later variants of the *Methuselah (see)* virus.

Senescence—*obsolete*; the process or condition of physical and mental deterioration associated with advanced age.

STD—a late-twenty-first-century acronym standing for "scheduled to die," in turn a colloquialism referring to those who have completed their dosage of Epilox™ and thus have a known prospective date of death. Not to be confused with an acronym for sexually transmitted disease common in the late-twentieth and early-twenty-first centuries.

Tripler—a colloquialism of the mid-to-late twenty-first century referring to someone over the age of one hundred; derived from triple-digit, as in age. *See also Lingerers, Doubler,* and *Lifers.*

VTOL—also **eVTOL**; vertical take-off and landing, usually referring to solar-powered electric prop-driven aerial vehicles widely used for personal and commercial travel in the mid-to-late twenty-first century.

ACKNOWLEDGMENTS

This novel would never have come to be without the inspiration provided by a number of nonfiction sources and the feedback and support of early readers.

I'm indebted for the former to Chip Walker's *Immortality, Inc.*; Andrew Steele's *Ageless*; Lawrence R. Samuel's *Aging in America*; David A. Sinclair's *Lifespan*; Peter Attia's *Outlive*; L.S. Dugdale's *The Lost Art of Dying*; Andrew Stark's *The Consolations of Mortality*; Lynne Segal's *Out of Time: The Perils and Pleasures of Aging*; and poet laureate Donald Hall's *A Carnival of Losses: Notes Nearing Ninety*. Anyone with a lingering interest in the scientific and philosophical underpinnings of this book's fictional world would be well served by these fine works of nonfiction.

No author knows what he or she is really doing without honest feedback, and for that I'm deeply indebted to many thoughtful and engaged advance readers, in particular Sarah Peck and David Lloyd, and to my wife, Courtney McWalter, whose inexhaustible faith and encouragement is a treasure to all who know her, but most of all to me.

ABOUT THE AUTHOR

Keith G. McWalter's first novel, *When We Were All Still Alive*, was published by SparkPress in 2021. His essays have appeared in *The New York Times*, *The New York Times Magazine*, and the *San Francisco Chronicle*. He's the author of two blogs, *Mortal Coil* and *Spoiled Guest*, which present his essays and travel pieces to a loyal online following. Keith is a graduate of Columbia Law School and earned a BA in English Literature from Denison University. He lives with his wife, Courtney, in Granville, Ohio, and Sanibel, Florida.

Author photo © Solunar Graphics

Looking for your next great read?

We can help!

Visit www.gosparkpress.com/next-read
or scan the QR code below for a list
of our recommended titles.

SparkPress is an independent boutique publisher
delivering high-quality, entertaining, and engaging
content that enhances readers' lives, with a special
focus on commercial and genre fiction.